TOMORROW
WE SPY

TOMORROW
WE SPY

SPY ANOTHER DAY series
Book Three

DURHAM CREST BOOKS

Cover design by Steven Novak

TOMORROW WE SPY © 2014 Jordan McCollum

First printing, 2014

Published by Durham Crest Books
Pleasant Grove, Utah
Set in Linux Libertine

ISBN 978-1-940096-10-0

PRINTED IN THE UNITED STATES OF AMERICA

For my children,
who mean everything

CHAPTER 1

I DON'T SPY. Even the CIA doesn't expect its operatives to work on their honeymoons. So every morning for the last week and a half, I've woken up reminding myself of three things:

1. I'm married to Danny (and it's okay to find him in bed next to me).
2. I'm in Paris (and it's okay to be in this strange apartment).
3. I'm currently on vacation (and it's okay to not be my usual paranoid self, though my station in Canada isn't exactly an espionage hotbed).

After a dozen repetitions, it's finally setting in. This morning I don't even remember my "affirmations" until after I finish making breakfast for my husband with our adorable octogenarian hostess, Sylvie. She arranges the hot chocolate carafe, fresh fruit and *pain au chocolat* on her tray while I load the rest of the food on mine.

"*Es-tu prête, Talia?*" she asks.

I smile to mask the anticipation flittering in my middle. Of course I'm ready. "*Allons-y.*" I lead us to the back hallway and the tornado stairs from her apartment to the one we're renting.

But my eager feet carry me up the metal steps too quickly, and I have to wait on the top landing for her. Maybe I'm not really hiding the giddy nerves over this admittedly silly breakfast-in-bed surprise.

"*Je viens*," Sylvie calls. She's coming. I glance out the lace curtains and for a second, despite all my affirmations, I forget who and where I am. A silver BMW rolls down the street, a click slower than casual. A steel cord laces around my stomach.

Watching my back every waking moment has tuned my instincts tighter than a twelve-string. The rational side of my brain can't put the reasons into words, but something isn't right.

No. I shake off the worry and the imaginary wire. Even if something isn't right, it's not my business. Not like I'm their target. Today I'm not Talia Reynolds, CIA operations officer. I'm Talia the newlywed, and I won't preempt someone else's problem.

Sylvie reaches the landing and huffs, murmuring something about her knees and the November chill. She sets her tray on the finely carved table by the door, then urges me to go on. "*Je vais au marché. As-tu besoin de quelque chose?*" *I'm going to the market. Do you need anything?*

"*Non, merci.*" I thank her again for her help and watch her down a couple stairs to make sure she won't fall. Once I know she's okay, I switch my heavier tray for the lighter one Sylvie carried, grab the hot chocolate and open the ornate paneled back door to our cozy studio apartment.

At my entrance, my husband rolls over in bed, and I take a second to soak him in, his dark brown hair just long enough to flip out behind his ears, his loving brown eyes, his amazing smile still fuzzy around the edges from sleep. Danny shoves aside the handmade coverlet and swings his feet over the side of the bed. "There you are. I was beginning to wonder if you'd been abducted."

"Not today—don't get up," I rush to say. "You'll ruin it."

Danny pauses at the bed's edge, one eyebrow sneaking up half an inch. "Ruin what?"

"The surprise."

He presses his lips together to hide his amusement, eyeing the food I'm carrying. Okay, yes, it's not much of a surprise anymore. I cross the few feet to the bed, planting one knee on the off-white bedspread for stability. I'm balancing the carafe of hot chocolate, and I really don't want to ruin anything in this adorably dainty flat.

Danny takes the food, beaming. "You made this? For me?"

"Me and Sylvie. And her freezer."

"My compliments to the Kenmore. And the cooks." He sets the breakfast on his lap and leans forward for a kiss.

I oblige, but tap his tray before he gets any ideas about putting off breakfast. "Come on; we've been working for an hour. It's your favorite, and it's getting cold."

"Okay." A laugh lurks in his eyes, but he obeys. I can't help practically bouncing while I wait for him to take the first bite.

He crunches into the flaky pastry and pauses to appreciate the warm, buttery layers. "Amazing."

I grin.

"But I thought *chocolatine* was *your* favorite."

"*Pain au chocolate*," I correct him (though I know it's a dialect difference.) I take the plate and the pastry and settle in to enjoy the gooey chocolate inside the croissant. "Tough luck."

Danny shakes his head, still smiling, and pours himself a mug of hot chocolate. Yeah, he knows I'm only teasing. I return the *pain au chocolat* to the plate and get his breakfast from the table outside the back door. One glance out the landing window shows the silver BMW down the block still.

Still not my problem. I return with the loaded tray: scrambled eggs with bacon and potatoes, lightly toasted fresh bread with melty Rocamadour cheese, and a croissant like mine, only stuffed with shaved ham and two more kinds of cheese, Emmental and chèvre.

"Whoa." Danny sits up straighter to take the heavy tray. "You *have* been cooking."

I take the other tray from his lap and scoot next to him again to enjoy my breakfast of warm semi-solid chocolate and warm liquid chocolate.

Paris in November might not be heaven, but you can't get closer than being here with Danny. (My husband—have I mentioned that once or twice? I'll never get tired of saying it.) Once he's sampled and praised everything, he wraps an arm around me, pulling me closer. I lean into him, automatically settling into the spot where I just fit.

"Remind me how you say it in Finnish?" he asks. Either he likes that I speak four languages (almost five, with his help), or he likes that I finally told him the truth about them all. Either way, we've been through this enough he doesn't have to explain what "it" he means.

"*Rakastan sinua*," I tell him. *I love you.*

"*Rakastan sinua*," he repeats.

I sit up to look into his eyes. "*Ja minä sinuakin, ikuisesti.*"

His eyebrows furrow in a tiny wince. "Did I say it—?"

"It means 'And I you, forever.'"

The worry he's messed up evaporates with his eye-crinkling, Talia-melting smile. My husband tilts forward to rest his forehead on mine. "Which part is 'forever'?"

"*Ikuisesti.*"

"*Rakastan sinua ikuisesti*," he says.

"Good." I give him a quick kiss then a quick tip. "Trill your tongue on the 'r' a little more. Three or four taps and you'll sound like a native."

"I'll keep that in mind next time we're in Finland." He takes a bite of the ham and cheese croissant, chews, swallows, and sighs. "I think you should make breakfast every day."

"And I think we should quit our jobs and never go home." I punctuate my proclamation with a bite of my own buttery, flaky, chocolaty goodness.

"I wish—but you know when you make these for me at home, they'll be called *chocolatine*."

"When I make these at home, they'll be *pour moi*."

Danny glances at me and does a double take. His gaze locks on mine, and no amount of food could distract us. He moves in for a long, slow kiss, and for a few moments, he and I are the only things in my universe.

I've never been a giddy, giggly girl—can't stand them—but I don't care how silly it is to lose myself so completely in his kiss I can't tell which way's right. I'm on my honeymoon; I've earned some time to let my guard down, especially with all the stuff Danny and I have endured for my job lately. A spy may not be able to take classified documents out of the office, but sometimes work tails you home.

We needed this trip for more than a honeymoon.

Danny finally pulls back with a final peck. "You had some chocolate on your lip."

"How embarrassing." I scoop a fingerful of chocolate from the middle of my croissant and smear it on my bottom lip. Danny's laughing and leaning in, and I'm doing the same—until a knock sounds at our front door. I freeze and bite the chocolate off my lip, like we've been caught.

"It's Sylvie," I whisper. But even without my full voice, the doubt comes through as loud and clear as if I'd said the "right?" at the end.

"Wouldn't she use the back way?"

"She was going to the market. Maybe she's stopping by on the way out."

My husband hasn't even turned away. "Nah. Must be the wrong apartment. They'll go away." His lips touch mine and I'm ready to forget that knock.

Until it comes again. In the suddenly tense stillness, we lock gazes and exchange a silent conversation. Not going away. We both look, neither of us willing to let go of one another yet.

He lifts his chin and his voice to address the caller in French. "We don't need anything today, thanks, Sylvie!"

Silence follows. With every passing second, my grip on Danny's T-shirt grows tighter, but neither of us move, not even to breathe.

That car.

No. Nobody should be able to track me down. I've done my best to curb all my extra paranoid little habits on vacation—no small feat. I'm safe. But someone. Is. Here.

Could be anyone. Could be nothing.

"*Monsieur Fluker?*" calls a man in the hall. So much for the wrong apartment theory. And this dude's French accent is bad. Almost as bad as this situation feels.

Danny releases me and I'm the first to ditch my tray and hit my feet. I peek out the window.

That silver BMW's parked across the street. I squint at the windshield. I swear I can see a man with binoculars. Pointed at our building.

My stomach drops and rebounds like I took a speed bump too fast. Now it's my problem.

Danny's out of bed, and before I can dash across the apartment, he reaches the door. He twists the knob, angling the door to shield me from whoever's in the hallway.

I'm rubbing off on him. Apparently I'm a bad influence.

"*Quoi?*" Danny asks.

"*Votre femme, est-elle ici?*" *Is your wife here?*

The skin on the back of my neck turns cold.

If I peek at the man in the hall, he'll see me, so I watch Danny, willing him not to check my reaction. He leans a shoulder against the door, releasing the knob to wave me away.

Whoever's on the other side of this door is bad news. I

don't abandon Danny to bad news. Ever.

"She went to the market." Danny switches to English. "Maybe I can help you."

"Let's just see what she thinks about that," the man replies, like he knows I'm here.

Happy thought.

"Okay," Danny says. "Leave a message, and I'll give it to her."

The man barks out a cynical laugh. I wish I could get a better read on him with any visual, but again if I can see him, he can see me. Danny waves me away, now more insistent.

He's a grown man. He's my husband. He wants to protect me. But I'm his wife—I'm a spy. I should do the protecting. I touch Danny's hand to let him know I'll take it from here, but he lets go of the doorknob again and plants his palm in my stomach. Stopping me.

"I need to talk to her," Mystery Man says.

"Like I said, she isn't here. If you don't want to leave a message, you'll have to come back later." Danny gives an apologetic shrug and closes the door. Yeah, that isn't suspicious.

"I can handle this," I insist. (Quietly. If Mystery Man gives up and goes away, I'm not about to cry.)

Danny takes my elbow and guides me across the room to the back door. He leans close. "Go."

"It's probably nothing." But my reply would *probably* be more convincing if I could raise my voice above a whisper.

He glances back to frown at the front door. I'm not fooling him. He opens the back door to the stairs. "If it's nothing, then let me find out for you."

Mystery Man knocks at the other door again. "Mr. Fluker, you're not fooling anyone. We know she's there."

We? My pulse accelerates. While I'm distracted, Danny picks the precise moment to push me onto the landing. But I'm not leaving him. I turn back. "Seriously." I pitch my tone and my eyebrows to convey stern insistence. "Let me do this, Danny."

He cuts off my protest with a quick kiss. "I can take care of him. He's old. And fat. I've made it through worse."

Before I can argue again, he closes the stairwell door—and *locks* it. I try the knob, but yeah. Locked.

Fine. I can go around. On the wrought-iron spiral staircase, I roll my feet to hide my hurried escape, barely pausing to knock before heading into Sylvie's perfectly appointed apartment. *"Sylvie? J'ai oublié..."*

My lie bounces off the creamy paneled walls and the parquet floor. No Sylvie. Wonderful. I start for the door out of her apartment, but I'm not even past the elegant dining table when Sylvie trots out from the bedroom, perching her perfect little hat on her perfectly coiffed, perfectly white hair. She's wearing gloves. Gloves. This apartment's still in 1964.

"Oui, ma chérie?"

Sylvie doesn't speak a word of English, and I've only been focusing on French for a few weeks, so communication between us is comical. I'm not in a joking mood. I need to go, but adrenaline isn't helping my language processing. How do I say I locked myself out? I send my brain through the paces and spit out a question to bide time. *"Allez-vous au marché?"* *Are you going to the market?*

"Mais oui. Veux-tu venir avec moi?" Sylvie invites me along but doesn't wait for an answer. She bustles off for the bedroom while launching into a lecture, probably about my disregard for my health by wearing nothing warmer than long sleeves in the fall. (It's cold, but we live in *Canada*. This is practically Indian summer.)

The minute she's gone, I'm ready to race out the door and up the main stairs to get this guy away from Danny. But before I turn, footsteps carry through the ceiling above me. I look up, like I can see through the embossed ceiling tiles. A second elephantine set of footsteps tracks after the first. No way that's Danny. A third set patters—no, that's my heartbeat racing in my ears.

The plodding steps track across the ceiling toward the back stairs. He's coming. I stare at Sylvie's door to the stairwell, not daring to move.

"*Y a-t-il un problème?*" Sylvie's voice comes from behind me. *Is there a problem?*

I pivot back with a smile. "*Bien sûr que non.*" *Of course not.* Little conversational phrases go a long way in a foreign language. I can fall back on them 90% of the time.

She holds out a black wool coat. Great—a disguise. I accept it without complaint, too distracted by the footsteps to protest anyway. Even Sylvie, who must've tuned out noise from her guests upstairs, stares at the ceiling to follow the heavier steps to the door. He's leaving.

Where do I go? Back to Danny, to make sure he's all right? (Not that there's been a single sound to indicate otherwise—no time to freak out.) Or tail the footsteps out of the building, and make sure this guy isn't a threat?

Either way, I need to leave this apartment. "*Allez-y,*" I say to Sylvie, gesturing for her to go ahead in case my French is failing me.

Her lips pinch and her gaze tracks to the coat she loaned me. What's the problem?

Sylvie tells me: "*Ce manteau ne suffit pas.*"

The coat's not enough? I'm in a hurry, woman. But arguing with her will chew through more time. My French falls into place faster—and we live in Canada, so I know the word for scarf. "*Un foulard?*"

She smiles indulgently at my efforts, then pulls a scrap of fabric from a side table. Oh. Right—Danny warned me about that Québecism. At home, *foulard* means a knit scarf. Here in France, it's the *other* kind of scarf, and the black and white polka-dotted one Sylvie hands me is fashionable and lightweight. (And somehow enough for this weather?)

Whatever. Let's go. "*Merci.*" I pocket it and walk her to the front door of her apartment.

Am I hurrying to check on Danny or chase Mystery Man? I urge Sylvie to go ahead, pointing upstairs to imply I'm checking on Danny. Sylvie heads out, but before I decide which way to go, I hear the back staircase vibrating under someone's footsteps. Got to be Danny. I crane my neck around the door to verify that.

Sure enough, his plaid flannel pajama pants appear on the staircase. I glance back at Sylvie down the hall—and the heavy-set, middle-aged dude jogging to catch up to her.

No, no, no. Dragging an innocent civilian into whatever this is?

"*Bonjour,*" Mystery Man greets Sylvie. He points at the ceiling. "*Vos voisins?*"

The neighbors. He's asking about us. I don't dare breathe.

Sylvie looks at him askance. "*Pardon?*"

Yes, his accent is indecipherable, but I can't have her engage with him. Sylvie has no idea this guy might be a threat or that he might have backup waiting outside. I've got to help her.

"Talia?" Danny calls softly from behind me.

I make eye contact with him. "I have to go. Start packing."

"But—"

"He's after Sylvie." And it's my fault. Danny is safe. Now I can't let Sylvie go out defenseless, unawares, alone, to face this guy and his crew. I have to protect her. I grab a pair of big round sunglasses from the table by the door. "If they come back, ditch our stuff."

"Wait—" Danny tries, but I'm already jogging down the hall. Danny will only go so far in his PJs. I slide on the sunglasses and tie the polka dot scarf over my long, dark ponytail. Bobby pins from my pocket tuck my bangs underneath the scarf.

Sylvie and Mystery Man took the elevator, so I dash down the stairs. They're already at the front doors when I reach street level.

I slide into my cover and the saunter I've seen on Parisian streets for over a week. By the time I reach the sidewalk, Mystery Man has peeled off, leaving Sylvie alone. She must not have said anything to keep him interested. I release a breath. Maybe she's fine. Maybe I can go back to Danny. Maybe we can figure out what's going on. But first, I have to be sure Sylvie's safe.

I scan the street, doubly grateful for the sunglasses. Paris isn't blinding in November, but as long as I'm facing the right direction, you can't tell where I'm actually spying. I'm free to search the area for anything or anybody out of place.

Nobody catches my eye, no actions screaming "surveillance," but you never know. I note the cars on the street, the BMW and the same little European numbers we've seen every morning, all stationary. Sylvie's halfway down the block before I hear the engine rattling behind us.

I toss my ponytail, turning enough to check my six o'clock. That silver BMW pulls out, coming my way. My heart freezes, but I purposefully don't look at the driver—or at least don't *look like* I'm looking at the driver. I can't tell much as he cruises past, other than he's wearing a suit. He heads the same direction as Sylvie, toward the market.

So much for getting back to Danny.

Yeah, all that stuff I said about not being a spy? I take it back.

CHAPTER 2

I RUSH TO SYLVIE while the BMW and Mystery Man are out of sight. When I reach her, I take her arm. She whirls on me, then squints and moves her head back and forth, like she's trying to focus on me. *"Stéphanie?"*

Oh, man. Am I triggering a dementia episode? *"C'est moi."* I lean in to whisper, "Talia."

"Ah, te voilà." She takes my hand and pats it. *"C'est incroyable comme tu ressembles à ma nièce dans ce manteau."*

I resemble her niece in this coat? Great—a ready-made cover. Today I'm Stéphanie. Sylvie chatters about the food at the market, and we walk on. I don't look to see if we're being tailed. Because now I'm not a spy. I'm not a honeymooner. I'm not a newlywed wife who just left her husband. I'm merely a girl shopping with her elderly aunt. I *am* this part because Sylvie's safety may depend on it.

That car circles the block to pass us again before we reach the market. As we get to the stalls, the increasingly familiar engine rattle grows closer. When Sylvie and I come even with the first vendor's baskets of eggplants, I make sure to stop at the perfect angle to check behind us. Hello, silver BMW.

Needles stab into my gut. I might look like Stéphanie to Sylvie, but my disguise isn't fooling somebody—or maybe they're following Sylvie. Oblivious, she evaluates the vegetables, and I make the appropriate conversational noises in the right places. But behind my big sunglasses, my gaze is glued to my new nemesis.

They *might* know who I am, but they have no idea who they're dealing with.

Sylvie moves to the next cart, examining the *haricots verts*. (Even "green beans" sound fancy in French.) I hurry to keep up.

"Are you bringing anything back for your sweetheart?" Sylvie hasn't exactly kept it a secret she thinks Danny's cuter than a cuddly little kitten, and that cuddling's my wifely calling.

Which I'd be doing if it weren't for the dude in pursuit. Speaking of—the silver BMW's door finally swings open. I don't move, and my eyes don't leave that car. A stocky man in a dark suit gets out.

I haven't ticked off any mobsters lately. So who's this guy, and what does he want?

Sylvie strolls past the next stall, which is bustling in pre-lunch preparations. A head of warm steam carries aromatic spices—Moroccan food. I push through the steam cloud to use it as a cover. "*Donc,*" Sylvie says like she thinks she's being subtle, "is there some trouble between you and Danny?"

"No, not at all."

"Then why have you left your husband after bringing him breakfast in bed?"

Pretending to be Stéphanie even helps my French. "He loved the breakfast, but he wanted to sleep longer."

I scan the market. The surveillance guy reaches the eggplant stall and surveys the white Chinese imports. Can I herd Sylvie along faster?

"Do you not want to spend more time with him?"

Who, Surveillance Man? Why would I?

Oh, she means Danny, duh. "While he's asleep?"

Sylvie sighs as if this is evidence my romantic prospects are going down like the *Titanic*.

"I just don't want to waste our last day here sleeping," I explain.

We reach another produce cart. Sylvie clucks at some sad, overpriced zucchini, and we mosey onward. "*Chérie*, you should be together."

"*Bien sûr.*" *Of course*. My attention stays with Surveillance Man. He skips the green beans. I skip my next two heartbeats, but smile at the next vendor Sylvie chats with, a baker. Sylvie pays for bread, and I pick up a nice market tote. I'm not what you'd call fashion forward, but this could come in handy. I check the lining—fully reversible.

Yep, definitely coming in handy.

I pay the vendor, but all of my senses fixate on Surveillance Man ten feet behind us. Feels more like he's breathing down my neck. He greets the Moroccan couple prepping lunch—with a loud, nasal voice. Decent French. Not the guy knocking at our door.

How extensive is this crew?

I could confront him—or I could see if I can draw him off Sylvie. I'm the one they want, right? With one more day in the country (and Danny hopefully packing our things now), we could escape long-term if I give him the slip on the way out of the market. But I don't take chances. I take precautions.

"Thank you for bringing me shopping," I tell Sylvie. "I'm going to sightsee for a bit."

She peers at me like she's super concerned about the perilous state of my twelve-day-old marriage. "I was married for forty-two years before my Georges died."

Did I understand that right, or am I too distracted by the guy on our tail? "I'm sorry for your loss."

"Your marriage is new; you must work together to build it. You're used to looking after your own interests, to living separately, but now you must work together."

"Yes, of course."

Sylvie pats my shoulder. "Danny's used to taking care of himself, and you have been on your own too long, too."

Apparently her apartment isn't the only place it's 1964. I need to make my escape, but I can't just walk away. "Sylvie, everything's fine with Danny."

"I'm sure it is. Remember, you've been responsible for your own life, and Danny has managed his, but now you must work together to build a new thing, this team, this marriage."

"We will. In fact—" I risk a glance at Surveillance Man. He's still behind us, still masquerading as a casual shopper, absorbed in the baker's pastry pitch.

Time to make my move. I turn to Sylvie. "Could you tell Danny to meet me where we had lunch yesterday? At eleven?"

Sylvie stops to consult her watch, and I have to take the opportunity. A small gaggle of über fashionable girls in their midtwenties stroll by. I take off my polka-dotted scarf and sunglasses and toss them in my tote before I join the chic group. Seems like they're not so much here to peruse the produce as to parade through. Bonus for me.

We tromp through the market a minute before I check on the people in my wake. Sylvie finishes looking for me and bustles off to her next stop. Surveillance Man's on the move, too. His gaze isn't locked on me—is he trained?—but he's headed my direction.

Perfect. Sylvie's safe.

A girl in my new group of "friends," a blonde, pivots to glare at me. (The sunglasses really undercut the effect of your death stare, sweetie.) I cock an eyebrow at her and maneuver past them, putting the girls between me and Surveillance Man. Once that shield's in place, I dare to look again.

15

Still after me. Sylvie might be safe, but I'm not.

Fortunately, I know what to do. I empty my new bag and flip it inside out to hold my accessories and Sylvie's black coat. I spot a stand selling knit berets and thrust what I hope is enough euros at the vendor before I pick up a yellow number.

Sometimes it pays to stand out. If Surveillance Man figures out the woman in the black coat changed into the woman in the yellow hat, all I have to do is get rid of my bright yellow beret beacon to slip under his radar again.

In theory.

I don't know this area well—okay, I don't know any part of Paris well after only a week—so I navigate on instinct. Years of routinely evading surveillance have built up a sense for "yes, go there," or "no, dead end," that translates even to a centuries-old European city. I avoid the first alley leading off the market, and duck down another street. The wide, tree-lined avenue has so little foot traffic it's eerie. My spy sense squeezes my lungs tighter. Any main road this empty feels like trouble.

Once I'm down the block, I casually turn my head. Surveillance Man behind me.

Big trouble. If I take a side street, I might find a shop or crowd or anything to get lost in. Or I might end up more isolated, giving Surveillance Man the opportunity to corner me.

I scan for a store. The cutesy sidewalk café isn't quite right. The ritzy chocolatier would normally be my first stop, but I don't think it's big enough for what I need.

Finally, I spot it: a clothing boutique, large enough to reach the back alley. Traffic's thin, so I jaywalk and head in. No point looking behind me: Surveillance Man will definitely follow.

I step into the boutique, nerves taking my stomach for a dip. I doubt I can afford haute couture—let alone carry it off—but this is what I'm here for. I pick up a hot pink shirt with faux-fur trimmed cuffs. (Please tell me this isn't "in" now.) The bored clerk rings me up like he resents my entire existence.

"Can I ask a quick favor?" I try in French, adding a timid smile.

The clerk snarks back something in French that I don't have a prayer of understanding. Before I recover, Monsieur Snootypants sneers and switches to English. "What do you want?"

Might as well shout his subtext: don't bother speaking French; my English is better than your offensive communication attempts.

So much for the charm route. Plan B: I slide a hundred euro note across the counter and slip into my best Aussie accent (more likely to get help than an American). "Let me out the back and you can keep the change."

He scrutinizes me, and I try to remember to breathe as the seconds tick by. Surveillance Man could be here any minute, but I hold onto my cover and my composure. Finally, the clerk jerks his chin for me to come on. He leads me through a suede curtain into a dank storage room, then unlocks three padlocks on the back door. "I never did this," he says in English.

"You never saw me."

The door screeches shut and the locks clack closed. Crud. Naturally, it occurs to me twenty seconds too late: I should've bought shoes too. My flats are good for roaming the city, but if Surveillance Man is as well-trained as I think he is, he'll surely recognize the shoes.

Hopefully I've already lost him. I check both directions of the alley. Both ends lead out to the street, one almost too close. Staying in this alley could be a dead giveaway, but Surveillance Man could guess my little game and round that closer corner. I hurry down the alley toward the far end.

Over my pulse, pounding for plenty of reasons, I hear a metal door slam behind me. Same sound as the one to the boutique. I don't dare turn back. I pick up my pace until I reach the corner.

When the building blocks my pursuer's view, I yank the

black coat and scarf out of my bag and flip it right-side out, not slowing a step. I tuck my stuff inside the bag. Once it's loaded, I pull on my (sigh) lovely new shirt and tug out my ponytail elastic. With a conscious effort to add a more casual spring to my normal gait, I ease on down this new road. The heavier crowd here is perfect to lose him.

I snag a table at the first café I find, positioning myself to monitor that alley. A waiter who sniffs like I'm infringing on his air comes over to sigh at my table.

Funny, the only rude Parisians I've met seem to be people providing customer service.

I try to tamp down the nerves buzzing in my belly. I *will* meet Danny for lunch, he *will* handle this situation okay, we *will* be fine. But for now I can't eat, so I order something I have no intention of drinking: "*Café au lait.*" (Yeah, Danny and I have gotten more than a few stares for avoiding coffee, tea and alcohol in Paris. What can we say? We're Mormons. We're okay with being weird.)

The waiter leaves. Man, I hate to be still now. I need to be going. I need to be running. I need to be dodging. Instead, I'm sitting. I'm waiting. I'm pretending to peruse an abandoned issue of *Le Monde*. My eyes dart to that alley between each unintelligible paragraph. But nobody comes out before my coffee arrives.

If he's hiding back there to lure me in, I'm not that dumb. I toss a few euros on the table and head out again. Nothing like real surveillance on your tail to make you keep moving.

I make my way down the street store by store, browsing new purses and baked goods and another restaurant's menu. Waiting for a stocky guy in a suit to show up in my virtual rearview. Peering over my shoulder. Ignoring the nagging tug that I've been in this *attractive* shirt for too long, and it's time to change disguises.

I know what I'm doing, and I will wait him out.

After an hour, I'm realizing that these cute flats have been okay for sightseeing, but they're no match for determined walking. Oh, and I'm beginning to accept that Surveillance Man is good and gone. I lost him.

Now to find out what's going on, who's following me, and how they tracked me down. I change course for the crêperie where we ate yesterday, hanging onto the hope that Sylvie conveyed the message, and that Danny remembers where this place is (and I do, too).

And the hope that this is about to become a distant memory.

CHAPTER 3

IF SYLVIE RAN A RESTAURANT, it would be this crêperie. The similarities run deeper than the lace-draped tables. Something about the air in here is simply . . . serene.

Yesterday, the peace was perfect. Today, it's aggravating. How long until Danny gets here, and we can figure out what's up? Mystery Man, Surveillance Man, searching for me—

Wait a minute. Surveillance Man's accent? American. Same with the guy at our door.

No reason springs to mind for my own people to want me that badly—or go about finding me that badly. I definitely don't have any "friends" in Paris. So the people going to all this trouble to track me down are . . . who?

Uneasiness prickles down my spine. This. Is. Bad.

"There you are." Danny echoes his greeting from this morning as he settles into the seat across the tiny table. I can finally release the worry I've been harboring since I left him at Sylvie's, the same sentiment reflecting in his warm brown eyes. He's safe, he's here, and he's my husband. I ruffle his dark half-curls where they flip out behind his ears, then pull him close. He kisses me, and the reality seeps in. We're *both* safe.

For now.

"Good to see you, too." I force myself to smile. We have one day left of our honeymoon, and I can't waste it worrying. Of course, I'm also trying to figure out where we should stay tonight, since Sylvie's is obviously not secure. All three of us will be safer if we're elsewhere.

Danny furrows his brow. "Could've avoided this if you'd listened to me."

I sidestep an argument (neither of us really wants to argue), going for a diplomatic tone. "Why do you say that?"

"We have an appointment at the US embassy at one." Danny passes me a business card.

"Really." My voice is the definition of disbelief. I read the card. *Noah Crystal*, a phone number, and "1 PM" in Danny's writing in the corner. "Did he mention what this is about?"

"Wouldn't say, just insisted he had to talk to you."

"And he came in?"

He nods. "For some reason, he didn't believe you weren't home."

"Weird." Could be a setup. I've seen this movie. I get out my phone—well, the cheap non-CIA phone I bought when we got to Europe. I've programmed the number for the embassy, but I didn't expect to need it.

"Embassy of the United States in Paris," the machine answers. I press whatever keys it takes to get to a real operator. Meanwhile, the grandmotherly woman who owns the crêperie comes to talk to Danny. She's so happy to see him that she must remember him from yesterday. Danny has a tendency to stand out. I mean, I already appreciate how handsome he is, but what really draws people to him is how completely, genuinely . . . genuine he is. He's the one part of my life that's real, through and through. Plus, apparently older women find his Québec accent endearing. (Or unintelligible. I was nearly laughed out of a classy place when I used the Québec pronun-

21

ciation of *beurre*, butter.)

I'm still navigating phone menus when the owner promises us the house specialty. By the time a human gets on the phone, I'm tapping my foot (for the operator and the crêpes).

"Hello, this is Tammi," says the operator. "Can I help you?"

"I need to speak to Noah Crystal. I'm told he works in the embassy."

"What department?"

I study the card, like that information would magically appear. "I only know he came by where I'm staying and tried to convince me he works there."

A beat of silence passes. No way could any one operator possibly know everyone in an embassy the size of Paris's, but I sense the concern carrying on the line. Smells like a scam. "Let me check," she finally says. "Can I put you on hold?"

"Sure."

Danny asks a wordless question with a lifted eyebrow, and I change the angle of the phone to answer. "Looking him up."

"Something's weird."

Yep. And Danny doesn't know about the guy who tailed me yet.

"Think he's lying?" Danny asks.

They've certainly raised enough warning flags. But something about this goes beyond criminal to just deeply wrong. (Something = Surveillance Man.)

"Are you still there?" Tammi returns to the line.

"Yep."

"Let me connect you with Mr. Crystal's secretary."

Okay, so he works there—but that doesn't prove he was the one at our door a couple hours ago.

After two rings, a man answers. "Noah Crystal's office."

"Apparently I have an appointment with Mr. Crystal."

"Okay," he says, instantly warming. "What's your name?"

Old habits die hard: I scan the half-full crêperie and lower my voice. "Talia Reynolds."

Danny clears his throat, and my gaffe registers. "Fluker," I add, way too late. "Talia Reynolds Fluker."

No answer for a long second. Two. Three. I'm about to check my phone to see if we're still connected when the secretary finally speaks again. "We'll see you at one."

Closer to a command than a question. "I guess so," I say, fighting the falling feeling in my stomach.

"See you then." He ends the call.

The scent of warm chocolate reaches me before a warm, delicate crêpe coated with Nutella does. I manage to thank the owner, but I'm not sure I can eat.

"Well?" Danny asks.

"We've got a date." Yippee.

As you might expect, the US embassy in Paris is pretty huge. Housed in a classically designed behemoth, it could be a nightmare to navigate, but of course they're expecting us. We surrender our phones and follow our escort through a maze of halls, a breezeway, more halls.

This isn't some paperwork problem we can resolve in the main chancery. It's something big. Every step, I'm holding Danny's hand tighter.

And every step, we get closer. I'm not clinging to Danny because I'm afraid of what we might be headed for. I'm clinging to him because I know exactly what we're getting into.

Okay, not "exactly," but enough to realize it isn't good. Though Langley would never confirm or deny anything about Noah Crystal across an unsecure line, bureaucrats aren't the only people in an embassy.

Which makes me wonder if Danny should be here. But I'm not letting go.

The guard leaves us in a sleek waiting area. The modern seating and polished receptionist desk are empty. The rest of the office is deserted. Even the drooping flag's creepy.

Tension still ties my heart in knots, but Danny instantly relaxes a bit. "Gee." He sweeps a hand around the office, which is only missing the Company seal. "Wonder why we're here."

"The CIA. We're subtle." My voice carries the same sarcastic twist. "Says so right on our letterhead."

Danny settles on the black leather couch, and I pace a minute until he beckons for me to join him. He slides an arm around my waist, but the closest I can come to comfortable, casual closeness is drumming my fingers on his knee. What does the CIA want that couldn't wait a couple days till I'm home and back at work? And what's with the scare tactics?

Finally a man too young to be an overworked bureaucrat comes bustling into the office. "Sorry to keep you waiting." He gestures for me to come along. I hesitate a split second, not quite ready to abandon Danny, especially here in the belly of the beast. The man stops and turns back, waiting for me.

Alone. It goes without saying.

I squeeze Danny's knee and stand to follow this guy. He leads me down a hallway. At the last second, I catch Danny's *what now?* expression.

Whatever this is, it'd better be quick. The dude leads me to his office. The glass desktop positively gleams. In front of it, a pair of cushy armchairs waits for a nice fireside chat. "Noah Crystal." He offers a hand with his introduction, though I sincerely doubt that's his real name.

I shake his hand, but obviously he already "knows" me. Noah pats the back of the blue chair farther from the door. I perch on the cushion, bracing myself for the blow.

Pessimistic, maybe, but this is the CIA. If they're begrudging my first vacation in too long—not just a vacation, my freaking honeymoon—it's probably *not* to give me that belated wedding gift.

"We need to discuss an assignment," Noah says. He settles into the other chair. As if the setup wasn't enough—not sitting opposite me across his desk, but in this tender little tête-à-tête—he arranges his light brown hair and his features to project a perfect air of competence and kindness. I'm not buying #2.

He senses the reluctance in my silence, because he adds, "An opportunity."

Again, not buying #2. "I'll stop you here. Answer's no."

"Ms. Reynolds, you don't understand."

I'm already on my feet. "Nope, I got it. Thanks for thinking of me and hunting me down in a very threatening way on my *honeymoon*, but I'm sure there are spies in Paris with less on their plates."

"Sorry about the approach. But we need to talk to you two."

I spear him with a sarcastic glare. "Who, me and my landlady? Your goons followed her, you know."

Crystal sighs through his teeth. "Never would've come to that," he mutters, "if Jim hadn't—"

He cuts himself off, but I've heard enough. Doubt his little scapegoat exists. Barely restraining an eye-roll, I head past his chair. Crystal doesn't bother to stand, letting me grasp the doorknob.

"You'll really want to hear this," he says. "You'll kick yourself the rest of your life."

I pause, and that split second's enough for him to strike. "It'll give you closure with Fyodor Timofeyev."

The name hits my back like a cold splash of acid. It's been three months since that case went horribly wrong—and Fyodor died. I'm still working through the aftermath, but I thought I was close to finding closure.

Still, I can't resist the question tearing through my thoughts. "How?" I turn and ask.

Crystal stands slowly. He doesn't acknowledge my question. Instead, he points toward the lobby we just left. "That was your husband? The aerospace engineer?"

My lungs jolt in panic, and I instinctively position myself at the door, ready to protect him. "Danny's fame precedes him."

"Just part of your file." Crystal turns to his desk, his voice deceptively casual. "Your husband met Timofeyev too, right?"

I give the smallest nod in recorded history. The instincts that have served me well today now growl like this conversation has taken a bad turn.

"In fact, wasn't he a victim of corporate espionage on Timofeyev's part?"

"Obviously you've done your research, Mr. Crystal."

"I like to be thorough." He flashes a grin, like his little laid-back pretense will build our relationship. "Call me Noah."

I'm done. I tug the door handle, but before I pull, he scrapes in a last-ditch effort. "Don't *you* like to be thorough? Wouldn't it bother you to leave a loose end dangling?" He lets that resonate before he lowers his voice to add, "Don't you want this put to rest at last?"

I eye him over my shoulder. He's moved to sit on his desk, ankles crossed in the picture of corporate casual. No way can he know how much this case affected me. If it weren't for that assignment, I never could've agreed to marry Danny. I wouldn't be here. I wouldn't be married.

I wouldn't have Fyodor Timofeyev's blood on my hands.

That very literal image—a memory—surfaces, and I'm gripping the door handle like it's a shield, a lifeline, the hilt of a knife.

I've gotten through this. I have. As much as possible. But it's only been three months, and I'm a spy, not an assassin. I know some people never escape that weight, that guilt.

"I'd want it closed. Over with," Crystal finally finishes. "I'd at least listen."

I release the doorknob and turn to him again. "Listening."

"We need to know if the plans Timofeyev stole from your husband's office made it back to Shcherbakov." He's already brought up Fyodor, but suddenly I'm in the deep end of the espionage pool. This isn't some superficial loose thread to tie up. This could be serious.

I recovered the drive he stole, but, hello, email? A file could've circled the globe twice before we knew it was gone. Granted, the stolen plans belong to Canadian defense, but I don't think anybody at CSIS, Canada's spy agency, would dare argue Timofeyev isn't my turf.

Apparently my full attention isn't enough for Noah. He hops off the desk and shrugs, walking away. "Your call."

I won't play his game. "Great. I'm sure you'll find someone to handle it." Someone *not* on their honeymoon, I don't add. I'm about to leave once again when Noah launches a heart-seeking missile.

"Do you trust your husband?" Now Noah circles around me, but he's not nearly tall enough to intimidate me with just his proximity.

"Duh?"

"No, no—I mean, of course. I just want to be sure *we* can trust him before we go any further. You know, with his allegiances to another country. Allegiances that could be exploited."

Danny's Canadian job and Canadian clearances hardly qualify. This time, I don't hold back the eye-roll.

Noah closes in to I'm-dropping-the-act distance. "All I'm saying is you need to be extremely careful of what lines you two will and won't cross. What'll happen if Danny has to choose between his country and his job? You and his job?"

I school my features into a stare of stone. I trust Danny.

27

With everything. "As much as I appreciate the marital advice, I think we're done."

Crystal ignores me. "And what if you have to choose between yours and him?"

"Is that what this is about?" I laugh, a single syllable without humor. "My husband or my job? Push me on that, and I don't think you'll like the answer."

Crystal's phone buzzes, and he glances at the screen. Like I'm not standing right here. He looks up with this little frown-smirk. "What I'm trying to say is this assignment isn't for you."

"That tactic won't work—"

"If you would stop interrupting, I could finish what I've been trying to tell you for the last five minutes."

Only one of us has been beating around the bush the whole time. I say nothing, letting Crystal finish so I can get out of here.

"The assignment's for Danny."

That's a joke. It has to be. I peer at him a minute, willing him to crack a smile.

None comes. I remember—Noah said "you two." You two. Me and Danny.

The silence spins beyond my control, and my stomach floats in zero Gs, like I'm at the top of the climb, the split second before the plummet back to earth. More memories assault me—Danny in danger. Danny facing off against a traitor. Danny at gunpoint.

I will never, *never* let that happen again.

"No." I hold up both hands. "No way."

"They're his plans. We need him to go to Shcherbakov."

"There has to be someone else. Technical officer. Anyone."

Crystal's expression finally breaks, but not into a grin—a grimace. "It's the only way."

I step away from the door, coming at Crystal. "Why are we talking about this? My husband wants nothing to do with the

CIA. We've made this clear to my station chief."

"I'm afraid this is out of your hands."

"My husband's involvement with *my* job is 'out of my hands'?"

Crystal holds his arms in a defensive position, and I realize my voice, my posture, my words are already on the attack.

Because I am. I *will* protect Danny. "My husband's already gone way above and beyond what any civilian should have to endure. You *cannot* put him in danger."

"I'm sorry, but it's too late."

What, because I said yes to the CIA and to Danny, my hands are tied on all decisions about the two of them? Heat builds in my chest and my cheeks.

This is my fault. He's in danger again because of me, because of my job. That's the only reason they can get to him.

I have to stop this. I have to. And I have one sure way to keep Danny away from danger. The idea hurts—physically hurts—but nothing's worth putting him in harm's way. Not again.

I stride to Crystal's desk and grab a pen from the holder. "Paper."

"Talia, listen to me—"

I rip a blank sheet from the ink jet printer on an ebony end table next to his desk and scribble out my message. *I, Talia Reynolds, resign from the United States' Central Intelligence Agency, effective immediately.* I sign and shove it at Noah. "Now you can't touch him."

Noah won't take the paper, but he won't take his eyes off it, either. "I can't accept this."

"Take it," I say through my teeth, though this must be way outside the correct protocol.

Yeah, well, so's recruiting my husband.

"You don't understand." Crystal tilts my wrist, moving the resignation out of his way. "Danny's already said yes."

CHAPTER 4

FEAR FREEZES ME ON THE SPOT. My too-hasty resignation still hangs between me and Crystal, but I doubt that's why he's swallowing hard and avoiding my gaze.

They want Danny—they want Danny—they want Danny.

Too bad. "You said it was an assignment for me. You said, 'You two.'"

"I said I wanted to talk to you two."

"Meaning you wanted to talk to him," I correct Crystal. "When did Danny supposedly accept this? We've been in here for five minutes, and he's still out—"

"He's talking to Jim Alison."

(Alison and Crystal? These guys lucked out in the operational name department.)

I back up until my foot hits those stupid blue chairs. "How could you possibly know he said yes?"

Crystal holds up his cell phone. Text message from Jim Alison: *He said yes. Where is the wife?* ("The wife"?)

I look down at my resignation. Thirty seconds ago, I was ready to give up everything, but if Noah's right, Danny's two steps ahead of me. I fold the paper in thirds, deliberate.

"Still want to give me that?" Crystal asks.

I shake my head slowly. I can fix this. I have to. Somehow. "I want to see him."

"But—"

"I want to see him right now, unless you've already packed him off to Russia." My voice is harder than steel.

"By all means." Crystal rounds me to open the door.

"Have you considered the logistics?" I ask in the hall. "He doesn't speak Russian. Rostov-na-Donu is no Paris."

"There's more planning in this than you might think," Crystal mutters.

"Yeah, I really get the impression of foresight when you spring this on me *by stalking me on my honeymoon*." Am I the only person who thinks this is a serious breach of human decency? I may have signed up to give my life if necessary, but that doesn't mean I have to give up any semblance of living one in the meantime.

"Look, I'm not the one you should be mad at. I told Jim we should talk to you first. I didn't realize you'd bring your husband with you."

"It's our honeymoon. And I'm not about to leave him alone with your goons tailing innocent old ladies to track me down."

Crystal grimaces. "Knew I should've been more specific when I told them to find you. I didn't have time to explain before Jim came in this morning. He insisted we should talk to Danny without you—I was trying to extend a professional courtesy here."

Okay, maybe Noah Crystal isn't the big bad guy. Still don't have to like this situation.

We stop at another office and Noah knocks. I can't miss the grim glance he exchanges with the white-haired man who answers the door. If I had to guess which was the Chief of Station, I was shunted off with a subordinate while Danny was left to backstroke with the Big Shark.

Speaking of Danny, he's sitting at the conference table behind Jim, staring at the door. He offers me a reassuring little grin, and I can't stop the answering rise of hope in my heart. Maybe they haven't gotten to the assignment part yet. Maybe he didn't really accept. I keep my expression neutral.

"I'd like to speak to my husband." I'm definitely pulling marital rank. "Alone."

Jim steps aside, allowing me in. I make sure the door closes behind him. Before I dare to speak, I check the room. The well-stocked bookshelves seem mostly decorative, but I'll bet they're hiding a camera or two. I join Danny at the conference table, maneuvering my back to the shelves, shielding my hands to signal the walls have ears—and eyes. I pick my tone carefully. "They said you accepted."

"Yeah," he says, the *of course* ringing through his words. "Wouldn't you have?"

I don't answer. I did nearly quit, but that was to protect Danny. Meanwhile he was agreeing to this scheme. "You didn't even think about talking to me first?"

His little grin falls, and then he swallows. His gaze slides away from me and grows distant. "Probably should've thought about that."

"That whole 'marriage' thing." I shoot for a hint of humor, but I think I miss.

The old me would freak out over this whole situation. With my family history of less-than-successful marriages, I might've been more paranoid about marrying Danny—well, ruining our marriage—than anything I've ever done.

But twelve days ago, I made a choice to take relationship freak-outs off the table. Even when Danny turns around and makes a Hail Mary free throw from left field for the wrong team. (I know that's three different sports. That's how discombobulating this is.)

I need to talk to him, for *real*, to understand what's going on. (Why, why, why would he say yes?) I lower my voice for the thinnest veil of privacy. "We *just* had the 'I don't want to work for the CIA' conversation a month ago. What's up with the one-eighty?"

Danny rubs each fingertip against his thumb in turn, as if he's rolling over his answer in his fingers as well as his mind. Weighing out what to tell me. "It's what you'd do."

Would I have accepted without talking to him? I'm not phoning him to consult every time a case or a target crosses my desk back home, but on my honeymoon? I'd like to think I'm smart enough to confer with Danny first.

"I thought that's what you *were* doing," he continues, still focused on the high-shine conference table. "I take it you didn't accept."

"I wasn't invited."

Danny scowls at the door. "Sure know how to spin a sales pitch, don't they?"

"It's our job." I lay my hands and my (metaphorical) cards on the table. "You want to do this?"

He finally meets my line of sight. "Do you not want me to?"

The reality underneath shines through his all-too-honest eyes. He wants to do this, and there's something more he isn't telling me. He's seen how badly ops can end. Firsthand. Recently. But it isn't the enthusiasm and excitement of a new adventure haunting him.

It's desperation. Easy to spot when my frame is vibrating with that same fear.

Whatever the reason, he *needs* this. I finger the folded paper in my lap. Danny's the most important thing in my life, and this means so much to him. How could I make him go back on his word?

But sending him out alone to do the things I do—without my training and experience? It's sending him to his death.

Palpable panic floods into my rib cage like sand filling an

hourglass. I can't. I can't. I can't. The deeper the sand, the deeper Danny's desperation grows, and I see that my choices are dwindling to A. killing his spirit or B. killing him.

He needs this. I give him as much as I can. "I—I have to see their strategy."

Danny smiles, but for the first time in the year and a half I've known him, there's something . . . false about his smile. Not forced or fake, but something in his expression absolutely doesn't match.

They're taking him from me already.

I've got to change this somehow without compelling Danny to go back on his word. There has to be a middle ground, right? "Hang on."

I pretend like I don't know they're probably observing the whole exchange and move for the door. Jim and Noah are chatting in the reception area on the other side. They stop and Noah shifts from leaning against the sleek receptionist's desk to standing.

I ignore their expectant eyebrows and ready my demands. "I get final approval on all plans."

Noah glances up at his boss. Jim shakes his head, his distinguished white hair barely ruffling with the movement. "No go. You don't have the right compartment."

"Seriously?" Perfect timing for politics to pop up. As if Top Secret isn't enough, we go adding "compartments," segmenting off the *really* secret secrets. "Read me in."

Noah shrugs in fake apology. "No more slots."

"But Danny gets one? Don't try this crap with me. Walk me through the entire plan now or we're walking out of here."

Noah checks with Jim. The Chief of Station gives me a frown, a very clear *correct me if I'm wrong, but haven't you already volunteered for all this?*

I step into the waiting area and close the door behind me. "I signed up for this." I jerk my chin to indicate the door and

34

Danny beyond. "He didn't. You can't drag civilians—"

"CIA spouses help with missions all the time."

"Is this *my* mission?" I challenge. Noah specifically said it wasn't, so I've got Jim there.

He sighs, resentfully capitulating, and turns to Noah. "Get Lori."

Noah marches to the back hallway. Jim turns to me again. "Heard good things," he says.

"So good that you're cutting me out of an op centering around my husband?"

"We're not cutting you out. You know you can't possibly go to Russia together, not while maintaining your cover. All it takes is one Google hit on your wedding photos and you're both dead."

Yes, my cover's delicate. That one Google hit would betray the whole setup and then some. Any foreign power associating my face and my name with my real job would destroy my cover. My real name and my real credentials—a Canadian law degree earned on the CIA's dime—are among the few things preserving cover for half a dozen CIA officers in Ottawa.

I could go to Russia as someone else, but all my current fake identities are thinner than October ice and twice as precarious, too closely associated with my activities in Ottawa. Generating new ones in, what, nine hours, with all the back-stopping and paperwork and lies? Not feasible unless this is a much higher priority than they're letting on.

I hate him for it, but Jim's right. Danny's got to do this alone, because I can't help.

I hope this isn't the beginning of a terrible trend: Jim being right, and me having every reason to hate it.

Noah returns with an iPad—sure, Paris gets budget and we get bupkis—and settles on the black leather couch. I shoot a pointed look at the door behind me. Danny's got to hear, too, and soon. (While we're at it, a timeline would be good.) Noah stands and starts for Danny.

As Noah passes, I eye his tablet. "Is the iPad 'Lori'?"

"She's on her way." Noah opens the door, revealing Danny, now standing. "If we go into this, of course, it's a commitment."

Danny clears his throat, and Noah turns to include him in the conversation. "Meaning I can't back out once you show me the plan," Danny says.

Noah nods, then looks from Danny to me and back again. I can't hide the attitude seeping out through my pursed lips and stance. It wouldn't do to fully brief a civilian only to have him balk, but does Noah think I'm stupid? "You don't have to sign his name in blood to give him the ten-thousand foot view," I say, automatically slipping into the idiotic Agency jargon that we usually avoid in our office. "We're entitled to that much."

Noah studies his iPad and pages through a couple screens. He sits at the table and turns the iPad to Danny, showing a sad, cement, Soviet building. We take seats and Noah begins. "Shcherbakov."

The company Fyodor worked for, headquartered close to the military establishment in Rostov-on-Don (i.e. where I lived as a missionary years ago). Shcherbakov's struggled to compete against the Russian government's conglomerate in their not-communist-but-still-command economy. Hence Fyodor stealing the spy drone plans from Danny's office, most likely with the intent to sell them, most likely to the highest bidder, most likely one of our enemies.

Until today, I thought we'd gotten to Fyodor and the plans before they got any farther.

I nod at the depressing factory on Noah's screen. "Why do we think the plans are there?"

He chews his lip and flips through a couple other screens on his iPad, clearly debating telling us the whole truth. He settles on the picture of Shcherbakov again. "Tech got some-thing off his computer."

The laptop that ended up in the charred wreckage? No wonder it's taken them three months to process.

I have to admit, their case for going in sounds better.

I wave for Noah to continue, and he does. "We're in the process of finalizing an on-site visit for Danny, on behalf of National Research Council Canada."

"To make sure our agreement with Fyodor made it back without him?"

Noah says nothing, but his eyebrows say he doesn't know what Danny's referring to.

Danny hesitates. "Does NRC know about this?" His employer deals with sensitive stuff, including the Canadian defense contracts Danny handles. Is this an acceptable risk?

Noah sets the iPad on the conference table and heads to the sideboard below the bookshelves. He picks up a small silver box, thinner than a deck of cards, and hands it to Danny. Danny flips it open. Inside, a couple dozen business cards. I pull one out. Exact replicas of Danny's real card, except the back has a Russian translation, and under his name, it now says—

"'Director of Research and Development'?" he asks. "They signed off on that too?"

"Yep," Noah says.

"I don't want a promotion," Danny says. "I like my job; I like my projects. I didn't go into aerospace to end up in management."

"I'll have them make it temporary. But if you're not a director or higher, nobody at Shcherbakov will meet with you."

Danny's gaze falls back to his new business card, and my stomach drifts downward, too. I hope he can see it—they're already demanding concessions. Already taking things he loves. Coercing him to do one little mission? Yeah, right.

We still have time to back out.

Danny snaps the card case shut. "So I'm playing ambassador. Reciprocal visit making sure our agreement's still okay."

Noah make a little *sure* gesture. "Right. I'm guessing you'll go through the usual paces of an on-site. Done that before?"

"On the hosting end." Danny pushes the card case away and folds his arms. Defensive? Worried? Cold? I can't say.

"Obviously, your real objective's to find the files, if they have them."

Danny's emotions finally become clear in a skeptical frown. "How sure are we that the plans are there?"

Noah's head bobs side to side. He's hedging. "We're not—but don't worry; we'll make everything easy for you."

"I've heard that before," I mutter.

Noah glares at me. Always an effective tactic for persuading my husband.

"Look, they're your plans." Noah sets aside the tablet to level with Danny. "Nobody can recognize them like you. You can see through any changes and variations by Shcherbakov."

"And you have access to him," I point out. *And me over a barrel,* I don't point out.

Noah reins in the dirty looks this time. "Granted," he admits.

I build on my momentum. "When would wheels-up be?"

"ETD is tonight, eleven PM."

So fast? A knock cuts off my next question. Noah answers the door. "Long lunch, Lori?"

"I came straight here," she says. Noah lets her in. Lori's about my age, though it's hard to tell because once she dares to cross the threshold, she fixates on the multicolored carpet. Between being a CIA officer and the shyness more crippling than a shrapnel bomb, you'd expect her to seem more fading-into-the-shadows. Instead, her deep red coat is accented with wide lapels and a matching belt. Her red hair is styled in an asymmetrical cut, one side chopped at chin-length and the other side nearly long enough to graze her collarbone. The incongruity's startling.

So why is the shy girl who's trying too hard to be noticed now on this case? Noah shepherds her over to Danny and they shake hands. "Lori, Danny," Noah begins the introduction. "Danny, this is Lori. She's an officer here, and she'll be your interpreter."

Lori makes eye contact for the first time—and it ain't with her boss or her coworker or me. Nope, that's my husband.

Danny's answering expression is just friendly, but yeah. Color me not happy. (And green.)

I fight down an incredulous eyebrow and stand next to Danny to face Lori. *"Ty govorish' po-russkiy?"* *You speak Russian?*

Uh huh. To test her language skills, I open with a yes/no question. Brilliant. But she should correct me for using the familiar form with her, a total stranger.

"Konyechno." *Of course.*

"Kogda v posledniy raz ty byla v Rossiy?" *When were you last in Russia?* I don't really care how long it's been—five years for me, so odds aren't great I can show her up. But I need to know if she's up to the task.

"Ya ne byl tam." She has to force the last word out, her eyes focused on my feet.

I. Just. Stare. Not only has she never been there *ever*, but the way she said it . . . no Russian speaker would phrase it like that. I try not to betray my surprise or the unease creeping up my spine. "But you're ready to interpret?" And, you know, make sure my husband doesn't *die*?

"Da."

Call me a control freak, but am I seriously supposed to trust my husband's safety to a woman barely confident enough to speak in complete sentences? This doesn't feel right, not at all. "Sorry, what was your specialty again?" I ask Lori.

Noah cuts in. "I don't think I said."

I smile with exquisite patience. "I asked Lori."

She swallows and focuses on the boring beige wall behind me. "I'm an analyst. A political analyst."

Fire flares in my chest, but I keep that patient smile plastered over a look so pointed it could give Noah a puncture wound.

"We need a walk," Danny jumps in before I actually perforate the dude.

"Yes." My voice is firm.

"You can't—" Noah starts.

"Pretty sure we can." Danny places a hand on my shoulder and maneuvers me around Lori to the door.

Noah hops up to intercept us. "You're coming back, right?"

"You'll find us if we don't." Danny's eyes say he's not sure what's coming, but he's behind me 100%. I hope.

Noah nods for Lori to walk with us. She hangs back to whisper, "Did I do something?"

My glare answers "Yes" to her question and "No" to Noah's suggestion. Lori stays. Her job title isn't her fault, but even among analysts, she'd be looked down on. Could they seriously want someone with *no* experience in Russia (or anywhere else) for Danny's backup—especially considering I'm right here?

My cover may be fragile, but if I have to sacrifice it—if I have to sacrifice my job—if I have to sacrifice *my life* for Danny, no contest.

As we pass through the wrought iron embassy gates to place de la Concorde, I glance at him. What if I'm not the one to make that sacrifice?

CHAPTER 5

Place de la Concorde's pretty enough, though all the leaves have abandoned the trees. Maybe it's me, but the air feels colder than this morning.

No, it's not just me—it's the distance between me and Danny. Broad sidewalks afford us way too much room as we stroll past the ornate fountains and Egyptian obelisk in the center of the square.

We reach the Seine and start across pont de la Concorde. The words weigh on my tongue—I've got to say this. But I can't, strolling down this street in the heart of Paris, between the classical lampposts and balustrades, with the Eiffel Tower looming in the distance, a reminder of a happier day not even a week ago.

"I'm sorry." Danny finally begins the conversation.

"Why didn't you think to talk to me?" Seriously. I expect major gaffes from me, who's hardly seen a functional marriage in action. But not Danny, who sometimes makes this relationship work singlehandedly.

He shakes his head in amazed disappointment, not looking at me. "I'm an idiot."

His excuse is hilariously far from the truth, but I let that slide. We reach the other side of the river, and a Grecian-style palace as suited to Paris as DC. I take a left to walk along the quay beside the river. "I can't let you do this."

It's his turn to stare at me, gauging my reaction, my sincerity, my intent. "Because you think I can't."

Because I *know* Lori can't. "I'd be surprised if Lori's ever worked in the field. At all." I try to keep the derision out of my tone—another vestige of Agency-speak—but fail. "She's a political analyst."

"What's wrong with being a political analyst?"

"Nothing." I think better of the lie. "It's . . . I don't know, the sanitation 'engineer' of analysts."

Danny grimaces.

"There's a universe of difference between the field and a desk." I could be wrong. She could be great. But I'm not going to bet my husband's life on it. "If that's the best they can do, I just can't—you can't."

"It's not supposed to be that dangerous. I don't even have to pretend to be someone else. It's a cake walk."

Between his famous-last-words and the temperature, I shiver. That's exactly what they want him to believe. But I don't say that.

"If you're that worried, why don't *you* come with me?"

I pick my words carefully, focusing on the ornamentation of the classical buildings across the street—reminiscent of Rostov. "I could. Doesn't mean it's a good idea. Might be even more dangerous."

Suddenly I realize why it seems so cold: we've held hands pretty much constantly since we've been here. But now, after that meeting inside and that unexpected blow, the invisible cable of connection between us has snapped.

I have to fight for us. I offer my hand and Danny takes it. "I couldn't go in as your wife," I explain.

"Why not?"

I casually check the tree-lined sidewalk, but nobody's paying attention to us. "Talia Reynolds—Fluker—barrister and solicitor, doesn't know Russian. She's never been to Russia. She has no business going with you."

"Not even on her honeymoon?"

It's so much more complicated than that. Word could get back—well, that part wouldn't be too hard to explain. "What if somebody at Shcherbakov phones NRC and mentions meeting your wife-slash-interpreter? They get curious, word gets around . . ."

"What if we didn't say you're my wife? You're just Talia Reynolds, cute interpreter I picked up in Paris."

I laugh off the compliment. "Talia Reynolds is also a lawyer in Ottawa who doesn't speak Russian." The disappointment even tastes bitter. Much as I want it to, that scheme won't work for a million reasons. I know that, I've been through them all, and yet I'm still making the same arguments as Danny in my mind, shooting them down like clay pigeons. But the truth? I do want this, because there's no way I'm letting him go there alone—or worse still, with Lori.

We reach a gap in the cement guardrail on the left, with stairs down to river level. I turn and lead Danny down. A memory snaps into focus, the two of us cutting through a break in a guardrail just like this, only half a world away, arguing our way down the stairs to the water. Breaking up.

"Where does that leave us?" Danny asks.

Somehow, I don't think he just means this assignment. "I dunno. You said yes, and I won't put you in a headlock until you go back on your word."

He pretends to size me up. "I'd like to see you try that."

I shoot him a get-serious look.

"Or you could ask. Not like I signed a contract."

No, but I did. I signed every part of my life away—except

him. And that's what it comes down to. I'm ready to sacrifice anything for my job but him. Now, not even two weeks after our wedding, that's the first thing the CIA demands.

Bodes real well for the long term. Am I right to resign?

"They *could* find someone else." I mean for this mission, to replace Danny. Or maybe I mean to replace me.

He doesn't answer, focused on the barge tied up by the metal railing. Despite Noah's insistence that Danny's the right guy, someone else could do this job. They wouldn't do it as well, but at least they'd be risking their lives and not my husband's.

"You want me to say no," he says. Like I haven't changed his mind, but I've still made the choice for him.

I may not have seen many healthy relationships growing up, but I did pay enough attention in my college Foreign Affairs courses to figure out unilateral decisions rarely make the other parties happy. I can't say no for him, and I still can't understand why he said yes.

So I ask. "You wouldn't agree to this on a whim. Why'd you accept?"

He offers a little smile and a sigh, like it's not worth explaining. "If you want me to say no this bad, I can say no. Backing out isn't illegal."

"Danny." I stop where the sidewalk dead ends at a narrow parking lot, tucked between the two-lane road and the wide river, and meet his eyes. "Tell me."

He monitors me, measuring his message, like he's worried he can't set it on my shoulders. Whatever it is, I brace myself before he finally speaks. "It's my fault."

Because he just said yes? Uh, duh.

"He'd never have gotten the plans if it weren't for me."

Oh. "You were only following protocol," I remind him.

"Protocol that I knew wasn't smart. I knew putting them on a USB drive wasn't secure enough, no matter what the rules said. Now anything could happen."

Though we can't go into specifics in the open, I know what Danny means. His drone's intended for recon, but it could be a dangerously powerful tool.

Or a weapon.

Nobody wants that.

"If I can stop that, I have to." He starts into the parking lot past the little guard's hut, as if that red and white striped boom barrier will hold back the past and its consequences.

Too late.

The single traffic lane's the only place to walk, and a little black Renault is coming our direction. We step out of the way, onto the cement barrier between two rows of cars, and I look up at Danny.

"You know you're not the only one with guilt." My voice is so quiet that I worry the passing car swallowed my words. Especially when Danny doesn't respond for a long moment.

"Believe me, I know." He has no reason to hide things from me, but I can see it in his eyes. Another reason lurks there, bigger than his own (questionable) culpability. He turns away, headed for the steel pedestrian bridge that crosses the river in a single span. I think we've been there before, but we've crossed nearly every bridge in the city it seems.

We reach the footbridge's shadows under the pedestrian paths that lead back to the street above us. A set of stairs rises from our level up through the middle of the bridge. I stop him here, the closest to privacy as we've gotten this whole walk. "I want closure, too, but it's not worth the risk—"

"What were you doing two nights ago at three fifteen AM?"

I blink at the sudden shift to the third degree. "Not sure, but I'm going to go with sleeping?"

He scrutinizes me, gauging whether to believe me. "No. You had a nightmare."

Now I know exactly which night he means. My gaze falls to

45

the cement at our feet. "Did I wake you?"

"I woke you."

I only remember the dream ending abruptly, Fyodor's vacant stare evaporating into the black. In the last three months, I've been through enough to fuel a life's worth of nightmares. We both have.

The rest of the groggy memory comes into focus. Danny asking if I was okay.

Me saying I was fine. A stressed-out dream about missing our flight home. A lie.

Finally, he pulled me over to lay my head on his chest. I stayed there until his breathing was deep and even again, holding still, holding my breath, holding in the tears.

"You wouldn't cry about *not* catching a plane," Danny murmurs.

I should've known he knew.

"That's why I have to do this."

"No, it's why you don't." I look back to him at last.

Earnestness shines in his eyes like a laser sight trained on me, and I want to look away. "Talia, it's my fault you went through all that, that you're still going through it. If I have even half a shot at closure—for you—I want to take it."

"I 'went through all that' to protect you, so you'd never be in danger again." I let the end of my argument play out in his mind: which is exactly what this assignment would be.

Danny inhales, slow and deep, and releases it, staring at the shallow stairs up to the bridge. "Puts us at an impasse, huh?"

He slides an arm around my shoulders and leads me up the stairs. The bridge is metal, but the stairs are covered in weathered wood. They get progressively shallower, becoming a ramp as we emerge into the sunlight.

Now I recognize this place. We came here our first day in Paris. Along the steel rebar of the bridge's guardrail hang hundreds and thousands of padlocks, inscribed with names and dates and messages from couples in love.

When we arrived here our first day in Paris, Danny's wedding gift to me finally made sense: a brass antique padlock with the brand name "INVINCIBLE" scrolled across the body. He'd had our names engraved on the back. We locked it on the railing and threw the key in the Seine, following the ridiculous, romantic tradition. (And updating it by sealing the keyhole with superglue. I know, they'll use bolt cutters if they want it off, but it's all about the sentiment.)

The large brown patinaed lock is hard to miss, and we naturally gravitate to that spot. I do not feel invincible.

We gaze out at the same river where we threw away that key. Even this morning, we were those same carefree lovebirds. Now my husband wants to run off on an adventure for my sake. To end my nightmares.

Let's be honest: how dangerous could visiting an aerospace company be? I've only been in trouble a couple dozen times in my whole career; true danger, a handful. Maybe he's right. Maybe it *is* a cake walk.

Danny tugs on my hand, and I turn to him. "Talk to me," he says. When I can't find the words fast enough, he presses on: "I've spent the last year tearing down the Great Wall of Talia. This morning, you were open. You were vulnerable. You were . . . silly."

"I'm never silly."

Danny casts an oh-really? look at the lock on the steel wire in front of us. He wins that point. "Now your shields are up again. Back at square one."

My shoulders fall. Withdrawal has always been my best defense—but I have to do better. "You need this?" It comes out as more of a question than I intended.

"I want to end it. Let me do that. For you."

Don't know if I can argue. Didn't Noah try the same closure tactic to tempt me?

If Danny's going to be the one who ends it, I have to be the one by his side. End of story. But how can I—

The plan hits me harder than an *avtobus*. I know exactly what to do.

Noah and Jim are desperate. Desperate enough to conscript Lori. Desperate enough to do whatever the mission takes. Desperate enough to try something crazy.

"All right," I tell Danny.

"You're giving me permission?" The wry undertone in his voice mocks the entire idea, like he's extracting a signature from me, the evil parent, for the next cool field trip.

I squeeze his hand. "I'm giving you support. Think that's okay?"

"Guess I can live with that," he jokes.

Oh, he'd definitely better live. I'll see to it.

CHAPTER 6

THEY PAGE NOAH WHEN WE RETURN TO THE CHANCERY, and the man must've run to greet us. I wait until he escorts us back to the CIA conference room to announce our decision to him, Jim and Lori. I step up to the head of the table, like I'm in control.

Because I am. "Here are the terms," I begin.

Jim and Noah instantly slip into skeptical masks. And yeah, a pronouncement isn't a great way to start collective bargaining, but they need to understand a few items are nonnegotiable.

"Danny's going." I wait one more second before I drop the news. "And so am I."

Jim and Noah stand to get me to see reason (or to throttle it into my brain), raising their red-flag objections so fast they talk over one another.

I hold up my hands to stop them. "I know—"

Noah breaks in first. "You'll blow your cover, and we can't sacrifice—"

"I wouldn't be me."

Jim takes the next turn. "We've already worked through the details. Lori's ready."

"Ready?" I don't look at her. Sorry, sweetheart. "She isn't trained for this. It's not fair to her or Danny."

"We don't have any other options."

I smile that perfectly patient smile again. "I'd love to write you a whole options paper, but *I'm not an analyst*." I let that sink in a second before I swing on Lori to continue with my argument. "Do you know where the hospitals in Rostov-on-Don are?"

Jim and Noah exchange a glance, then we all look to her. She stares at the high shine wood grain, and in her reflection, her eyes grow wider. No response.

"Can you get there on your own?"

Silence. Jim and Noah slowly sink into their seats.

"Could you get Danny there in the dark if necessary?"

Danny's eyebrows jump. "Hoping to avoid a Russian hospital."

"You have no idea," I return in the same tone. "But we have to be prepared for when things don't go according to plan. Do you know where the jail is? What you shouldn't say to a Russian man? Where you shouldn't shake hands?"

Noah's breaks in. "We can brief her on social customs."

"You can brief her, you can run simulations, you can hook up a virtual reality Rostov—and it'll never be as good as someone who's really lived there." (For six months, five years ago.)

Jim folds his arms. "All right," he concedes. "You've made a valid argument. Don't think we haven't thought this through ourselves."

Uh huh.

"And," Noah interrupts, "what if you have to choose between him and your job?"

Okay, someone's obsessed with that idea. "That's the beauty of this. I won't have to choose. He *is* my job. Basic executive protection."

Danny folds his arms and frowns. Before I can address him,

Jim waves away the topic. "We've had this exact conversation with Langley, and the final decision is it's too big a risk. All it takes is one wedding photo—"

"This is why covers and disguises were invented." I've got him there.

Ooor not. "You can't just use one of your fake names from back home."

Maybe they really did go over all this and back again—but I have one trump card that's never occurred to them apparently. "Don't need a fake name. You already created a perfect cover." I cast a meaningful glance in Lori's direction.

Jim catches my drift and considers it. "What about your disguise—you going to wear prosthetics and face paint the whole time?"

Obviously he doubts the power of cosmetics. (Men.) "Ever see Kim Kardashian without makeup?"

Jim's brows knit together. I might've taken the wrong tactic. "Kim who?"

"Or any American celebrity. Like in a grocery store tabloid. They're unrecognizable." I hold out a hand as if to finish the phrase: *just like I would be.*

Noah stares at his boss from the corner of his eye, clearly not understanding me. It takes half a second, but Jim's grin grows to mirror mine. In unison, we swing to Lori. Does she see she's being cut out?

She blows out a long breath, and for a second, I think we've deflated her. Then she finally looks up. Tears shimmer in her eyes.

Great. I'm the villain of her little spy dreams.

"Oh my goodness," she says. "Thank you."

"What?"

She doesn't answer, but hops up from her chair and snares me in a hug. "Thank you," she murmurs again. The reality lands in my gut like bad borshcht.

I'm going with Danny. I'm going to Russia. I'm going to have a lot of prep work.

It's a long afternoon until we're finished at the embassy, but I'm far from done with my planning. Normally, CIA officers are ready to travel at a moment's notice (well, an hour's notice), and if I'd been home when I got this assignment, I'd probably be on a plane already. Today, our travel plan doesn't start for a couple hours, and preparation abhors a vacuum.

As soon as we walk in our apartment, I'm ready to pack. But our suitcases sit on the elegant handmade bedspread. I hurry to check—they're full.

Did they come in here while we were at the embassy? I riffle through my clothes.

"You said to pack," Danny says from behind me.

"Oh." I stop mid-shuffle. "Right." Jumping to conclusions. I laugh at myself. Still, I need to get ready. I dig out my nicest pair of pants and both skirts I brought. "Do you have a travel sewing kit?" (Eagle Scout. He's prepared.)

"Always mend before a mission?" Danny plops onto the bedspread and digs in his bag.

"Sort of." I reach into my jeans pocket and pull out some of the equipment Jim and Noah provided: a lock pick set, actual picks plus improvised and repurposed tools (and yes, there's a use for bobby pins in lock picking, but probably not the one you're picturing). "I need to sew these into my clothes."

He raises an eyebrow, but doesn't comment further, surrendering the plastic sewing case. I make quick work of the stitches, and by the time Danny heads to the bathroom for our toiletries, I'm onto my next prep step. I go to an ornate side table drawer filled with scattered odds and ends. Cautiously amused, Danny leans against the bathroom doorway to watch me. I grab a handful of small items and arrange them on the cream-colored tabletop. I pick up the first object (a thimble) like I'm examining it, switch it to my other hand, then set it down. Next, I lift the second thing (a stubby pencil) inspect it and put it back.

"Interested in Sylvie's junk drawer?" Danny asks.

"Fascinated." I move the third item, a standard six-sided die, to my other hand before I snap up the fourth thing, an expired *Paris Visite* transit pass. "Should we finish packing?"

"I guess."

I return the pass to the table and look up. Danny studies me. Yeah, too slow. I drop the die on the tabletop and rearrange the things to repeat the routine. This time, I keep the pencil.

Gotta do it again. I take the die again. Almost there; almost fast enough. One more time. As soon as the pass touches down, I pivot and start across the room. When Danny takes stock of the table, I slide the die into my pocket.

"Are we playing a game?" Danny asks.

"No, why?"

He nods toward the table. "The die's missing."

Dang. Still too slow. I take it out of my pocket. "Ever do magic tricks as a kid?"

"Did you?"

"My brothers did."

His squint still seems skeptical. "So you'll never reveal your secrets?"

"It's not magic. Sleight of hand."

He goes to his suitcase and pulls out three or four USB drives. (They're multiplying.) Seems like he's been keeping careful track of these things these last few weeks—since one of his was stolen. "Let's try that with something more practical."

I roll the die over my palm. Is he asking to learn a magic trick, or . . . more? "Why?"

Danny shrugs. "Could be useful?"

I'm not buying the casual act. I observe him for another minute, as if he has a reason to lie. I believe him—I do—but I don't want him to need even something as boring as these skills.

"Okay," he says slowly. "If you don't want to show me—"

"No, I can show you, but . . . maybe we should leave this to me?"

He contemplates me a long second. I'd need something better than a real-life decoder ring to decipher that expression. (Not to mention the fact we discontinued those rings decades ago.) The tension stretches out.

I need Danny. He's the thing that keeps me sane in the spy life, the wilderness of mirrors. But I'm supposed to keep him far from that life. Have I made a serious mistake?

I wheel away and change the subject abruptly. "Did you bring any warmer clothes?" We've already been briefed on current climate conditions in Rostov-on-Don: roughly the same as the weather back home, and a little colder than Paris.

"I'll survive," he says. He slides his USB drives back into his suitcase and stays where he is, across the room. Not daring to come closer. "Are we planning on stealing something?"

"Not planning on it, but—"

"How does that make you better than him?"

I don't have to ask which "him" he means. Fyodor Timofeyev. The man who stole his plans—the man I had to kill to protect Danny. I muster the courage to approach Danny, because I can't answer his question above a whisper. "Maybe I'm not. I don't remember saying I was."

"I understand he broke the law—"

"*We're* about to break the law. Day one, lesson one at the Agency: spying is illegal in every country of the world." I search his eyes: normally warm, now worried. I can barely breathe my next words. "Do you know what you're getting into?"

I mean what he's getting into accepting this assignment— no, not an assignment; they can't *assign* civilians anything. But in the silence spinning between us, Danny looks away, subconsciously rubbing his wedding ring.

A metal band just as solid cinches around my stomach. Aside from a crappy family history of happy, lasting marriages, I work in a job with a divorce rate of approximately 163%.

I turn to the side table, yank the drawer open harder than I mean to, and brush all the practice props back inside. But the nervous energy doesn't dissipate, and I'm pacing the little apartment, finally settling on stuffing the tool-laced clothes back in my suitcase.

The only thing left to pack is the thing I'm dreading most. I ease off my engagement ring and wedding bands, three rows of channel-set diamonds that we haven't had time to solder together. I couldn't wear them no matter what my cover ID was—CIA officers always travel "alone"—but I'm not ready to give them up.

"Hey." Danny's hands land on my waist. I glance over my shoulder at him. "It's your job. I might not like it, but I get it."

"Thanks." Even I can tell my grin's weak.

"You all right?"

I open my fingers to reveal my rings in my palm.

"Guess I should get used to that," he says.

"I hate that idea."

Danny takes my rings and pushes the suitcases out of the way. We sit on the bedspread. He twirls one wedding band between his thumb and index finger.

"I can wear them till tonight." I offer my finger. It already feels . . . naked.

Danny holds my hand. I stare at my bare finger next to the

band on his, aircraft-grade titanium with a carbon fiber inlay (pretty sure he married me and not aerospace).

It's only been a few seconds, but that's long enough. "You planning to put that ring back on me?"

Danny lifts my left hand to replace my first wedding band. "Worried?"

My gut does a double backflip, but my cocky grin is self-mocking. "Hey, it's me."

"So yes? Perpetually?"

I elbow-nudge him, though he isn't wrong. "Danny, if I didn't think I could handle this, we wouldn't be doing it."

He frowns at me for a long second, and I mentally back-pedal. What did I say wrong? Danny focuses on sliding my engagement ring and my second wedding band on.

"Hey," I say, leaning down to his line of sight. "Who's playing sullen now?"

He shakes off the sadness. "Sorry. You said *you* could handle this."

"Well, yeah, I hope so."

"Not 'we.'"

I'm not sure it's the pronoun choice bugging Danny. "Of course 'we.' I'm not leaving you after I fought so hard to go with you."

He nods, staring at the tufted headboard instead of me. "Sure about this?"

"So far I have a perfect 100% mission survival rate."

Danny meets my gaze, a challenge in his eyes. "What a coincidence. So do I."

I smile at his joke and lean in to kiss him, sliding my arms around his neck. At the last second, I realize the challenge hasn't faded, like it would if he were joking.

But Danny kisses me back without hesitation, and I push away every thought but enjoying the last minutes of our honeymoon.

CHAPTER 7

THE TAXI ROLLS UP TO THE AIRPORT, and I assess the glowing building. I don't think we realized it, but the minute we accepted the mission, our honeymoon was over. I'm already in operational mode: thinking in Russian, checking for surveillance every fifty feet, running through Moscow Rules, readying for this test.

I've been a CIA officer (we don't use the term "agent" for ourselves) for four years, but Canada pales in comparison to Russia. Though the Cold War's long over, Russia's still an important operational area. And maybe my biggest challenge yet.

Danny gets out of the cab and helps me out. I've done all I can to debrief him. If I'm honest, the nerves dancing in every major organ aren't just for his sake—they're for mine.

I've faced off with foreign intelligence, recruited high value targets, even taken down a traitor, and still it feels I have to do this to prove I have what it takes as a CIA officer.

As if I'll ever stop proving myself. Ever stop striving.

Danny and I check in at the counter, and he gets his changed itinerary. My tickets still fly to Ottawa (apparently thirty-six hours away). I scan the crowds out of habit.

Man, I hope Lori's up to this.

Once we're past security, we have twenty minutes before I have to spring into action. The gates to Moscow and New York are nowhere near one another, so we grab snacks from an airport café and linger between our destinations until our muffins are long gone.

"Have a good trip," I say, slightly louder than I would in real life. "Show 'em how to aerospace."

Danny almost laughs. "Travel safe," he says before he plants a kiss on my forehead. "*Rakastan sinua*," he says softly.

"*Hyvä*," I whisper back, praising his punctuation. (Finnish for "good.") "*Ja minä sinuakin, ikuisesti.*"

"You'd better," he finishes, back to English for the part someone else might hear. (Also, we've exhausted his Finnish vocabulary.)

It's much easier to leave my husband of less than two weeks knowing I'll see him tomorrow, but I'm definitely not saying no to his slow goodbye kiss. A distinct perk of honeymooning in Paris: nobody's offended if you're in love.

He pulls back. "Better go."

"Yeah." I clamp down on the inward wince at leaving him. After one last kiss, I slip away, glancing back for surveillance. Danny's the only one watching, so I give him a little wave.

Halfway through the terminal, I find my real destination: a women's bathroom. And it's crowded. Good thing we've planned for that contingency. I join the queue waiting for a stall, puffing out a bored breath. I monitor the slow-moving line, willing a redhead in a red jacket to appear.

Finally, when I'm nearly to the front, she joins us.

Action time. I'm next in line, and I take a stall. Off with my black jacket and aviator sunglasses (cliché, maybe, but they hide more of my face). Out of my jeans, revealing black slacks underneath. Trade out my worn-in sneakers for shiny black flats. I hoist my carry-on onto the rack above the toilet.

The costume change doesn't take long, and I'm repacked well before Lori's ready. After what feels like forever, black patent flats pass by my door, then back again. I wait until she's clear before I throw open the door. *"Désolée, désolée,"* I apologize. (Probably marking myself as a tourist, but half the people in the airport are foreigners, right?)

Another woman in line starts forward and my lungs clench—but Lori backtracks to slide in the stall first. The other woman scowls and troops back to the line. I deliberately scrub my hands, including under the nails, still mostly manicured (at my mother's insistence) from my wedding.

I take the same care drying my hands, then examine my makeup in the long mirrors. We have to keep this up while the line clears out, but I'm not sure how much more I can delay when I finally glimpse the right stall door swinging open. Lori, with a long dark braid, jeans, sneakers and my black jacket and aviators, strides out to the sinks.

"Pardonez-moi?" she approaches me. *"Est-ce la vôtre?"* She rolls my carry-on to me like she found the bag I "forgot."

"Ah, oui, merci." I scan the line, the women leaving the stalls—nobody should see Lori went in a redhead and came out a brunette. I duck around a corner into the bathroom's mirrored alcove and open my bag. As planned, Lori added regular and black diplomatic passports and her boarding pass for a direct flight to Rostov-on-Don to the rest of my supplies: a red wig and gorgeous red coat. I pull on the wig cap and wig, making quick adjustments in the mirror. There's enough time to secure it with a dozen hairpins. I finger-comb the strands into place, arranging the long bangs to the right, as close to Lori's asymmetric cut as possible (which she eventually confessed was designed specifically for this mission). With the long red coat, I'm suited up to be somebody else.

I walked in the bathroom Talia, but I walk out Lori Dolman. It's been a long time since I flew undercover internationally, but since we're already past security, the hard part won't come until we hit Russian customs. I've got some strange stuff in my bags to (not) declare—and that's just what we were comfortable with me flying in. It doesn't count the things I'll retrieve or buy in Rostov (or the tools too small to set off metal detectors, sewn into the lining of my pants and Lori's jacket).

I'm ten feet from the bathroom when the first obstacle grabs me by the arm—literally. I whirl around to find Lori. *"Mademoiselle, avez-vous vu un alliance dans les toilettes?"*

Did I see a ring? Oh. Crap. I forgot to exchange a key item: my rings. Lori asked if I'd seen one in the bathroom. Decent cover, and definitely something I can work with. I lead the way back to the bathroom where we made the switch.

"We shouldn't have contact," I murmur, though it's my fault she's had to track me down. I pretend to hunt around the sink. When I bend down to search the tile floor underneath, I tug my rings off. *"Voilà!"* I hold them aloft, then press them into her hands. "Try not to lose them again." My eyes are twice as serious as my tone.

Lori nods and slides the rings onto her middle finger—they're too big for her ring finger, and that's the closest we can get to secure. I'm not losing those.

I give Lori some lead time, scrubbing my hands again after touching the floor. (Public bathrooms in Europe? Yeeeah.) Once I'm sure she's clear, I rush out of the bathroom. I reach my gate on time and trot to the tarmac for my tiny plane without any problems—until my phone vibrates. I check my phone. A text. From Danny.

Lori says Zverev emailed. Wants to see us when we get in.

That's fast. Don't recognize the name from the company profile. *Who is he?*

Dunno. The guy I'm meeting at Shcherbakov.

Which makes him our target. *Hope you said yes. Gotta go.* I scan the tarmac as I close in on our little jet. A couple others are headed this way. I navigate to the secret CIA app better than a factory reset. Once it's wiped, I remove the SIM card.

Almost done—now to make this look good. At the bottom of the stairs to the plane, I drop the phone and it skitters underneath. Although the wand waver dude beckons for me to come away, I chase it. Seems like you can never destroy a phone when you want to (though if it falls a mere foot at home, it's ruined). This time I'm in luck: spider-web cracks cover the touchscreen. I leave the phone where it is and hurry to the stairs.

Inside the plane, I slide the SIM card into a mini battery pack in my pocket. It emits a barely noticeable buzz, and the SIM card is erased, reformatted, and short circuited. (Or something like that. Do I look like a tech guy?)

I've severed the last link on me to Talia Reynolds. Even my luggage is labeled with Lori's name.

My bags are only the beginning. When I land, I'll have six hours to reacquaint myself with Rostov, procure my last provisions and scope out Shcherbakov. Granted, an actual building penetration would take months to plan, but preparation might as well be my middle name. (More fitting than Rosalie, for sure.)

Six hours to prep. Then Danny arrives in Rostov, and the real challenge starts.

CHAPTER 8

RUSSIA'S COLDER THAN I REMEMBER (which is saying a lot). I huff out a fogbank as I hoof it to the gates of the Cathedral of the Nativity of the Virgin. The white towers topped with gold onion domes and Orthodox crosses feel so familiar, like coming home.

You know how you can never come home again? Yeah, it's not the same. I have to remind myself I don't need to find my missionary companion or approach people to share the gospel, though the pressure already hangs over me. Serving as a missionary was hard work.

This mission could be much harder. And it starts now, by finding my contact here.

At the cathedral gates, I drape my fashionable scarf over my head, a requirement for women in Orthodox churches. The sweet smoky scent of incense hits me as soon as I walk through the doors. Once my vision adjusts to the dim lighting, I glance up at the gold-tinted icons—paintings of Christ, Mary and the saints. My favorite, Our Lady of Kazan, gazes out with her Mona Lisa smile in that "iconic" Russian style.

The morning services will begin soon, and the cathedral's

busy with worshipers attending to the various icons, praying, lighting candles, kissing pictures. It's so different from Mormon services that it was hard not to stare when I visited before. But today I observe disinterestedly before I take my place in the women's side of the pews, where other worshipers stand waiting.

My Agency liaison in the city should be here. I've already checked in at my hotel and reacquainted myself with major landmarks. Now I need to touch base and ask a quick favor.

"*Devushka?*" someone whispers. I turn to the man in the aisle. He holds out a small leather-bound book. "*Eta tvoya?*" *Is this yours?*

I've only seen his picture for a minute, but I recognize the salt-and-pepper hair and beard, and friendly smile lines at the corners of his eyes. He presses the prayer book into my hands and I accept it. "*Da, spasibo, dyadya.*" (That's "uncle," and I'm not ad-libbing a cover this time; it's a term of respect.)

Are we staying through the whole church service? I gaze-point at the doors.

My liaison gives an almost imperceptible nod. I check behind me once as he meanders out. I linger a minute before I follow.

He's waiting on the sidewalk and starts walking toward the *rynok*, the open-air market by the cathedral, as soon as I reach him. "You should button your coat," he says as a Russian greeting. Yep, he's been here a while. I heed his pestering. It's everybody else's business whether you're dressed for the weather here. Everything is everybody else's business.

"Was the flight too terrible?" he asks.

"Always." Doubt he knows how much I hate flying. I try not to make it a big deal, but I wish Danny had been there to distract me from the vicissitudes of aviation.

My liaison's quiet until we've rounded the corner to the cathedral's side. "Name's Semyon," he says in English.

A Russian name. Uh huh. "Lori."

"First time in Russia, Lori?" he asks. "Or just Rostov?"

"Neither, actually."

"Welcome back." He monitors the straggling worshipers hurrying to the doors. "Need anything?"

"Another suit and a couple skirts. Shoe polish. Sponge."

"Measurements? European sizes?" He starts walking toward the market again, trying to look like we're not together.

I tuck my coded list of requests—fall weather wear and another business outfit—between the prayer book's pages. "*Cheritishop* is good." James Bond might wear a newly made, freshly tailored suit, but in the real world, you draw a lot less attention with normal, local, gently worn-in clothes. Real spies shop thrift stores: nothing too new, nothing too nice, nothing too foreign.

"Delivered to your room, *tsaritsa*?" That would be *empress*.

I pretend he isn't being sarcastic. "Sure. Hermitage Hotel." I pause to admire a table of lacquer boxes (cheap knockoffs, not the real kind painted with a single squirrel hair) (seriously). Semyon wanders on, and I take a few minutes before I catch up.

"You all set?" he asks. "Any tools or anything?"

Gadgets and gizmos are kind of cliché, but I do have a few—and more than a few standard-issue tools on board. "I'm going shopping, but I'll let you know if I need anything else." This time, I amble ahead, and he reaches me between two stalls.

"So, how'd they task you with executive protection? No offense," Semyon adds quickly. "Just that I wouldn't have pegged you for the type."

"That's why I make the perfect bodyguard."

"Got a point there." He hands over a SIM card. "Text me the room number; my number's on there."

Good thing I packed a spare phone. Though I'd love for our communication to be more secure, I'm sure he's got our calls set to be rerouted until they're next to impossible to trace. He'd

64

better—he's the only thing in Rostov linking me to the Agency.

I walk a couple feet ahead, past a booth selling spoons and shoes. "You have a good cobbler?" I ask. Doubt English slang for a document forger translates.

"Yep. Need something?"

"Backups never hurt."

"I'll pull your files." He glances around, and the chilly air changes. Something's coming.

I let the prayer book slip from my hand and we both stoop to pick it up. "Don't know if they told you in Paris," he whispers just before we stand, "but we believe there's an FSB officer in Shcherbakov."

F. S. B. *Federal'naya sluzhba bezopasnosti.* Russian domestic intelligence. Yeah, that's a pretty big deal. "Didn't mention it." Before I dragged my husband into this company. Thanks a lot, Paris.

Semyon takes the prayer book and rises. "Deep under. Recruiting an agent or maybe keeping tabs on their imports and exports."

I don't know him well enough to judge whether he's trying to downplay this, but the implications stream through my mind. Danny could be in more danger than I anticipated—both of us could. My pulse speeds up and I suck in a slow breath to cool it, slowly starting a circuit back to the cathedral.

Semyon takes the lead and pauses around the corner of the cathedral—a blind spot. We have maybe thirty seconds to wrap this up. "Top priority's executive protection," he says, "but a close second: find that officer. We know something's up, and we can't figure out how to get at it. Haven't been able to recruit any Shcherbakov employees from outside."

"Figured out where in the company the officer works?"

"We've narrowed it down to R&D. Stay on your toes."

"You think?" I've always operated on *my* home turf. I'm doubly on my guard just being here. Now I need to step up my game again. I promised Danny we'd be fine—but rather than keeping me apprised of the details, the CIA and its secrecy are biting the hand that spies for it.

"What sector are you meeting with?" Semyon asks.

"R&D."

He smiles for the first time. "Starting in the right place."

"Speaking of starting." I hand over my extra room key. "Thanks, 'uncle.'"

Even with Semyon's help, again, I've got a lot of work to do before Danny gets here.

I've refreshed my Rostov recall and stocked up on the stuff I didn't ask Semyon to supply—and I could spend another week on prep, easy. Whether I'm ready or not, my time's up, and I'm back in Rostov International Airport. It feels like a huge, temporary shed that was used for so long, people forgot the "temporary" part and added on. Classic Russia—and pretty confusing. Danny had better arrive okay. The airports in Moscow are about as English-friendly as we get here, and even then, navigating alone without a word of Russian? Yeah.

His flight should be here by now. I scan the crowd. After four or five forevers, my heart rate's accelerated enough I could be the next flight departing the runway. He has to be here. Unless he's stranded in Moscow. What would we do? Would they send someone after him? How fast? How long do I wait before I text Semyon? Nerves invade my stomach like angry *kuznechiki*—grasshoppers—getting madder by the minute.

And then Danny strolls in, scanning the signs like he reads Cyrillic. As usual, all my worrying is a waste. He's here. He made it.

I should run up to him. I should throw my arms around his neck. I should kiss him. But I can't. I'm Lori. Not Talia. I'm normally good at compartmentalizing my professional and private lives—almost too good sometimes—but today, Danny has been tossed into my CIA box, and even I'm not sure how to make this work.

He walks past me—hardly surprising, given I'm in the disguise and (some of) the makeup I'll be living in for the mission. I march up behind him. "Mr. Fluker?"

He jumps a bit and turns. I wait for the exact second it registers that underneath this flashy red coat and the almost too-stylish red hair, it's his wife—

No. I can't be his wife. I'm his interpreter, and that's how I introduce myself. "Lori Dolman. I'll be your interpreter."

"Hi." He shakes my hand, barely veiling the amusement in his eyes. "Call me Danny."

"Let's go get your bags, Danny, and head to your hotel."

We reach the depressingly bare gray walls of the baggage claim. Never thought I'd miss advertising. I watch for his luggage on the conveyor—well, I watch him watching. I'm not supposed to recognize his bags. "Done much business with Russians?" I ask.

"Not a whole lot."

"I'm sure you've read the typical advice: have your business cards and documents translated, be punctual, use an extremely firm handshake."

Danny stoops to get his suitcase and turns back to me. "Define 'extremely.'"

"Most people use the term 'bone-crushing.'"

The laugh and the smile I love shine in his eyes again, but I avoid his gaze. I'm Lori, not Talia. And I'm also not kidding about the "bone-crushing" part. They'll go easier on a woman, but with guys, it's like a middle school game of Mercy.

What else does he need to know? "Oh, names. Naming structure's important. When you want to address a superior, someone you'd call Mr. Jones, here, you'd use his first name and patronymic. That's like his middle name, but it's formed from—"

"His father's name. I know what a patronymic is."

I snap my fingers like I'm remembering something. "Right. Rocket scientist."

"Yep." He flashes a grin and grabs his other bag.

I lead him toward the exit. "You address people at your level—business acquaintances—by their whole first name. You'd call friends by the short form of their name. They'll tell you what form to use."

"And more than friends?"

We pass through the glass doors to the outside, the icy blast chopping the conversation short before I can read his expression. I answer him anyway. "Close friends and family members usually use a diminutive form, like a nickname," I say, conspicuously skipping over one important category. "So a woman could be Natalia Petrovna at the bank, Natalia with business contacts, Tasha to her friends and Tashen'ka to her grandma."

"Tashen'ka," Danny repeats like he's mulling it over, not quite looking at me.

Another teasing response springs to my lips and I almost literally have to bite it back. This idea suddenly feels really stupid. Not only does Danny not belong in my CIA box, but seeing him is the one thing that seems to tell my subconscious it's safe to relax in my "private life" box. Can any amount of compartmentalization hide our real relationship, my real identity?

We have to. I straighten my shoulders, all business. All Lori. (My version of her.) "We'll drop off luggage at the hotel and get changed. Then I hear you're meeting with Mr. Zverev?"

"Yep." We hit the outer doors and the humidity and chill—feels like home for a whole new set of reasons: this is exactly what the weather's like in Ottawa now, and to have Danny at my . . . well, not at my side. I monitor Danny and his first glimpses of Rostov. He peers up at the milky sky, a reminder of the winter closing in (as if the freezing temperature wasn't warning enough). "You'll want to button up." I nod at his jacket, too light for this weather. We didn't pack for a Russian detour.

"I'm fine."

I give him an okay-but-you'll-regret-that expression and look to the curb to scan the cabs (and for surveillance). If you're taking a taxi while traveling abroad, I don't envy you.

"What are you looking for?" Danny asks, studying the cars.

"Something standard, marked. A company I recognize." Cabs are a classic way to trap tourists, extort them, mug them, or . . . worse. I lower my voice and angle my head for him. "And surveillance. Get in the habit of checking behind you and scanning crowds for familiar faces."

Concern flickers over his features, and I add, "Keep in mind that if anyone knew why we're here, we'd be in trouble."

The concern in his eyes deepens to a frown, but before I interpret that, I spot a cab marked *Lider*, a company name I know. Danny follows me and loads his bags, and we get in.

The cabbie, an elderly man with curly white hair, turns to us. He's missing a few teeth, replaced with gold ones. Cabbie's got a grille? Welcome to Russia. Somehow the gold makes him endearing instead of threatening.

Not that I trust the guy completely. I give explicit instructions in my most polite Russian, including the exact route to the hotel. The cabbie knows how to get there, but now he also knows I'm familiar with the route, and if he deviates from our course by one turn, I'll be able to tell.

(He doesn't realize I'm trained to leap from a moving

vehicle, but that's probably best kept on a need-to-know basis.)

The cabbie confirms my directions and pulls out. When he makes a sharp left onto the street, Danny slides across the seat with the turn, ready to slip his arm behind my back.

The second he starts moving, however, my reflexes kick in, and I plant a hand on his hip to stop him. Danny jumps, eyes wide with surprise, and the daggers I'm staring at him aren't communicating clearly enough. I eyeball the cabbie (the witness). He's still on my set course, not spying on us in the rearview (that's my job). But for all we know, he speaks English.

So I say the only two words I can to communicate the message to Danny. "Mr. Fluker."

The realization slowly dawns in his eyes—what he's gotten himself into. I'm not being mean. I'm being Lori. This is exactly what we signed up for.

He shifts away, looking down. "What else do I need to know about Russians?"

Whew. He understands. We both know this is only a few days, but yes, I will have to put my job first. For both our sakes.

"Don't smile without a reason," I start the list. "You'll come off as an idiot. Be on time."

"You said that."

"Glad you're listening." Before either of us make this into an inside joke, I resume my list. "Dress your best—suit, polished shoes—but I'm sure you can handle yourself."

His eyes stay fixed on the window. "You really think so?"

I wait until he looks at me to smile. "Yeah. I do."

He smiles, contemplative, and I take his hand for a surreptitious squeeze. This mission is going to be great—no, it'll be perfect. I hope.

CHAPTER 9

THE CAB LEAVES US AT OUR HOTEL, its mint-colored exterior and white pilasters and molding like a mini replica of St. Petersburg's Hermitage (transplanted a thousand miles to the south). I lead Danny under the awning, through the oak doors and up the half-flight of stairs to the lobby. It's not huge— nothing about the hotel is—but the finishing touches are nice, from the tray ceiling to the gold drapes and sofas, to the gleaming ochre tile. Danny's lips form a somber line, but he nods his approval.

"Have you worked with an interpreter before?" I ask.

It bugs me I don't already know the answer to that question. I should, right?

"Not formally." He focuses on the gold Cyrillic script floating on the wall behind the (empty) walnut and marble reception desk.

"Well, keep in mind it's my duty to translate everything verbatim. So if you say, 'I think he's a jerkface,' I say, 'I think he's a jerkface.'"

Danny finally looks at me, one eyebrow quirked. "Can you translate 'jerkface'?"

"Guess I'd have to think about it." I allow myself a little smile. "Why, planning on calling someone that?"

"Only if that's the next custom you're going to brief me on."

"Russian insults are an art form. Not sure 'jerkface' qualifies." I give him a wink just before a clerk arrives at the desk. I step up to get him all checked into room 302, next to mine.

The clerk gives me the keys to Danny's room. I pivot back to him. "All set."

I show Danny to the elevator alcove. "The 'verbatim' thing cuts both ways, so if they ask how the magnetic storm's treating you—"

"As in the geomagnetic storm?"

"Uh . . . I don't know. That's a real thing?"

Danny casts me an amused smirk and takes the paperwork for his room. He indicates the fancy Cyrillic script logo on the letterhead. "Can you read that?"

"*Ermitazh.* Hermitage. Name of the hotel."

He sends me an um-duh? look. Right. Rocket scientist. "Obviously," I add belatedly.

Danny makes an effort to keep our fake small talk alive. "Where are you from?"

I pick one of the many states I've lived in for an answer. "Oklahoma."

"Sooners fan?"

"Not into sports." The elevator finally arrives to rescue us from this awkward chat, and we board. No one else joins us, and the doors slide shut on our silence.

"Sorry about the cab," I finally try.

"My own fault." The words echo across a stilted distance, as if we really are strangers. But it's only awkward because we have to keep up this front.

The elevator slows to halt at our floor, and the doors slide open to reveal two overstuffed armchairs, deep red with gold stripes. I take one of Danny's bags for him and march down the hall to our rooms. Once I've unlocked the door, I give him the key. (No comment on where the other key went.)

Danny deposits his suitcase between the desk and another of those red-and-gold striped armchairs. I follow him to park his other suitcase there. Not much space anywhere else in the nice but narrow room. I keep my gaze on the obnoxiously rosy two-tone walls—do they have ears? Or eyes?

He holds out a hand, but until I can answer my question, I have to turn him down. "I'll let you get changed," I say, ready to make for the hall again.

"Can we talk?"

"About what?" I keep my voice neutral to play dumb, but when Danny and I face each other, I give an exaggerated shrug. I don't know if the room's a safe place to talk. One of a dozen things I would've done if I'd had more time to set up.

But I'm not totally unprepared. "Remember, there's no such thing as business casual," I tell him. "I'll be back in a minute."

He gives me a thoughtful "hm" before I hurry to my room. I've got to change, too. In Russia, no respectable interpreter—no respectable *woman*—would work in a professional environment in pants. (You can wear them whenever you want, but if you're doing business, buck tradition at your own peril.)

I didn't bring business attire on my honeymoon, but between Lori and Semyon, I've got a decent wardrobe and my makeup case is now ridiculous. We're talking the works: moisturizer, toner, primer, foundation, concealer, highlighter, contouring powder, lipstick, lip liner, lip gloss, three shades of eye shadow, two kinds of mascara, loose powder, fake eyelashes, and the latest edition of PhotoShop. (Kidding.) (Kind of.)

But I'm not here just for the costume change and a fresh coat of paint. I raid one bag for another handheld device. Normally, I don't have a whole lot of gadgets in my job, but this one's important. The size of a deck of cards, the scanner doesn't have external labels or indicators. You have to be in the know to understand the LED display lights on this bug detector.

With the scanner in hand and the cool-weather gear Semyon provided for Danny over my arm, I return to his room. I give Danny's door a perfunctory knock, then pop the key in the lock. Before I open it, I remember who I am: not his wife. His service provider. (And not *that* kind of service.) I withdraw the key and wait for the door to open any second.

It doesn't.

I ignore the nagging, irrational worry and knock again. The door opens less than a second later. "I said I was coming."

"Sorry; didn't hear you."

He buttons the second and top buttons of his dress shirt, and it strikes me once again how handsome he is. He's even wearing the suit he wore for our wedding. (Without the vest today. Still. The effect? Good.) I want to wrap my arms around him and kiss him.

Apparently Danny isn't the only one this will be a challenge for.

He's stepped back from the door, but he's observing me, too. I doubt someone else's clothes and haircut and face has nearly the same effect on him. I couldn't really pass for Lori, but I don't resemble me, either.

"You look . . . different. Really different."

"Thanks?"

He opens his mouth to respond, but I shake my head. I'm not actually offended (I think). After another second, he raises both eyebrows. "You coming in?"

"Sorry." I shut the door behind me and hold up my signal scanner, wiggling it. Danny tilts to take a closer look, intrigued. I drape the coat over the chair and switch on the scanner.

"We're too far away to see the Sea of Azov, right?" he asks.

"Yeah, it's twenty miles downstream. Why, do you have a view of the Don?"

"Yep. Aren't you next door?"

"Building's in the way." We fall into silence. After a second, he moves to grab his tie: the dark red one from our wedding. (Is he doing this on purpose? Or did he only bring one tie?)

I pick up our safest conversation from earlier. "Basically," I say, "when I'm interpreting, you should act like I'm not there."

Danny pauses in measuring the position of his tie's knot. "You want me to ignore you? Not sure that's possible."

The LED display finally registers its reading, each segment of the line lighting up, turning green. I keep the conversation going as a cover. "I mean, when you talk to someone else through me, address him, not me. Pretend like I'm part of the scenery, the furniture."

Barely suppressing his amusement, he focuses on his Windsor knot.

Two more LED bars. "Again, I'm bound by ethics to translate verbatim. I can explain cultural concepts, connotations, that sort of thing, but I can't provide analysis."

"Aren't you an 'interpreter'? What good are you if you can't *interpret*?"

"Sorry. It's my job to translate, not advise."

He glances at me, barely reining in a look of pure mischief. "Okay, can we—?"

I hold up a finger, waiting for the color on the last bar of the scanner. After two tense seconds, the final bar on the scanner lights up—red. The back of my neck drops twenty degrees. I can't even flip the display to him, because red means audio *and* visual bugs. It means this room isn't private.

I'm surprised, but I'm not. I'm an American spy in Russia. Is anywhere supposed to be safe?

I'll have Semyon send somebody in to exterminate the bugs as soon as we can. For now, we need to live our covers.

Danny contemplates me, his frown settling in. He rephrases his question. "Will we have time to do anything at

Shcherbakov today?"

"Might as well stop in if we're here, right?"

He pulls on his suit jacket and buttons it. Finally, he replaces his wallet in his back pocket, then reaches for his phone.

"Doesn't work here," I remind him. "Yet. We'll get you a SIM card." Which was on my list for Semyon, but not in my room with the rest of his deliveries. I pick up the coat Semyon *did* come through on. European cut, heavyweight fabric, black. It'll blend in perfect. The pockets are loaded with a hat and gloves. It's even reversible. "You'll want this."

"It's not that cold—not even below freezing. My jacket's fine."

"Not here it isn't." I try to fight back a smile and offer the coat again. "Just trust me."

Danny comes to stand behind me at the desk, meeting my gaze in the mirror. "I do."

My nascent smile fades, and we stare at our reflections. Thirteen days ago, he was dressed like that, and we stood together for wedding photos. Today, I'm wearing twice as much makeup as I used to look my best in photographs, the blood red coat, and the way-too-much-maintenance copper hair that tapers from short on one side to long bangs on the other.

Danny's right. I look different. But I don't just *look* different. I *am* someone else.

And yes, that's smarter and safer. But, man, do I hate it.

I note Danny's reaction. He needs me to take the lead. So I do. "Ready?" I ask.

"Sure."

I hand over his coat and walk out first. In the hall, I slip my scanner into my pocket. Once we're alone in the elevator, Danny puts on the coat while I check the scanner display again. Green lights. Clear. "There's a listening device in your room."

He puffs out a breath. "Twenty minutes in the country and they're after us already?"

"No." I stuff the scanner back in my pocket. "I just want you to be as paranoid as me."

"Is that even possible?"

I scan him a long minute, trying to read that inscrutable tone and expression. Is this supposed to be teasing? Or is that how he feels about my job, my quirks—*me*?

I'm almost afraid to figure that out—and if I obsess over this internal temperature taking, I'm sure to miss something important.

"Look," he says. "We just got to the point where you're not using a cover with me. I don't want to go back to that." As if that's not a bolt to the heart, the watchfulness in his eyes, like he's worried we're starting over, hammers the arrow deeper.

I don't have a comeback for that. Instead, I raid his coat pockets for the gloves Semyon provided. "Put these on." I reach inside the coat to retrieve the knit hat from the breast pocket.

When I try to put it on him, however, Danny ducks away. "No, don't—"

"Seriously, you'll want it."

"It's only November. I can figure out whether I'm cold."

I go after him again, and he catches me by the waist, his grin teasing. He pulls me close, and the hat's the last thing on my mind. I tilt my chin up, anticipating the kiss, but then the elevator stops. We both turn to the gold doors. My reflection, my hair, my makeup: they're window dressing for the real difference. My eyes are the same, and yet fundamentally different.

I'm not his wife.

And that's what I hate most.

Danny releases me and I stumble a step. The elevator doors slide open—either I missed the chime or it's broken—and the glare of the setting sun slices between us.

"Here's your hat." I shove it at him and stride off the elevator, pretending to not notice that Danny pockets the hat. And he still hasn't buttoned his jacket.

He's right: it isn't all that cold, and we're as used to cold weather as people get (that is, though we curse the day winter hits, we can deal). But I'm not kidding when I say he'll want it.

The icy air creeps into my coat while we walk to the main road, as if the incident in the elevator didn't leave me chilled enough. After dismissing a couple good Samaritans offering a lift (not unusual, but I'm not trusting them), we hail a real, marked cab. I give the driver exact directions to Shcherbakov.

"Why do you do that?" Danny mutters once we're in.

"So we're both clear we know where we're going." I focus on the cabbie's back and drop to my volume. "And we'll know if he tries anything."

He scrutinizes me another minute, calculating whether to believe me, or what I mean, I'm not sure which. "Wow" is all he says, and I don't think he's impressed.

The cabbie interrupts. *"Dolzhny nosit' shlyapu."*

I toss Danny a told-you-so expression and reply to the driver. *"Uzhe eto yemo skazala."*

After a minute, Danny clears his throat. "Interpreter, you going to help me out?"

I fight back the smirk. "He says you should put on your hat."

Danny closes his eyes for a second, like he's praying for patience. When he opens them again, my gaze locks on his. "Trust me," I breathe.

"I do."

But the hat stays in his pocket, and the lurking look of uncertainty stays on his face.

So much for this mission being "perfect."

CHAPTER 10

THE CAB PULLS UP TO SHCHERBAKOV, and it's obvious Noah's picture in Paris is out of date. If we're supposed to get the lay of the land, here's where to begin: the façade has been updated to über modern with narrow transparent rectangles, stacked randomly, forming the windows. The effect would be cooler if it weren't for the Soviet-era gray cement brick forming the rest of the exterior. Blue neon letters stand atop the building, spelling out the company's name in bold block print: Щербаков.

The juxtaposition of old and new is . . . weird. And not in a hey-cool-post-modernism way, or a purposefully-disorienting-and-whimsical way. More of a were-they-on-drugs-when-they-thought-this-was-a-good-idea? way.

We climb out of the cab and stand on the sidewalk, taking in the "eclecticism." We're alone: my last opportunity to smooth things over with Danny—and warn him. "When we know we're alone and clear, we don't have to pretend. But the rest of the time, I. Am. Lori. Okay?"

"Okay." He leans in as if to seal that deal with a kiss, but I retreat.

"We're not alone." I nod at Shcherbakov.

Danny glances down at his outstretched hand. "Oh," I say. "Right."

We shake on it (belatedly) and start for the vintage-1972 doors. "Show time," Danny whispers. "You ready?" He's fixed on the building in front of us, subconsciously biting his lip. His first undercover op. It's far from my first, but the same nerves echo in my jittering stomach. For me, it's not (just) fear—it's anticipation.

"Always ready." And why wouldn't I be? I'm in Russia. I'm here with Danny—working with him. I was *made* for this op.

We march to the doors in sync. We're more than prepared. We're a team (thank you, Sylvie), hitting on every cylinder, ready and willing for any challenge.

Why did I ever think this was a bad idea? I can't think of anything more perfect. I belong here.

I swoop a hand over my hair, making sure none of the strands from the longer side have strayed, and pause at the door to let Danny open it. "Thanks. Always get the door for a woman."

"Hey, I do try," he jokes.

The lobby's open to the top floor, but it feels more like we're at the bottom of an elevator shaft than in the foyer of an international aerospace company. Danny and I both crane our necks to trace the light up to the skylight overhead.

"Is it normal for me to bring my own interpreter?" he asks. "Or weird?"

"Normal," I assure him, though lining up an interpreter through the hotel would probably be even more normal. I hunt for the coatroom. It *is* weird—and rude—to wear your coat inside. Ruder to not tell us where the cloakroom is.

The receptionist finally looks up from her desk a few feet away. "*Da?*"

I take over in Russian, including using the proper form of

Danny's name to introduce him (though I don't try to form a patronymic for him—Terryovich?). "Fluker, Danny, from National Research Council Canada, here to see Director Zverev."

She scrutinizes me and Danny and me again, moving only her eyes. I instinctively stop breathing, waiting for her response. "I'll call his secretary down."

"*Spasibo.*" I release that breath and back off. The thanks is overly polite, but at least I'm not smiling. Russians really do think you're up to something if you're grinning without a specific reason. Danny's not smiling. Good. (Probably the first time I've ever thought that was "good.")

The receptionist picks up the phone. Danny turns to me. "*Spasibo*—thank you, right?"

"Yep."

"What's 'you're welcome'?"

"*Pozhaluysta.*"

Danny repeats it under his breath before another woman emerges from the also-vintage-1972 doors in the shadows behind the receptionist desk.

As soon as this woman steps into the light, I see my definition of "business attire" is about three decades too conservative (though the secretary's about my age). Her white skirt's precariously short, and only a tailor or a magician could make her deep purple buttoned shirt fit like that. Her platinum blond hair either receives weekly salon treatments or is actually natural.

And, PS: this is Russia, so she's supermodel gorgeous. I check Danny's reaction and see the smile already starting. "Don't smile," I remind him, a little snappier than I need to be.

He schools his features into a more neutral expression by the time the secretary reaches us. "Obolenskaya, Nadezhda Vasilyevna," she introduces herself. I handle the introductions for me and Danny, and Nadezhda pivots to lead us into the

81

belly of the building. "Oh." She waves dismissively toward one hallway. "You can hang your coats down there."

I take Danny to the cloakroom. "Try not to drool too much," I murmur.

"I wasn't drooling. I wasn't even ogling."

"Let's keep it that way, okay?"

He winks at me, and I realize I've dropped the façade unintentionally. One problem with the whole undercover/not undercover idea? Shifting between identities and boxes. Cover. Cover. I. Am. Lori. And I will not slip up again. I hang up my red coat, the only brightly colored one in the room (and the only brightly colored one on the streets). Hiding in plain sight.

They could search my coat pockets, so I grab the signal scanner, small enough to hide in my skirt pocket. We return to Nadezhda, and she leads us through the second set of doors, Danny falling back to take up tail position. Nadezhda stops at an elevator and pushes the button. Once again, all the best in mid-1970s decor. She glances back to appraise Danny for a second (not rude in Russia). "He doesn't speak a word of Russian?" she asks me without taking her gaze off him.

"Pleasantries." My voice is too terse, and I try to readjust.

Her face impassive, she turns her back to him to wait for the elevator. "He's young. Cute. You're lucky."

I examine Nadezhda from the corner of my eye. Hard to miss the overtones there. "He just got married." (So much for losing the curtness.)

"Is that why you're so on edge?"

I must've telegraphed my trepidation. Or maybe I'm telegraphing a whole lot more. My stomach makes one slow twist.

Danny, not entirely oblivious, gives me a meaningful glance in Nadezhda's direction. "Everything okay?" he asks in an undertone.

"Absolutely." I make sure Nadezhda isn't watching and

dismiss her with a wave.

The elevator finally arrives, and the interior's gleaming, jerking us into this century again. "Is Director Zverev in his office?" I ask.

"No. He'll be with you shortly."

Shortly, of course, is code for "whenever he feels like it." Do I mention that to Danny?

We reach the third floor, and Nadezhda leads us down the drab hall. (Like they've only updated places customers might see, trying to hide the corporate rot.) We stop at a corner office. Assuming that's as prestigious in Russia as in the States, how high in the company is this guy?

Before we reach the door, it flies open. A man leans out. Even from the head-and-scarily-broad-shoulders view, you can tell he's practically a giant—and he can't be much older than Danny and me (though he's got the baby face of a twelve-year-old). "*Vidish' moya—?*" The man cuts himself off to think a second, then ducks into his office.

No way is this Director Zverev. I'm expecting middle-of-the-road, middle-aged, round middle. Russian hierarchy is tied to bureaucracy, seniority and *svyazi*: connections, not talent.

Danny and I hold a silent conversation in little more than a glance. He's thinking the same thing. (Also, didn't Nadezhda say he wasn't in his office?)

"*Direktor,*" Nadezhda calls.

The boy-giant reappears at the door, dispelling any doubts, his eyebrows lifted high enough to disappear behind his over-grown hair. "*Da?*"

"Your Canadian visitor is here." Her accent's heavy, but her English is correct.

Her facts, however, aren't. Again, Danny and I share a split-second exchange. We never said we were Canadian, but we're definitely not correcting her.

"Come in, come in," Zverev summons us—also in English—

before he turns to his office. We approach the door hesitantly. Zverev's rummaging through stacks of papers on his desk. A jumble of cardboard tubes nearly buries a pair of office chairs, while pile after pile of paper rings the office. Guess that whole "clean desk policy" fad hasn't caught on in Rostov quite yet. It's so much paper I wouldn't know where to begin organizing. Maybe with a match?

But I don't have to organize it. I have to search it—a true target-rich environment. And that's even more daunting.

At his desk, Zverev accidentally knocks over a pile, launching a miniature avalanche, knocking half a dozen USB drives off the corner. My heart rate kicks up, as if I haven't already recovered the drive Fyodor stole from Danny. Still—I want those. (And it seems he's worse than Danny in accumulating those things, like they're the stray dogs of the engineering world.)

Before we can move to help him, Zverev's rebalanced the stacks and shoved the USB drives back in place. He approaches us, hand outstretched. Danny holds out his hand as well, but doesn't move from the doorway.

Crud. I nudge him forward, all the way into the office. I whisper the explanation I didn't give Lori, Jim and Noah. "Where you should never shake hands: across the threshold."

He doesn't acknowledge me. Once again, he's smiling. "Don't smile," I remind him.

He obeys and frowns—at me—before looking back to Zverev.

"Zverev, Borislav Vyacheslavovich," he introduces himself with a broad grin. (And I finally get a first name for the guy.) "Nice to meet you, Mr. Fluker."

"Nice to meet you too." Their knuckles both turn sufficiently white for a good business handshake. Danny's a tall guy; Borislav's got a good three inches on him. Not that it bothers Danny. "You speak English?" he asks.

"Yes, here we learn English from third grade."

Great. Guess who's superfluous. Well, with him. Not everyone here will speak enough English to get by.

Borislav swings to me, still beaming. "We don't have many people bring their sweethearts to the office."

"I'm his interpreter," I correct him. Or have we already blown our covers? I hold my face muscles as still as possible to hide the rising panic.

"Naturally." Borislav moves on, and my premature panic peters out. He looks back to Danny. "Good to bring her. Come, sit." He gestures to the office chairs buried in stacks and rolls of paper.

I inspect the nearest pile. My eyes land on the line TIMOFEYEV, FYODOR OLEGOVICH.

The air rushes out of my lungs like I just got a kick to the chest. I check the next pile, and the next. Fyodor's plans, his approval, his signatures. His work, his life.

I thought I was dealing. I've talked to CIA counselors, co-workers, my station chief. The memories and nightmares come less and less. But to be here? Don't know why it didn't occur to me before, but I'm standing in the office of the man I killed, staring at his paper ghost.

"Or perhaps we stand," Borislav finishes.

"Standing's great." Danny smiles. But he checks my reaction, and his smile instantly fades. "Are you feeling okay?"

His voice sounds far away—in the present. And I'm drowning in the past. I shake my head. "I need water."

"Oh!" Borislav practically leaps over three paper piles. I have to backpedal to dodge him. I bump into Danny, who steadies my arms. Borislav fills up a plastic cup at the water cooler half-buried in papers and holds it out eagerly. "Can I get you anything?" he asks Danny.

"No, thanks."

I take a sip from my brimming cup. Russians aren't inhospitable—with friends. Which we're not. Falling all over yourself for a stranger? Strange.

Borislav backs off a step. "You're my first visitors. But you—you hosted Fyodor Olegovich, yes?"

I nearly drop my cup, and water sloshes onto the closest stack, instantly blurring Fyodor's signature. "Sorry," I say quickly. We both drop to swipe at the puddles on the pages (much easier once Danny takes my cup).

"Dinyushka!" Borislav bellows—a form of Nadezhda's name. But not a standard short name like Nadia. A pet name: Naddiekins, practically. There are more intimate forms, but this is definitely not what a superior normally calls a secretary.

Of course, Russian gender politics could be in play. He's her boss, so even if something's going on, it doesn't necessarily mean the relationship's reciprocal.

Nadezhda appears at the door. Borislav sends her off to fetch cleaning supplies. A minute later, she reappears, towing a janitor's cart. The three of us just gape at her, silently responding with a chorus of *Seriously?!/Ser′yozno?*

She ducks out again. Once she's gone, Borislav murmurs, *"Durochka Dinochka."*

I gape at him a second. He's using an affectionate form of the adjective and her nickname, but "that fool Naddiekins" isn't exactly a term of endearment. I glance up at Danny. "Explain later," I mouth to him.

Borislav finds his secretary's stupidity cute, and comments to us about it. Another strike.

Nadezhda brings a towel, and we mop up the last of the water.

As we stand, I barely catch the little gesture: Borislav's hand touching the small of her back. He bows his head toward Nadezhda's, and now he isn't a giant towering over her. Something's definitely going on there, because that's not just a supervisor steering a subordinate.

Nadezhda starts from the room, but stops halfway to the

door. "Oh, should I file old requisitions by supervisor or amount?"

Borislav studies her a minute. "They have a file number—you know, I'll take care of those, too, just bring them in."

Nadezhda doesn't turn our direction on her way out, and I can't interpret anything about her posture or pace to put more context into her side of the "affair."

I don't need another reason to cast Borislav in suspicion, but this isn't exactly a point in his favor.

"I apologize," Borislav says. "Reorganizing the office is difficult, and Fyodor Olegovich had so much . . ." He trails off, gesturing around at the piles littering the room. "Obviously we did not plan for this."

"Of course," Danny says.

Borislav takes a let's-move-on-from-that-unpleasantness breath, then slaps back on the grin. This guy's *not* a normal Russian. I've met hundreds—thousands—of Russians, and I've never been treated this warmly until we became much better friends. (Then, you're part of the family.)

So why is this dude so eager to embrace us foreigners? My suspicion seismograph registers a tremor.

"How are you liking Russia?" he asks us.

Been a great two hours. Danny comes up with a better reply: "Can't wait to see more."

"Very good." Borislav claps once and gestures for the door. "We have a short time, so let's get started."

Danny follows Borislav out. In my pocket, my phone buzzes and I take it out, along with the listening device scanner. Before I slide that back in, I spot a blue light—the blue LED.

The room's bugged. Audio.

My sternum presses down like I just put on all my Russian winter wear. I fixate on Borislav outside the door, discussing something with Danny, both of them earnestly conferring (and grinning) while they wait for me. Would a subordinate dare bug his office—or would the FSB recruit from the top? Either Borislav records meetings for his reference, or this is the *real* reason he got the promotion.

That giant talking to my husband has got to be an FSB officer.

And I'm foundering like a boat in the shallow Sea of Azov.

"Everything okay?" Borislav asks when I reach them.

"Yep." I tear my gaze from them, sure my eyes are betraying me. The only logical thing to look at is my phone, still in my hand. The message flashes on the screen, giving me a valid excuse. "My phone's out of battery."

"Oh." Borislav takes it. I force myself not to snatch it back as he pushes past me into his office.

An FSB officer took my phone. My CIA-issued phone. He'll plug it into his computer, which will conveniently clone it while we're out touring whatever, and he'll know everything.

My pulse escalates. I have to get it back. I approach him. "That's okay. It'll last until we're finished."

"I insist." Borislav rummages through his desk. Finally, he produces a charger—an AC adapter. Oh. While he plugs it into the outlet closest to the door, I wipe my screen clean so I can tell if anyone touches it. Borislav gently hooks up my phone, setting it on another stack of papers. "There you go," he says.

"Thank you."

"Naturally." Borislav pats my shoulder, and it seems like he has to bend over to reach that low. He edges past me to re-join Danny; they start down the hall we came in. Nadezhda watches us pass, and I nod to her. She squints at me, like she doesn't understand the gesture.

Borislav picks up where he left off. "We specialize in fixed-wing applications, though we want to delve more into developing lightweight composites—but my special area of interest is unmanned aircraft."

I monitor Danny's reaction. He maintains cover, not casting a meaningful eye my direction. The plans Fyodor stole were for a next-gen drone with a hyperspectral camera. (Danny's explained it like X-ray vision and seeing the past rolled into one.)

We know he had electronic copies because we found Danny's USB drive in Fyodor's things—but could he have sent hard copies, too? I look back, as if I could see the stacks of paper littering Borislav's office.

An uneasy weight settles in my gut: dread. This is going to be a very long search.

CHAPTER 11

I SPENT THREE HOURS OF MY FLIGHT studying Russian aerospace vocabulary. Seems like a waste as we sit in the glossy conference room. Borislav personally translates the entire sales-y PowerPoint (pirated?), the standard "Welcome to Shcherbakov! We're Successful®! Let's Make Money Together!" spiel.

He's nearly done when there's a knock at the glass door. A dude in his mid-forties stands there, eyeing me and Danny. This guy's pinched face is full of suspicion.

Borislav gets the door. He invites Kita in (short for Nikita, and yes, it's a man's name). I feign boredom, staring past them into the hallway. Kita holds out a sheaf of papers. "Could you review these?" The deference, even reverence, of his half-bow is unnerving.

"Certainly." Borislav accepts the papers. Just what the guy needs more of.

"Customers?" Kita asks in an undertone. "Overseas?"

"Business partners," Borislav corrects him. "I'll get back to you tomorrow." I try to draw Borislav's attention to finagle an introduction (so I can get to Kita later). But Borislav doesn't notice and returns to the screen. Kita lurks in the back, his gaze lingering on me and Danny.

Speaking of unnerving. The sensation slithering down my spine is way more than being watched—and if it were normal checking out, you'd think he'd be less interested in Danny (or me, you never know). He divides his time in observing each of us.

Borislav jumps back into his PowerPoint. After loitering (totally creepy), Kita leaves. Definitely sticking a giant mental red flag on that guy, for our safety if nothing else. By the time Borislav finishes and leads us out of the conference room, it's well past five.

"I want you to meet our design team." Borislav cranes his neck to survey the sea of cubicles, most empty. (No Kita.) "In the morning, perhaps. Let's get your phone."

We trail after him to his office. He retrieves my phone (no signs of hacking), and he and Danny continue their animated conversation. Can I get away with coming back tomorrow if Danny really doesn't need me?

Borislav chats Danny up the whole way to the parking lot. I have to analyze every word, figure out his motives for small talk a normal Russian wouldn't feel so compelled to make. Trying to sneak intel out of Danny? Borislav offers as much information as Danny does, though, so I can't be sure. I can hardly wait until the cab to talk to Danny.

"I hope they're putting you somewhere decent." Borislav doesn't slow as he passes the first row of cars.

"Hermitage Hotel," I provide.

"Oh, good." He gestures to his black Jeep Cherokee. Clearly they're already paying him well if he's driving an import. "I'll drive you."

There goes our chance to talk. Danny holds out a hand for me. "You can take the front."

"That's okay. You two obviously have lots to discuss." I take his hand to climb into the backseat. Jeeps aren't particularly high, but in this skirt? I'll take the help.

As soon as Borislav folds himself into the driver's seat, he picks up his conversation with Danny. "Not sure what to do with you now," he says.

My lungs capture my next breath and keep it. Threats?

"This is really the first time I've hosted a guest. What is customary?"

Oh. Yeah. He mentioned that. I relax (on the outside).

Danny doesn't seem to notice. "Don't know how it's done in Russia." He pauses to check with me. I gesture for him to go on. "But at NRC, we take the opportunity to build the business relationship. Maybe take them out for dinner, show them the sights if they've never been to the city before—just try to get to know them better."

"Ah." Borislav considers that a minute. "Then where did you go to school?" He's testing Danny's cover. He has to be. He's suitably impressed at Danny's University of Michigan pedigree. (He should see Danny's transcripts.) Danny reciprocates the query.

"*L'Institut polytechnique des sciences avancées*, in France."

Oh. Crap. My stomach inches toward the upholstery. Could this be a coincidence? Or has Borislav's innocent small talk been fishing after all?

"*IPSA?*" Danny asks. "*A Toulouse ou à Paris?*"

"*Tous les deux. Parlez-vous français? Oh, bien sûr—Canadien.*"

Yep. They both speak French. (Though once again, Danny doesn't correct his assumption that he's Canadian.)

And yeah, this isn't the conversational stuff I can manage: within seconds, we're up to our antennae in aerospace jargon. I pick up on "canard" and "ailerons," and I'm reminded how many English aviation terms are borrowed from French.

They keep up the French the whole drive back. The aerospace terminology peters out, but the camaraderie doesn't. At our hotel, Borislav lets Danny out with an enthusiastic handshake. "Tomorrow, we will see better things," Borislav vows. (I dunno, that PowerPoint was awfully impressive. Animated and everything.)

"Counting on it." Danny helps me to the curb, and again, I appreciate the support. Once I'm firmly on the ground, he settles into holding my hand way too comfortably.

Holding hands is such a small gesture, a tiny symbolic connection. You get used to it so fast—and you never expect to miss it so much. I want to interlace our fingers, but instead I pull my hand away, swallowing a sigh.

Borislav's smile doesn't slip so if he notices, he may not care, considering his relationship with Nadezhda. We bid him goodbye and head into the hotel.

The elevator doors slide shut. Finally alone. (Like November isn't a popular time to visit Russia or something.) I'm weak: I take Danny's hand. "So Borislav speaks French," I observe. "What a coincidence." My flat tone conveys my skepticism.

Could Borislav have orchestrated Danny's visit? Doubtful. But he could speak half a dozen languages and fished for something Danny spoke to cut me out of the loop.

"Come on," Danny says. "That guy? A threat? Even you couldn't be *that* paranoid—"

"Okay." I cut him off, pretending that little dig doesn't cut like a dagger. "Did he say anything pertinent?"

The elevator reaches our floor and the doors slide open. No one's waiting to get on, so Danny takes two steps for the hall. We're not done with this conversation. I tug him back into the elevator and push the button for the fifth floor. The doors slide shut and the elevator rises again. "Did he?" I reiterate.

"Not really. Didn't react when I mentioned hyperspectral imaging."

"How'd you slide that in?"

"He wants to work on infrared signatures. I said I had

experience after a hyperspectral imaging project."

I squeeze his hand. That Danny. He can be tricky. I appreciate that—but is he tricky enough to outmaneuver Borislav?

Should I tell Danny exactly how much danger he's in? I'm staring at him, and he pivots to me, waiting for me to speak.

He doesn't know. Paris didn't tell him about the FSB officer. I'm beginning to think they didn't know, and Semyon saw an opportunity to get in somewhere he's been targeting for ages.

I trust Danny, but that doesn't mean I should throw all my secrets on him. We both know they're a privilege and a burden that aren't his.

This is exactly why I came here: to protect him.

"I know you know," I say, "but seriously: watch what you say to him."

He scrutinizes me for a long moment. "You don't seem to like Borislav."

"I can't afford to like people."

"All he's done is be nice."

"Exactly."

He doesn't say anything, but his eyebrows express his disbelief.

"Never known a Russian to be so friendly. That's just . . . not who they are." Unless they've got a good reason. AKA an ulterior motive.

"Okay." He draws out the word, making me sound even crazier. Clearly he didn't get the subtext. He changes the subject. "If my room's bugged, why don't we jam the signal?"

"The logistics can be tough—but the real problem is if someone's listening and the feed goes suddenly haywire, it attracts attention. Attention is risky."

The elevator slows to stop at the fifth floor. "What percentage of your job is looking like you're not doing your job?"

"Seventy-five. Ninety." I shrug and release his hand.

"Depends."

The doors slide open, revealing an elegant elderly woman with a fur-lined coat waiting to board. She moves aside to let us off, and we oblige, staying silent until we reach the narrow back stairwell. We stop on the fourth floor landing, and Danny draws me close.

Technically this meets the definition of "alone," but I can't relax till I check the bug scanner. We're clear.

Danny tilts my chin up to kiss me. I kiss him back, but something's different. In Paris, everything was veiled by a newlywed haze of happiness. But kissing in a Russian hotel stairwell, his kisses taste too much like danger.

I pull away suddenly. Danny's eyes fly open, as surprised as I feel. This is a gamble, and I can't gamble with his safety—his life.

"What's wrong?" he asks.

That question is what's wrong: he doesn't understand. And why would he, when I've basically said we don't have to play spy when we think nobody's around?

I extricate myself from his arms and sit on the stairs. He has to see how serious this mission is. "Ever heard of Moscow Rules?"

Danny's gaze wanders away as he searches his memory. "Maybe?"

"Legendary operational rules for Moscow as the center of Soviet power. Google will tell you it's things as basic as 'Trust your gut.'"

"Sounds like Des Moines Rules." He leans against the wall, settling in to listen below a flickering light.

"Right. In other places, reasonable caution's enough. In Russia, you have to be so careful you don't look like you're being careful. The real Moscow Rules are stuff like . . . assume everyone's an agent or officer of the enemy. You are under constant surveillance, so on the street, never, ever stop. Don't turn around. Don't tie your shoes. Don't check your reflection in a store window. Don't do anything anyone could construe as looking for surveillance."

"How do you work?"

"You walk. For hours. And hours. And when you're about to drop, you do something so totally normal no one would blink twice."

Danny scrutinizes me. "Are we in Moscow?"

"No," I admit. He has a point: Rostov is Russia's the tenth largest city, and it's a port with military and aerospace connections, but still, it's not like 10% of the FSB is roaming the streets.

"You realize the USSR broke up over twenty years ago, right?" he continues.

"Remember the last time you tried to tell me that? Aboard a certain boat?" The unspoken component of the context hovers above us: when a certain Russian had taken us prisoner. After he stole Danny's plans.

He shifts his weight against the wall, looking away. I have to drop the other shoe, make my last point—Borislav's the enemy, whether Danny wants him to be or not. But Danny's taking too much pleasure in picking on my paranoid proclivities lately. If I make that accusation, Danny will chalk it up to more paranoia.

And he'll still be in danger.

I shoot for a kicker as close to the truth as I can get while still within the realm of believability for Danny. "You want to trust me on the whole international politics thing or not?"

He regards my feet. "You know I trust you."

"Yeah." I stand and wait till he meets my gaze. "I know."

He leans in to kiss me—but a door above us opens. I jerk free of his grasp, on my feet before that door slaps shut. Danny follows me down the stairs. "Sorry," I murmur at our floor.

"I know." He winks and opens the door. We emerge into

the hall, stepping back into our roles.

We reach our rooms, but Danny doesn't go in. He moves closer—close enough to kiss—to lower his voice. "Borislav said there's a cool restaurant on the river. Dinner?"

"Sure." I subconsciously glance at his lips.

Yesterday, we were on our honeymoon. Today, we're supposed to be new acquaintances. But I'm closing in like I'm succumbing to the inevitable pull of his gravity.

This cover whiplash is going to cause more than soft tissue damage.

"Let me know when you're ready." He straightens and unlocks his room, leaving me hanging.

"You did that on purpose," I say.

He tosses a grin over his shoulder before he shuts his door.

Well, that's plain evil. I unlock my door and consult the bug scanner. My room isn't safe either.

My phone buzzes. A text message with a series of random Cyrillic letters. Classic. I hunt for the program to block the data signal and decode the encrypted message.

There's an app for that, at least at the CIA. We usually disguise it in a boring game, and I find the right icon in the menu and enable the Easter egg code. Within thirty seconds, I'm reading Semyon's message in ungarbled Russian.

Ul Krasnoarmeyskaya, 168. 1815. I'll find you.

Now my heart rate's high for a different reason, but my stomach sinks. The app deletes the data from the phone: encrypted message, decrypted message and single-use key. I check the time. Quarter till six. Enough time to get ready, get in an SDR and get there safely.

So much for dinner with Danny. Sigh.

Tonight's sweater and jeans are less businessy and a heck of a lot warmer than a skirt. I apply yet another coat of paint, this time an evening look. (Thanks, YouTube tutorials.) I pack my extra coat into a fashionable (reversible) tote, in case I need to change disguises.

Once I'm ready, I'm left to the task I'm dreading most—telling Danny we won't be eating together after all. I quash the instinct to walk into his room and knock instead.

He answers the door, smiling. "Ready?"

Ouch. "Sorry," I begin. "Just realized I can't take you to dinner."

"Why not?"

"Meeting. They should take care of you in the restaurant downstairs."

"Oh." That sounds less like disappointment and more like distaste—and I doubt he's got anything against the hotel restaurant.

What can I do? I scramble for an excuse or a reason or . . . whatever Danny needs. "Work stuff, you know."

"I thought I was work this week."

I try to go the silent conversation route, shooting for *give me a break here*. His shoulders slip down a centimeter.

Ignoring the jolt to my heart, I switch tacks. "I can order room service for you."

"I'll figure it out. I can even tie my own shoes, you know." He's teasing, but . . . something there isn't a joke.

I know Danny's an adult, and it's not like he's helpless. "I mean—"

"I'll survive."

"I'll come by when I get back."

"Have a good meeting." He peers over his shoulder, like he'd say more if it weren't for his room's listening devices.

You and me both, dude. "Stay safe." I let my eyes convey how seriously I mean that.

He releases a silent sigh, as if he lost some internal battle. "You too."

A small reassurance, but I'll take it. I shoot him a wink before he shuts the door, and I head into the night alone.

As soon as the corner store clerk's occupied with someone else, I step into a secluded corner of the *produkty*, my last surveillance detection stop. I pull out my dark coat. My tote flips inside out to hold my red coat and wig. In under sixty seconds, I'm ready to meet Semyon, I'm on time, and I'm black. (Free of tails.)

I troop down Bol'shaya Sadovaya street. I don't know if it's the streets I spent so many months walking, or the familiar routine of the SDR, but something about this . . . fits. Like I'm finally in my element again.

That thought makes me flinch as I check behind me again. My element is Ottawa, I remind myself. My hands in Danny's, his arms around me, my lips against his.

I reach the Rostov Administration Building and turn, barely allowing myself a glance up at the familiar sight. A glance is all I can afford, since the ornate façade with filigrees, cherubs and shells makes me think of Paris. Which makes me think of Danny.

Where I really fit. Right?

Now's no time to worry about that. I keep my pace brisk, both to make my meeting, and to get off the dark street.

Maybe I should've brought Danny. Well, not Danny, but someone. Last time I was in Rostov, I never, *ever* went anywhere alone. Like I said, I can take care of myself, but usually that means *not* wandering alone in the dark. (Not that I'm asking an untrained civilian to be my bodyguard.)

I reach the address. On the outside, the building seems like just another brick in the strip-mall wall. Inside, however, it's clear they're trying to distinguish themselves with a blend of modern industrial (exposed ducts and can lights), eclectic (mismatched dining sets) and shabby chic (with repurposed, artfully worn furniture).

On a weeknight, the atmosphere is subdued, but the trendy twentysomething crowd must pack in here on the weekends. I hesitate at the antique entry table—more shabby, less chic. No hostess in sight, so I take a seat at a tiny black coffee table with a good view of the door.

I scan the harmoniously mismatched table arrangements, but Semyon's nowhere in sight. How much have Moscow Rules changed? No contact in public? Probably should've mentioned that before he arranged this morning's meeting.

The waitress takes my drink order and disappears. A man a couple decades older than me strolls through the door. I scrutinize him to be sure it's not Semyon, but it takes me a second too long, and he spots me. He comes to sit in the overstuffed armchair beside me. Which is okay in Russia—but not with me. Unfortunately, I can't run away without drawing more suspicion.

My new friend offers his name: Lyosha (also a man's name; short form of Aleksei). He takes my nod as a conversation invitation. I keep the small talk far from the truth, or any of my covers. The waitress gives Lyosha both of our drinks, and he passes my Perrier with pomegranate juice and honey. (Oh my goodness, I nearly forgot about Russian honey. They're obsessed with the stuff—but their honey deserves the devotion.)

"And where are you from?" Lyosha asks.

Before I can lie, Lyosha turns to accept the bread from the waitress and orders a traditional starter, oliv'ye salad, for both of us. I never liked the potatoes, veggies, eggs and chicken in mayo, but I hardly care—I'm definitely not eating.

"Moscow," I finally answer. I scan the restaurant casually. Still no Semyon.

"I thought you were from Kyiv. The most beautiful women in the world are from Kyiv."

Without my Lori disguise, I do *not* buy the obvious line.

The waitress returns with our food, and she's careful to place the bowl in my hands. I immediately figure out why: she tucks a piece of paper between my fingers and the dish. I wait until Lyosha is absorbed in his meal and use my bowl to shield the paper from his view.

Басков дураки. Literal translation: *Basque fools*. Using actual words will hopefully be enough to throw any Russian speaker off the scent, but the real message is there. Басков = Cyrillic B + ACK. Back. And дураки = *dur*aki = door.

I set my plate on the table. Wish I could make the getaway cleaner, but I can't afford to abandon both my coats here. (Bye-bye, one on the coat rack). I make a show of searching the pockets of my tote bag, like I'll need something in the bath-room—makeup, feminine hygiene products, any excuse will do—and hitch the strap onto my shoulder. "I'll be right back," I say to Lyosha.

He must know it's a lie, though I hope he can't guess why.

Normally, I'd tap into the CIA's social engineering skill set to get out the back, like in Paris, but nobody notices me in the kitchen, so I walk to the quiet side street.

Crap, it's cold without a coat.

A beat-up, boxy beige coupe sits halfway down the block, facing me, someone in the driver's seat. Tension laces through my shoulder muscles. If this isn't Semyon, this isn't good.

I go that way, not looking at the driver. My pulse climbs with every step closer to that car. I don't even know what Semyon drives.

When I come even with the front bumper, the engine starts. I barely manage to not jump. The headlights stay off, but the dome light flashes in the car, illuminating the driver a split second. The fedora's misleading, but there's no mistaking the salt-and-pepper beard: Semyon.

Whew. He rolls down his window. "Get in," he calls in a mock whisper.

"Duh. You think?" I mutter, and hop in. I have to avoid a briefcase on the floor on my side, and hold my tote on my lap.

He drives onto the main road before he switches on the headlights. "So," he says, one eye on the rearview. "How was your first day at the office?"

"Slow. Can you get me another coat? Had to sacrifice one in there."

"Sure. I'll have one in your room tomorrow. Any leads?"

I flip through the few people I met today: Nadezhda, whose boyfriend/boss calls her dumb. Kita, the lingerer. Borislav, the guy who's way too friendly with foreigners and strangers. "Oh, I think so."

"Sweet."

I glance at him, surprised at the wrong-decade slang (has it been that long since he's been home?), but he's too busy scanning the street. I check my side mirror: squarish headlights behind us.

Semyon taps my elbow, drawing my attention. He's holding out something the size of a thick credit card with a USB plug. I don't use this device often, but I recognize it. A hard drive cloner. A low thrum of adrenaline begins to build in my stomach. This isn't just a gadget: it's an assignment.

How soon can I get some alone time with Borislav's CPU?

For now, I slip the cloner into my tote. "Our hotel rooms are bugged. Audio and visual."

"Par for the course. I'll have someone sweep when they bring your coat. But we can't take all the bugs out. Attracts more suspicion."

Of course. "Need a SIM card for my executive, too." The standard term for someone you're protecting. Even Semyon doesn't need to know who he really is.

"Didn't I tell you about the dead drop?"

"Nope."

He sighs at his forgetfulness, patting his pockets. He pulls out a slip of paper. An address, then the words *ozherel'ye, varezhki*, like it's a shopping list (for a necklace and mittens). But the items aren't things to pick up: they're a code. "Necklace" is the cryptonym for a postbox, and "mittens" means the dead drop concealment device is disguised as a rock.

I slip the paper into my tote's pocket, too. Like I've hit the end of a silent countdown, the familiar jitters steal into my legs. That's not Restless Legs Syndrome. It's only been a few minutes, but if we need this level of secrecy, this car meeting can't last much longer. I need to get moving.

I'm about to get up when Semyon starts the conversation again. "When you find the officer, let me know. We'll take it from there."

Not like I have time to do more anyway, leaving the day after tomorrow. "Sure. Turn here." I point at the next right and grab my bag. "This is my stop."

We both know we're nowhere near my hotel, but Semyon obeys. He takes the right slowly—slowly enough that once the building provides cover, I can escape safely without stopping the car. By the time anyone can peer around the corner, Semyon's door is shut, the briefcase I nearly stepped on is in my seat and opened, and the pop-up dummy inside makes it appear I never left. Meanwhile, I've yanked on my red coat and tucked my bangs under my wig. I move the cloner to my pocket. The quick-change act only works because my coat covers my dark braids, which I don't have time to pin up properly. I'll straighten it out.

Maybe Danny and I can get a quick dinner, but then I've got another appointment—face time with Borislav's computer. And Danny might be my ticket in.

CHAPTER 12

AFTER STOPPING AT SEVERAL RESTAURANTS along the way back (not many options at this hour and part of town) to fix my wig and make sure I'm surveillance-free, I reach the Hermitage again. The lights shining up on the façade throw the green and white decor into deep relief.

Deep relief sounds wonderful right now.

Too bad I've got other plans. I go straight to Danny's room and knock, proud of myself for heeding the right protocol the first time instead of my instinct to walk in.

He doesn't answer. "Mr. Fluker?" I call, knocking again.

Still no answer. After my third attempt fails, cover or no cover, I'm going in. I fumble the key into the lock and let myself into the dark room. It's barely seven; could he be asleep?

Then again, with all the time zone changes and red-eye flights we've endured in the last two weeks, who knows what time it feels like to him? I switch on the lights. "Danny?"

No Danny on the bed. No note on the desk. No sign of room service trays or trash in the can. I glance at the bathroom. Empty.

Fear flickers to life in the corners of my mind. I verify the room number on the open door: 302. Like they accidentally switched my room key with a universal one. I step in. His bags are still by the desk.

It's okay—*he's* okay. He has to be.

I told him to go to the restaurant. Maybe he got caught up with some new Russian friends. (Which could be trouble, but probably not danger.) He just hasn't finished eating yet.

I lock up and head down to join him for dinner—which I could use, too, since I didn't choke down even a bite of my oliv'ye salad. Which happens to me way too often.

The small restaurant's warmly lit, the gold walls accented with white molding, both playing off the navy and white tablecloths. Reminds me of somewhere Fyodor Timofeyev took me to dinner, in fact. I suppress a shudder and scan the tables for Danny's familiar longish hair or dark suit.

Nope.

I fight the tide of worry rising in my mind again and wander in for a better view, murmuring something to the maître d' about meeting someone. Every table, every chair: not him, not him, not him.

The maître d' is reading his reservation book when I approach. "Is Fluker here, from room 302?"

"*Nyet.*" He turns back to his book.

No in Russia is usually a knee-jerk response to any request for concessions or help—yay, decades of Soviet bureaucracy—so I can't be sure he's sure. "We're supposed to meet for dinner." I brush my long copper bangs aside, carefully arranging them. (Calling attention to a positive physical attribute is almost required to get your way as a woman in Russia—when you're not a missionary.) I describe Danny quickly, what he was wearing. "Have you seen him?"

"*Nyet.*"

My stomach drifts down an inch. One consolation: in Russia, I'm not obligated to thank him for not helping. I pivot to the lobby, slowing to a stop at the reception desk.

Danny's—no. I can't let myself even think the words. I march up to the desk and wait for the clerk, Natalia. "Have you seen Mr. Fluker, room 302?"

She searches her memory. "I don't think so."

"He didn't leave a message?"

"No, miss."

The chill starts in my scalp and creeps down my neck, but I try to act normal, nodding to her.

What do I do? He can't just pop into a restaurant next door—the hotel's centrally located, but in a residential area off a main thoroughfare. He can't negotiate with a cabbie or understand a *marshrutka* driver. His phone doesn't even work.

He couldn't go wandering off in a foreign city alone, right?

But if he's not alone—

My knees nearly give way, and I steady myself on one of the lobby's gold sofas. The buzzing at the back of my brain turns into full static. I can't block out the thought this time.

Danny's gone.

I sink onto the couch cushions. After two weeks of marriage, I've lost my husband.

I lost Danny.

He can't be gone—he can't. I vault to my feet again. Pointless, maybe, but I have to search a city of over a million. I have to do *something*.

I have to save Danny.

I canvass every restaurant, *produkty* (corner store) and *apteka* (drug store) I can find, scouring a range far beyond a normal SDR. I loop back to check the hotel every fifteen minutes.

Every time I reach our floor, the hope sparks up again. And every time, his room is empty and dark. The last ember of hope is fast dwindling.

I strike out again, taking a different side street—all residential. I hurry down the block, scanning the pedestrians around me, like Danny wouldn't say something if I passed. At the corner, I open a door to yet another *produkty*. I have to look twice to make sure he isn't in line. But the images in my mind aren't of Danny standing at the counter, being waited on by the clerk. They're memories I never want to face again. Danny's wrists in ropes. Danny flinching away from a gun aimed at his head. Danny bleeding, broken, shot.

The last one wasn't really him, but a memory of my partner twisted in a nightmare to be Danny. I have worked so hard and risked so much to keep that from becoming a reality, to keep Danny safe. That possibility slips through my fingers with every step, every stop, every failure.

Next, a *napitki*. Nothing. Yeah, shocker, he's not in a liquor store. Unless he's tied up in the back. Should I be barging into the stockrooms of every shop?

No, I should be trying to figure out who could've done this. I'm not law enforcement, but a few obvious suspects leap to mind: Borislav. Kita the lingerer. The FSB officer.

Before I know it, I reach the merchants' entrance to the *tsentral'nyy rynok*—the open air market square downtown. This courtyard is bustling every hour of the day and every season of the year, but now it's quiet. Above the rooftops loom the gold onion domes of the cathedral where I met Semyon this morning. The cathedral's clock tower shows it's been over two and a half hours since anyone has seen my husband.

The truth finally smothers the last little bits of belief, of hope. I don't know where to go. I've already failed, and even a band of bloodhounds wouldn't find him if he's already tied up, spirited away, or even—

Even dead.

I drag myself back to the Hermitage one last time, but his room's still silent, dark, empty.

I drift back down to the lobby and sink into a gold couch. Defeated.

The reality crystallizes like ice in my bones. I lost Danny. I lost Danny. I lost Danny.

The worst-case scenario was *not* supposed to be an option on this mission.

Like I flipped a switch, the pain and the panic shut off. Too much. I can't handle it. I can't deal. I'm still sitting on that golden velvet upholstery, staring up at the tray ceiling, but this can't be real, this can't be happening, this can't be my life.

No, it's real, and I have to—I have to—I don't know what. Everything's so wrong, no course seems right. Track down Borislav and . . . what, beat him? Not harsh enough.

Do I call Semyon? The *politsiya*? Normally I wouldn't come within twenty meters of them as a spy on their turf, but it would look weirder if his interpreter didn't.

What did Danny say about a whole lot of my job consisting of looking like I'm not up to anything?

I can't do these mental gymnastics. I can barely keep my brain from running through the memories—real and invented—of all the times I've put Danny in danger.

I lean forward on the couch and bury my face in my hands, like I can hide from those nightmares.

Footsteps trail past me, through the lobby, toward the elevator. The dimmest hope glows in my heart: maybe the kidnappers are back to search his room. I barely dare to look.

Danny strolls out of the lobby, his back to me as he heads for the elevator alcove.

Am I imagining this? Pasting his suit and hair and gait on a stranger in psychic CGI?

Against my better judgment, a full blown sunray of hope sends new energy into my exhausted muscles, and I practically leap up. I fly across the tiles to the elevator alcove. Just as the doors slide shut, I catch a glimpse. Danny. Not even close to dead.

I'm gonna kill him.

I run up both flights of stairs, but Danny's already down the hall when we get to our floor. He unlocks the door and I swoop in behind him. He steps in and turns to close the door— and then he sees me and startles. "Oh, hey. You're back."

"I've been back. Where have *you* been?"

"Dinner." He steps aside to invite me into the room.

"Where?"

Danny gives me a smile that says *not sure where the aggression's coming from here.* "Floating restaurant on the river."

"The one Borislav mentioned? Why not downstairs?"

"He called and invited me five minutes after you left. You could've come too, if you'd been around." His voice carries no accusation.

Good, because I'm still on the attack. "You didn't leave a note? You didn't think to call?"

"I did leave a note, under your door, and I don't have a SIM card. Or your number."

"You—" Crap. He's got me.

"You want to talk about disappearing?" Judging from his tone, his genial façade is reaching its stress limit. "Where were you? Do I want to know?"

"That's immaterial."

He scoffs, like I'm so unbelievable it's amusing. "When I worry, it's immaterial, but when you worry, it's the end of the world?"

"When I worry—!" I strangle off the shout and press a fist against my lips. I can't break cover. I can't fight with him. I can't let myself yell—

I'm angry, but the heat in my chest's covering the real reason I'm upset.

I really thought I lost him.

If Danny thinks being silly was me being vulnerable, he has no idea what my real weaknesses are.

"We need to talk." I pivot and practically jog away. Danny's key rattles in the lock behind me. I reach the stairwell and drop to sit on the top stair. Danny's through the fire door before it closes, and his footsteps pause behind me.

He settles on the step next to me. He tries to reach for my hand; I hug my elbows and don't let go.

We're alone. I'm supposed to be Talia. I promised to drop the cover here, but I'm in no mood for cute. These identity flip-flops are more dizzying than any clothing quick-change.

I need to be Lori. Lori, the interpreter. Lori, the stranger. Lori, the person who isn't his wife.

I have to be Lori. Even when we're alone.

"Sorry," Danny murmurs. "Didn't mean to scare you. I tried to let you know—"

"I know." My voice holds too much emotion, and I try to swallow that down.

"Come here." He holds out his arms, waiting to hold me.

I need that—I need *him* so badly. But I can't. I hold up a *stop* palm. "That's exactly what I need to talk to you about: I have to be Lori. All the time. It's too hard to jump back and forth."

"Okay." He sounds like he's buying time while he constructs a better plan.

I'd love to hear it.

Nothing comes. We sit there, the silence growing stale, until I gather the courage to turn to him again. He's shifted away, and my whole side's cold where he should be next to me.

My job is pushing us apart. It's pushing him away. Stealing

him.

I can't sit anymore. "Well." I rise to my feet. I came back to use him as a cover to get into Borislav's office, but the new plan falls into place as I speak. "Since you've already eaten, I'd better finish my rounds."

"'Rounds'?"

I cock an eyebrow, daring him to ask for details of my spy escapades deep in enemy territory.

"You don't want me to come with you." It's not a question.

I shake my head and start down the stairs. If I had my way, I think I'd lock Danny in his room for the rest of this trip. Better for me to be out after dark alone than risk a repeat of tonight.

But Danny doesn't turn for our door. I stop on the stairs and pivot to him. "Stay."

He pins me with a raised-eyebrow, dropped-jaw *I can't believe you seriously did that.* "I'm sorry, did you think you brought your pet dog with you?"

"Danny, I—" —totally treated him exactly that way. The realization lands in my gut like a sucker punch.

I'm not trying to be a jerk. He knows what I mean, after what I've been through. The anger and fear of ten minutes ago threaten a resurgence, and I stuff them into the furthest corner of my mind and lock them down. But I can still hear them in my voice, breaking as I almost beg him, "Please. Stay."

"Where are you going?"

I have to give him something. "Shcherbakov. I'll be fine."

"When I worry—"

The door to our floor swings open, and we both fall silent. The maintenance man in navy coveralls doesn't make a point to look at us or avoid our eyes. I watch him the whole way down the stairs. Don't recognize him, but not like I know every FSB officer. Jumpsuits are a classic way to blend in.

Potential enemy operative leaving our floor. Who knows

111

what he might've done in our rooms? Or found in mine?

Danny's won this argument—no way am I leaving him here alone. Back to my original plan, I guess. I start down the stairs. At the landing, I turn to Danny, still on the floor above, waiting for me.

With an exasperated sigh, I nod for him to come.

"Do I dare ask what changed?" he asks when he reaches me.

"Maintenance man. Could've gone through our rooms, left a trap." For all I know, Borislav took Danny out to give this guy time to get into his room, and the maintenance man either hid when I checked there (been there, done that), or I missed him.

"Or," Danny draws the word out. "He could've done *maintenance*."

I'm silent as long as possible, then begrudgingly admit, "Maybe."

"Are our lightbulbs safe? Should we check on them?"

I shoot him a mock glare. Cute? Sure. Cautious as we should be? Ha.

He pursues me down the stairs, into the cold and up the hill to the thoroughfare. We'll need a real cab again, and I hail one. I give the driver detailed directions once again.

We're not alone, and we shouldn't talk—but I have one more detail to settle before we get to Shcherbakov. Like Borislav said, they learn English from third grade these days. The cabbie might be too old to qualify, but he hasn't made any attempts at English. After several tense seconds slide by, I decide it's worth a shot as long as I monitor the cabbie (and the mirror). I lean over to Danny. "Give me your watch."

"Going to let me in on the plan?"

I beckon for him to give it up. Silently grumbling, he un-latches the wristwatch I gave him as a wedding gift—more bells and whistles than . . . I don't know, a bell tower in a whistle factory. It's been a long day, okay?

"Thanks." I slip the watch in my pocket and it clicks against the hard drive cloner. Anticipation builds in my chest again.

We're going in. We pull into the parking lot. The cabbie agrees to wait for us underneath the blue neons of the Shcherbakov sign, and Danny and I march up to the glass doors. I glance at Danny. Earlier, his cover was the truth. Now, I'm trusting a ton of this cover to him—a lie.

Suddenly, I almost wish I'd stolen his watch and let him freak out over losing it. But no going back. My heart rate hikes before I give Danny his story. "You lost your watch and think it's in Borislav's office."

Though he doesn't make eye contact, Danny confirms the story. We stride through the doors and find a security guard kicking back at the reception desk. He stands and waits for us to speak.

"Tell him" is all Danny can manage. So I explain how we visited Direktor Zverev, and Danny's missing his watch, and we have to find it before the cleaning crew finds it (i.e., steals it). The night watchman listens to the entire spiel impassively. He isn't the slightest bit moved until I smooth my long copper bangs and tilt my head to smile up at him.

He unlocks the inner door and leads us in. Danny follows me close enough to lean in and mutter, "Not sure whether I hate that or love you even more."

I meet his eyes. I want to wink—but I need to be Lori. My gaze falls.

The guard escorts us to the conference room where Borislav gave his PowerPoint, but obviously our search comes up empty. (At least it looks good for the cover.) I paint on that small smile again and turn to the guard. "We were also in Borislav Vyacheslavovich's office."

The guard frowns at me, but takes us to Borislav's office and opens it. "*Dve minuty*," he says.

I translate. "Two minutes."

The guard stands in the door, though we don't need the supervision. Two minutes isn't nearly long enough to search with the state this place is in. I direct Danny to look next to the desk, and I round it, to get at the computer underneath. A fairly recent model. Good. With the desk shielding me from the guard's view, I plug the cloner into a front USB slot.

Okay, now I need . . . another minute?

Danny comes even with the edge of the desk in his hunting, but he doesn't say anything to find me fiddling with the CPU. "Any luck?" he says. Hope the guard can't interpret the heavy irony in his voice.

"Not yet." I try not to think about the clock ticking in my brain. (Finish up, cloner.) "Did you check by the door?"

He puffs out a breath, playing his cover. "I'm so dead."

"Afraid of your wife's wrath?"

"You know, one thing I love about her is that she's a fighter. And that's who she is sometimes even with me." He moves over by the door, and I'm not sure whether the resignation in his tone has more to do with me or our little charade. "Still love her."

I command myself not to look up, but I don't hide the smile.

The green light reflects under the desk—all done cloning. (Don't you wish your external hard drive worked that fast? We're putting the "flash" in "flash memory.") I slide the cloner out of the computer and pick up the watch. "I've got it. Under the chair."

Danny releases his relief in an audible sigh. "Thank you."

"Yep." But I stay on the security guard. He hasn't given any sign of understanding us, and that doesn't change. I start past the desk, but "accidentally" bump a paper pile, triggering the same avalanche Borislav did this afternoon. His USB drives clatter to the floor.

Danny's still focused on putting the watch on, so I drop to my knees to clean up my mistake. All my practice in Paris ensures the maneuver goes smoothly, and the pile of flash drives is back on the desk by the time Danny finishes latching his watch, with one of the USB drives concealed in my palm. Danny helps me up, and the security guard marches us back out to our waiting cab.

My gaze settles on the side mirror, fixed on the maroon car with round headlights behind us. After about two minutes, I can't take the quiet any longer. I might have to be Lori, but that doesn't mean we have to sit in awkward silence. "Was dinner good?"

"Yeah." Danny finally turns away from his window. "We had . . . *pirozhki?*"

"Yum. What kind of filling?"

He relents a little. (The power of good food.) "Minced beef and mushrooms, and—wow. Borya recommended that and the appetizers, but I didn't catch the name."

Oh, but *I* caught the name. "Borya, is he?"

"He said I should call him that." Danny tilts his head a fraction of an inch, making his expression cautious. "Why? Did I do that wrong?"

"No, you're fine. Short form of the name. It just means you're real friends."

Danny considers that. "That's okay, right?"

Okay? An FSB officer building trust with my husband? Um, no. But I think I've overdrawn the your-paranoia's-cute account with Danny. "What did you pick up about him?"

"Not much. Was I supposed to?"

I hold out a hand to say *duh.* Can I blame someone so wholly genuine when it's not second nature to him to spy?

He rolls his eyes, and I direct mine back to the side mirror.

And a set of round headlights. A chill that has nothing to do with the cold slinks down my back. The same maroon car?

Should've known our afterhours visit would attract attention. I scan the blocks of buildings on either side of us. I didn't specify what route to take, but this one's okay. Though I haven't scouted this street, it's familiar, like I walked it a lot when I lived in Rostov.

A maroon car follows us through another light. Where can we stop for surveillance detection? Bank—closed. Karaoke bar—no parking. Boutique—closed. With a cabbie who's already done something unusual for us, we're running out of options faster than a "traitor" sentenced to the gulag. My pulse revs up to run. I stare at the mirror, watching those lights.

I look for a stop again, and the block of buildings gives way to a huge hotel. I know exactly where we are.

And exactly what to do. Usually, I use boring errands to determine if someone's tailing me. But sometimes, all you need to detect surveillance is a single background with enough contrast.

"Turn right," I tell the cabbie in Russian. He obeys. I concentrate on the mirror the whole way. The headlights follow down the next block, too.

"Turn again," I order the cabbie. Something's different—new stucco across the street?—but I don't have time to analyze. This is our alley. "Stop here."

"Are you sure?" the cabbie asks.

He's right to doubt a foreigner telling him to let her out beside some random alley, but I know what I'm doing. "*Da.*"

I pay the cabbie extra and practically drag Danny out. He looks at the dark passage between two buildings. "Remember how we talked about *not* getting into danger?" False brightness lights up his whisper. "I liked that plan."

"New plan." I take Danny's hand—more as a guide than a girl—and tug him into the alley. In the near-dark, you can still see the rust on the apartment balconies and ductwork, the neglected windows and graffiti, and every other sketchy detail.

Behind us, headlights round the corner and stop. Parking. Searching for us.

I can't tell if I'm hearing actual footsteps or my heart pounding in my ears. I can barely hear Danny: "Tell me you know where you're going."

Can't blame him for the weariness in his voice. I lead him faster. "Go with it."

We dart between the buildings and cars till we reach our destination, a two-story building. The lights are on. I check behind us. No headlights. But we can't let our guard down. They could be waiting for us. We have to get into disguise.

Footsteps. Not my pulse. I swear I hear footsteps approaching. "Hurry." I run the last few feet to the door. Please, please, please let it be open. What if no one's there? What if it's locked?

I pray that it isn't, that we'll get in and out without anyone suspecting.

The door opens and I pull Danny inside. I try to tow him through the tiny foyer as fast as I can. He wouldn't recognize the white tiles and walls, but as we pass, he does a double take at the familiar painting of Jesus Christ. "Tell me we're not where I think we are."

No time to argue. We need to get changed and back on the street fast to avoid suspicion. "Just go with it." We hurry down the hall, but the kitchen's locked. (Why, people, why???)

With no other choice, I drag Danny into the bathroom.

CHAPTER 13

"**U**M?" DANNY EYES THE STALLS—even in Russian, pretty easy to figure out where we are. "What exactly am I going with?"

"Take off your coat."

He couldn't be more confused if I were speaking Russian. "What?"

"Just do it—it's reversible." I turn to the mirror. If I can get this makeup off, I'll look different enough to get away. I consult Danny's reflection. Not moving. "Come on, hurry up. A fast change and they won't believe it's us."

Danny slowly starts on his buttons, but he's still gaping at me. "'They'? 'They' who?"

"The people tailing us." I grab a paper towel and run it under the faucet.

"What are you talking about?" He finishes unbuttoning his coat and shrugs it off. "Nobody's tailing us."

"Maroon car, round headlights, behind us." My pulse throbs in my throat through every second. I scrub off the sculpting face paint from everywhere but my eyes (way too messy), turning myself back into me.

Danny flips his coat's sleeves inside out. "And you've seen this car before?"

"No, but they followed us around the corner, and round headlights came down the alley after us."

"Round headlights? That's it?"

I check on Danny in time to catch him gaping at my reflection like he doesn't believe me. "How can you be sure it's the same car?"

We don't have time for this. I pivot on him. "Sorry I didn't get the license plate number, sir." I yank that gray knit cap out of his coat pocket again. "No arguments this time."

He takes the hat without a comment, but it's obvious he's not on board.

I stare at him. "Don't you trust me?"

"I wish I knew how." His words echo off the vintage tile and through my chest like it's just as hollow and empty.

I have spent months—more than a year—letting down every wall for him. I've told him the dangerous truth about what I do, I've sacrificed the things I thought were protecting me, I've given up every secret I can. The only ones I'm keeping now are to keep him safe.

I have nothing left to give. And this is still how he feels?

I'm in trouble, and it's not because of the headlights pursuing us.

"Guess we're screwed." My sharp response bounces off the tiles, too, like icy shrapnel.

"I didn't—"

"Forget it. It's fine. I know what you meant." If what he meant = exactly what he said.

I try my wig, but half a dozen points of pain in my scalp remind me I'm so not done. "Come on," I mutter, tearing a couple more pins free. Finally, the red wig comes off. I tug the wig cap off and undo my braids. My bangs are plastered to the side, and I try to fluff them like I was going for that sideswept look.

Danny's switched his jacket from black to red-flecked gray. "What about your coat?"

"I'll go without." Like my wig, my solid red coat definitely stands out—which means nobody will recognize me without them. I shed the coat and grab the bottom hem at the back. With a sharp jerk (and a silent apology to Lori), I tear out the stitches holding down the lining—my stitches from this morning. Between the lining and the shell, I basted in the market bag I picked up in Paris. I rip it free and stuff all my stuff inside.

Wish I had other shoes, though the car behind us hardly could've seen them. Danny's coat is on my shoulders before I can reach for the door handle. "I've got a suit jacket."

"That's not enough."

"Let me do this for you."

I'm ready to argue, but I know that look. I've given it to him enough. Insistent. Serious. Because he wants to take care of me. Even if he's not sure how to believe me.

The ends of his hair poke out under his hat brim. I tuck them in, then slowly let my gaze lower to meet his. I can give him this much. I have to. "All right. Give me a full minute before you follow. Make it look like we're not together, but stay on my tail. We'll take a *marshrutka* back."

He doesn't acknowledge my plan, instead sliding one hand back to cradle my head. Once again, there's no way I can say no to him as he leans in to kiss me. His lips move over mine and for one minute, I forget about the hurry and the danger and all our problems.

"Good to see you again," he breathes against my lips.

I draw back to meet his eyes. Yes, we've got issues to work through, but maybe we can make it. As long as we make it out of this mission alive.

"You're lucky I love you," I whisper. Though it's the other way around.

"Yeah, I know." He smiles a second before planting a peck on me again. "I'll follow."

I have to wipe off the grin before I open the door and slip into the hallway. And I'm not alone. A man stands five feet away. Staring at me.

A cold shock hits me like a smack.

They found us.

I have to lead them away from Danny. I have to act like nothing's wrong, though this guy's ogling me with more than a hey-cute-chick leer.

"Sestra Reynolds?"

Ice threads through my veins. That's. My. Name. Not just my name—my name and title as a missionary. Here. In this building. Five years ago.

If we were being tailed, this surely isn't the guy. But something else has caught up with me: the past. I take two breaths to calm my racing heart and turn toward this man.

The minute I take a closer look, I recognize his square-cut features and premature gray hair. A gasp escapes. Could it be—? I move forward, a smile stealing across my lips again.

Before I say anything, the door behind me opens, and now everybody's confused. Danny, to find me here with a stranger, I'm sure. The man in front of me, to be seeing me (and then a guy coming from the women's bathroom). Danny takes my arm, stepping to a protective posture.

But I don't need protection. Finally I find my voice. "Valya," I breathe. This isn't just some dude I ran into on the street. I visited his house weekly. I taught his wife, helped her learn the gospel and decide to join our church. I showed their daughters how to shinny up a drainpipe (yes, in a skirt). I played the piano at his wife's baptism.

"Sestra Reynolds!" Valya cries again, then he grabs me out of Danny's grasp into a bear hug.

"Valya!" I half-choke on his name, my throat suddenly

filled with emotion. *"Kak dela?"* *How are things?*

"Normal'no." Yep, that's "normal."

I pull back, still holding onto his arms. I have to see the rest of his family too. They should be here. *"Gde Ksena? I Svetusya, i Melanyushka?"*

Somewhere in his eyes, his smile grows sad and strained, and he's suddenly ten years older. *"Ne zdes'."* *Not here.*

Before I think about asking for details or everyone I want updates on, someone else runs up from my right and plows into me, seizing me in an even bigger hug. My heart hits the afterburners again, but I only have half a second to panic before he shouts, "Sestra Reynolds!"

Who the crap? Danny moves in to help again. I struggle free, protesting in Russian and backing toward the foyer. When I see who my would-be attacker is, my jaw nearly hits the carpet. I don't know whether to jump for joy or safety. Heavy-set, swarthy, and the last person I expected to find in a Mormon church. "Garo?"

"You did not forget me?" he asks in English. "You have come to marry me! Finally!" He lunges for another hug, and, I'm betting five hundred rubles, a kiss.

I sidestep his advances. "It's great to see you *here*, Garo." I point at the white tile floor to show I mean that literally, because the last time I lived in Rostov, Garo was a lot less interested in Jesus and a lot more interested in me and my companion.

"Yes, yes, good to see you too." He throws his arms around me again. I have no retreat and not enough of a reason to hurt him, so I just brace myself. Handshakes aren't the only greeting in the Russian gesture vocabulary that's bone-crushing.

Valya and Danny both try to intervene, though it doesn't seem like Garo's paying any attention to them when he releases me at last.

"I'm not here to marry you," I protest.

Garo laughs, because, duh, why else could I have traveled five thousand miles?

"What brings you back to Russia?" Valya matches our English—and saves me. (Thank! You!)

"I'm interpreting." I nod to Danny, still hovering nearby, amusement and uncertainty warring in his eyes. "My friend came on business."

Garo was never one for subtlety, but even the truth, spelled out clearly, isn't enough to deter him. He sweeps me into his arms yet again, rushing into the tiny foyer to spin me around. "You have finally come back!"

I doubt the man's pined away for the last five years, but, yeah, it's likely he won't listen to my logic. "Garo," I start with a warning in my tone.

We abruptly stop spinning. I'm not naïve enough to hope Garo's heeding to me.

Nope—Danny's got him by the shoulders. "She said to let her go."

Danny couldn't know this, but reminding a man that a woman said no and he'd better straighten up? *Big* deal. Though it seems like he's only playing, and he is, Garo's treading on razor thin Russian ice. Respect for women is more than "nice"; it's an inviolable social law.

Chagrinned, Garo releases me. By some subconscious maneuvering, we end up with Danny not quite between us, and yet ready to intercede any second.

Speaking of social laws—I run through the introductions, keeping Danny as my "friend." (Luckily, Danny is here as himself—and it's normal to skip last names in this context.)

Valya finally steps up to run interference as well. "Our music night ran late," he says, switching back to Russian. "We had to stay to stack the chairs." He gives Garo a skeptical glance once more and turns to me. "Do you need a ride anywhere?"

"That would be great." Even more perfect than my original plan. I gesture for Danny to follow, and we bid Garo goodbye.

"No, no," he says before we make our exit. I freeze for a second. I can't let this escalate.

He pulls a business card from his pocket and writes on it. "Here is my mobile number. You must call me before you go."

That's a big no. I don't even want his business card—way too dangerous for him if our FSB "friends" find it on me. But I take the card without any promises, knowing that it's the only way to get away fast. In my peripheral vision, I catch Valya's gaze flick heavenward, though he also says nothing. I understand: Garo's still Garo. Try as my missionary companion and I might years ago, we never could convince him we weren't interested, weren't here to date, and certainly weren't going to date him. I have to wonder if Garo figured joining the church was the best way to troll for American sister missionaries, or if he actually, truly converted.

Which is pretty horrible of me, isn't it?

Valya holds the door, and Danny and I finally make our escape. Once Garo's out and Valya's locked the doors, he points out his car, a boxy Moskvich Aleko hatchback that's got to be twenty years old, more rust than metal. For a second, I worry it won't start, but it does, and this is even better than running from Garo or surveillance.

It's too much to ask Valya to take us to see Ksena and the girls, though maybe I could find an hour tomorrow night to get away. At the thought, a happy sigh gathers in my chest. But that's tomorrow. "Could you take us down to the river? I want to show Danny the Don."

"Certainly." He looks at Danny in the rearview and asks me in Russian, "Should I ask why he was in the women's bathroom?"

I try to laugh his suspicions away. "I should've been there to guide him, but I wasn't."

"Ah." Valya looks to the rearview—to Danny. "And what is your . . . business?" I see why he switched to Russian—his English is halting at best.

"Aerospace."

"Ah." But he's squinting like he doesn't understand what Danny said.

Time to do my job and interpret. "*Aerokosmicheskaya promyshlennost'.*"

"Very nice." He slides into Russian as well. "Smart young man. Over the head of an old soldier."

I relay the message, but there's not a whole lot to say other than thanks. Could I bring Danny with me to meet Ksena and the girls? Might be awkward for him, but I've met friends from his mission, and I know Danny understands that soul-level connection.

"So you're not married?" Valya's pitch implies we should be. An instinctive flinch clenches my gut—but wait. He used the "*ty*" form of the verb, meaning just me. If he were implying Danny and I were "traveling in sin," he'd use the plural "*vy*" form.

"No," I say, trying to keep my tone light. "Marriages in my family don't last."

Valya nods sadly. Russia has the world's highest divorce rate, so he knows a lot of people in the same singlehood boat. But Valya's been lucky. "And where is Ksena?" I ask after his wife again. I'm definitely getting away to visit tomorrow. I can almost see her smile.

"She died, two years ago." Valya's delivery of the sad fact is so Russian: sadness mixed with acceptance. Life is hard, but it's my life.

A vise slowly squeezes my heart. She's gone? This woman whose life I helped to change all those years ago? Here I am, imagining seeing her, and I'm years too late to say goodbye. My shoulders slump automatically, like even my muscles are powerless. "Valya, I'm so sorry. I . . . What happened?"

"Cancer."

Not that unexpected for a woman who smoked for pretty much twenty years straight. I glance at the rearview. No headlights. Like that makes it safe to talk. I barely dare to ask about his daughters. "How are Svetusya and Melanyushka?"

"Svetusya is wonderful. She wants to be called Sveta these days. So grown up. Learning to play the piano. Does so well in school." Pride shines in his eyes, but it can't hide the pain. Just over Ksena?

"And Melanyushka?"

Pain wins out. "She is sick. Cancer also."

The same emotion that caught in my throat earlier strangles me again. I do the mental math: she has to be, what, ten? There's no such thing as "fair," but this is cruel.

I want to *do* something. I need to. "Can they treat her?"

"We do what we can here, but the wait is long for the better treatment center, and they say her prognosis is bad."

"Is there anything else you can do?"

He focuses on the road (and I check the rearview—still clear). "Pay to be treated sooner, or go to Germany, but we cannot afford either."

"The church—"

"Helped so much with Ksena's treatment. I will not ask more. I can't. Everyone has trouble." He half-hums out a sigh of resignation. "They help in other ways. Tyotya Gala tutors Sveta in math and makes sure Melanyushka doesn't fall behind."

"Aunt" Galina isn't any relation to Valya. She's a professor of math in the congregation. But she'd do that for any child who was willing to work. There has to be something I can do.

My stupid brain draws a blank.

"It's awfully late. Are you sure I can't take you back to your hotel?" Valya asks.

I don't want to leave; I want to help. But my stupid, stupid brain is still in spy mode. "My friend will like the lights on the river, and we need to talk."

He peers back at Danny, and I swear Valya looks like he knows too much. Then I remember—walking's how you get to know someone better in Russia . . . when you're dating.

The man already knows who I am; is thinking I'm interested in Danny worse?

"Enjoy your walk," Valya says to Danny. He pulls over to let us out.

Still not ready. I have to find a way to help his daughter, stop sickness from stealing another of Valya's girls. "Can I come see Melanyushka?" I ask.

"She will be at the hospital for treatment tomorrow evening. How about Thursday?"

"I leave Thursday. I could come to the hospital, if that's okay."

"If she's up to it," he says. "Hospital number one."

"Will you bring Svetusya?"

"Sveta." He winks. "Certainly."

I switch to English for Danny's benefit. "Thank you, Valya. It's so good to see you."

Valya hesitates, but finally speaks in Russian. "Seeing you again means a lot. After Ksena and Melanyushka . . . sometimes I worry God forgot old Valya." He smiles at last. "Then he sends me you, to say, 'See, Valya? I cannot forget you.'"

I know he's right—I *know* it with every brain cell, blood vessel and bone of my body. It's no coincidence I ended up at church tonight. But at the same time, I'm totally unworthy. I've done nothing but lie to this man, my friend, since the minute I saw him tonight. Now the best I can do is to be the symbol that God still remembers him, even as He takes everything away?

I have to do more. But all I can say is "I'll see you tomorrow, Valya."

I get out of the car, and Danny follows my lead (even using

127

spasibo with Valya, though I'm hardly surprised Danny's polite). Once Valya's off, we start down the street.

Not sure where we stand, so I let Danny begin the conversation. "Is that a Baskin Robbins?" He's squinting at a bright pink hut between us and the river.

"Probably a knockoff. You need to try the Russian ice cream. Their dairy products are more . . . dairy."

He raises an eyebrow at my awesome description. "Is that why Borya insisted I needed so much butter?"

"No, that's to fatten you up to make it through the winter."

He looks at me like he's waiting for me to laugh, but I'm not joking. "Oookay. So those were friends from your mission? Or . . . more than friends?" He's grinning, because Mormon missionaries aren't allowed to date (so Garo's advances were doubly inappropriate).

"Sorry. Garo's never been good at understanding subtle social cues—you know, like when we said, 'no, we can't marry you, and we don't want to.' But he's harmless."

"I know the type. Guess I was just delusional to think I was the first to ask."

I flash him a smile, then scan behind us. We can't stay out long without a coat for Danny, but once I'm back in disguise, I can return his. And I do need to get back into disguise soon. Talia isn't staying at the Hermitage; Lori is.

"Is the guy who gave us a ride another ex-boyfriend?"

I give his joke a single hiccup of a laugh. Valya looks older than he is (late forties?). "No. When I knew him, he was married. I taught his wife." I take a deep breath. Danny will understand the magnitude of this blow. "Just found out she died a couple years ago."

Danny slides an arm around my shoulders. "You okay?"

I don't pull away, because there's more. "Their daughter— she can't be older than ten—she has cancer, too. Sounds aggressive. I want—I *have* to help."

Regret rings through my voice, and Danny squeezes my shoulder in a side hug. "I know. Not a lot you can do," he says.

I steer him around another corner, but the truth sinks into my stomach.

There *is* something I can do. Valya isn't just some "old soldier." He's a *podpolkovnik*, a lieutenant colonel, stationed at the Russian Ground Forces' district headquarters. I can get Melanyushka treatment, get her to Moscow or Germany, get her cured. I can fulfill their obligations and maybe manufacture a few miracles.

I just have to get Valya to be a spy.

CHAPTER 14

IT FEELS SO MUCH LATER THAN IT IS, it's almost a shock to find stores open. We duck into the nearest McDonald's (we're awful Americans) to change out of our disguises. Well, since our disguises are us, maybe it's the other way around? Once we're safely in our "regular" clothes, the professional barrier goes up again. More whiplash.

We meander back to the hotel with as many surveillance detection stops as Danny can handle. No one's in pursuit, but there's something about being out, even in the dark and the cold. It's the last thing you'd expect in Russia, but when the alternative is your hotel room, buttoned down and boxed in and bugged, the air outside is filled with freedom.

By the fourth errand, Danny's exasperation shows in the set of his jaw. I pay for my Alyonka chocolate sticks with delicate chocolate wafer filling (this is *my* hunt for Red October—the candy manufacturer) and lead him to the street.

"Do you get frequent freak-out miles from the Company or something? Tax break? Claiming a new pair of shoes every month as a business expense?"

The same message lurks behind the jokes—you're

paranoid—but I have to admit it's funny. I share a couple chocolate sticks. "You realize only one of us is wearing heels, right?"

"You realize that's your own fault?"

I pretend to be exasperated with myself. "You know, you never finished telling me what you learned at dinner."

"Are we clear?" he asks.

I won't respond to the exhaustion in his voice—though I think he's less tired and more just tired of this. "Yes." (Though I have one more stop before we finish.)

Oblivious, Danny launches into his report from dinner. "Borya's local, went to Toulouse for grad school. This promotion was unexpected, but apparently he was handpicked as Timofeyev's successor."

"By Timofeyev?" We stop at a street corner, but traffic's light enough we can jaywalk.

Danny half-shrugs. "Sounds like it—sounds like Timofeyev was anticipating a promotion himself. Borya's modest about it, but the way people treat him—did you see it? He's the golden child, this protégé they kind of envy, kind of resent and kind of love."

Kita's awe and reverence and fear today flashes through my mind. Danny was paying attention, and the assessment could be spot on. But if he's so dedicated to aerospace, why is Borya with the FSB, too? "You discuss anything work related?"

"After we finished, he started talking up his vision for Shcherbakov, and—what's OAK?"

"*Obyedinyonnaya Aviastroitel'naya Korporatsiya,*" I reply, guiding us around another corner, another semi-residential side street. "United Aircraft Corporation. The government formed a coalition of aerospace companies and left Shcherbakov out. They get the government contracts. Timofeyev said it makes life hard for Shcherbakov."

"Yeah, Borya feels the same. He says before OAK, Shcherbakov was on course to take over the industry, but several other companies had . . . *svyazi?*"

"Connections, usually in the bureaucracy. Typical Russian attitude, blaming the establishment when you can't get ahead. Though it's the government's fault more often than not."

"Borya seems to think he can reverse that, though. Sounds like he's got a specific way to make it happen."

I give a sneaky, slow sideways glance. "A way that involves plans for a spy drone with a hyperspectral imaging camera?"

"Yep, told me all about it." With that much sarcasm in his voice, his eye-roll's redundant.

"Was it just the two of you at dinner?"

"Yeah. Why?"

"No reason." The lie is out before I can stop it, but I backtrack to correct myself. "I think he's dating—or maybe not 'dating'—Nadezhda."

"'Not dating'?"

I make another turn, debating the best way to explain the double standard. Respect for women is paramount—but maybe "respect" is the wrong word. Men have to be polite and accept no for an answer, unless they have some sort of power over a woman. To say no to your boss could be tantamount to professional suicide (or actual suicide). "Sexual harassment can be pretty institutionalized here."

Danny contemplates that. "Quick move for a new boss."

"Maybe." An hour of interaction isn't enough to analyze all the power politics that might be in play. Could be sending a message to the rest of his new subordinates, some of whom might've been passed over for the job.

We reach the corner, and I finally recognize the cross street—the one Semyon's note mentioned. The street with the dead drop.

I check my back once again. Rostov's a big city, but it's been dark for hours, so it feels later than it is, and most people have gone home. Only a few people are out on the sidewalk: two grandpas shuffling away from us and two young couples clustered together, chitchatting softly half a block away. Nobody's paying any attention to us. "Come on," I murmur.

Danny takes on that single lifted eyebrow that's become shorthand for his favorite question today: what now? But he follows me around the corner.

The blue box is mounted on the beige brick wall at the opposite end of the street. I wait until we're close enough to read the Почта России sign to search the ground nearby. A grapefruit-sized rock sits nestled in a sidewalk divot by the building's foundation.

My rib cage slowly turns to steel. I scan behind me once more. All clear.

I retrieve the rock. A little lighter than you'd expect. The seam between the halves seems like a natural crack. Well-made concealment device—but we work on these from the time we arrive on the Farm, so it's hardly a surprise Semyon's is good.

No time to admire his workmanship. Careful to angle it so nothing falls out, I twist the halves apart to reveal the hollow compartment and its contents. I hand the SIM card to Danny and pocket the passports and mini USB drive cloner. The tiny hard drive cloner and the USB drive both fit in the compartment.

"Oh," Danny whispers. "I was beginning to think you didn't take anything."

I purse my lips, but don't respond to that. "That's your SIM card. You're welcome." I screw the halves together and set it in its divot, brushing the cigarette butts around it into place.

As soon as it's secure, I'm off—but not running. A steady, casual pace. Danny matches me easily. "Do I dare ask what you just did?"

"My job." We round the corner to the main road.

"Stealing trade secrets?" His question from yesterday

echoes back in his tone: how does this make me any better than Fyodor?

I'm not better than him, maybe—but I'm not stealing secrets. "Just making sure ours haven't been stolen." I glance behind us again, pretending like I think we dropped something. Nobody back there to appreciate my act. But ahead, a guy across the street peers at us too long. I resist the urge to pick up my pace (though my pulse takes the opportunity to spike).

We stop in the nearest *produkty*. The clerk fusses at us that they're getting ready to close for the night. I put him off, claiming we're warming up for a minute. I browse the freezer cases, biding my time long enough that the guy across the street has to either come in or wait on the street a suspiciously long time.

After a couple minutes, he hasn't tailed us. The sidewalk's empty when we leave the store—though I make sure that's still the case every twenty feet or so.

Danny catches my gaze with his frown of disapproving skepticism. "Glancing over your shoulder is making me nervous."

"I'm glancing so you don't have to be nervous."

"Crazy thought: we could work together on watching our backs."

I laugh. "Thanks, but I got it. Besides, this is normal for a woman on a dark city street."

"Guess I wouldn't know. Appreciate the vote of confidence, though."

Ouch. I change the subject, pointing to the high-rise apartments down the block. "Recognize those?"

"The ones by our hotel?" His inflection says that's mostly a guess, but he's right. He takes the cue to drop the subject now that we're on approach (though I do make one last stop to check for surveillance). We reach the forest green hotel awning and march in. Once we're at the elevators, I can finally breathe easy. Man, it feels good to be done with walking.

"What's on the docket tomorrow?" Danny asks.

"Tour Shcherbakov, roll with the punches." The elevator arrives, and we step on. "Didn't 'Borya' tell you the plans?"

"Yeah, we're looking at composites, and then he recommended sightseeing in the afternoon while he's in a meeting."

With his superiors at the FSB?

I have to tell Danny. Dread gathers in my middle like a coming blizzard. I want Danny safe—he *has* to be safe—but with the way he talks to and about Borya, he won't like the truth.

"Sounds like he's got something to show off." Danny's words downplay the enthusiasm glowing in his voice and eyes. "Borya says that if we want, we could see—"

"You should be careful about listening to what 'Borya says.'" Before I can explain, we arrive at our floor. I reach for the button to continue up, but Danny gets off the elevator.

I hurry to follow. "I don't trust him," I mutter once I'm in range. There's only so much I dare to say in this hallway.

"Picked up on that one." Again, Danny's light tone doesn't match his words. We get to his door, and he doesn't stop to think whether we might be safer talking in the hall or letting me search his room after that "maintenance" call. He heads in and pulls off his tie. "Any reason you don't like him?"

At least he isn't using names. I linger in the doorway. "He's too nice."

Danny tosses his tie on the desk, then approaches me again, his face and his footsteps cautious. "'Too nice'? What does that mean? Next you'll stop trusting *me*?"

"Whoa, no—"

"I get you don't like him."

I flounder in silence, my mouth moving a second without sound. "I guess I don't."

Danny nods, looking at his open door. He wants to say more.

And if he isn't saying it, I'll bet I don't want to hear it. "Even if I'm wrong," I allow (though I'm not), "it'd be safest if you didn't go off alone with him again."

He gawks at me, incredulous. "And it's safest for you to roam the streets alone?"

"That's different. I—"

"Can take care of yourself," he finishes for me. (Not quite what I was going to say.) "So what does that say about me?"

The kick to the chest leaves me reeling. "You—I—Danny—"

He closes his eyes. "Let me know when I can come out in the morning."

Before I recover enough to stop him, the door's between us.

I didn't even get to tell him about the FSB. And would he believe me?

I turn for my door and draw in a breath. Two more days.

How have we only been here one day? It feels like a lifetime—and a lifetime of walking.

I'm physically, emotionally and mentally drained. All I want is to curl up with Danny, the one thing that reminds me every day that the sacrifices I make are worth it to protect people like him.

People who apparently think I'm on par with a common criminal and totally patronizing.

I glance back at his door one more time, willing it to open, for Danny to take it all back.

Nothing.

I'm exhausted, but I doubt I'll get much rest tonight.

CHAPTER 15

AFTER TWO NIGHTS OF SCARCE SLEEP, I definitely don't have the energy to continue the fight in the morning, and my 3 AM run to cache a disguise or the two-hour time change from Paris isn't the real reason I tossed and turned. Even Semyon's encrypted text doesn't cheer me: *B has contacts in Libya, Iran, etc. May have drone plans. Expect another package.*

Not solid enough to present to Danny. I avoid the argument and phone his room to have him meet me at the lobby bar's breakfast buffet. We're civil—or as friendly as Danny and Lori should be—over our kasha porridge and *syrniki* (fried pancakes made with the firmer Russian version of cottage cheese) with honey. At Shcherbakov, the receptionist waves us through and we make our way to Borya's office alone.

The elevator's extra uncomfortable. Yesterday, an elevator ride with him meant a few seconds to relax our covers. Today, it means a few seconds it's even harder to pretend.

"I heard you had an adventure last night?" Borya greets us outside his office. He doesn't bother hiding the amused smile. "The security guard tells me you came by."

"I lost the watch my wife gave me for our wedding," Danny

says. "Must've fallen off."

Is it me, or is there way more than mirth behind that smile of Borya's? "Good thing it didn't happen while we were at dinner, then. You'd never see it again."

The back of my neck turns cold. That's got to be more than amusement. Did he notice Danny's watch at dinner? It's a nice watch, but . . . Do we need to be even more careful?

"I know," Danny says. "Thanks again for dinner; much better than sitting around my hotel."

I pretend I honestly don't care about this conversation or Danny needling me for ditching him. What am I supposed to say? *Yes, honey, please come to all my Top Secret CIA meetings?*

"Only doing what you suggested. Hope I didn't cause you any trouble. Or worry." Borya's glance at me is lightning fast, but I still catch it. He knows. He knows I left Danny. He knows about our fight—over worrying.

Because he's listening to the bug in Danny's room. He has to be. My rib cage shrinks.

Yep. We're in his sights.

And now we get to spend the day together. Yippee. Borya turns for Nadia's desk by his door, but she's not there. He rolls his eyes. "She must have confused six hours and sixteen hours on her alarm clock again."

Danny glances at me. "Sixteen hundred?" he mutters.

I nod.

Borya smiles at us. "Don't worry; she'll be here to take care of you in the afternoon, while I'm in my meeting."

Keeping his girlfriend far away from his meeting with his FSB superiors? Uh huh.

He claps. "Let's get started."

Danny agrees, and they file past me to begin the day.

I hate how much I have to stare at Borya to be ready to translate his chatter as we make the rounds with the design team. Unfortunately, I don't have X-ray vision, so I can't see through him. After we've met half a dozen people, they delve into design details. With Borya translating, I'm left on the fringes of the group, hovering in the "hall" between cubicles. They're not talking loudly enough to hear, but at this distance I see the way the designers treat Borya. He makes a point, and they hurry to nod. He cracks a joke, and they guffaw with gusto. He disagrees, and they backpedal. I didn't spend much time in corporate environments as a missionary, but like Danny said, the reverence and awe these guys show Borislav is . . . unsettling. Is his affiliation with the FSB an open secret?

Then I feel it, that familiar tingling at the base of my skull. Like I'm being watched, and not just by the FSB specter hanging over the whole building. I lean against the cubicle wall, puffing out a bored breath, and slowly scan the hall as if for some respite. When I see the man behind me, my jump is only half fake.

Kita, the lingerer. Danny's absorbed in a conversation and computer monitor, so I turn back to Creepita Creepyev. "Nikita, yes?" I ask.

"Call me Nikisha." He finishes the command to use a more intimate form of his name with a leer.

I'd rather call him Nikikha, the derogatory form, and dismiss him.

"And you are?" he finally asks.

"The interpreter."

"Ah." His eyes take the scenic route over my body: hair, sweater, skirt, boots, and back up, taking his time to reach my face again.

Checking someone out isn't rude in Russia, but inspecting me like I'm goods for sale in the *rynok*? Different story.

I cross my arms to shield myself, my defenses rising. "You need something translated?"

"No." But Kita keeps staring. Could this guy be the FSB

officer? The evidence is definitely in Borya's favor, but Kita's got that pinched look I'd attribute to an American Fed (though constipation may not be a side effect for all federal agents).

The design huddle breaks, and Borya and Danny reach the "door" of the cubicle. "Oh, Kita," Borya says. He's suddenly closed and unreadable. "Need something?"

"Simply getting to know our visitors."

Borya indicates each of us. "Lori Dolman. Danny Fluker."

Kita acknowledges Danny, but his gaze stays on me. (Suspicious?) He doesn't leave, blocking Borya's exit from the cubicle. Borya waits, but Kita doesn't move. "Did you want to come with us to *aerodinamicheskaya truba* to see the *skorkot*?" Borya asks him at last, carefully picking each word (including the ones I can't translate).

My shoulders fall and my stomach follows. Whatever an "aerodynamic tunnel" is, it's not my idea of fun. I'm guessing it's these guys', though.

Kita accepts eagerly, and finally lets Borya and the other designers past. They start off without telling Danny where they're going, but turn back like they expect him to come.

I touch Danny's elbow to get his attention. "Aerodynamic tunnel, to show off the *skorkot*."

He glances at my hand, and I realize this is our first physical contact today.

That's depressing.

"*Skorkot*?" Danny asks me, pursuing Borya, Kita and the designers.

"Not sure. Have you heard about a fast cat?"

"Oh, I think he was telling me about this yesterday."

Could this be the ace up Borya's sleeve for Shcherbakov? "What did he say about it?"

"Three-surface aircraft—canards, wings, tailplane. Can increase your maneuverability if you do it right."

I slow down, dropping back from the crowd. "Borya's

secret weapon to save Shcherbakov?"

Danny squints, thinking. "Doubt it. He told me about this in the car yesterday; didn't mention his plan until later. Plus, this stuff hasn't been cutting edge since the mid-eighties, at the latest."

Borya and company hold the elevator, and we end up with the designers between us and Borya and Kita. I regard Danny the whole way down, examining him as these people see him. Not the man I love, but a talented aerospace designer trying to broker a research collaboration. That expertise is exactly why the CIA recruited him for this mission—and exactly why I love it and hate it.

On the ground floor, Borya leads the group out the back doors, through an icy blast in the breezeway and into a long, low building. Inside, the smell of chemical fumes, metal and grease is overpowering. Clusters of machines are scattered throughout the room. Jumpsuited workers busily spread epoxy on a miniature airplane's wings, maybe six feet across.

I check: the jumpsuits are gray, not the navy of the "maintenance" guy leaving our floor last night. (Proves nothing.)

Borya calls a greeting, and one worker waves without looking up, all three concentrating on the surprisingly delicate task. "We'd like to show our visitor the Fast Cat model in the aerodynamic tunnel," Borya tells them.

Ah. A wind tunnel. The oversized pipe running around the edge of the room now makes sense, and I spot what must be the testing part of the tunnel, a huge gray box with a steel exoskeleton. Duh. Danny's shown me NRC's wind tunnels in Ottawa—all six of them—should've figured this out sooner.

"Sounds like you're seeing the mini Fast Cat in action," I murmur to Danny.

"Cool." But he's still staring at the nearest model, his eyes alight like . . . well, like an aerospace engineer in an aeronautics

141

model shop.

"Do we go *in* the wind tunnel?"

He shrugs. "Sometimes."

I wait for Danny to see the problem. Finally he looks at me, and I point at my skirt (not to mention my wig).

"Oh. Yeah, that could get awkward."

No more awkward than standing around the model shop alone.

Unless this is a huge opportunity. I turn to Danny again. "Okay if I leave you for a few?"

"You don't want me alone with Borya, but when you feel like it, leaving me with them is okay? They're *less* likely to gang up on me when it's ten on one?"

"Thanks for reminding me the numbers aren't in your favor." I fold my arms and sigh, like I'm trapped here in DeathByBoredomVille (population: me).

"Go then. Believe it or not, I *can* take care of myself."

I choose not to acknowledge the edge of annoyance in his voice and approach Borya. "Borislav Vyacheslavovich, I need some air—the fumes are . . ." I gesture at my head and grimace.

"I apologize; certainly."

Now the *coup de grâce*. I put on my I'm-so-innocent-you'd-give-me-your-firstborn-and-your-keys face and a tiny smile, smoothing my long copper bangs once again. "I could . . . wait in your office?"

For a very long heartbeat, Borya scrutinizes me from the corner of his eye. Like he isn't used to being flirted with? Or like he doesn't trust me? I count the seconds, careful to maintain my neutral/innocent/hopeful expression.

Three seconds. Four. Five.

At last, he pulls a key ring from his pocket, offering me one key in particular. "You can wait for us. If you can find your way."

"I'll manage, thank you." I smile again, even if a Russian

wouldn't, but not just at his generosity.

I have unfettered access to an FSB operative's private office. Field day for a CIA officer.

Any FSB officer worth his salt—or harboring stolen plans— would know better than to open his office to *anyone*, and especially not some random American interpreter. Until just now, Borya's never seemed the slightest bit suspicious of me.

Always a poor strategy. I let myself in his office. Still Paper Central. Once the door's locked behind me, I stick the first USB drive in my minicloner. While it works, I home in on the closest paper pile. *Zayavka. Requisition.* Dated six months ago. Nope. I flip through the stack and lift off the top couple inches of papers. Seven months ago, also a *zayavka.* I try two more spots in the pile. Can't be sure, but short of checking every single paper in the stack, this method's the best I can do. The dates move further back in time. I have to assume these papers stacked together, all the same type, are just that.

I work in a circle, clockwise around the room, switching USB drives between each paper stack search. They all seem legit along the first wall, none of them pertinent. The office chairs hold purchase orders. The cardboard mailing tubes hold plans. I know right away they're not Danny's—kinda easy to tell a drone from an actual plane (no seats in a drone)—but I should take pictures anyway.

I get my phone and set up the photo op: spread the plans by the desk, steady my elbows on the desktop, make sure I'm not casting a shadow on the papers, snap the photo. I repeat the process for each of the five cardboard tubes. One or two of them I can't dismiss out of hand, and I try to note where they fall in the photo order—tubes three and five, pictures twelve through fourteen and sixteen through twenty.

Once those are done, I've still got half a dozen USB drives to copy, but I need to tackle the pachyderm in this place: the personal computer. We cloned his hard drive, but what didn't that cover? I hop behind his desk and wake up the computer.

Parol', it prompts me. *Password.* I glance around, as if he'd be stupid enough to—and there it is, right in front of my nose. A pink Post-It note on the monitor. His login is Зверев6, his last name and first initial, and underneath that, Динус91: Dinusya, his nickname for Nadezhda, with a netspeak 91 for the я.

As soon as I type the password, suspicion sets in. An intelligence officer who lets an American not only have free rein in his office—but also posts his computer login and password so obviously? With survival instincts like these, it's no surprise the FSB squirreled him away monitoring imports/exports in an aerospace company.

Unless, of course, this is a trap.

A risk I'll have to take? Maybe—as long as I keep my computer activities to something I can explain away.

My favorite spot to start is always email, but that might have to be second. I doubt his afternoon meeting has anything to do with what we want—not like he's Skyping with Libyans from work (unless it's actually work, but . . . why?)—but I have to go for the low-hanging fruit.

I'm curious. Sue me.

I check his calendar. "Tsurenko" is all it says this afternoon. Ukrainian?

Okay, email it is. I open the email client and search for Tsurenko. A couple emails come up. I skim them. Oh. He's a supplier, outsourcing new fiberglass something or others.

Next tack. I open the contact list. Borya couldn't possibly

be dumb enough to keep Libyan contacts in his email program, right?

I look at the pink Post-It note askance. Really no telling.

Not sure I'd recognize a Libyan name. I pick out mostly Russian surnames with a couple Tatars and Armenians mixed in. A group of Georgians. Ukrainian names, could be Russians. Nothing jumps out as Arabic or African or anything interesting.

He's smart enough not to use his work email with his *other* work contacts. Could he have another email address? I pull up a browser and hunt through his bookmarks. Mail.ru, right at the top. The most popular web-based email in Russia.

I've done something right, because the site automatically logs in to his inbox. I scan the emails. Only a handful of messages, mostly spam.

The outbox, then. Most people don't think to empty that. I scan the recipients.

Al-Ansari? Definitely not Slavic. More like Arabic. Bingo. I click through to the message. It's in French. French?

Wait, don't a few countries in Africa speak French, some strange vestige of European colonization? Yeah—Morocco, Algeria/Algiers, Burkina Faso (random fact, but I *do* know the country home to Ouagadougou speaks French when they spell the capital like that).

I look back at the message to al-Ansari. *L'offre n'est pas assez. The offer isn't enough.*

Whoa, whoa, whoa. Borya's telling his French Arabic contact the price is too low?

Icy fingers trail down my back. What is this? I scan the sent folder for al-Ansari.

A key jams into the office door. My heart jams into my throat. Caught.

I race to kill the browser window. I need a cover. Russian computers have solitaire, right? Adrenaline makes my fingers

145

fumble on the mouse.

No, not enough—it's too suspicious I'm on his passworded computer at all. I hit the monitor power button and the screen goes black.

The door swings open. I spin 90° away from the computer and slap on a bored look.

Nadezhda stands in the doorway. "What are you doing in here?" she demands in Russian.

My pulse races faster than those jets I just photographed. I instinctively cover my phone in my pocket, but I don't dare take my gaze off Nadezhda. "Borislav Vyacheslavovich told me I could." I go for the respectful form of address. I'll use any respect I can beg, borrow or steal.

"He did?" She prowls over to the desk. I concentrate on her, careful to keep my eyes away from the monitor, on the off chance it hasn't already occurred to her to switch it back on.

She appraises the piles of papers, but reaches over them— reaching for the monitor. Every muscle in my body goes rigid, and my brain scrambles for a distraction. "He and Danny are in the aerodynamic tunnel."

"Hm." She doesn't stop. She doesn't even pause. Her hand closes the last few inches and I can't breathe.

But she doesn't touch the monitor. She goes for the tiny picture frame beneath the screen, flipping it face down. I barely have time to glimpse the happy couple. Borya and Nadezhda?

"The fumes were bothering me," I explain, as if I didn't see her. "Borislav gave me his keys so I could wait here." I place them on the desk.

Nadezhda squints at them. Does she not believe me, or does recognizing her boyfriend's keys take that much of her brain power? "It *is* strange to find you in his office. Alone."

Awesome. If I hadn't brought attention to it, *Durochka Dinochka* wouldn't have noticed.

"Yeah, didn't think about how boring this would be." I try

the same wide-eyed innocence that got me here in the first place (without the overtones of flirting).

Nadezhda buys that without comment. She isn't being overly friendly, but her standoffishness seems to be normal Russian reservation rather than real dislike or suspicion. She inspects the stacks of paper on the desktop, as if I'm dumb enough to leave out evidence.

I'm not—and fortunately, that makes one of us.

She finishes her search and turns back to me. "You're very formal with Borya," she observes, using his short name for the first time (with me). "And very informal with 'Danny.'"

"'Danny' doesn't have any other form of his name, or a patronymic." I stand, shrugging like that will cover up the awkwardness of her observation.

"What about Daniil?"

"His name is just Danny." Wait—does that come up a lot in conversation? It was weeks before I teasingly called him Daniel and he corrected me. "He told me to call him Danny."

She thinks about that. I get the feeling this might take a while. "You like Danny?" she asks at last.

"Sure." But I don't know if the casual tone and shrug are fooling anybody.

The set to Nadezhda's features turns knowing instead of uncomprehending—as if she sees too much as she looks me up and down. "Unsolicited advice: stay away from offices that belong to other people—and men who belong to other women."

"Good advice," I murmur. Because I'm Lori. Not Talia.

And apparently I need to work harder to remember that if I'm here to protect Danny.

CHAPTER 16

NADEZHDA LEADS ME OUT OF BORYA'S OFFICE. I assume we're going back to Danny and Borya, possibly so she can tattle. Makes the elevator ride awkward.

At the ground floor, Nadezhda takes the same hallways we did to the wind tunnel. Maybe her "friendly advice" is opportunity's knock. She may not be in a relationship with him by choice, but she's likely in Borya's confidence—and she just extended the first tentative understanding to me. *Durochka Dinochka* could be a major asset.

I hurry to match her pace down the hall. "Have you worked for Borya long?"

She startles slightly to find me next to her, surprise replacing her blank expression for half a second. "We've worked together for almost a year, but he only became the director in August."

"How'd he snag that promotion? Aren't there more senior managers?"

"His predecessor was poised for his own promotion. He'd made it clear he wanted Borya to replace him."

We round the final corner to the glass exterior doors.

Danny and Borya are on approach. (No Kita. No loss.) We wait.

My last chance for questions. How can I imply there must be another reason he got this job? (I.e. the FSB.) "Does Borya have *svyazi* in the company? Or . . . ?"

"No, Fyodor was the one with *svyazi*. And he had to go and get himself killed."

The suspicion in her typical Russian bluntness is enough of an accusation that my stomach pitches like an ill-fated test plane. Before I can worry that Nadezhda will see my reaction, the doors swing open. Danny and Borya pass between us, laughing over some aerospace joke. I watch Nadezhda: her gaze tracks after Borya, and deep in those blue eyes I see the longing for the littlest recognition.

I glance after Danny. I know how she feels.

When he's a couple feet past us, Borya casts a quick wink Nadezhda's way.

Danny doesn't turn back. I'm not disappointed he's playing his cover. I told him to treat me this way, and he's on-mission. It seems bad, but it's actually good.

At least, I really want it to be good.

Nadezhda and I fall into step behind our men. (Okay, she doesn't know that.) "How long have you been 'seeing' Borya?"

Her eyebrows flinch, but beyond that, Nadezhda betrays no emotion. "Almost a year."

Since before the promotion? Then does she know he's FSB? Or was he recruited more recently? I toss another lure into the water. "He seems like a good man." Not.

"Very." She fixates on the back of his head, and I can't tell if she absolutely does or absolutely does *not* believe herself.

Yep. She's the cashew I've got to crack.

"I'm sure he treats you well," I say, though I try to leave a question in my tone, like I'm concerned about her well-being after seeing too many of these relationships go south.

She gives a quick noncommittal nod. Danny and Borya

hang a left and we follow.

"He must trust you. And like you a lot."

"Both, I hope," she says. "What about you? How long have you been an interpreter?"

I play my cover easily. "Four years. First time in Rostov-on-Don, though."

"How do you like the city?"

I borrow Danny's diplomatic tack. "I like what I've seen, but that's mostly the hotel and here."

"We'll fix that. We have your sightseeing excursion this afternoon."

That's right. More time to trick her into talking about her boyfriend. (Totally not above that.)

Danny and Borya stop ahead of us and take a left into an *"ugleplastiki"* lab. (Angle plastics?) We observe them through the lab's window, not invited to come along.

Nadezhda props her arms on the sill, watching Danny and Borya and the other workers in the lab. Borya holds up a piece of black fabric, obviously pretty proud of himself. Oh, right. He promised composites. "Why do people complain learning Russian is difficult?" The tone of Nadezhda's small talk matches her vacant expression. "It is so easy even babies learn it here."

"Um." Wow. I see why her boyfriend thinks she's stupid. "Was English difficult for you to learn?"

She breaks away from staring at Danny and Borya's silent conversation to me. "That is different."

"Yes." Only not.

"Was Russian difficult for you?"

"Somewhat. Being in the country helps a lot."

Skepticism settles in the lines around Nadezhda's squint. "Is this why you have been working in Russia for four years?"

"No, mostly it's the people." No hesitation. It's the thing I've missed the most. Valya, Ksena, even Garo—people I served and taught and laughed with and loved. (Though maybe not quite how Garo wanted me to.) I turn back to Danny and Borya, talking to someone in a lab coat, all huddled around another computer.

"Did you need any specialized training for your job?" Nadezhda asks.

My suspicions creep up a notch, like the hairs at the back of my neck. What's she fishing for? "Yes," I lie. (Spy.) "I'm certified."

"Where do you work in Moscow?"

So glad I didn't go rogue with this support mission for Danny. The CIA's already fully backstopped my legend— meaning they've provided the documentation and bribes necessary for people to verify my story, so I can say this without worrying. "InterpretiRossiya."

"Do you work in the Moscow office?"

"I work wherever they send me." I know she's trying to make small talk, and I'm all for the relationship-building exercise, but I only like playing Twenty Questions when I'm the questioner. Now it's my turn. "Why do you ask?"

"Oh." Nadezhda blushes and looks back to the window. "I don't mean to bother you. I've always wanted to interpret."

"English?"

"Ukrainian."

"I could see if there are any openings."

She looks at me, and a small smile shines in her eyes. "*Davai na ty*," she says.

Tough concept to translate. In Russian, like Spanish, French and most European languages, there are two forms of "you": the formal one for superiors and strangers, and the informal one for friends. Nadezhda's offering to move me from the first category into the second.

"*Da, davai*," I agree.

"Call me Nadia."

You know, I kinda like her. Not that I'll let that block my

objective. She might even help.

I glance at Borya and Danny passing a miniature black plane wing back and forth, chatting up the lab workers—my husband and the FSB officer who might have his stolen plans. I'll take all the help I can get.

After half an hour, Borya wraps up the facility tour and takes us to lunch at 16th Line, an art gallery/restaurant. Even as Lori I'm not cool enough to be here. The exterior is painted in hipster-style graffiti, giant graphic faces, while the industrial chic interior is all black, steel, chrome and mirrors. Oh, and alcohol. Walls of bottles in every shape, color and vintage.

The hostess guides us back to a corner table. I step right up to the best vantage point to see the door, and Danny gets my chair for me.

Not tuning out the barrage of aerospace chatter takes serious effort: watching, waiting, protecting Danny. At least they're using English. Nadia has perfected the patiently, indulgently, vapidly bored look. Maybe I need to work on that. Or maybe it comes naturally to her.

The waitress has brought us water and vodka (gee, thanks) by the time the topic of correcting tailplane instability finally winds down—but Borya's just getting started. "So, the University of Michigan," he begins.

He's testing Danny's cover. Again.

Fortunately, it isn't a cover. Danny sips his water easily then smiles. "Yep."

"A very good school."

"They worked us hard."

"And an expensive school, too, from what I understand? That was the biggest shock of studying outside Russia, the price."

Danny gives a little laugh-nod (that's actually really cute). "I was spared the brunt of it: in-state tuition. I'm from Michigan."

Borya slowly pulls his bottom lip through his teeth, and something tells me he isn't pondering international tuition system differences. "You're American, then?"

"Yeah."

So much for the Canadian-employee's-Canadian-himself charade, though it's hardly worth the effort without that back-stopping. Borya's gaze slides away, thoughtful. Trying to find something else to trip him? Pondering what to do with an American? My palms grow clammy.

"Did you know any Russians at university?" Borya asks.

Danny rubs at his cloth napkin, also thinking. "Can't think of any. A friend go there?"

"Yes, for his Master's. Oleg Kollerov?"

I don't dare signal an answer to Danny. Maybe Oleg did go to U–Mich, and maybe this is the obvious test. Or maybe Borya's even cleverer. Maybe there *is* no Oleg, and he's baiting Danny. If Danny says yes, his cover's blown.

One of the most important ways a spy obtains information is through elicitation: getting answers without asking direct questions. You flatter your new best friend. You pretend to be dumb. You lay a trap of misinformation.

"When was he there?" Danny's gaze is still distant, like he's still searching his memory.

"Would have been . . . eight years ago?"

"Probably wouldn't have run into him. I was an undergrad then."

Borya accepts that answer. Danny's incredibly lucky—no, he's lucky he doesn't have a cover to play, that he can tell the

153

truth. Their talk moves to Paris's *Musée de l'air et de l'espace*, and it's my turn to play my cover as someone who wasn't there last week.

"What was your favorite exhibit?" Borya asks.

Danny doesn't wait a beat, settling back in his sleek black chair. "SO.9000 Trident."

"Oh?" Borya's gaze wanders skyward as if he could actually look through his memory. "I don't recall that one."

"Experimental hall, interceptor from the fifties. I have a thing for scrubbed prototypes from that era." (I swear, if Danny mentions the Avro Arrow, the Canadian plane with an eerily similar history that he's *obsessed* with, I cannot be held responsible for what I may do.)

"Ah, your pet project. I'm eager to hear more."

Yeah, he'd better not.

"What was your favorite exhibit?" Danny asks.

"V-1 flying bomb, from the Great Patriotic War. I have 'a thing' for unmanned flight." This is sure to be riveting. But when Borya leans forward, enthusiasm sparkling in his eyes, my brain jumps to full attention. "Have you worked much with drones?"

My heart also hops to high alert.

"Worked with almost everything." Good thing Danny's used to being vague about his Canadian defense contracts. He guides the conversation in a different direction. "One thing I love about my job, the variety. Every week's a new challenge."

"And is that how you worked with hyperspectral imaging?"

I swallow hard—or I would if I could. That's the drone Fyodor stole. Sure, Danny mentioned it to him yesterday, but at the time Borya had never heard of it.

I'm sure my gaze is drilling into Danny, but his is fixed on his cobalt blue glass. "Oh, yeah. That was a while ago. Our latest projects are on de-icing."

"Ah." Borya takes the answer, but I can see it lurking

behind his acceptance—the subject is far from dropped. "You're coming back to Shcherbakov this afternoon, yes?"

"Yep."

"Then I can't wait to hear more about that."

Why, why, why did I not tell him who Borya is? Danny knows better than to spill classified secrets, but what about everything that's okay to tell a business partner but not an FSB officer (i.e., *everything*)? We've got to grab a minute alone.

The waitress finally arrives to take our orders—an "ox fillet" is just beef, right?—and heads away. Customer service isn't the aim of Russian restaurants, so it could be a while before we see her.

As soon as she's gone, Nadia takes advantage of the interruption and leans over to murmur something to Borya. They both glance my direction with wary eyes.

Oh, crap. She's telling him about finding me in his office. She has to be.

But he gave me his keys. He has no reason to suspect me, and it isn't news to him. Still, my pulse ticks up a notch.

"Wait." Borya slips back to Russian and turns to her. "They need me to do what? Why?"

Oh. My pulse returns to normal—after another minute of discussion shows this business note for what it really is: my chance. I catch Danny's attention and point to the *Galereya* sign across the restaurant. "There's a gallery upstairs. Why don't we let them work?"

Borya acknowledges us with a nod and focuses on Nadia.

I lead Danny upstairs. He immediately maneuvers closer. "'Great Patriotic War'—World War II?"

Not the topic I was planning. "Yeah. Still a big thing here. I mean, Rostov was besieged twice, Volgograd was practically leveled, and despite that, they won. A big deal."

I try to make our browsing seem casual while steering him away from any prying ears. When we're the only ones admiring a photorealistic painting of a beggar on a cracked sidewalk, I kick off that classified conversation. "Be careful what you say to him."

Danny eyeballs the destitute man in the picture. "Doubt he's gonna talk."

I spear him with a patented Look, and Danny relents (and sighs). "You can't be serious."

"I am serious, thank you."

"Obviously he's harmless. He's just an engineer."

"Like you? Like Timofeyev?" I.e. the man who stole Danny's plans.

Danny presses his lips together. Really, we still can't confirm Fyodor was doing anything other than "normal" corporate espionage, but in this case that should be more than enough.

"There is an *officer* at the company." I add extra emphasis so he knows I'm not talking about an executive.

He shakes his head, focusing on the painting again. He opens his mouth, then closes it, rethinking his response. Instead of speaking, he walks to the next painting, a shaggy dog in psychedelic colors.

I follow, keeping to whisper range. "Are you listening to me?"

"Oh yeah, I'm listening." His tone makes it clear he doesn't like what he's hearing.

"He's trying to extract information. Don't you see that?"

"Don't *you* remember drones are his specialty, the topic of his thesis? It's a coincidence. I don't know why you'd think—"

"I told you." I scan the gallery. No one's close enough to hear, but I'm not getting specific. "Nobody's this friendly with strangers without an ulterior motive."

Danny points a thumb over his shoulder. "Have you seen his office? If he had anything, even he wouldn't know."

I can't fault his argument or logic or how he avoids mentioning sensitive intel, but my brain shouts to not buy into this.

"So can we *not*?" Danny asks. "We're here, we're looking—isn't the real assignment enough?"

Now I'm the one whose mouth is working without an answer. I don't believe for a minute that Danny's siding with a dude he met yesterday over his own wife (of two weeks).

And for the first time, it dawns on me: we were married two weeks ago today. Last week, that seemed like a milestone worth celebrating. Now, we're lucky to make it this far.

I'm silent too long and he pivots away. "Here's a plan: wait until we have one shred of evidence before we overreact."

I need to figure out how to subtly remind him I *do* know what I'm doing. "Trust me."

Instead of the tired line he gave me yesterday, Danny studies me. "I—"

I pick up an incoming person in my peripheral vision and hold up a hand to silence him before I look. Nadia. I give Danny a we-are-sooo-not-done face and wheel on her. "The food has come," she informs us in English.

We thank her. As soon as she turns, Danny leans close. "Try to look normal this afternoon, okay?"

"Fine."

We return to our table. Back to the waiting FSB officer. Back to our covers.

Back to the invisible wall between us.

I don't have much of an appetite—which is fine because I don't trust Borya and Nadia with my food. But Borya behaves himself the rest of lunch, unfortunately, seriously undermining my argument with Danny. Every minute, I watch my wonderful, devoted husband become better and better friends with the enemy, only stopping when Borya bids us goodbye to take a taxi for his meeting, and Nadia takes his Jeep for our tour.

But our first stop's within walking distance: unsurprisingly, Nadia's top pick is the Eternal Flame, the World War II memorial—sorry, the Great Patriotic War Memorial. (Did you know Russia won the war for us? Yeah, I didn't either until I lived here. I'd joke about how kind that was of them, but I'm guessing the reality is some blend of both our versions of history.)

Nadia can speak English, but defaults to letting me translate, keeping me busy. Probably the purpose of this pursuit, eh? I relay the monument's story as we walk around the roofless rotunda. Opposite the entrance, a woman's stylized, sad face is sculpted next to one hand, holding an olive branch.

"This is the only Great Patriotic War memorial to remember the women and their contribution to the fight." Nadia finishes her monologue, and I finish repeating it to Danny.

Nadia's not done. She stares up at the woman's bronze features, but that isn't who she's talking about. "When something momentous happens," she says in Russian, "you can be assured a woman is behind it."

Before I reflect that to Danny, for the briefest second, *Durochka Dinochka* pins me with an all-too-knowing look. My gut flash freezes, but almost instantly, her expression dissolves into her usual, slightly vacuous one. "Don't you think?" she finishes.

The look's gone so fast I immediately doubt myself. But if I saw what I think I saw, she knows exactly who her boyfriend is. And she won't help me go after him at all.

Danny cuts in on my thoughts, moving closer to me—closer than a business associate would stand. He bows his head toward me to murmur, "What was that?"

I pull back to the present and turn to Danny—and he is way too close. His uncertainty and pensiveness fall away in an instant at that range, like he's forgotten all about our argument earlier.

"Um." I falter. I doubt Nadia's message was intended for him. "Nothing."

He eyes me a minute longer, silently asking if I'm *sure*. To really dismiss the subject, I let the sarcasm flash through a yeah-right lip-purse/eye-roll combo aimed at Nadia's back before I force myself to walk away.

Nadia sweeps past us. I hope she missed our exchange. She makes no mention of it on the kilometer to our next stop. In the meantime, I try to play Nadia right back, but she neatly shuts down my most oblique references to Borya. She won't even tell me where he's from, something he told Danny freely.

Next up on our magical history tour is Teatral'naya Square and its monument obelisk to "Soldier-liberators of Rostov-on-Don from German-Fascist invaders." (Nazis, for those of you playing at home.) The tower is 200 feet tall, with stylized wings swooping out at the top. According to Nadia, the gold statue up there isn't Mother Russia but Nike, Greek goddess of victory.

I translate for Danny. He keeps the appropriate distance, with the appropriate responses, the appropriate cordiality. Which is great, I tell myself. Wonderful.

Next, Nadia leads us through the pedestrian tunnels, decorated with mosaics, underneath the main thoroughfare. We emerge on the other side of the street, at the Park of the Revolution. It's more than a city park with a carousel, a small zoo, tons of birds (even swans, peacocks and flamingos), rides, and an ice rink. Nothing's quite as cool in November (except the weather), but apparently Nadia's real goal is to regale us with history.

I wait for any opportunity to ditch Nadia and talk to Danny or vice versa, but she controls the grand tour masterfully. When we've seen the aviary, we circle back to the large fountain near the entrance. After all our stops in here, I'm sure we're not being tailed—though we *are* being ferried around by an FSB officer's girlfriend—but I can't shake the feeling. Of course we're being watched.

We reach the fountain and Nadia launches into another history lesson. I'm keeping up with her stories when someone veers a step too close to me. With Danny on my left, I don't have time to move. I brace myself for the bump.

Instead, the stranger maneuvers past me, barely brushing my coat, touching my hand. But not just touching it—something drops into my fingers with the quietest of clinks.

I close my fist around a key chain, keep my features still and do *not* search for whoever executed that brush pass. Nadia hasn't missed a beat, so I don't either, slipping the key in my pocket when she isn't looking.

In a lull in Nadia's narration, Danny's hand lands on the small of my back, cracking my concentration. He leans in to whisper again. "Why are we still excited about the communists winning this war?"

I signal for him to hush. That is not a topic of discussion, especially not for Americans. "I can't explain why, but Lenin is still revered as a hero."

He keeps his voice down. "We're allowed to talk about Lenin but not communism?'

"Pretty much." I move even closer. "Stalin is He Who Shall Not Be Named."

"Russia's history is Harry Potter?" Danny smiles at his joke.

I always call Danny's smiles Talia-melting, and this one is that and more. I manage to smile back, but mine holds a sadder note.

No. I am Lori. I will compartmentalize this. I will not flirt with my husband—and what we're doing now could look like any interpreter joking around with a client. Right?

Nadia brushes past us again, and I move away from Danny. My waist turns cold where his warm hand was, as if I could feel his touch through my coat.

When I catch up to her, Nadia casts me a sideways glance. "If you're not careful," she intones in Russian, "someone will get hurt. Badly."

I don't answer, just keep my head down and match Nadia's

speed to the car.

She may be *Durochka Dinochka*, but she's also dating her boss. How hard would it be for her to assume I'm dating mine? And how dangerous?

CHAPTER 17

NADIA RETURNS US TO BORYA'S OFFICE—where he *isn't*. We're a little later than planned, so he should be finished with Tsurenko. Where could Borya be? Danny cranes his neck to check the two halls that converge on the corner office. "Is he still in his meeting?"

"I'll find him." Nadia marches off for the elevators again.

I hate to risk another entry into his office, but if we don't look for those plans, our mission will definitely fail. This is an opportunity gift wrapped in a whole lot of office paper. I scan the hallways twice more before I slip the travel lock pick set from my waistband.

I'm not great with picking locks, but this one offers all of five seconds' resistance. It's open before Danny appears at my shoulder to ask, "What are you doing?"

I give him an eye. "My job."

"Don't make this about him."

I stand there, gripping the knob for a very long second. What is he asking me to do—or not do? "Why? Because he's nice?"

"I get that's why you don't like him, but in the real world, being nice is actually a positive thing."

My heart sinks like a star-crossed Soviet submarine. He still doesn't believe me. My own—

I can't afford emotion. I don't have time. They'll be back any minute. "Fine," I tell Danny. "You be lookout." I turn the handle and step into Borya's dim office.

With Danny on my heels. "He isn't the only person working here. The odds against this are astronomical."

"Stay there." I point back at the door.

"Does it say 'Fido' on my forehead?"

I trip midstep—but stay on topical target. "Are you trying to stop me?"

He silently invites me to go right ahead with a gesture at the cardboard tubes in front of the desk.

Already looked there. I snap the next USB drive into my copier and start where I left off in the piles along the wall.

"What are you hoping—?"

I whip around to unleash a glare at him, indicating my ears, and then the walls.

"If what you think is true," Danny says, very carefully guarding his words, "why would he do that to himself?"

I choke back a frustrated snort and focus on the stack of still more requisitions.

"Could you be logical for one minute?"

"Sorry I'm not Dr. Spock." I move on to the next pile, the seconds until Borya gets back beating through my brain louder than my pulse.

"Mr. Spock. Dr. Spock is the baby expert."

I glower at Danny's correction and move on to the desk— and the real issue. "Whose side are you on?" I turn back to the desk and start on the top papers. Personnel lists.

Danny rounds the desk to stand opposite me, pushing the chair out of the way. He leans down to my line of sight. "How about *sanity's*?"

"You want to do the sane thing?" I point back at the door to tell him to stand lookout. When he doesn't move, I plant my hands on those personnel lists, and three different stacks slide in three different directions. Danny and I both shift into damage control mode, him ducking to catch two piles, while I pin down the one avalanching toward me. One of Danny's piles hits the mouse, waking up the computer. I crane my neck to see the desktop appear. Still logged in? He can't have gotten far, and now we've wrecked his office.

I shove the papers into place. Then I hear familiar laughter echo in the hall. Borya?

I yank the USB drive free of the copier and dash to the door, but I can only see down one hallway. I barely dare to venture far enough to see around the corner—Borya's five feet away. He spots me immediately, and my ribs turn into steel girders.

"Borislav Vyacheslavovich," I exclaim a touch too loudly. Danny had better hear that.

"Here you are." Once again, mirth is practically doing a mambo in Borya's eyes. "We were ready to search."

"Sorry." I have to save Danny. I block Borya's path to the door. "It was all my fault; I—" I cut myself off when confusion flickers across his face.

He was kidding, probably about us getting back late from sightseeing. Good one, Talia.

He waits for me to move aside, pulling his keys from his pocket. Danny's pinned down without an escape. I can't extract him. I need a cover. A distraction. "Where's Nadia?" I ask.

"'Helping' someone with paperwork, as long as she doesn't make that worse. Let me get something and we'll start the final negotiations." He grins, all patience and kindness. No guile at all. He's so genuine, he almost reminds me of Danny.

That thought blocks out any other ideas for distraction tactics.

Borya is not Danny. He's not. He's a very well trained FSB officer trying very hard to play on my American sympathies, and he'd be doing a very good job if I weren't careful to keep my guard up. I bring my brain into a mental boxer's stance and focus on Borya again.

He's eyeing the already-cracked door. "I'm certain I locked this."

"We found it unlocked." I try to sound concerned. "Might want to ask around."

My lie does nothing to slow him. He pushes through and flips on the light. "Danny?"

"Borya, hi, afternoon." Danny straightens the pile on the desk one last time. "We were just looking for you."

That friendly smile's gone, replaced with a hurt frown. "At my empty desk? Without the light?"

"My fault," I jump in. "My phone charger wasn't working last night, and Danny was helping me find yours."

Borya scrutinizes me, waiting for my cover to crack. Not happening.

He has no reason to suspect me. He sent me here alone earlier. He should still trust me. No matter how many seconds pass, I can hold this cover of damsel in telephonic distress.

After a long minute, he nods and goes to his desk. Danny steps back to give him room. Borya fishes the charger from a top drawer and offers it to me. But as he slides the drawer closed, the tremor reactivates all the fault lines between the piles, and another landslide sets in, this time knocking the USB drives down.

Borya swears under his breath. I'm there in a heartbeat to help him clean up. Too easy. Pick up one, switch hands to place it on the desk. Pick up another, and another, put them on the desk. Pick up two more, deposit them on the desk. He doesn't seem to notice the one hidden in my left hand as I grab another drive and stick it on the desk with my right.

Danny arrives in time to scoop up the last few and finagle them into the only carefully engineered (ha) configuration that keeps them all on the corner of the desk.

"Apparently that takes a rocket scientist," I mutter.

Borya and Danny both reward me with wry almost-smiles. "Two," Danny says. He turns to Borya. "Sorry for the intrusion."

"A misunderstanding." He waves away our concerns. He misses a big one of mine: is there any way he *doesn't* know this scenario is exactly how Fyodor stole Danny's plans in the first place?

Borya surveys the desk and picks up a tablet. He glances at the office chairs, still filled with paper. "Conference room again?"

"Sure." Danny lets Borya pass to lead the way, and I fall in behind them. But two steps in, Danny pivots back. Without a word, he presses a USB drive into my palm—and his eyes say it all. *I'm doing this for you.*

I give him the smallest smile and try to communicate wordlessly, too: *Thank you. I understand. I love you.*

He squeezes my hand, and I close my fingers around the USB drive. Half a dozen out of, what, twenty drives taken or copied? Not great odds, but better than nothing.

But Danny holds my gaze a minute longer, and now I can't read the message in his eyes. Or I don't want to, because that certainly looks like he's letting go of more than a USB drive, or his side in the argument three minutes ago.

What does Danny think he's losing here? I'm not sure I want to know.

Borya presents a reasonably good but obviously Shcherbakov-slanted collaboration agreement, and Danny negotiates exactly what they're willing and able to share. They both promise final offers in the morning, and we're done at Shcherbakov for today.

I don't know if I've ever felt so good to be finishing a mission. I will *not* be sad the last time I see Shcherbakov in the rearview.

But that's tomorrow. Today, we're back to the hotel. We get out of the cab, and Danny starts in. I don't. He turns back to me like he's waiting for the next body blow.

It doesn't hit him. It hits me: I don't know if I can trust him alone. "I have something else to do," I tell him. "We both do."

"Okay." No hesitation or argument. Only an attitude of *I can do that*.

I really, really hope so. I start for the main road and get out the key chain I received in the brush pass. The short brass key is stamped with 468. The blue silicone bracelet and plastic card on the keychain both read АРБАТ-ФИТНЕС. *Arbat-Fitnes*. A gym. I flip it over to find the address, number 74 *1-ya liniya*, and the number 3175.

"We're picking something up," I tell Danny. And for once I don't have to walk everywhere. "Let's catch a tram."

A surveillance detection run, a ride on the vintage 1989 electric tram, and another SDR later, we're safe to pick up this package. We head down the right street, down the hill, down into an industrial park. I'd worry we were going the wrong way if it weren't for a huge billboard at the end of the street for *Arbat-Fitnes*. We walk through the gates and pass an office building before we find the big white gym.

I spot a cement bench by the office building doors and gesture to the newspaper abandoned there.

"Is that our package?" Danny asks

"That's where you'll wait."

He shoots me a *seriously?* look. Huh? He's gone with traipsing through a park, riding a tram in silence, picking up new hats, and our stops at a drug store, a convenience store, a pharmacy, a corner kiosk, even a karaoke bar. All I'm asking him to do is sit, and now he balks?

He shakes his head and marches to the bench. Could be worse; at least I'm not towing him after me like toddler. I march into the gym. To my left, a gray tiled wall bears the gym's name in carved block Cyrillic above black leather couches. To my right stands the registration red granite counter with cubbyholes behind it. I get close enough to peek inside. Numbered. Half of them hold the same blue rubber bracelets as the one in my hand.

And the rest of the bracelets are red.

The pieces snap into place a second before the admin turns to me. The bracelets must be color coded to the men's and women's locker rooms. I read the admin's nametag. She's Yekaterina, but I'm more interested in the tag itself: logo, job title, name; black ink, white paper, plastic holder on a lanyard. Easy to fake.

Yekaterina's waiting for me, pleasant and patient. Now I just need a plausible reason to come here and leave. "How late are you open today?" I ask.

"*Do dvadtsat' dva.*" *Until twenty-two.* (Ten PM.)

Not that it matters to me. I beat a retreat out. When I reach Danny, he lowers his newspaper. "Done?"

"Does the hotel have a business center? I need a computer. And a printer." Though if I'm careful I could make it by hand.

"Dunno, what for?"

I glance around; we're alone. Still, I step closer and hold up the blue bracelet. "A nametag. I need to get into the men's locker room."

Again with the *seriously?* look. Danny watches me another minute, waiting for me to get . . . something. But I don't. So he grabs the bracelet from my grasp, taking the card and the key, and strides off for the gym.

"Wait a minute." I hurry to keep up. "You can't—"

"You need in the men's locker room." His fixed stare silently tells me to fill in the blank.

And he's a man. Duh, I knew that, but I . . . have no excuse. So I rack my brain for a way to stop him. We reach the doors, and I've got nothing. He walks straight to the desk and gives Yekaterina the card. Will they scan it? Is there a photo to match?

She looks at the card. I don't dare breathe. She looks up at me, then to Danny, then hands the card back. Crap. We failed.

Then Yekaterina welcomes him to the gym. "*Spasibo*," Danny says, and he starts for the marble stairs to the locker room.

I replay the sequence in my mind from Yekaterina's perspective. She must think I was asking how late the gym was open for Danny's sake.

Good enough. I jog to keep pace with him. "You sure about this?" I murmur.

"Think I can handle opening a locker."

"Without drawing suspicion." I point at the signs marked with a man's silhouette, signaling him to follow. We reach the end of the tiled wall, revealing a juice bar. "I'll wait here."

He disappears up the stairs.

I spend the next eternity reading the menu until I can recite it from memory. But I can't eat with nerves gnawing at my gut. On the clock above the counter, minutes crawl past. Not biting my lip or my cheek or my fist takes all my willpower.

How long can opening a locker take? Two minutes? We're close to twenty.

Something's gone wrong. Someone could've been watching the locker. They could be spiriting him away to the local version of the infamous Lubyanka Square now, and I'd have no clue.

The clock shows it's been thirty minutes, and I've exhausted every trick Langley ever taught me to look calm while I'm freaking out under the surface. I'm done waiting. No time to make my own nametag—maybe I can "borrow" a worker's tag. I'm on my feet, my pulse screaming for me to run to him, when Danny comes into sight on the stairs. His coat and his suit jacket drape over one arm. He's doing his top button, his tie hanging loose on his neck. His hair's wet. Relief releases the tension in my back. He's fine.

I reach him and make sure no one's in eavesdropping range. "What took so long?"

"Wouldn't it be suspicious if I came right back?" He starts on his tie.

That should've occurred to me, but no, I was too obsessed with the massive error of letting him out of my sight. "Good thinking."

We drop off the locker key, Danny dons his coats, and I wait until we're outside before I ask, "You get it?"

"Yep. Tablet." He taps his coat pocket.

With everything we copied off Borya's computer last night? Has to be. Now we don't have to deliver the USB drives I cloned today to Semyon. Perfect.

"Did you really take a shower while I was out there worrying about you?" I ask.

Danny laughs softly. "No, I just wet my hair."

"Sneaky." And that's a compliment. I'm so thrilled to get us through this okay, I could dance all the way back. I spring for ice cream cones (available year-round in Russia; don't ask me why you have to button up but can eat frozen foods), and then kvass at a corner kiosk (yum, yeast soda; bread-based drinks are my *fave*) before we stroll off the main thoroughfare.

Four SDRs, a successful dead drop pickup and Russian treats? When things are clicking, I'm unstoppable. As soon as the elevator doors close, I catch Danny in a celebratory hug.

"We did it," I whisper.

"I love you too." He pulls back enough to look at me, and I can't help the sharp little gasp at the instant connection of our gazes. A wave of pure adrenaline hits me that has nothing to do with fulfilling our assignment as spies.

You know what? We're alone, and we're fantastic. So I kiss my husband like we just survived a lot more than an innocuous pickup. Only when the elevator slows do I step back (reluctantly). We stroll to our rooms, Danny's smile reflecting exactly how satisfied I feel.

"I assume we're going through these files," Danny says at his door. "Room service?"

"That sounds—" Oh, crap. I'm meeting Valya and his girls tonight. I stop short, a disappointed sigh escaping. "Sorry. I can order you something, but I have another errand to run. Can't take you this time."

The smile and the satisfaction drop from his face. "'Take' me."

"Yeah. Sorry." My voice is as sincere as I am, but he just studies me carefully. Then he heads into his room without a goodbye.

Wait, how did that plan backfire? Defeat settles on my shoulders. I let myself into my room and empty my pockets onto the dresser. New hat, brochure from *Arbat-Fitnes*, receipts, change. Pocket litter, living my cover down to the details. I'll need to get rid of the evidence of *Arbat-Fitnes* so no one's suspicious. I tear the brochure to bits and flush it.

A memory nags at me—something left undone (and not just with Danny). Something I should've destroyed. What was it? I took it from someone.

From Garo. His business card. My stomach shrinks. Bad, bad, bad—how did I slip?

I attack my dresser first, sorting through the papers and

trash from every walking expedition. Nothing. I shuffle through the leaflets and receipts again, then stack them one by one. No business cards.

Garbage. Empty.

I scrutinize every horizontal surface in the room, rip off the bedsheets, shine my flashlight under the bed.

I rock back on my heels and run my hands through my hair, tugging at my wig's hairpins. Did someone take Garo's card? Did I throw it away? That's not secure.

One last hope springs up: maybe I gave it to Danny. Or maybe he took it. I practically run to pound on his door. "Danny?" Panic rises even in my voice.

He answers quickly. "You okay?"

"Dunno." I push past and beeline for his trash. Also empty. I scan his dresser, moving papers till I find a stack of business cards. Shcherbakov, Shcherbakov, Shcherbakov. My hands can't keep up, and several cards flutter to the ground.

"What are you doing?" Danny asks slowly.

"I'm missing something—something important."

"A business card?"

I whirl on him. "How'd you know? Have you seen it?"

"Not that I know of." He closes his door, gesturing at the flurry of business cards left in my wake. "Whose card?"

Like I can say that aloud. I point to the walls to remind him of the bugs. "My friend we ran into yesterday."

"Okay, we'll find it. Checked your pockets?"

"Yes." I start on his dresser drawers, which are empty. Could I have stuck it in my suitcase? Doubtful.

Danny pulls out his wallet and adds to the messy stack I just left. "I'm sure we can get his number."

"But I need the card—the card itself." My stress levels spike with my blood pressure. If someone found that in my room, Garo could be in trouble. In danger. I may not love the guy, but I'm not trying to get him arrested. Or worse.

"Hey." Danny's touches my shoulder. "Calm down."

You know the worst way to calm someone down? Telling them to calm down. I jerk away. "You don't understand, I *need* this *card*. Now."

Danny studies me in silence a minute. "Don't they have phonebooks in Russia?"

"That's not the point—if I don't have that card, then I don't know who does." I enunciate each word, trying to make my real meaning clear: anyone could've come in our rooms and gotten it, and Garo would be a target.

Danny backs up a step. "Yeah," he admits, his tone begrudging, "but you could've dropped it anytime you took your coat on or off. It could be in the garbage somewhere."

"No" is all I can say out loud. I can't bank on luck. In the field, you'd never keep contact evidence for anyone to find. With actual agents, officers memorize their numbers. They don't keep business cards. They don't use address books. They definitely don't put them in their phones. To leave a number lying around where someone could find it could be a death sentence.

Danny stares at me a minute longer but turns away. I attack his nightstand. The single drawer's empty. Is someone targeting me? Did they search our rooms for this? I press my fingers to my eyes. What have I done?

A hand lands on my shoulder and I whirl around before I can tell myself it's Danny. He stares at me like we're strangers, then finally holds out his other hand—a card. I snatch it: Garo Mirzoyan.

"It was in my coat pocket."

Now that my lungs are free, I suck in oxygen. "Oh. Right." Because I was wearing Danny's coat when we ran into Garo.

"You could use a night off," Danny says. But he sounds uncertain. Like he's not sure what I'll say? He's still staring like he's never seen me before.

"I need to go." I slide Garo's card into the secret pocket inside the lining of my sleeve.

"Can't it wait?"

My shoulders fall. "My friend's daughter is in the hospital. If I want to visit, it has to be tonight."

"Oh." He nods, subdued, but that's enough to launch my latest guilt trip. Everything was perfect five minutes ago. Why can't I do anything right? Why can't I make things better?

But you know what? This assignment will be over tomorrow, and we can figure it out then. We have to. "It's not far. I'll be back as soon as I can." I head to the door. "Stay safe."

"You too."

Awesome.

I shuffle to my room. The extra coat from Semyon waits on my desk. I stuff it in a bag. One benefit of hardly sleeping last night: the rest of my disguise is already cached and waiting—something a lot more conservative, a lot more like what I wore when I was a missionary. I can't leave a bugged hotel as Talia, and I can't walk up to Valya as Lori, but I can change en route to the hospital.

I shake off the stress of losing the card and the situation with Danny. I've got enough stress tonight: recruiting Valya. Once I'm safe on the street, I can text Semyon about recruiting him. I take the stairs down and march through the lobby. A short man with dark hair sits on the gold couches, chatting on his cell phone. He finishes his call and stands as I pass. He stays with me, jogging down the stairs to the entrance to open the front doors.

It's normal Russian manners for a man to get the door for me—but to jog to do it? Could be chivalry. Could be a coincidence. Could be surveillance.

I wait to see if he asks for a date, but he barely acknowledges me.

My gut creeps downward. This guy pings my paranoid

radar. I brush past and march out, like I haven't already spent all day on these heels. (So glad I cached a pair of sensible shoes.)

Maybe my subconscious takes me to the *rynok*, as good a place as any. I buy the first sunglasses I find, but I'm not really shopping—I just need a good crowd. I maneuver behind every pair and trio of people I find.

Halfway through the market, I pause to admire a table of real lacquer boxes, but really I'm turning to see if my eager friend's still back there.

Short, slight and swarthy? Yep. Eager Igor's still on my tail.

I thread my way through the milling masses, putting as many people between me and him as possible. Odds aren't in my favor when I'm the only person in a bright red coat. I can't risk retrieving my disguise too soon, so I'll try to lose him the easy way. At the other gates of the *rynok*, I stop to discuss honey with a vendor. He insists his linden honey's worth every kopeck, while I subtly scan the crowd around me under the cover of my sunglasses. I'm not buying anything, so I let the vendor win the argument and walk away.

Because Eager Igor's still behind me.

I may be running on fumes after two sleepless nights, but the energy in my system spikes. Gotta do better.

I move to the market gates and remember *Vkusno Lyubov'* (*Delicious Love*), the café with fantastic blini across the street and down the block. My chance to lose him. Plus, I skipped lunch, and I haven't had authentic blini since we got here. I jog across the street in a gap in traffic. From inside the shop, a rundown little refuge, I scan the windows for Eager Igor's approach.

Not there.

Whew. Still, I opt to keep my coat close instead of hanging it on the rack before I get in line. On my turn, I order a blin—no, two blini with blackberry, smetana and honey filling. I pick a table in the corner closest to the door and lay my coat over a chair. My blini are in front of me in less than two minutes, and I take my paper plate and bottle of water.

The sour, tart and sweet of the berries, honey and smetana (kinda like sour cream) blends perfectly against the earthy wrapping (kinda like a crêpe), and I sigh after the first bite. It's even better knowing I lost my tail.

After my third bite, the door swings open. It's not the sub-arctic blast that makes me stop eating. It's the man standing in the door. Eager Igor.

My heart dips.

Now *that's* training. At that realization—that threat—my stomach also takes a dive. He's FSB, and he's after me. I set down my blin. Amazing what surveillance does to your appetite.

He doesn't look at me, but he doesn't move to the counter, either. He hesitates in the doorway, blocking my escape.

Joy.

Finally, the shopkeeper shouts at him for letting in a draft, and he walks in. Not to the line. To a table.

He'll get fussed at again for taking up a seat without buying anything, but he settles in. Waiting me out.

I need to eat—but I'm not staying here. I need to move, I need to go, I need to run. I need to step up my game.

I take one more bite, then tug on my coat and grab my water bottle and bag. I push through the door, taking a long draught of water.

The first trash can I pass, I toss the water without slowing. I check my peripheral vision. He's back there.

I shouldn't dart out in front of a car to avoid surveillance, but there's no traffic at this end of the block. I cut across the street diagonally, and he crosses at the same time. The light next to him turns green, and he has to watch cars. While he's distracted, I pivot on my heel and hurry back to the corner past the café. The yellow Dumpsters are still here, still full (lost a great disguise in Ottawa that way once). Nobody behind me. I extract the parcel wrapped in black plastic from behind the Dumpster.

Leggings from my cache slide under my business skirt, making it easier to change into the knit maxi skirt. The balancing act of not letting anything or any body part actually touch the filthy ground or Dumpster makes me wish I'd taken up yoga. Once I've changed my coat and shoes, I pull off my hairpins, wig and cap, pull out my braids, then pull on a hat that nearly matches my dark braids. My other clothes and bag fit in my cached backpack and two makeup removing wipes later, I'm ready.

Ready? In these flats, I could walk a surveillance evasion marathon.

Once a turning delivery truck provides cover, I hit the street and pass the café again. The shopkeeper's busy with a customer. Eager Igor? My heart seizes—but it's not him. Unless he's got a disguise that makes him forty years older and even shorter.

And my blini's still on the table. I'm still not hungry, but I need the food. I slip in and pick up the blini. With Eager Igor out there, I'll let myself out the back. I venture down the dark hallway. The bathroom door swings open, and out walks my pursuer. Despite my pulse's spike, I keep moving like I know where I'm going, like I don't care he's there, like I can breathe and think and walk normally.

Like I'm not hunting an FSB officer in Shcherbakov, undercover as my own husband's interpreter.

The guy doesn't look twice. He's searching for a woman in a bright red coat, not a long dark one. I reach the end of the hallway and the back door—locked.

Great.

I could go back to the shop, risk running into my follower

again, or I could try to get through. The door's protected with a grate, but a rusted silver padlock holds it shut. Padlocks are ridiculously easy to open. If you're good at picking locks. If you can find a good-sized rock. If you've got a shim.

With my usual luck at lock picking (this afternoon was a huge exception), and without a rock (plus the noise will attract attention instead of avoid it), I've got one option. Luckily, I'm prepared as ever.

I take off my backpack and hunt for my other clothes. Once again, I've sewn the right tool into my clothes. My tweed business skirt lining yields a thin sheet of metal I fashioned in Paris from a soda can. It's all cut and ready, except that I need to bend it to make it work better. I curve it around the shackle. (MacGyver's not the only one who uses improvised tools.)

The shaped metal slides into the narrow gap between the shackle and the lock body, and the lock springs open.

See you later, Eager Igor. I slip out the door and into the alley that leads back to the *rynok*. That honey vendor engages me, at the same price. "Two hundred rubles!" he squawks.

I pause. I know better than to pay that much for that tiny bottle. "One twenty-five," I say.

Speaking Russian—speaking it well—always cuts your prices. The vendor agrees and recognition never flickers in his eyes.

I stop by a florist's booth and pick up something for Melanyushka. Flowers are standard gifts here, but always odd numbers unless you're at a funeral, and no yellow ones, and be careful what kind. Russian flower symbolism is more complex than Victorian England's. The florist helps me pick out a bouquet of five pale pink flowers. I leave the *rynok* and catch the first *marshrutka*, which is like a big passenger van crammed with as many seats as possible.

I could swear I was a missionary again. I almost look around for my companion. Last time I lived here, I never went anywhere alone.

But the women I was assigned to live with 24/7 as a missionary, Sestra Carter and Sestra Bulovskaya, aren't in Rostov. And they're not my companions anymore. Danny's supposed to be.

Not sure what he thinks of me right now. I only know that I feel very alone.

CHAPTER 18

EVERY TIME I COME TO A RUSSIAN HOSPITAL, I swear it'll be the last. I don't know what it is about the lights in hospitals here, but no matter how bright they are, it feels dim. Or maybe the lights just reveal how dingy things are, dirt no amount of scrubbing will clean. And then the smell. After five minutes, all I want to do is escape that odor of disinfectant and desperation.

Even using all my spy skills, it takes a while to track down Melanyushka's building. Bureaucracy might be the best defense against espionage. By the time I've found the right room, I've figured out that Melanyushka's doctor is Yulia Yakovlevna, her diagnosis is throat cancer and her time is severely limited. (Health care privacy? Where do you think we are?)

From the door, I can see four beds in the room, but only one's still occupied. Facing the bed, Valya sits in a cheap chair, animatedly telling a Russian fairytale. "'I'll never leave my beloved village,' Maryushka told Kashchei."

Hardly seems coincidental that the diminutive form the character in the story uses alludes to Melanyushka's nickname.

"And the evil sorcerer was so upset, he cast a spell. Maryushka transformed into a bird. Not any bird—the *zhar-*

ptitsa."

I step in to see Melanyushka, smiling feebly at the mention of the mythic firebird. Plugged into IVs and tubes, she seems both older and younger than I remember. Her eyes are still wide and blue, but all their innocence has faded. Underneath them, dark circles bloom like bruises, pitiful and pleading. She's reclining on pillows, like holding her head up is getting too hard. An embroidery hoop sits in her lap, forgotten as her father relays the dramatic story.

"Maryushka grew long, beautiful tail feathers that glowed orange and amber and gold, like the embers of a bonfire. Before she could fly away, Kashchei transformed himself into a falcon and swooped down on her." Valya uses his hands to mimic the falcon's dive.

He calls himself an old soldier, but anyone can see he has a storyteller's heart.

But he *is* a soldier, too. And that's a big reason I'm here, to recruit him. Unless he decides to report me. A double-edged sword: the exact thing that makes him perfect for an agent makes him dangerous.

"And he captured Maryushka the firebird to carry her away from her village," he continues. "But Maryushka was true to her word. She could never leave her beloved village, so she shed her beautiful feathers, one at a time, as they soared over the land, leaving a piece of herself with her home. When the last feather fell from her tail, Maryushka died in the falcon's claws, escaping Kashchei forever. But the firebird's feathers burn on, appearing to lovers of beauty, and those who have lost hope."

Kinda grim (Grimm?), but most Russian fairytales are in the old-school macabre mode. Far from the worst thing a kid dying from cancer can hear.

"Tell 'Vassilisa and the Firebird,'" prompts another voice. I take another pace into the room to see Svetusya in a wooden chair by the bed's head. She's about twelve, just growing into that awful gawky phase, but she looks weary and older than her age, too. She picks up her sister's embroidery hoop and starts to work.

Valya begins the requested story. "Once, in a fairy tale—" He suddenly spots me and stops short to beam at me. "You came."

I return the grin. "Naturally. Hi, Svetusya—Sveta, Melanyushka."

Melanyushka regards me warily. I offer the flowers. "You don't remember me, do you?"

She accepts the bouquet, squinting at me. Valya jumps to help. "Sestra Reynolds was one of the missionaries who taught your mother."

Sveta leaps from her chair and runs to throw her arms around my waist. "I thought so, but I didn't think that was possible!"

"It isn't," I say. "But things that just don't happen—"

"Happen in Russia," Valya joins me to finish the saying from Tolstoy or Peter the Great. (A favorite among missionaries adjusting to a "land that can't be understood, only believed in.")

Melanyushka, who might be too young to remember me, gestures for me to sit on her bed. Sveta and I do. "Can I see your embroidery?" I ask.

She flips it to me, an amazing picture of a red and gold bird with flowing tail feathers. The firebird. Though it sounds like a phoenix, and there are stories where the firebird doesn't die, I don't *think* the firebird is associated with rebirth. I mean, he just finished a story about the creature dying. Is he preparing his daughter for the inevitable?

I certainly can't. "Do you remember Sestra Carter?" I ask, searching for a distraction of my own. "She has twin boys now."

Sveta giggles—Sestra Carter wasn't shy about her fear of children. But things change.

I look to Melanyushka and Valya. Things certainly do change. And I didn't come here merely to see the girls. I came here to do what I can to change things for the better.

My phone vibrates and I check it quickly, in case Semyon has something important for me. But it's not Semyon. It's Danny. *Need your help. Labels in Russian.*

I apologize to Valya and the girls before I respond. *At the hospital now*, I tell Danny.

How far?

2 km? Which doesn't tell him how long it'll take me to get back, what he probably really wants to know. I'll be back soon enough. I turn back to Melanyushka. "How are you feeling?"

"Tired," she rasps. She takes a breath to say something else, but instead she coughs, hard.

Sveta and Valya watch her carefully, patting her back. I hold her free hand, and she squeezes.

"You are very brave," I tell her once the coughing has subsided.

"As brave as she must be, she always says," Sveta repeats. She sets the embroidery aside, and curls up next to her sister on the bed. "Too brave for a little girl."

I remember the incident the day of Ksena's baptism— Melanyushka climbed on their apartment building's roof that morning, because the girl never understood fear. Valya and I take turns telling and embellishing the story, till the building's twenty stories tall, and Melanyushka isn't just prohibited from playing up there, she was expressly forbidden by every adult on the planet, and she isn't just sitting on the roof, she's swinging from the flagpole. Melanyushka can't say much, but her silent laughter is more than enough.

We all spin tales of friends-of-a-friend-of-a-friend who defied their parents or less immutable laws, like gravity. All of us except Melanyushka, though I'm not sure whether she's too weak to talk or it hurts. (It's *throat* cancer, after all.)

We've barely begun our second round of storytelling when Melanyushka's eyelids droop. She fights to stay awake through her dad's story, but we all know she's done for the night. The nurse bustles in and unhooks her IVs, dismissing us without a word.

"Come, she needs rest." Valya kisses her on the forehead, then beckons Sveta to bring the cheap wheelchair from the opposite corner. "The treatments leave her weaker than the cancer."

Valya lifts his daughter into the chair and herds us into the hallway. "Sestra Reynolds, you must come to our house. I'm sure Sveta can find some dessert."

Melanyushka isn't the only one who had to grow up fast. Valya's military assignment here left them far from family, and with her mother gone, Sveta must be running the house at twelve.

"I can't impose." I kick myself mentally. This is a terrible, terrible insult. "I have to get back to work. My friend needs my help tonight."

"Your friend," Valya repeats. Nothing about his expression or his voice betrays his skepticism, and yet, it's still there. You'd have to be an amazing friend to fly halfway around the world, huh?

"Come," Valya says, "let us walk out together."

I follow them to the elevator. Melanyushka rests with her head in her hands, while Sveta reports on the other families I knew when I lived here, the few teenagers at church. The account is stereotypical Russia: the good and the bad, triumphs and struggles, victors and victims. Life here is hard, but they love life and they love their home.

With each story of Sveta's and each story of the building, we get closer to our farewells. My opportunity is slipping through my fingers. I still don't know how to approach Valya, though I've pinned down his motivations and values. (Hint: she's sitting in the wheelchair.)

The congregation's small enough that Sveta finishes the catch-up before we hit the ground floor. My stomach keeps heading down.

My last chance to pitch him. To get help for Melanyushka.

I let Sveta get ahead of us in the elevator alcove. One quick glance at my bug scanner: green. Clear. I grab Valya's elbow and my chance. "Can I talk to you for a minute?" I cast a meaningful look in Sveta's direction, then down at Melanyushka's back. "Alone?"

He cocks an eyebrow but calls his older daughter. "Sveta, take Melanyushka to the car."

Sveta hurries back. Valya gives her the wheelchair and the car keys. I lean down to give Melanyushka the customary kiss on the cheek. "Be strong." She doesn't open her eyes to see the silent postscript in mine: *I'm doing all I can. Hold on.*

Hope it's enough.

I bid Sveta goodbye, too, and she starts for the car. Good. Hopefully privacy helps me build this proposition carefully, instead of heeding the adrenaline beating in my pulse. Someone else could eventually do this, yes, but it would take months to get acquainted with him and build up trust—months Melanyushka doesn't have.

All I've got right now is that he already trusts me and I know his values and motivations: his daughter.

"You want to do more for Melanyushka," I begin.

"Certainly."

"And she'd get better treatment in Moscow, or abroad?"

Valya sighs, resigned. "We could never afford it. There is no money."

I make sure my breaths stay at a deliberate pace, but it still feels like I'm rushing.

Of course I am. Who wouldn't rush to save a dying little girl? "What if I got you money?"

"Sestra Reynolds, we couldn't ask that."

I give him a sad smile. "Wish I had that kind of money to give you."

"Then what are we talking about?"

Up to now, I've been standing on the shore, tracing a path across a frozen river, picking out the transparent trail of ice where it's safe to tread. I've mapped the territory as best I can from a distance. Only way to find out if it's passable is to move forward.

With anyone else, I'd still be working on a relationship of trust. I'd still be gauging his reactions. I don't know what Valya's will be, but I do know that his daughter's life is worth this tiny risk to my own. Cold pitching an active-duty, no-reason-to-be-disloyal soldier? Not my best idea. But our only choice. "I have friends who could help. A lot."

"Members of your congregation?"

Hadn't crossed my mind, and maybe—but that's not guaranteed. Mine is. "No." I meet his gaze. "I'm not an interpreter."

I order my lungs to work against my ribs' iron grip. I'm vulnerable, but more than that, I *need* Valya to say yes. Melanyushka needs him to. I focus all my attention on drinking in the fire hose of his nonverbal feedback.

Silence slips between us. Valya stands there, disbelieving, but I don't have to explain. This is Russia. I'm an American. What more do I have to say? The city's newspaper ran front page articles profiling missionaries, speculating about whether we worked for an American church or the American government. (Only one sends teenagers to do its work.)

The set to Valya's jaw hardens to steel. "Were you always—?"

"No," I say quickly. "I was a missionary. You know that."

He pivots on his heel, takes three steps out of the alcove, and then turns back. "You're saying . . ."

186

I follow to keep my volume down. "You work at the district headquarters, don't you? You have access—"

"*Nyet.* I cannot. I won't." He raises his gaze to the ceiling, like he's remembering Melanyushka's treatment upstairs. Or maybe he's thinking of Ksena. Or God.

I'm still in observational overdrive, soaking in every gesture, searching for something to help my case. "It's for Melanyushka. I'd never ask otherwise, but it's the only way—I just want to help."

Valya starts walking without acknowledging me. I keep pace with him. "Please, let us help. No one will get hurt, and she'll have the best care, we'll take care of everything, no danger—"

"Only to my career. Only to my integrity. Only to my soul."

"I'm not asking—"

"Aren't you?" Valya stops at the doors and glares at me. "The answer is no," he says in English, as if he wasn't getting through to me in Russian. He pushes through the glass doors to the street. "Find someone else to do your dishonest work."

"Wait." I follow him five feet, concentrating on him one more eternity, pleading, praying, imploring. If I thought begging would help, I'd be on my knees.

But every second I stare at him, the hatred runs deeper.

I was only trying to save Melanyushka. And I failed. I close my mouth, fall a step back, shut down my hyperfocus and let him go.

Valya's ten feet away when I hear the footfall behind me.

My breath crystallizes in my chest. Did I not escape Eager Igor? Is Valya in danger?

Am I?

My brain tries to switch to self-defense mode, but it just keeps flipping through the pages like that chapter's missing.

Valya's rejection might not be tonight's low point.

CHAPTER 19

FIGHT OFF THE URGE TO WHIRL AROUND AND LOOK. Not yet—I have to make sure Valya gets away at least. I stand there long enough to make sure he's out of sight, then, shaking a finger at myself like I forgot something important, I pivot.

And run right into the person behind me. The streetlight behind him casts a shadow across his face, but that's not the only thing menacing about him. He's just standing there, waiting for me to notice him.

Panic crawls up my throat—and then I recognize him. Danny, buttoned up, scarf and hat and all. I don't need to be afraid, but I'm still not sure this is good news. "What are you doing here?" I ask.

"Didn't want you to have to visit your friend alone." He glances after Valya. "Tell me that's not what I think."

"You heard one sentence." (One sentence that anyone who doesn't know who I am wouldn't understand.) "Don't take it out of context."

Yeah, once I say it, I detect the massive rationalization.

"Put it in context."

I scan the streets. It's after dark, so foot traffic isn't heavy, but we're far from alone. I consult my mental map of the city. Major landmarks wouldn't move in five years, but I don't think a hospital or a jail is a good place to talk.

A cemetery. There's a cemetery around here. Those are kinda hard to move, right? I start in the general direction. It's past the university—I check across the street. The university. I think I can find it now. "Let's walk," I say.

I lead him across the street and down the block to the cemetery entrance. Cemeteries in Russia are always interesting, though the Jewish Tatar cemetery is kind of specialized. Not too many Heroes of the Soviet Union or cultural icons with sculptured gravestones in here, but if I remember right there are a few interesting memorials that might attract tourists (us).

Not that we'll have a lot to see in the dark. We stick to the path. I maneuver closer to Danny. I'm not sure whether I'm trying to protect him or help him protect me. There's no one (alive) around, but privacy can be a paradox. Yes, you're safe from prying eyes, but sometimes you need the safety of other people if something worse, bigger, scarier comes along.

Hopefully they'll stay out of the graveyards, though, right?

I kick off the conversation. "How did you get here?"

"You'd be amazed what being nice to the concierge gets you."

The location of all hospitals within two kilometers? Apparently. "Nice job."

"You don't have to sound so surprised. I'm not totally helpless, thank you."

"Did I say you were?"

"It's not what you say."

"I—" I guess I have a bad habit of separating the people in my life into CIA/not CIA boxes. Being in the latter—mostly clueless civilians—is often not a compliment. "I'm just trying to do my job."

"With your friend?" Danny jerks a thumb the way we

189

came. Where Valya was.

I glance around and still can't see anyone. I slow to a stroll. "His daughter needs better treatment. Her cancer's aggressive."

"That's not 'dishonest work.'"

I sigh and watch the condensation cloud dissipate before I dare respond. "We'd pay him."

"You mean, if he works for you."

Every muscle in my body tenses, and I snap to search the shadows. We're still alone, but I need to check my scanner. The cemetery's got to be bugged, remnants of the KGB era. I'm not sure even the dead are allowed secrets.

Green lights. Whatever's out there isn't active. We're clear, but we may not be safe. "We aren't a charity," I murmur.

"Uh huh. And what about that 'honoring, obeying and sustaining the law' thing?"

Great. The guy's quoting scripture to me. And yes, Valya is under that obligation—but so am I. "What about me?"

"What about you?"

I stop short and search the dark cemetery trees once again, though there's no sign of life. "Illegal everywhere, remember?"

"There's a world of difference between you and him."

"Is there?" I fold my arms, but stay close, barely breathing out my next words. "Day one, lesson two: our objective is to recruit spies and steal secrets. Am I supposed to worry about their morals, too?"

In the streetlight filtering through the trees, I can't see much of his expression, but I don't like the steel there.

"This is part of my job," I say. "All of it. If you find it distasteful—"

"I find you doing your job with a friend from church distasteful, yeah."

The words sting like a slap, and I'm stunned into gaping silence for a moment. "Probably something you should've thought of two weeks ago," I manage. "Sorry I don't get to operate on the same moral compass you do."

"Convenient," Danny says, not quite as careful to keep his voice down. "Your 'moral compass' is 'different.'"

"It *is*. And if you want to talk convenience, which of us gets to live in a world of absolutes and easy answers?"

"Lecturing me on morality, after what I just saw?" His scorn is louder than his volume.

I turn to leave the cemetery, but he blocks my path. "After what I did for you today?"

"What do you mean?"

"The USB drives."

I roll my eyes. Filching a couple flash drives from an FSB officer is a different axis on the moral scale compared to inducing someone to pass along secrets. Especially to save his daughter. Does Danny want to explain that to Melanyushka?

But he doesn't have to, and neither does Valya now. "Guess it's a good thing he said no."

"Yeah, it is."

Where does that leave us? The things I do are completely illegal—and they don't cause me a moment of lost sleep. Can Danny live with that? With someone who's made peace with living like that?

That's a question too terrifying to ask. I wheel away and scan the dark grounds.

"What are you looking for?" Danny demands.

I turn back, keeping up my pace. "Zombies." The eye-roll (and the truth) is unnecessary.

"No one. Is. Following. Us. We're the only people here. We're *fine*."

"I was followed on my way out of the hotel. *Today*. I'm just trying to keep you safe."

"Keep . . . me . . ." He slowly pulls back, studying me with a frown that grows more serious by the second. "They're always on your tail, aren't they?"

I barely dare to meet his gaze, heat rising in my chest. "Excuse me?"

"You run like someone's chasing you everywhere. You stop at grocery stores and restaurants and post offices on your way to the bathroom—"

"You're exaggerating."

"Barely."

Once again, I'm reeling from the verbal blow. Danny's teased me about my professional paranoia before, but the anger in his voice—I had no idea he resented it so deeply. Something that's saved my life more than once. Today. "If you really think that's true, that it's in my head and I'm crazy, then say my name. Right now."

Even when I let my cover down, he's never called me Talia since we left Paris. Not once. Somewhere, on some level, he must *know* this is real, the threat.

But Danny scoffs, his march not missing a beat.

I can't believe this. "Is this a game to you? You get to play at my job, while I keep us safe, and you—"

"Keep us safe? Are you kidding?"

Now he doesn't believe me? "You keep saying you trust me." I hold my volume to a controlled whisper. "But you question every single move."

"No, I don't—"

"Every move that involves your new BFF, you do. You know who invented 'Trust, but verify,' right?"

"Reagan?" Danny snarks.

"Russia. *'Doveryai, no proveryai.'*"

Danny stops again, a few feet from the entrance. "When do we get to the 'verify' part? Do you have a single shred of *anything* that proves he's who you think he is?" He pauses to search my face. "Or is it just you?"

The words sink into my stomach like depth charges. He doesn't believe I need to be this cautious. Even here, where I absolutely cannot afford let my tradecraft slip. He thinks I'm overreacting. Jumping at shadows. The bad kind of paranoia.

"Please." His voice breaks on that syllable, and the shards of the word hover there like the cloud of condensation between us. "I've tried—I've tried to be okay with this, but I'm not."

I have to think through the blood rushing in my ears. No. This is a three-day mission. I'm not going to let it ruin our real lives. "Look, I know this is hard right now, but it's only for twenty-four more hours—"

"No, it isn't. The restaurants, the food, the claustrophobia, the constant stops—it's the rest of my life. I can't live like this."

He . . . can't . . . ? What is he saying?

But the frost shooting through my chest tells me the truth. I already know. My parents. My mother, three times. Two of my brothers. Half my coworkers or more. Divorced.

No, no, no. He has to understand. "Danny, I have to, especially now, especially here—"

"It's fine—it's *great* that you want to keep us safe here. I'm down with that. But watching you over the last day, I'm seeing what you do at home. I've tried—"

"*I've* tried. I started keeping food, I stopped worrying so much about restaurants, I—" I have nothing else to list. I haven't given much, but it was all I could.

"You skipped lunch today," he finishes for me. "Because they were alone with your food. Right?"

The truth is not my ally, and my sarcasm is spent, so I resort to silence.

"Isn't it exhausting? Aren't you tired of looking over your shoulder?"

"Exhausting? It's a mental marathon every time I walk out the door. But it keeps me alive." We're close enough to the street and its lights that I can see the argument building behind his eyes again. I cut him off with some of that aircraft-grade titanium in my tone. "We. Are. Working. And when you're on assignment with me, you *have* to live by the rules."

He moves an inch closer, and drops his voice to the edge of a whisper. "You going to pull rank with me when we get home, too?"

I gape at him, but he answers his own question. "It won't work there."

How is this backfiring? How is this getting worse with every second? I can't even face him any longer.

Danny catches my elbow. "Please," he says again. "You're going off the deep end with the paranoia. Being here is just making it worse."

I yank free and start walking. "You have no idea what you're talking about."

"Maybe I don't." He follows. "But you can at least hear me out. Because I really have done my best to follow your rules, so I think I've earned that much."

I nail him with a go-ahead-and-*try*-to-sway-me expression, which I know he can see when we reach the streetlight.

And when we reach the streetlight, I can see his face too. The pain and the pleading in his eyes cracks my concentration—and my heart.

"Please stop," he says. "Please come back. You know I've been here before." He pauses to let that sink in, the real underlying message.

The only "here" I can think of would be his relationship with his ex-fiancée. The one who had a serious mental illness, who screwed up Danny's life for way too long, who tried to kill herself to get him to take her back.

My paranoia doesn't reach the level of a personality disorder. Does it?

"I think you still have a choice. You can still stop it; you can still come back, now, before it's too late. Please." He inhales before he takes the final plunge. "Please choose me—end this."

I try to swallow, but I can't. I try to speak, but I can't. I try to process this, but I can't.

I've tried to be his wife—but maybe I can't.

Slowly Danny's gaze falls. Whatever he was expecting me to do or to say, I didn't. I couldn't. I'm just . . . *not*. Not enough. Not who he thought.

He shakes his head a tiny bit, like he's trying to renege, trying to say something, but all that comes out is the last two words again. "End this."

He starts down the street, and I can't stop him. I don't dare. He walks out of sight, on a straight course back to our hotel. (Fortunately, it *is* easy to get back from here.)

As he disappears out of sight, the dread hits rock bottom in my gut. The worst part is that I don't know what "this" I'm supposed to end.

No—the real worst part? I think I know exactly which "this" he means. It's all my nightmares, worse than even Fyodor, come true.

CHAPTER 20

ONCE I'VE CHANGED INTO MY LORI DISGUISE, thanks to my backup makeup kit, I start my surveillance detection route back to the hotel. Though it's less than a kilometer away, suddenly it feels like marching to Moscow.

How is this my life? A life that yesterday felt so perfect is now pretty much pulverized.

I kind of feel the same way. I don't know how to get Danny back. If I even can. If he even wants me to.

Two nights without sleep, now this? I think I've earned a bus ride.

I check the street for any form of public transit, and that's when I see a broad-shouldered beefcake veering across the pavement. Toward me.

In the States, it would be odd to have a stranger approach you on the street to get your number. (Or it was for me. Or it would've been, considering it happened exactly no times.) In Russia, that's normal. Not that I got propositioned a ton (well, not by sober men . . . this really isn't helping my self-esteem, but it's not like I can sink lower). Still, it's not completely out of the ordinary to have a guy come up to a woman and flirt with her or even ask her out, though she's a perfect stranger.

Fortunately, it's also not completely out of the ordinary for the woman to say "No" and the man to get lost.

I monitor Tall, Dark and Hulking, bearing in mind that I'm still wearing lots of eye makeup and heels and that copper hair. I'm Lori (with PhotoShop). The guy reaches me at the corner. "*Devushka*, may I make your acquaintance?"

"No, thank you." I pause half a second to pick a route around him. He doesn't make a move either direction, so I take the corner to see if he'll follow. Hoping he won't.

He does. *Also* not completely out of the ordinary for a guy to ignore a "no."

I don't like anybody pursuing me, even if it's because they think I'm cute. I hug my market bag, running a mental inventory for a makeshift weapon—something that'd draw less attention than pulling a gun on a guy trying to get a date. (Pulling a gun = compromising the mission. Which is why I don't carry a gun.)

My attention stays focused on Tall, Dark and Hulking, concentrating on his footsteps behind me. Not too close, not too far. At least we're not alone on the street.

I'm halfway down the block before my hand grips an engraved metal Shcherbakov pen in my bag. Perfect. I slow to give the guy a chance to reach me. Just before I draw and wheel on him, a pedestrian down the block straightens from leaning against a building. He's staring at me.

Okay, yeah, I look nice with the makeup and the wig and all, but that's too much. I race through my mental map of the other pedestrians. There's another guy behind my pursuer, and two men chatting in the streetlight at the corner. Everything about these guys is innocuous.

Too innocuous.

My tongue goes drier than the arid Russian steppe.

I can fight this—this paranoia, this overreaction. For Danny.

Five men on a street do not automatically constitute a crisis. I keep moving forward, trying to put more space between me and Tall, Dark and Hulking.

I study the buildings for stops to lose these guys, though they haven't converged on me yet. Dry cleaner, closed. Place for rent. Bank, closed. (How late is it?) Running out of options.

No. It's fine. I'm fine. Everything is totally routine, and the warning bells ringing in my brain are wrong. The guy in pursuit weighs enough to crush the life out of me, but I reach the corner without running. (See, Danny? I can be normal, even if in practice it seems more like being stupid.) (Please still love me.)

A black sedan swoops to the curb. My warning bells turn into a cacophony, and my heart turns to solid ice. I grope for the pen again, willing this panic to be wrong, to be an overreaction.

"Lori," the man behind me calls.

Yep. Well past time to run. Glancing over my shoulder, I feint a dodge to the right. When the guy goes for it, I switch directions to take the corner and run down the street.

He's faster than a guy his size should be. His hand clamps on my elbow. I flail to wrench free, but he's got me good.

I search the street for someone to shout to, someone to help, but the guys I thought were his cohorts are gone, and the nearest pedestrians can't get here in time, half a block away.

Tall, Dark and Hulking's other meaty paw seizes my other elbow, and he pulls them together so I can't resist. He rotates me toward the car, my waiting prison. Though this is nothing like my memories, my brain keeps dredging up images of the only time I've been taken prisoner. By Fyodor Timofeyev.

My pulse skyrockets. Did Danny fall into their trap, too?

The sedan's back door swings open, and my lungs instinctively seize, prepping myself to once again find Danny at gunpoint.

Borya sits in the backseat. Alone. Waiting. Like *won't you join me?*

As if I have a choice. My meat-fisted friend thrusts me forward, ducking my head to shove me into the backseat. (Because apparently he's done this before.) The door shuts, and the car joins the flow of traffic.

One-on-one with an FSB officer. I should be smarter than to fall prey to a classic rendition, snatching someone off the street. Even if I was a little distracted.

"Hello, Lori." Borya smiles like he didn't just abduct me. "I see you've met my cousins Anton—" he gestures at the driver, then back at the street— "and Evgeniy."

"Pleasure." Now what's the smartest course? If I leap from a moving vehicle or give him attitude, like I did Fyodor, I'll tip him off I'm not some poor interpreter. If I can lull him into that sense of security, maybe I can figure out what this is about.

I regard Borya with wide eyes. "What's going on?"

His smile turns sinister. "I suppose I should ask you the same thing."

My heart hovers, waiting for the other shoe to fall, waiting for him to say my real name, waiting for him to call me on my real relationship with Danny. But he says nothing.

Ah, silence. The interrogator's BFF. Not falling for that trick. I didn't know if it was physically possible, but apparently I *can* make my eyes even wider and more innocent. "What will you do to me?"

Borya flinches. (And I ignore a flash of victory at throwing him off his game.) "Who said I was going to do anything to you?" he asks.

I cast a pointed look at the door, as if we haven't already left Tall, Dark and Hulking well behind us. "Is that how you get a woman in a car with someone she knows? You couldn't ask?"

"We did. You said no."

"Doesn't count."

Borya relaxes into the leather upholstery. "Well, should we drop you off at your hotel?"

"Yes, please."

His laughter dismisses that possibility. Yeah, that bodes well. "We have much to talk about first."

Oh boy. But to keep my cover, I dangle the bait I pray he won't take. "Don't you want to talk to Danny?"

"This doesn't concern him, unless he was the one trying to hack me."

Danny's (hopefully) at the hotel inspecting those hacked files. Is either of us safe? "No idea what you're talking about."

"Did al-Ansari send you?" Borya springs the question like he can startle me into confessing.

"Sorry, still don't know what you mean." I offer an apologetic shrug though I know exactly what he's talking about: his email buddy.

"You or Danny logged into my email on my computer. Did you think I wouldn't notice?"

Um, yes?

"Registry files show a USB device connected to my computer with an afterhours time stamp yesterday when you and Danny came back to the office to search for his watch."

I squint like my memory scan came up empty. "I didn't see anything like that, sorry."

"Tell me what you know about al-Ansari."

Now would be a good time to lie. "Al Ans-what-i? I guess it's . . . an Arabic name?"

"Do you know who he is? Do you know what he does?"

"I didn't know 'he' was a specific person." I fixate on Borya, but I try not to lock on his gaze too long.

"And you are not working for him?"

"No. Never heard of him." I look around, like I'm expecting a candid camera crew to jump out.

"What did you read in my email?"

"Nothing," I say quickly. "I didn't even mean to log in. I just wanted to check my email, but yours popped up."

Borya eyes me. I hope he'll chalk up any deceptive indicators that subconsciously sneak past my defenses to innocent nerves. "What's your login?" he asks.

"To—to mail.ru?"

"Yes. You went to mail.ru to read your email. So what's your login?"

I rub my seatbelt. The real Lori's account would be the best answer, if she had one. I'll go with something I can sign up for as soon as I get out of here. (I'm getting out of here, right?) "LoriDolman87."

"Why don't you log in?" He holds out his giant screen smartphone, Mail.ru's page already loaded.

This is a test. And I'm going to fail. I take the phone, my brain paging through possible excuses. I type the login I gave him, and a few random characters as a fake attempt at my password. Not too surprisingly, it gives an error message: *Nevernoye imya pol'zovatelya ili parol'. Invalid username or password.* I barely have time to see it before I hold it out to Borya.

He takes his phone back and consults the screen. Without moving his head at all, he looks up at me, the classic librarian-over-the-glasses glare. "It didn't work."

"No?" I feign surprise. I take his gloved hand wrapped around the phone and tilt the screen to me. My shoulders drop. "I just changed my password. I haven't memorized it yet. You know how InterpretiRossiya is with security. I'll have to look it up again when I get home."

"They make you use your work password on your personal email?"

"Of course not. I like to only have one password to remember at a time."

Is it me, or does that excuse sound even lamer out loud?

But it should be good enough for the dude who keeps his password on a Post-It on his monitor. Unless that was a trap.

Borya purses his lips. "That is not good security, either."

Is he calling my bluff? I've got to play the cover harder. I cover my mouth. "Oh my gosh, please don't tell them." I go for the wide-eyed innocence he fell for earlier, and add a twist of neurotic fear. "They'll fire me—please, I can't lose this job."

He waves away my hysterics. "Endanger their security however you want." He puts away his phone, and the tension in my shoulders releases.

"So now are you going to tell me where you're taking me?" I ask.

"Where I'm taking you?" Borya nods at the windshield. The Hermitage Hotel looms ahead down the street.

I'm almost free? I draw a silent breath. But I can't leave without trying to exploit this opportunity. "So who is this al-Answari guy?" I trip on his name on purpose.

"Al-Ansari," he corrects me automatically. "And he's none of your concern."

"Okay," I say slowly. "You practically kidnap me to accuse me of stealing your files for someone who's none of my concern? Do I need to tell Danny about this?"

"No," Borya answers so fast he almost cuts me off. "If you mention this, it will bring trouble. I doubt that's what he's paying you for."

I don't respond to that. "And *not* mentioning getting snatched off the street is supposed to keep him out of trouble?" I shake my head in fake wonder. "I guess Danny's wrong about you."

"Hm?" Borya can't hide his piqued interest.

"He kinda can't stop talking about you. He thought you were becoming good friends. Hope I'm not getting in the way."

He contemplates that a long second, and I can *see* the fight. He wants to give me something, for Danny's sake. "Keep him away from ulitsa Novatorov tomorrow afternoon."

Not sure where that street is. We pull to the curb, but I'm not done. "Wait, what's tomorrow?"

"The less you know, the better," Borya says. He focuses on my floor mat, and something about his flat tone raises a yellow flag of worry in my mind.

I lean forward. The upholstery creaks beneath me. "And Danny? Does he know too much?"

"Danny knows nothing. Keep it that way, and you'll both be safe."

"From you?"

"From al-Ansari." Again, his tone is oddly flat. Either he's lying, or something else is going on.

"Are *you* in trouble?"

Borya brushes off my concern. "No. I'm fine. And you will be too, if you do as I say."

Oh, I will. But I'll also be calling Semyon as soon as Borya drives away. "All right." Would an interpreter take control of a client for the day? That seems awkward (even if your client doesn't hate you). "If you really want to keep Danny safe—without getting his suspicions up—you should find something for him to do at Shcherbakov."

"Our visit ends at noon."

"I'm sure you can find something else—"

Borya shuts me down, flicking away my argument. "I will not be there, and no other directors are available."

Right. "Okay, I'll figure something out."

"See that you do." He signals the driver and the door locks click. Unlocked. I'm free.

But this still feels like one for the loss column. I bite my lip, staring at him from the corner of my eye. "Are you *sure* you don't need help?"

"Absolutely. Good night."

I'm good and dismissed. Fine. I climb from the car without

saying goodbye. Borya's driver pulls away.

I take a steeling breath and stare at the Hermitage's façade. What will I tell Danny?

I exhale, and all the adrenaline and energy seems to leave my body in this condensation cloud. Danny's only with the guy until noon tomorrow. Then I can take him somewhere and keep him safe and out of custody. Then tomorrow night, drone or no drone, we have a flight to catch.

Somehow, the logical plan doesn't leave me reassured. Mostly because things never go according to plan.

I wait until Borya's car is down the block and around the corner before I move. I don't know what to say to Danny yet, and I need to get this message to Semyon. I trudge into the hotel garage (or whatever this entrance is for). The text takes thirty seconds to type, encrypt and send to Semyon: *B is doing something with al-Ansari on ulitsa Novatorov tomorrow afternoon.*

I lean back against the cement wall and just . . . breathe. It's done. This is the last piece I need, and it confirms everything (as if the rendition wasn't enough proof). Borya's FSB. He's the biggest threat. I was right all along.

And he wants to keep Danny safe, too. On one little front, that makes Borya and me . . . well, co-combatants. Not friends.

Besides, what can I do? Run up to Danny to crow *I told you so*? I have the trump card I need, but no witnesses, nothing better than my word to prove this isn't my paranoia talking.

No, he needs to know he's more important than my paranoia. Even if all I've done is tried to keep him safe—

Because my paranoia *is* me choosing him. Maybe not how he wants, but the best way I know. I don't have to mention my tiny triumph tonight. He can keep his illusions, even about Borya, and I can look wrong and crazy and everything else—as long as he loves me.

Please let him still love me.

CHAPTER 21

I GATHER THE TATTERS OF MY STRENGTH and drag myself back to street level. Somehow, walking in the main entrance of the Hermitage takes more courage than anything I've done today. But I make it in the door, up the steps, through the lobby. I'm in the elevator when my phone buzzes. Random Cyrillic— Semyon. The decryption app spits out the message: *aA is an arms dealer.*

I knew it. I knew it. Vindication vibrates through me, even after all tonight's defeats and fatigue. I seriously doubt Shcherbakov's working with al-Ansari on de-icing or composites or turbines. He's an arms dealer—an arms dealer whose price is wrong, apparently.

What's Borya selling?

My job to find out. I don't have the heart to tell Semyon about Valya yet, so I delete his text and put my phone away.

I make it to the hall at Danny's door. Closed. Locked. And he hasn't called or texted.

Before I figure out what to do, my phone buzzes again. I barely have time for my hopes to lift before they're dashed: another text from Semyon. This one translates to *Exterminated video bug in exec's room. Audio intact.* Probably best to keep their suspicions down. Now we have a little privacy. I thank Semyon and he texts once more. *Ready for a PCS?*

My stomach twists tighter than a babushka's scarf knot. PCS = permanent change of station. Which = moving to Russia.

On one hand, I'm glad to make a big impression. Yeah, I'm in the country two days and I'm recruiting a new agent (unsuccessfully, but Semyon doesn't know that yet). Most officers couldn't do that. Developing contacts, building relationships of trust, pitching: all take time. When you already know people, you can cut to the chase. *Svyazi* at its best.

I should be thrilled I'm being scouted for Russia. If I'm honest, a good 50% of applying to the CIA was the prospect of coming back. Not necessarily to Rostov and the people I knew here, but to the culture, the type of people, the type of friendship I had here. Maybe that was unrealistic; a missionary and a spy have different objectives. But I'd be lying if I said I wasn't a little disappointed to end up in Canada, especially for so long.

And just yesterday, wasn't I boasting how much I *belong* here?

On the other hand, Canada's where Danny is, and our house and our life and our dreams. What do I do, leave him there for possibly *years* while I run off to fulfill a fantasy?

I refocus on Danny's door. In Paris, I was ready to resign for him. But that was when the Agency was targeting him. Do I have the courage—the strength—to decline something I've always wanted, all for him? For someone who wants me to "end this"?

My final defeat of the night: I turn for my own room.

I throw my gloves and hat on the dresser, but they slide off and land on a suitcase, my "probably won't use unless it's a *real* emergency" bag.

Too bad I didn't pack for a marital emergency. Doubt the carabiner or the climbing rope or anything else in there will help. I step to my bed, ready to sink onto the bedspread.

Can I really give up this easily? Russian assignment or not, I came here to fight for Danny. I didn't bargain on fighting *with* Danny, but if that's what it takes to keep him and keep him safe?

I still can. I have to. I unzip my emergency bag. The pad of quick-dissolve paper is exactly what I need. Once I tear off the first sheet—can't leave impressions—I scratch out a message.

I knock at his door, though I can hardly bear to look at it while I wait.

Danny answers, and the circles under his eyes make him look like he's slept less than I have since we took this assignment. Before things can get awkward, I keep the cover in place. "You said you needed help?" I ask, gesturing toward his room.

"Russian paperwork." He lets me in and closes the door. "Listen—"

I gesture at the wall and my ears. We can't *say* anything. He examines me. Disbelieving? "Sorry I snapped at you." He pauses for about seven eternities. Finally, he adds, "Lori."

The name he hasn't used yet crashes down on my heart. Welcome to the world's hollowest victory. Ugh. Am I always such an idiot with relationship stuff? How'd I ever get married?

I hold up my note and he takes it to read. *I have chosen you. I have since we first met. I've always tried. I'm sorry it's not enough. I don't know where to go from here.*

Wish I had some solution or something more eloquent to tell him, but the truth is my last refuge.

I demand the paper back with an impatient hand. He obeys, rubbing his eyes. I add to the note, using the door for a backing: *I have to do this. I have to protect YOU & there's nothing I won't do to do that.* I hesitate, but finally tack on: *Nothing I won't sacrifice. Even us.*

When he finishes reading, he's the one gesturing for me to give him something. I shake my head—I don't have anything.

Finally, he takes the pen from my fingers. Oh.

He scribbles something and flips the paper back. He circled my last word, "us," and wrote _NOT on the table._

I take the paper and pen back. _You said to end this._

Again, he scribbles a note and holds it up for me to read. Again, he's circled the last word, "this," and added _≠ us!!_ He pulls the paper back to add more exclamation points. I put my hands over his. "I got it," I mouth.

He surrenders the paper and pen. "Sorry, I—I just . . . I miss my wife," he murmurs.

"I understand."

He meets my gaze, and the feeling passes between us. Then he grabs me in a long, tight hug.

It feels like days—weeks—months since we've been this close, since he's held me in his arms. I had no idea how much I needed this until I'm here, clinging to him just as tightly, drawing in the comfort and strength of being with him. We may not have everything perfectly worked out, but we're not going to give up yet.

He pulls back, taking my hands and staring at them. "I've been going nuts with you out there by yourself."

Is he saying what I think? "Why didn't you call?"

"And say what? 'I'm an idiot. You're still alive, right?'"

Before I can gaze-point at the walls, he grimaces. "Sorry."

"It's okay."

He moves to neutral conversational ground and offers me the tablet. "Ready for paperwork?"

"One minute." I duck into the bathroom to flush the note, though the quick-dissolve paper's gone before I hit the lever. As I turn for the room, I catch a glimpse of myself in the mirror. I smooth my long copper bangs to the side, half-hiding my face. But that's not the real reason I look different.

I am so tired of being Lori.

I scrub off my eye makeup and rip out the dozens of pins

holding the wig on. Then I undo my braids, shed the red coat, tug off my high heel boots. I consult the mirror.

There I am. Lost myself for a second.

Danny's sitting on the bed, propped up with both pillows, and he doesn't look up from the tablet when I slip in. I perch on the other side of the mattress, then he finally meets my gaze. The recognition is instant: he knows what I'm trying to say. But more than that—his wife is back, if only for a few minutes.

He beckons me closer. I'm all too happy to oblige. I crawl across the queen-sized bed. Danny holds out an arm, and I curl up beside him, resting my head on his chest, where I fit perfectly.

"What do these say?" He indicates a column of Cyrillic by a list of percentages.

"*Titan, alyuminiy, vanadiy, palladiy, zhelezo.*"

He nods, then gently, silently, plants a kiss on top of my head. I arch my neck and pull him close for an equally silent kiss.

"*Rakastan sinua,*" I whisper.

"I know." He winks. "What do you say back?"

"*Ja minä sinuakin.*"

"Yeah, that."

I settle into the crook of his arm. "I'm guessing your list is—"

"Titanium, aluminum, vanadium, palladium and . . . iron?"

Okay, the first four are obvious, but *zhelezo* sounds nothing like iron. "How'd you guess?"

His shoulder shifts in a shrug. "The percentages are similar to a standard alloy with iron, but the palladium's new—guess it makes sense in Russia." He trails off into sciencey-thinky-land, and I let my eyes drift shut. I sigh out the air I've been holding for two days, it seems. Still a lot to work through—sometime when we can have a private conversation—but tonight I'll settle for a truce.

The next thing I know, I'm waking up to light streaming in the window—and an insistent knock at the door. "*Gornich-naya*," comes a woman's voice from the hallway. The maid.

Oh, crap. We overslept.

Oh, crap. I'm not supposed to be in Danny's room.

Oh, *crap*. I'm not supposed to be *me*.

I hop away from Danny, who's scrambling to get up, too. We're still dressed from yesterday. At least there's that. My brain jumps back into paranoid mode faster than I can blink. If the room is bugged, is anything here safe? Who knows who the maids are reporting to?

I point to the tablet on the bedspread. He must've dropped it during the night. Danny stuffs the tablet under the mattress. Not a great long-term option, but good enough.

Another knock.

"Just a minute!" Danny calls.

Uh yeah. Privacy's not found in the Russian conceptual vocabulary. Centuries of communal farming built up a deeper value on community and interresponsibility than private space. (This is why strangers fuss you out for not buttoning up, too.)

Out the window or into the bathroom—and dang it, I left my rappelling equipment in my *other* hotel room. I race into the bathroom and ease the door halfway shut so it seems vacant.

The housekeeper opens the room door, and Danny's there to stop her. "Oh, we don't need anything today. I mean, I don't—I don't need anything."

No time, no time. I pin my bangs to the side and twist up my long, dark hair. In this much of a rush, I hold it in place while I awkwardly wrestle the wig cap on. The wig is next. I only have time for a quick adjustment before I snag my coat and check the door.

"*Ne govoryu po-angliyskiy,*" the maid says. She doesn't speak English. "*Polotentsi?*" She mimics drying her hands and shoulders. "*Polotentsi?*"

She wants the towels? She's coming in here. My pulse does a freaking polka. I call Danny's attention over the housekeeper's head and gaze-point into his room.

He understands perfectly. "Oh yeah, over here." He turns to lead her into the room, like he has any idea what she's after.

I open the bathroom door and sneak out. The room door's still open, but if a team of maids is working in the hall—

My feet hit the hallway carpet, and no one's there to spot me. I'm safe. I take a silent breath—and then it registers.

There's a reason I can feel the *hallway carpet.* Because my shoes are still in his bathroom.

I pivot back to the open door and knock. Too late; the maid's already invaded the bathroom. I glance at Danny. He watches me warily, unsure what's wrong.

I push the bathroom door and find the housekeeper examining my high heel boots. "*Akha, tam oni!*" I exclaim. *There they are.* I bring Danny in on the cover. "I must've left them here last night."

"Yeah," he says, "you left in a hurry. Figured you'd gone to bed, and you could get them tomorrow. Today."

I take the boots from the maid. Let's get rid of her before she finds anything incriminating. I address Danny. "Do you need towels?"

"Not today."

I dismiss the maid as politely as possible and refrain from shoving her out the door. Danny closes and locks it. We exchange a wide-eyed, that-was-close expression.

"Bringing your tablet?" I nod exaggeratedly to supply his

answer.

"Yeah. Fell asleep before I finished reviewing that paperwork." He flashes me a look of *did I screw up too bad?*

I shoot him a nah-you're-good face. "We might have time later."

"Are we late?"

"Don't you have your watch?" I can't help the smirk.

Danny rolls his gaze heavenward and takes his watch from the nightstand. "Eight forty-five."

"When's your first meeting?"

"Nine."

"Better run." I can skip one shower. I duck into my room to change clothes, rebraid my real hair and put on makeup. (Now I need it, breaking out after two days of this shellac.)

I pause at my door. Facing off with an FSB officer? Better come prepared. My emergency bag's too conspicuous, but I grab the market tote still full from last night. In three minutes, we meet outside his room and rush downstairs.

We're almost through the lobby when I notice the businessman on a gold sofa, perusing a newspaper. Semyon. If he's here, it's big. Too big to text. "One minute," I tell Danny. I stop by Semyon's chair and ask something totally innocuous. *"Kakaya pogoda?"* How's the weather?

"Khudsheye zima v gody," he says. *Worst winter in years*— what they say every year. He sets aside the paper's first section. I pick it up, eyebrows arched to silently ask for it. He nods.

"Spasibo." That's all I have time for before we half-run out the door.

And holy CRAP, Semyon wasn't kidding. It wasn't this cold even last night. Nothing like contending with Russian winter on your last day in the country. I button my coat and huddle closer to Danny. We don't have time to wait for a marked cab today. The first car to pull up is a Lada, with a guy in his twenties behind the wheel. I open the back door to talk to him.

"*Kuda?*" he asks. (*Where to?*)

"Shcherbakov," I tell him our destination. I give the address too.

He winces. "Eight hundred."

That's outrageous. I have to haggle. "Three hundred."

"Four."

I'll take it. I give my very specific directions so the dude knows not to deviate from the direct course, and Danny and I pile in the backseat, tripping over one another's legs. Danny chuckles, and I can't help it, I join in.

The driver asks if tourists should be more careful with their vodka, and I don't bother correcting him. It just feels good to be around my husband. Even if I'm still not me.

"How do you like Russia?" The driver cuts into my thoughts in English. We need to be careful.

"Loving it today," Danny says. I glimpse his real, eye-crinkling smile. I'm loving it too.

I flip through the newspaper and find a folded piece of paper like the one we used for our notes last night. Great. I have to eat this.

I open the folded slip. *Paperwork ready. You belong in Russia.*

Suddenly, the prospect of the paper's sour taste isn't the only thing turning my stomach. Not loving the day so much.

Danny can read the English as easily as I can. (At least the newspaper shields us from the driver.) The laughter leaves Danny's gaze, and he looks to me.

"I'll explain later." I rip the paper in half and pop the side with the message in my mouth when I'm sure the driver won't see my lips pucker at the taste. (It's bad.) I pocket the blank half of the quick-dissolve paper before we roll up to Shcherbakov's wacky façade. We pay the driver and hop out. Danny checks the time. "Five after."

"Crap," I mutter. We should never, never, never be late. We

hang up our coats, and I stow my bag. (Have fun looking through my clothes!) Danny keeps the tablet in his suit coat, and we stride through the interior doors.

Once we're alone in the elevator, Danny finally broaches the topic of the note. "What paperwork?"

I cut my eyes at him and touch a finger to my lips. "Transfer." I try to make my whisper dismissive and factually neutral to settle the issue. "My company is pushing for it."

Danny turns a hard, shocked stare on me, but before he can speak, the elevator doors slide open. Score another one for temperamental elevator chimes.

Maybe we'll get a minute alone at Borya's office. But no, he's waiting for us, and I mentally kick myself again (and not just because I can't snag any USB drives). He's caught us arriving late—and I wasn't quite ready to see him face to face. "I was beginning to worry," he says. He's all smiles today, though he's conspicuously *not* addressing me.

"Sorry," I apologize. Neurotic Lori is definitely taking the fall. "All my fault—"

"It's okay. However, my meeting has been moved to eleven," Borya tells Danny. "Time zone misunderstanding. Teleconference. So we may not have much time this morning."

Borya spots me observing him from the corner of my eye, and he snaps away fast. Maybe this is awkward for him too.

"Shall we?" Borya gestures down the hall toward the conference room, and we follow.

He peers over his shoulder at me, and this time I play the cover harder and give him a why-are-you-looking-at-me? look.

This *is* because of last night's little scene, right?

Before Borya fully turns back, Danny detects our strange, silent exchange. He shoots me a question in the quirk of his eyebrow.

I give him a helpless, sorry-your-bestie's-a-freak shrug. I'm choosing not to tell him the full truth about our unromantic rendezvous for obvious reasons, but . . . even if Borya weren't here, would I tell Danny? Would he believe me?

"Everything okay, Lori?" Danny asks as we reach the conference room's glass doors.

I give a benign let's-get-on-with-this smile. "Yep."

He scrutinizes me a long minute, weighing my words. We might have gotten to a good place last night, but there's still more to settle.

"Okay," Danny says. His eyes are solemn, and I get the neon flashing message: *I'm trusting you.* Hope we have a chance to get this worked out before even our truce fails.

CHAPTER 22

ONCE THEY'VE STRUCK A MORE BALANCED AGREEMENT ready for the bureaucratic gauntlet of Shcherbakov and NRC, we troop out of the conference room. Borya and Danny may be all grins, but I'm trying to convince myself the mission wasn't a failure (tablet files notwithstanding).

Before I can think of an excuse to visit Borya's office to snag another USB drive, someone steps between me and Danny and Borya. They continue down the hall, chatting, and I look up to see who cut me off. Kita, pinched and skeevy as ever. "Yes?" I ask.

"Where should we go to dinner?" Kita finally replies.

Oh. He's just interested in me? (A dancing bear would get hit on in this much makeup.) "I fly back to Moscow tonight." I start to brush past him, but he stands his ground.

"Lunch, then."

Lunch dates aren't a thing in Russia. "I'm working."

Behind Kita, Borya consults his watch and flinches, then says goodbye to Danny. Kita's still not moving. Danny catches the awkwardness. I don't need a decryption app to get Danny's message: *what about this guy? Couldn't he be the officer?*

Maybe I can rule Kita out. I bat my eyes at him. "So you're an engineer?"

"Um." Kita swallows. "I work in personnel services."

HR? Not R&D, where Semyon said the FSB officer worked. I give Danny a quick save-me glance. He's there in an instant. "Let's go, Lori."

I give Kita an it-can't-be-helped shrug, and join Danny. "Not him," I mutter.

Fortunately, he accepts that. By the time we have our coats and my bag, the receptionist has a real cab waiting for us. Danny opens the taxi door. "You sure everything's okay? Things seemed . . . weird."

I take a seat in the cab. "With Kita?"

"With Borya."

Do I tell him? Not in front of the cabbie. I scoot across the backseat to make room for Danny. "Just relieved to be done," I murmur. "Anything you'd like to see today?"

"Nothing springs to mind. Things I'd like to talk about," he finishes under his breath.

What does that mean?

"You have been to *rynok*?" the driver asks in heavily-accented English.

"The what?" Danny asks.

"The *rynok*," I repeat. "The market. If you want souvenirs, it's the best place." Not to mention food, clothes, accessories— it's like a handmade Walmart.

"Sure," Danny says. He opens his mouth to say something, but looks at the driver and changes his mind.

Nerves worm their way into my veins. What did I do wrong? Do I need to tell him about Borya?

The taxi driver drops us off outside the *rynok* entrance. I brace myself for Danny's topic choice, but he's craning his neck to get a better view of the market through the gates. "Am I allowed to tell my parents I came to Russia?"

I glance left and right. "Of course," I say softly. "Why not?"

Danny leans down. "Absolutely no reason," he murmurs. I turn to him, and his face is inches from mine. Lightning rockets down my spine, landing in my stomach.

Why do I have to be Lori?

I adjust my bag on my shoulder—and then the idea pops into my mind. An even better way to kill time keeping Danny away from ulitsa Novatorov. "Tell you what," I say. "That café's good." I point to *Vkusno Lyubov'*, the place where I lost Eager Igor. "Let's start there and then we'll check out the *rynok*. Matryoshka dolls are always nice . . . samovars—you know, the Russian tea kettle-type things—"

"Yes, I know what a samovar is."

"Right. Honey's also big. Pity you didn't come in May. There's an entire honey festival."

"Yeah," Danny jokes. "The honey festival's the top reason why it's better to visit Russia in May than November. That's it."

I laugh and reach for his hand. For a split second, we're on our honeymoon again—but then I stop myself. I have to get out of this disguise first.

And see what he wants to talk about.

We reach the sidewalk in front of the little restaurant, and Danny gets the door for me and a stooped old babushka. But instead of thanking him or walking in, she snaps at Danny, shaking a finger an inch from his nose with every harsh word.

He jerks back, aghast. She goes in for a second round, but I quickly cut her off. "He's a foreigner," I tell her in Russian. "He doesn't understand."

The babushka scowls at Danny, the deep lines etched on her face carving into critical canyons. But she says nothing else and marches into the shop.

Danny finally steps in after me. As he helps me with my coat, he leans down. "What did you save me from?"

I turn to him. Even through the curtain of copper hair

218

separating us, I can see there's something strangely subdued about my husband. Because of the babushka? "She said you need to button up. 'It's cold out, don't you know that?'"

"Good thing you're here to protect me." He shakes his head, like that's a joke. Doesn't sound like he's kidding.

Could whatever he wants to talk about be no big deal?

Danny hangs my coat next to the same brown one that was left on the rack yesterday. We let the babushka take her turn at the counter, then I order blackberries, smetana and honey again. I look to Danny, and he gives a palms-up helpless gesture, like *I have no idea what to get.* So I order my favorite savory blin for variety: smetana and beef.

I explain what we're getting to Danny, and he listens like this recipe will save his life. "You like Russian food?" he asks.

"It's not bad. Except *kholodets*—two words: meat jelly."

"Oh, like aspic?"

I can't hide my horror. "We have the concept of gelled meat and fat in English?"

"My grandma's favorite. I couldn't touch it."

"Whew. For a minute there, I was worried we—" *couldn't be married.* I cut off the joke for a host of reasons (not just my cover), the biggest two being that 1. I don't actually find that funny, and 2. the owner arrives with our blini. I can almost pretend we're back in that Paris crêperie, with slightly different crêpes and fillings.

Danny and I sit, and he pulls out the tablet. I put a hand over the screen. "It can wait."

"Something more important come up?"

"Nothing until our flight at seven," I reply. That's all Danny needs to know. I don't have to tell him about Borya's deal or keeping Danny away from ulitsa Novatorov. Like that'll even be a challenge.

Before Danny can bring up his subject—I'm guessing it's not something he needs to talk to "Lori" about—I come up with a cover.

"Tell me about your meeting." I get out the biggest piece of quick-dissolve paper, like I'll be taking notes between bites. Danny furrows his brow a split second, but launches into a fairly generic description of the model shop, the machinery inside, and Shcherbakov's manufacturing capabilities. All good stuff for the CIA to know (we like to keep tabs)—but I'm not taking notes on Danny's observations (which he'll report directly during our layover in Paris tonight anyway). When he's done, I finish off my last bite of my blin and hand off the "notes." "Proof that and see if it seems correct," I say. "Have to run to the restroom."

He immediately studies the paper. And he should. Because he needs to follow those instructions to a Cyrillic T to make this work.

The note says Danny should finish his blini, get his coat (reverse it, button up and wear a hat, both as a disguise and to avoid the wrath of babushki everywhere), and go into the *rynok.* He can browse for a few minutes, but then he has to make his way to the honey vendor he passed on his way in.

The last line tells him to drop the note in my water bottle. Because it's all on my quick-dissolving paper.

By the time I leave the restroom, having ditched my usual disguise and waited long enough that Danny's gone, our table is clear, and I don't seem suspicious. I leave my coat with the other abandoned jacket (for now) and head to the first honey vendor at this entrance of the *rynok.* Buttoned up and gray hatted, Danny's focusing on the vendor's broken English and his description of the wonders of Russian honey. (He's not wrong.)

I reach Danny's side and beam up at him. "American?" I ask, like I don't already know.

"Yeah," he says. Anyone else could write off the amusement shining in his eyes as a general, cultural inside joke.

I turn to the vendor and to Russian. "One twenty-five." Which is fair, since I'm sure he's willing to come down more.

The vendor frowns. "Weren't you here yesterday?" he asks.

He could be an FSB informant—but what's he going to tell them? We'll be gone in seven hours. "Yes, and that's how much you charged me."

He huffs out a groan. "Fine. One twenty-five."

I inform Danny of the new price and he fishes out two one-hundred ruble notes. "Thanks," he says to both me and the vendor as he accepts the honey and his change.

I wink and start for the next cart. "Stick with me and we'll get you what you need."

"Apparently," he mutters.

That gets my attention. "What's wrong?"

He takes a deep breath, either thinking about what to say or thinking about whether he wants to say it. "Do you remember two days ago when you said I could handle myself here?"

"Sure."

"Did you mean it?"

I know I should say yes. But he needs the truth, so I try to remember the exact conversation. After three seconds, Danny shakes his head and keeps walking. "Forget it."

"No, wait—"

"Seriously, forget it. Stupid question."

"It's not a stupid question."

But before I can figure out how to move this conversation forward, a vendor jumps in front of us with a tray of *kholodets*. We decline, and I glance up at Danny to share the inside joke. But he's staring back at me, serious. Sad. Like he needs more than walking with Talia Reynolds, cute interpreter.

I study him a minute longer. It'd be tough for the casual observer to recognize Danny with the hat (and actually buttoned coat), and nearly impossible for anyone without advanced facial recognition software to identify me. My paranoia screams for me to keep my distance—but more than that . . .

Danny obeyed my instructions perfectly, though they were paranoid precautions, and he didn't hesitate or complain or argue that this is exactly what he begged me not to do last night.

He's giving me that. I don't know what's the matter, but I can give him this. I take his hand.

Danny looks at our hands and back at me. He smiles, but it's not the full-on eye-crinkling one I'm anticipating. Instead, his expression is tinged with sadness.

What am I doing wrong now? We keep moving through the *rynok*, racking up deals on Russian gifts (and things I can legit have at home, since it's kind of a secret I lived here). Though he's obviously trying to hide it, the melancholy lingers.

I'm about to ask him what's the matter again when I see someone I really, really don't want to. Not Borya or anyone from Shcherbakov (thank goodness), not Semyon or anyone from the CIA (though I don't know anyone else from the local office).

Valya. My stomach lurches worse than at the idea of *kholodets*.

He's eating lunch. The *rynok* is a major lunchtime draw, and the district headquarters are less than a kilometer away. Running into him isn't a major problem—but I'm the last person he wants to see today. After Danny's reaction to my pitch, even with Valya's unequivocal rejection? Yeah. This could get awkward fast.

I try to monitor Valya without Danny noticing, steering us clear of him, changing up our speed to make us harder to track. For a few minutes I think I've successfully navigated those treacherous waters—until I catch Valya two stalls behind us once, twice, three times.

Either he's making his way through the market at the exact same slow/quick/slow pace (yeeeah), or he's following us.

My pulse shifts into the fast lane, and hope and dread battle in my heart. Could he want to smooth things over? Could I have another chance to apologize?

We reach the arched gates to the street, and Valya hangs back. I tug Danny through the gates, then step closer to tell him, "I need to change. Can you get back to the hotel?"

"Sure." Not like he suspects something's up. Not like he thinks I'm crazy paranoid. Like he's willing to do anything I ask. His eyes search mine, and I have to know what's the matter.

"What's wrong? You act like you're leaving me here forever."

"Uh, yeah? 'Paperwork ready. You belong in Russia.'"

Semyon's note. Danny's spent all morning thinking— "Danny." I'm so tired of weighing and measuring every syllable. If I've learned anything, it's to not hoard the truth. "My contact's trying to convince me to transfer. It's been good working here, but . . ." I lift our hands and tighten my grasp. "*This* is where I belong."

Danny tilts my chin up, and I don't think he even pauses to think—he just leans down and kisses me. Once again, I should dodge, I should stop him, but that's the last thing I want.

Instead, I breathe him in and kiss him back like I might never get the chance again. He pulls back all too soon. "Sorry," he whispers.

I sigh. "For kissing me or stopping?"

"Neither." He plants one final peck on my forehead. "Guess that's not the only thing we need to work out."

Like the fact he hates a major part of my life? "Yeah." But looking into his eyes, suddenly I'm not worried. He's my husband. He loves me, and I love him so much I hardly have room to breathe. I don't know how, but we'll figure it out.

But first things first: "We need to check out of the hotel within the hour. I have to change—can you get there on your own?"

He studies my eyes a moment. "Yeah, I think so." He squeezes my hands once more, then starts off to do just what I said. I watch to make sure he heads the right direction before I double back to the *rynok*.

Valya's ten feet behind me. And he seems . . . chagrined. For intruding on that private moment? I don't know. I don't bother acting surprised to see him, though, and approach, passing through the gates. "I'm sorry," I start, but Valya shakes his head.

"No." He stops, and in the silence, pain haunts his face. "You are right. Melanyushka needs more help."

As if being right is any consolation. A little girl—a little girl I loved—is dying, and there's nothing I can do to stop it except make her father betray Mother Russia. Who wants to be right about that?

Valya shifts his gaze to mine again. "It's the only way." But his eyes beg me to come up with an alternative to save him, to save his daughter. His pleas echo in me, but I can't—I can't care or I'll crack.

In a couple hours, I get to fly out of here, but Valya's torment will just be beginning.

"I will do it," he says at last. "Tell me what I need to do."

Normally, recruiting an agent is a major victory. Celebrating the agreement together is fairly routine. That's anything but appropriate here. "Thank you." My empty words bounce around my chest cavity. I find Semyon's number in my phone, then write it out on the last corner of the quick-dissolve paper. I doubt Semyon gave an officer in town for a three-day assignment his permanent local number, so I can't be certain how long this contact is good for. "Call before seven o'clock today. My friend will tell you what to do next."

Valya takes the paper and studies the number.

"Destroy the paper. It'll dissolve in water."

His shoulders fall even further at his first tiny peek into the world of espionage. I want to snatch the paper away and stuff it in my mouth before he can memorize the number, he's so broken and defeated.

Just before I snap, Valya tucks the paper in his coat pocket. "I will call."

"All right." In any other recruitment, I'd be glad enough to hug him. I know Valya better than any other agent I've ever had—and that's exactly why I can't bridge the gap between us. I don't dare.

What have I done?

The thought seems to reverberate in Valya's stare a long time.

"If I knew any other way," I breathe.

"We do what we must. For those we love." He glances over my shoulder after Danny.

I knew Valya was behind me, but I didn't think I was exposing a vulnerability—not like he is. I look back, like Danny will magically reappear, then turn back to Valya, confirming his guess.

"You'd have to be good friends to come this far," he murmurs.

"Yeah."

Everything we need to say, but can't, and the things we've said and shouldn't have, hover over us like clouds bearing a blizzard, heavy with snow, threatening to fall and crush this tenuous understanding. But neither of us speak. Not because we don't want to break this feeble détente—I don't dare imagine our friendship will ever be the same. We both understand how awful and deep these circumstances are, and no words can change that.

"Thank you," I whisper again. Before he responds, I walk away.

A week for hollow victories.

225

CHAPTER 23

ISTART ON MY SDR BACK TO THE HOTEL, changing in an alley in between the café and McDonald's. (As if changing in the street wasn't humiliating enough.) Wish it were that easy to shed the memory of Valya, what I've done, what I'm making him do.

For Melanyushka. All for her. But the shard of guilt that wedges into my gut doesn't heed my logic.

I have one stop left when I get a text. I almost hope it's Valya, reneging. But it's Danny. *Think I found something*, he says. *Hurry back.*

Almost there, I reply. *Let me pack up first.* I try to shift my mindset to the person I need to be. Not Lori, though I do need to be her—but Talia, CIA operations officer. Like I told Danny, stealing secrets and recruiting spies is the job description you get Day One. Might as well be printed on the Agency seal. And yes, what I do isn't pretty, but like any undercover cop, law enforcement officer or soldier, I signed up to take greater risks and do awful things to keep people like Danny safe.

Yeah, I don't want to hear that any more than he did.

I made my peace with this long ago. I do have to make

exceptions to my moral standards—but again, like any under-cover cop or law enforcement officer or soldier, I do things a regular citizen shouldn't have to, all to keep those regular citizens safe. If the price of freedom is me lying, yes, that's not generally a "good" thing to do, but I believe God's smart enough to figure this out, and to see my intent, my heart's in the right place. Even if sometimes it feels like a very wrong place.

All for Melanyushka's sake, I remind myself. That's why Valya's making this sacrifice. His choice.

So why am I still trying to figure out how to undo it?

I'm almost back to my hotel when a beat-up, boxy beige coupe cuts me off. I recognize the car: Semyon's.

As soon as my door shuts, we pull away from the curb. "Okay, debrief," Semyon says.

He may be the local station chief, but he's not really my boss. After Valya, I don't have the will to pick a fight. "Got the tablet yesterday. We're going through the files. Danny says he might've found something."

"Great. They'll love that in Paris. How about the FSB officer?"

"Still points to Borislav Zverev. Bugs in his office. He alluded to conversations Danny and I had in the hotel. Oh, yeah, and he rendited me off the street last night."

Semyon nods, his friendly eyes now pensive. "You've gotten a lot done in, what, two days?"

"Feels longer."

"About that PCS—"

One more thing first. "One more thing: I recruited an agent."

Semyon stops more abruptly than necessary to obey the red light ahead. "You did what?"

"I recruited an agent," I repeat. Sounds clear to me.

"You mean you found an agent for us to recruit." His tone

227

sounds sure, but his face is begging me to agree.

"No, I pitched him. He accepted." I try not to picture Valya. "I told you about him. Didn't I?" I was going to text him while walking to the hospital—and then I picked up Eager Igor.

Oh, crap. I didn't tell him.

"Think I'd remember that." Semyon fumes, exhaling loudly, barely containing his fury. The light turns green and we jolt off the starting line as if fueled by his anger. "You cold pitched someone you just met, no idea—"

"I've known him five years. He's totally trustworthy—he rejected me at first, but he needs the money for his daughter. She has cancer."

"You fall for every sob story and outstretched palm that comes your way in Canada?"

"I approached him. He had no idea I'm CIA, and I'm pretty sure I ruined our friendship."

Semyon practically chokes on his scorn. "Heartbreaking. Glad to know your priorities are straight. And I'll bet we now have excellent access to, what, Rostvertol?"

The local helicopter giant must have a few agents in place. "How about the headquarters of the Southern Military District?"

"Okay, he works there, but does *he* have access? Or is he some low-level desk jockey?"

I assume he's high up. We saw him in the Victory Day parade, riding in style instead of marching. But beyond that, I can't be sure.

"Do you know his rank? Specialty? Branch?"

"*Podpolkovnik.*" As of five years ago. My voice is subdued.

"We haven't vetted this guy—I don't even know his name." Semyon whips down a side street and parks. "We need people who can follow protocol, because here our lives depend on it."

Everything inside me shrinks three sizes. Either I obey the rules too well and alienate my husband, or I've gone totally rogue. Complete no-win.

Semyon isn't done. "Go do your own thing. Seems that's what you're good at. Enjoy your last day here." His tone isn't nearly as generous as his words.

Guess I won't have to turn down that PCS. I'm so clearly cut loose, goodbye's unnecessary.

The worst part? All Valya's gone through is for nothing. He doesn't even know it.

I get back to the hotel with enough time to pack before we need to check out. And somehow I'll scrape together the will to keep moving.

I head to my room to gather my things. In a couple hours, this will all be over. I don't know whether to be relieved or guilty.

Guilt wins, besieging my gut like a German-Fascist invader. I shove aside the disappointment and worry to scoop up my dirty clothes and clear my bathroom counter. I need to keep moving. I have one chance not to screw something up on this mission: all I have to do this afternoon is keep Danny away from ulitsa Novatorov. Hope I can manage.

The front desk should hold our bags until we go to the airport. I ring for a bellhop. Once I've double-checked my room and lined up my bags by the door, the bellhop arrives. He loads the bags on his cart, and I ask him to wait.

I knock at the door. "Danny? You ready? I have a bellhop."

He doesn't answer. Must not hear me. Maybe he's in the bathroom. I pull out my key to his room and unlock it, hoping the bellhop doesn't notice or note the abnormality. Like security's one of his big concerns. (Hint: it's on the same end of the scale as privacy.)

"We'd better get going. Check out time," I say as I walk in Danny's room. He doesn't respond. The overhead light is off, though the lamp by the bed is on. But the lighting isn't the only thing that's . . . off.

I turn to the bathroom, dark beyond the door. I return to the hotel room, scanning like he's hiding in a corner.

He's not. I ignore the cold twinge at the back of my neck. "Danny?" I call, like he's under the bed or in invisibility mode or something. (No, we don't have a gadget for that.)

He's fine. Just like he was two nights ago. Just like always. He's fine.

Then it hits me: Danny's not the only thing missing. His bags are gone. His stuff's not on the table. I switch on the bathroom light. The sink and shelf are bare.

The chill spreads up my neck, tingling over my scalp.

"*Devushka?*" the bellhop ventures. "Is everything okay?"

I don't care if Danny would hate me for this: I don't trust the bellhop. "Everything's fine." I march to the door and slap a five-hundred ruble note in his hand. "Take the bags to the front desk and hold them."

The bellhop nods. I shut the door to the room and to the panic threatening to close in on my brain. I'll figure this out. I'll get through this. More importantly, Danny will get through this. He'll be fine. He has to be.

The telephone on the table rings. I jump and whirl on it before I dare to answer. "*Da?*"

"Missing something?" returns a female voice in Russian.

The cold twinge bursts into a thin layer of frost across my back. I don't respond to the question; clearly she knows the answer. "What do you want?"

She laughs, a patronizing arpeggio, and then I place the voice: Nadia.

Has Borya recruited her? Is she working for him?

"What do you want?" I grind out again.

"After the way you two always stared at one another, I assume you'd like Fluker back."

I hesitate. Obviously, DUH, I want my husband back. But Nadia doesn't know how much he means to me—I hope. And if

230

she doesn't, I won't jeopardize his life by letting on. "I'd never work again if I lost a client like that," I say. "What's this about?"

"I think you know," she says. "I think you know a great deal more than you pretend."

Oh, yes. She played me.

But I'll still play my cover.

"What do you mean?" When someone threatens you for knowing too much, playing ignorant is almost funny. You know, when the most important person in your entire world isn't at risk.

"For example," Nadia continues as if I didn't say anything, "I think you have information about locals working for the CIA."

Valya's face when he finally agreed to spy for us, not thirty minutes ago, flashes through my mind. For a split second, I let myself feel just as broken, pleading, and defeated.

I would do anything for Danny. I would protect an agent with my life. I have to. How can I save them both?

I have to stay in cover. "I work for InterpretiRossiya. I don't know what you're talking about."

"Say what you must," Nadia says. "But if you do not produce a list of CIA contacts in Rostov-on-Don in one hour, you'll lose more than your job."

She has no idea how much I stand to lose. She can't. My heart shrivels at the thought. "Please—I can't get that for you. I can't promise that. I'm just an interpreter."

"You have played it well thus far, but your cover will not work any longer. I hope you know not to involve the *politsiya*. They will only cause you more trouble."

Yeah, calling the cops isn't a great course for a spy.

"I can't—I can't—" Not sure whether the stammering is part of my cover or the real failure to understand coming through.

Play. My. Cover. Harder. "I barely know this guy. I don't know if this is worth it."

"I can always send him to Lubyanka Square."

The deep freeze reaches my stomach and it turns to ice, falling faster than a doomed Russian dynasty. Lubyanka was once where the KGB tortured and executed thousands. Now the FSB is headquartered in the same building. Could there be two FSB officers at Shcherbakov?

Or did I guess wrong?

But why else would an aerospace executive meet with an arms dealer?

They're in it together. They must be. And I have to get Danny away from them. "How do I know you have him? You could've watched him go to lunch and then come on this fishing expedition. Which is off the wrong pier, by the way. I don't have what you want."

The saying doesn't translate, or maybe she doesn't hear it, because she doesn't respond. There's still some sound on the phone, though, and I strain to make out the muffled words in the background. "No, thanks."

Danny's voice. Time stops, and so does my breath, my brain, my heartbeat.

She has him.

My mental clock restarts and fast-forwards to real time, replaying the minute I missed: Nadia telling Danny, "Say hello, anything."

"Hello?" Danny comes on the line, full voice.

I grip the receiver, take in air, steel myself. I can do this. I have to.

"Don't worry," I tell him.

"Why would I do that?" he mutters.

More shuffling, then Nadia returns to the line and to Russian. "Satisfied?"

"I still don't have what you want."

"Do you know *Svyato-Iverskiy Zhenskiy Monastyr*?"

Saint Something women's monastery? "No."

232

"Find it. Bring the list on a USB drive to the Cathedral of the Holy Trinity there. One o'clock. Come alone, or you'll be explaining why you've returned to Moscow alone."

"Please, I don't have any way to get that, and Danny—" I cut myself off before the emotion rising in my throat can. But it doesn't matter. She's already ended the call.

And then the reality knocks my knees out from under me. I sink onto the bed. After all the precautions, all the pleading, all the paranoia, they still got him. They have my husband, *my Danny*, and the only way I can get him back is to betray everything I've vowed to protect.

I could give her Valya's name—by the time she verified that he isn't an agent, we'd be safe. But I can't betray Valya, or any other CIA contacts—I *can't*. I don't know anyone, and not only would that mean selling out my own country—exposing those assets would cost their lives.

As if that wasn't enough, the loss could leave American intelligence crippled for decades. Regardless of how valuable Valya's intel might've been, a ranking military officer exposed as a spy? The CIA would have to leave town if word got around we can't protect our assets, and the FSB would see to it that word was splashed across the front page, probably in Valya's blood. With that chilling effect, we'd lose so much access and intelligence in this country—and that would doubtlessly cost more American lives.

I'm a horrible person and a worse CIA officer, but how can I weigh even a hundred American lives, and any amount of Russian agents', against my husband's? I can't. I can't.

I have to.

I know of exactly one CIA (would-be) agent in Russia (not counting Semyon—he's an officer, not an agent, and I seriously doubt he'd respond if I call). I find myself pacing outside Melanyushka's hospital twenty minutes later. Like I can run upstairs and tell her father not to bother—like he's there. Like I can take back everything.

My mind follows the tight circles of my feet, around and around the same logical arguments. There's no CIA scale to weigh out personal feelings versus professional ones. Even if I could take emotions out of the equation, Danny's supposed to be the one person who can keep me sane, keep me grounded, keep me from drowning in the paranoia that was supposed to save us both (ironically).

But all the precautions in the world weren't enough. Because we're American. And everyone assumes Americans in Russia are CIA. Nadia might have even kidnapped Danny thinking he was—but if she's turning to me for intel, she must have ruled him out as an officer.

He's more valuable than that to me. Danny's my concrete connection, the thing that reminds me all the sacrifices I make for this job are worthwhile, because I'm protecting people like him. When I come home at the end of the day, exhausted and broken, he's supposed to be the one person who sees what I'm giving up and reminds me that it's worth it. Nothing is worth losing him.

Not even Valya. But I can't sacrifice him, either. He's more than a (would-be) agent. When you get to know people as well as I knew Valya and Ksena and Svetusya and Melanyushka, when you forever change their lives for the better, when you help them become different, better, happier . . . they don't just get under your skin. They're part of your soul.

I reach an intersection and snap to attention before I wander into traffic across from the Jewish Tatar Cemetery where Danny and I argued.

The solution dawns on me like the sun on the Don.

I don't have to choose. I only have to put one person in danger. I can save Valya *and* Danny.

I just have to sacrifice myself.

CHAPTER 24

I CAN'T REMEMBER EVER FEELING MORE ALONE as the cab pulls up to the convent gates, like the façade amputated from a church. Orthodox crosses decorate the blue doors, only one standing open. Obviously the cab isn't supposed to go any farther.

I'm not the first woman to come here as a last resort, but I could be the first to do it carrying such a deadly secret.

The cabbie leaves me, and I pass under the blue-roofed, gold-domed steeple to the road into the convent. Immediately I see a problem: on my right, there's a big white church with black curved roofs and gold domes on its towers and farther down the road, another church that matches the blue-roofed gates.

My deadline's closing in, and I have to get to the Cathedral of the Holy Trinity. No one's around to ask which building that is.

Before I figure out where to go, a black sedan rolls around the bend in the road ahead of me. I wait for the sedan. It'd be fitting if it were the same car Borya used, but I can't tell. I check the road. Still nobody around. No witnesses.

I should be scared to face the enemy alone. I should fear for my life. I should be petrified. But there's only one thing I'm afraid of: not getting Danny back. Not getting Danny out. As long as I do that, nothing else matters.

When you accept your fate's out of your hands—when you let go—you reach a point past fear. And it's almost peaceful. I'm okay with whatever happens to me as long as I get Danny to safety.

The sedan's driver is short and swarthy: Eager Igor who tried to tail me the other day. (I make friends wherever I go.) I get in the backseat and look at him in the rearview mirror. As soon as my door shuts, he flips a U-turn.

Asking questions isn't worth my breath. Ready to accept my fate, I grip the USB drive in my coat pocket, holding in its fatal secrets.

"Good to see you," he says. "Here, especially."

I raise my gaze to his in the rearview again, and I can see his smile lines smirking. Yeah, super clever, dude. I keep my expression neutral and move only my eyes to stare out the window.

I don't know how Eager Igor got clearance into a convent, but I don't see any tourist cars around. We turn off the paved road to bump over a rutted track until we reach the back gates. Eager Igor suddenly isn't so eager, taking his leisurely time to open the gates before we roll onto a dirt road, and then close them behind us.

Yeah, okay, you've got something over me, and I'm not going anywhere.

Our dirt road becomes paved, and we pass typical Russian houses: cinderblock, brick and cement. But the "neighborhood" thins out into a dense thicket right away. We reach the end of the paved road, back onto another gravel and dirt path, clearly in an industrial area. We pass several electric gates before we reach the one Eager Igor wants. The metal gates swing open for him, and we weave between the neglected warehouses.

I try to swallow and to not think about my last face-off in a warehouse.

Only a few cars are around. Eager Igor narrowly misses a white van as we swing around to park in front of a squatty concrete building—a World War II—era bunker. My fingers cramp and I realize I'm gripping my door handle too tight.

I force air into my lungs and pry my fingers free. It'll be okay. I have a plan. Everything will work out—for Danny. That's all I need.

Eager Igor gets out and rounds the car to get my door. I smooth my copper hair and compose my heavily made-up features into a mask of cool indifference. I'm not Talia Reynolds—or Talia Reynolds Fluker. Most of all, I'm not Danny's wife.

I am Lori Dolman. Coming with a list, I have to admit I'm CIA, so I have to construct a new identity to keep the real me— the real Danny—safe. The interpreter job is now exactly what Nadia thinks, a cover for Lori Dolman, CIA Operations Officer.

I ignore Eager Igor's offered help and climb out of the car. He leads me up to the door in the concrete building. We pass into the interior's shadows.

A single light switches on at the far end of the room, illuminating the counters ringing the walls, stacked with test tubes, beakers and scientific equipment. My heart falls a foot. What have they done to Danny—and what will they do to me? Nadia leans against a table at the front, her arms folded across her chest. (We've got a lover of theatrics.)

Eager Igor shoves me forward. I don't dignify him with a glance. I know how to handle this. I fall into my new cover: detached, distant, dispassionate. I straighten my back and shoulders, lift my chin, and march across the open cement floor. Each clack of my boots' heels echoes off the walls, Eager Igor trailing after me. I don't take my eyes off Nadia. She's the threat. She's the one with the power.

If she's in charge here, what does that make Borya? Her subordinate at the FSB, and her superior at Shcherbakov? Or is he even higher up at the FSB?

"Search her," Nadia commands. "Do it first this time."

At least someone here isn't on their game. Eager Igor pats me down. "Why would I bring a weapon?" I ask. "My list is all the protection I need. You can't shoot me before I hand it over—it's encrypted. You'll never access it without me."

Nadia waves, calling off Eager Igor. I move forward, stopping beyond the circle of light pooling on the concrete floor. "You have something for me," I say, like I'm in total control.

Nadia grins—no, she leers, because she has all the power. (Or so she thinks.) "And you have something for me?"

I laugh, one little syllable. "Do I seem stupid to you, *Durochka Dinochka*?"

Nadia barely flinches at her cover's cruel nickname. "You seem many things, but not stupid."

Yeah, thanks. "Bring Fluker out first. I have to see that he's safe and unharmed."

"No." She doesn't bother explaining her reasoning.

Did something happen to him? Did something go wrong? Did—I can't think like that. I shove the terror screeching through my mind into a tiny box and lock that part of my brain fast.

I will show no fear. I shrug. "Fine." I hold up the USB drive from my pocket. "Your loss."

Nadia's draws in an almost silent breath at the sight of her prize. I slide it back in my pocket and wheel away, playing the bluff to the end.

"Wait," she says. She looks to Eager Igor, then nods to the left. He obeys her signal, following in that direction to the back door of the room.

We're alone in the silence. For a minute, I meet Nadia's eyes, and the pretenses fall away. We see one another for who we are: equals. Counterparts. Spies.

She might be the one making the power play, but she doesn't hold enough cards to wield real control. No matter what happens here, I *will* ultimately win. Our façades might come down—she's not just a secretary, and I'm not just an interpreter—but my real cover stays firmly in place. She will never know who Danny is to me. She might've suspected I had a crush on him, but there's no way she can know how badly I need to save him.

I will get him out of here alive if it's the last thing I do. In fact, I'm pretty sure it might be.

The door opens again to interrupt our moment. He's here—is he okay? Relief and anxiety lace through me, alternately cool and volatile, but I rein in the tumult of emotions. Eager Igor returns with another guard, towing Danny between them. Danny—my Danny—is hooded and handcuffed in front of him. (Crap. I should've taught him how to get out of those. Of course, with guards around, that might not have done him much good.)

Eager Igor reaches the table and stops Danny. He pivots Danny to face me, but I don't address him. I sneer at Nadia. "Do you think I'm an idiot?"

"Excuse me?"

"Take the hood off," I insist. Danny's surely heard my voice, though he doesn't understand my Russian. And, duh, I can recognize my husband's stature and walk and coat and just *him*—but I want to see him, see if he'll be okay.

Nadia snaps at Eager Igor. He obeys and yanks the black hood off Danny's head. Danny sees Eager Igor first and shoots glare-daggers his direction.

"You okay?" I ask, fighting to keep the real concern out of my voice.

"Sure." His acidic sarcasm isn't directed at me. He's fine (or close enough). Now I need him out of here.

"He is unharmed." Nadia's speaking to me, but using English for Danny's benefit. "Satisfied?"

"Not really," Danny interjects. "This won't sound good in my report when I get back."

Nadia doesn't even acknowledge him, turning to me and back to Russian. "Will it sound better than explaining *you*?" she asks. She nods for me to translate for Danny.

Yeah, right.

After a minute, Nadia turns to Danny. "Will it sound as good as explaining you brought a CIA spy?"

Oh, crap. My stomach makes one slow, sick barrel roll. Please, please, please let him keep our real covers safe—though he can't know what they know—

He gapes at me. "You're . . . what?"

Whew. Still safe. I don't acknowledge Danny, fixing Nadia in my sightlines. She holds out a hand. "List?"

I pull out the USB drive for the briefest glance, then slide it back in my pocket, ready to negotiate.

Danny beats me to the punch. "Whoa, whoa, what's this?"

Nadia and I both turn to him. "What?" she asks.

"Don't I deserve to know what I'm being bought for?"

She looks back to me, a condescending smile accompanying her response in Russian. "*Vasha tsena dorogaya. Kazhdiy agent v Rostove-na-Donu.*"

I say nothing. How can I get this over with faster?

"*Skazhi yemu,*" she snaps. *Tell him.*

I wish I could lie, but Nadia speaks enough English to tell. She's making me translate as part of her twisted power puppetry.

If it'll get him out of here, I'll dance for her. I focus on Danny, calm, like every second we're surrounded by probably armed Russians *isn't* driving me insane. "She says you com-

241

mand a high price. Every agent in Rostov-on-Don."

Again, he gapes at me, but this time the horror in his gaze is very, very real. "You can't—you can't do that."

My words walk a tightrope. "Do you know what I stand to lose if I don't?"

"I can't let you. Not for me."

I wave a hand, dismissing his concerns. "My call. My head." I snap my mouth shut. I have to be beyond careful what I say. If Danny has any idea what I'm planning, he could so easily give us both away, even by accident. If he had any idea what I'm planning, he'd never willingly leave this room. But everything I'm planning depends on that.

"Now are you satisfied?" Nadia asks me, still in Russian.

I stick to English, because Danny needs to understand this. "Let him go first. I have to be sure you'll keep your word."

Nadia's expression doesn't change. I repeat myself in Russian.

Now her jaw hardens. "How can I be sure you'll keep yours?"

And this part's something that Danny needs to hear too— but if he understood the full implications, it would bring my plans to save him crashing down. I choose Russian. "I'll stay," I say. "I'll stay until you can guarantee that he's safely clear."

Nadia contemplates the offer for five beats too long. Finally she gives a sharp little nod to Eager Igor, along with the command to make it happen.

Eager Igor unlocks the handcuffs. Danny jerks away, rotating his wrists. More than anything, I want to run to him, make sure he truly isn't hurt, kiss him one last time.

But I can't. I stand there like my boots are buried in the cement beneath my feet, praying Danny keeps the cover, too.

"Thanks a lot," he says to me.

I think—I hope—the sarcasm is for show (again). "Sorry to drag you into this."

"Yeah." He rubs his wrists. "Are we free to go?"

"You are. I'll catch up."

After a long minute, I realize I'm trying too hard to maintain eye contact and sell the lie. I rip my gaze away. "What's the best way out?" I ask Nadia.

She gives directions, and I reflect them to Danny. "Leave the complex the back way." I point south. "Turn west and you'll hit the main road in a couple hundred meters. The word for airport is *aeroport*."

"Okay," he says with a hint of hesitation. Danny starts out, but instead of heading through the door they dragged him in, he strolls toward the door I used—toward me. I stay trained on Nadia as he approaches. When he reaches me, he stumbles and bumps into me. The contact jars my arm, knocking my hand from my pocket, sending that precious drive to the cement floor.

"Sorry." Danny stoops and retrieves the list before I make it there. He presses the list in my palm.

I stare into his eyes, and not because I'm trying to prove I'm not lying. I'm trying to memorize him, make this moment last forever, let him know what I can't say.

I love you.

Goodbye.

I take the USB drive and slide it back in my pocket.

"Well," Danny says on a sigh. "Thanks for everything."

"Just doing my job."

He nods, focused on the floor. Then he walks away. I observe his retreating figure cross the full length of the bunker. Finally, at the door, he looks back. "Oh, hey," he calls, his tone casual, light. "I almost forgot: *rakastan sinua*."

I bite back the smile and tears that threaten. Hopefully Nadia's not among the 1% of the world who speaks Finnish. I swallow before I speak, trying to keep my voice neutral for the response. "*Minä sinuakin, ikuisesti*."

"What's that?" Nadia interrupts.

"American joke." I dismiss the exchange. I wish Danny knew more Finnish, so I could tell him everything else I need to say—but if I told him, he'd stay.

So I think it with every fiber of my being. *Be happy. Be safe. Goodbye.*

I can't say that. I can't say anything. Because I'm not his wife.

But because I *am* his wife, I have to let him go.

Danny flashes the briefest smile, a shadow of his true, eye-crinkling, Talia-melting one, and still my heart stops for a split second, like I can stop this mess from getting any worse, stop the inevitable outcome, stop time.

I can't. And I can't watch him go. I turn away before he slips out the door. One swallow to bury the emotions under the surface, and I'm ready to face fate.

CHAPTER 25

NADIA HOLDS OUT A HAND. "He's free. I've fulfilled my side. The list."

"Not until I know he's clear."

"Fine," she sneers. She turns to the table behind her and picks up a tablet (larger than the one we gave Danny, so no worries there). She swipes the screen for a minute and then offers it to me. "See for yourself."

I approach and take the tablet. She's tapped into the complex's security cameras, trained on the bunker's door and the white van parked outside. Danny walks through the gravel lot at a good pace, probably hurrying to get out of the cold. Maybe even thinking the sooner he gets to the airport, the sooner we'll get out of here.

One of us will. I watch until Danny walks into the next building's shadow and out of the frame, passing underneath the camera. Not safe enough. "He has to make it to the main road."

"You cannot possibly believe he'll save you." Nadia laughs. "What will he do? Call the *politsiya*? They would *applaud* me."

Actually, I think he'd try to find the nearest American consulate (and he's out of luck—gotta go to Kyiv or Moscow). "I want to make sure you don't tail him."

Nadia grumbles, but taps the screen until we switch views to a camera aimed at the street outside the complex. After a minute, Danny emerges through a gate onto the sidewalk. I wait until he disappears from view. My heart strains against my ribs like it's trying to follow him, but I clamp down on the ache with an invisible fist and give the tablet back to Nadia.

She sets it aside and holds out her hand again, but I need to give Danny a little longer to get clear. I glance back at the tablet on the table behind her—next to a phone. Danny's.

Great.

"I believe I warned you about becoming too attached," Nadia says.

The best thing I have to distract her from the man I love is a secret about the one she loves. I don't know how much she knows, so I start small. "Getting too attached? Is that why you're here instead of at ulitsa Novatorov?"

"You're stalling." Nadia pulls back her long black coat to reveal the gun in her waistband, cowboy-style. Eager Igor takes the signal and draws his own weapon. (Guess it's a little late for them to worry about compromising the mission with me.)

Two Russians, two guns—too many variables. But I just need two more minutes to give Danny the chance to run.

I'm about to make a second volley, when I see Nadia's eyes—curiosity's getting the better of her. I wait for her to come to me.

"Why ulitsa Novatorov?"

That's not a leading question—she really doesn't know. I allow a wicked I'm-enjoying-this-too-much smile. "That's where Borya's meeting al-Ansari."

"*The* al-An—wait, how do you know?"

"He warned me to keep Danny away from ulitsa Novatorov now, and he asked me if I knew al-Ansari."

Nadia searches the floor as her brain tries to make sense of this. "Did you?"

"Know al-Ansari? No." I don't bother explaining; it's clear Nadia already knows who he is. And as an FSB officer, she's got to want al-Ansari for the exact opposite reason Borya does. For all I know, our arms-dealing friend's on the local most wanted list.

She glowers. If I'm the target of her anger now, I think I'm merely a proxy for her boyfriend. "I could just arrest you, you know."

"But you won't." I hold up the USB drive. "No me, no encryption key. Or," I say, drawing out the word, lifting her hopes and mine, "you could let me go and go after al-Ansari."

"Shut up. Let me think." Nadia calls me a few nice names, like that's helping her process.

And then it all makes sense. Unless meeting with al-Ansari is an elaborate sting operation even Nadia doesn't know about, Borya isn't FSB. Meeting with an international arms dealer is a big deal. Would he dare betray his country—and his girlfriend— if he knew who Nadia was? "He doesn't know, does he?"

Nadia whirls on me, scowling. "What are you talking about?"

"He doesn't know you're FSB."

"And we're going to keep it that way."

We? Yeah, right. Can I make a run for it?

"Finish our business," Nadia commands. "Give me the list."

Sure. I pull the USB drive from my pocket, and slap it in her hand. But as the plastic leaves my fingers, light hits the stripe of blue on the casing.

That's supposed to be all black.

My plan just hit a patch of turbulence, and my stomach pitches accordingly.

My mind rewinds and then fast-forwards through my last seconds with Danny—him bumping into me. The USB drive hitting the ground. Danny picking it up, placing it in my palm—

hiding it until I closed my fist. So I couldn't see what he'd done.

I never got to teach him sleight of hand before we left Paris, but apparently he didn't need lessons. Because this isn't my USB drive.

My heartbeat halts, and the seconds stretch out, my mind spinning out of control as Nadia plugs in the drive. She'll see it's not the list. She'll know exactly what happened.

What's Danny doing? Why would he take my list, the one thing that—that bought his freedom. The realization sweeps over me like a coating of ice. He's trying to save me from sacrificing these agents for him and getting me out of here. What's his plan when they catch him? Using that bargaining chip?

Danny's doing this for me. He's trying to save my life. But what he doesn't know—he's ruined everything. Now we're both in twice as much danger.

"What is this?" Nadia hisses. "Expected expenditures? Itineraries? Sights to see?" She flips the tablet screen to me, and I verify the file titles—our honeymoon plans. In English. Obviously not lists of Russian names. And under the author column—Danny Fluker.

Time to run. I look for an escape, but find only Nadia's intense eyes. Every ounce of fury in her system aims at me. She jerks the USB drive out of the adapter and hurls it at me. Even *Durochka Dinochka* could find the list.

"Where's Fluker?" she seethes, advancing on me.

I fall back a step. "How would I know?"

Nadia reaches out. I retreat again, but she's signaling Eager Igor. He appears behind me. I maneuver so he isn't aiming that gun *directly* at me, but that's the best I can do now.

"Hold her," Nadia commands. "Keep her hidden."

"Where are you going?" Eager Igor asks.

"To get my list. And if I don't . . ." She draws back her coat, planting a hand on her hip, brandishing her gun again. Her gaze meets mine. "I will hunt *you* down."

Nadia backs away wearing a smug grin, her other guard in tow, both staring at me until she reaches the door.

She can't get to Danny. Right?

The fear already in my veins shouts the answer: yeah, right. I told him where to go, in front of her.

That noble sacrifice I planned to make? Moot. Danny may be trying to save me, but the flaw in his plan is very big, very bad, and very fatal.

The reason I knew I was going to my death with this bargaining chip list? Every. Single. Name. Came off a Jewish Tatar gravestone.

CHAPTER 26

THE DOOR CLOSES BEHIND NADIA, and I can finally deal with Eager Igor. This is Nadia's plan, not his. Maybe he can be bought or bullied or beaten.

Odds aren't great for any of the above, but I have to try something. "I'll give you five hundred thousand rubles to let me go." (Not quite $15,000. Believe me, I can get that if I need it.)

He snorts in derision.

"A million."

He laughs. "You're wasting your words."

"Okay." I move a pace closer, invoking the universal tone of *I'm leveling with you.* "I'm not going anywhere. Not worth getting shot."

Eager Igor casts a wary eye my way. As he should. I don't exactly *enjoy* having a gun aimed at me, but I doubt this will work out for him like he thinks. I keep my gaze on his while my brain runs through a visualization. Normally, I'd wait for an opportunity, but today there's no time. If I act first, I have the advantage—I might even be able to end the conflict before Eager Igor figures out what's happening.

I take a deep breath, commanding my muscles to relax.

Can't let the energy already streaming through my system give me away. One more breath. One more mental run-through. One more second.

Go.

I seize his gun hand and wrist. I whip his arm up and smack him in the face with his own weapon. While he stumbles backward, I grab the barrel and wrench away the gun.

Now it's safely in my grasp. Eager Igor recovers enough to give me a scowl that could cause second-degree burns.

He lunges for me. A sharp strike to the temple with the butt of the gun brings him to his knees. I'm running before I hear him grunt.

I slam through the door, scanning the parking lot, but Nadia's vanished into frigid air. Picking up speed with every step, I start toward the next building. Did Nadia get a car?

That van in front of the bunker. It's gone.

Finally, I reach the gate to the street. A white van roars past, headed the same direction Danny did. He's long gone, safely in a taxi by now, and I've got to keep moving too. I trail after the white van. By the time I reach the main road, the white van's ridiculously far ahead, off in the distance, barely discernible amid traffic. Escaping.

Danny could be anywhere, but realistically, unless he went back to the hotel, he has to be going to the place I just told him to go: *aeroport.*

I.e., the place I just told him to go right in front of Nadia. Right in front of a rival spy.

I grab my phone, but before I send a message, I remember— they took his phone. I've got to find him. Taxis dot the afternoon rush. They're great when you know where you're going (and how to get there), but I can't rely on a taxi driver to speed and maneuver to safety. If that's even possible. Nothing like a car of your own when you need to turn as soon as the impulse hits your spy intuition.

Do I risk stealing a car or searching for someone kind enough to leave their keys? Try CIA mind tricks to convince someone to loan me their car? Do I know anyone I could call?

Wait. I *do* know somebody who lives on this side of town. I even have his number. Garo.

I pull his business card from the hidden pocket in my sleeve lining. Within a minute, my phone is ringing. Please let him be around. Please let him answer. Please let him help.

"*Da?*"

"Garo, it's Sestra Reynolds." I wince inwardly at using my real name, but my options are dwindling.

"You have called! You—"

I cut off his celebrating without trying to correct him. "I need a favor."

Normally, I'd try to make this favor sound as insignificant and easy as possible—but I have neither the time nor the inclination. "I need a car. Do you know anybody who has one?"

Garo hesitates for a moment. "To borrow?"

"Yes." As long as I survive.

I check traffic, like I'll catch Danny's cab circling this block, while Garo sits in silence. "Is this a joke?" he asks at last.

"I wish it were."

"Well . . . all right. Two of my neighbors have cars. Let me phone them."

"Thank you." Already the idea of waiting has me bouncing on my toes. "Would they have their cars at home?"

"One of them, probably."

"I'll head that way. Thank you," I say again. I turn up the street for Garo's building. Doubt he's moved since I lived here—not how it works in Russia—plus he'd mention that, right?

Every second, one word repeats in a low thrum through my brain: Danny. Danny. Danny. I scan my memory of Garo's building, trying to drown out the fear. I think the only time we tried to talk to his neighbors, a screetchy lady stalked us door to door until we had to leave. Fortunately, it's a short trip to Garo's, just long enough for me to text him and ask for confirmation and his friend's apartment number. I run straight up to number 27 and knock.

And then, it hits me: I'm in disguise. If Garo described me to them to let them know what to expect, or if they mention the kind-of-inescapable fact I'm (currently) a redhead (as opposed to the brunette he saw two days ago), things will get weird.

Too late. The neighbor answers, a bright-eyed babushka.

"I'm Garo's friend," I start.

"Certainly, come in."

"I'm so sorry, I'm in a hurry—it's an emergency."

She opens her mouth to protest, and my heart clenches. I don't have time for chitchat when Danny's life is on the line. But at the last second, the babushka pauses and cocks her head to the side, studying me. "All right. Let me get the key."

"Thank you," I say, repeating it after she gives me the key.

"It's a Škoda Yeti. Parked on the street. It was my son's."

I have no idea what kind of car a Yeti is, but I thank her one more time and start to go—but wait. I turn back. "What's the fastest way to the airport from here?"

The babushka's bright eyes take on a twinkle. "You must not take Koroleva prospekt. You would think it would be faster, but you must take ulitsa Vavilova to ulitsa Nansena. You can cut your trip by ten minutes with traffic at this hour."

"Thank you!" I shout one last time as I run from the building. I could save a lot more than ten minutes with a shortcut. I could save my husband's life.

A Yeti's a small SUV, and Garo's neighbor's directions are spot on. My pulse pounds so hard I have to switch on the defrost. After only twenty minutes, I'm closing in on the airport ridiculously fast.

Not fast enough to turn time backward, of course. Danny's probably already here. Nadia too. Can I get to him first?

I don't know—but I do know I'll be spotted the minute I pull into the airport in this disguise. I shrug off my red jacket, shoving it out of sight of the window. My other coat's back at the hotel. I can face the cold—but if I have to get out of the car without a coat, I'll attract a lot of unwanted attention.

What if Nadia's already got him?

No. I can't let myself think that way. I start on the hairpins holding my wig in place. I'm almost there.

What will she do to him? Will he give up the "list"? *Then* what'll she do with him?

Focus. Focus. I try to keep up with traffic, the current speed limit, and the last of my hairpins. Anything to keep my mind too busy to spiral down the slippery slope of speculation.

Even with the shortcut, do I have any hope of finding him before she does?

I finally free the wig and tug off the wig cap as well, releasing my braids and bangs. That may not be enough to help, but I'll take any little semblance of a disguise.

Hope sprouts in my chest. Could Danny have donned a disguise? I don't know where he would have gotten one— where are his bags?

I reach the final turn into the airport and spot something to fry that fragile shoot of hope: a white van, turning ahead of me. Nadia? I have no idea—and no time to stop.

I cruise the road, but scan the parking lot, the sidewalk in front of the terminal. Too many taxis—no chance of telling which might be his. If he even made it this far.

Stay positive. He's here. I'll find him—before Nadia does. I have serious advantages: I could recognize Danny from any angle, and quite possibly through any disguise.

I slow to watch more closely, but none of the pedestrians on their way to the building have the same stride as Danny. None of them have the same height and build, none—wait. My lungs frost over, and not just because the temperature has to be somewhere south of freezing.

The gait, the height, even the coat and hat. It's the inside of the reversible jacket I gave him. And he's heading up to the terminal.

I gun the engine and whip around the taxi pulling in front of me, cutting him off—and I overshoot and jump the curb. Nobody will notice the crazy lady driving on the sidewalk, right?

No such luck: half a dozen pedestrians gawk at me, backing away. I lean across the seat to roll down the window. (Power windows? You're cute.) But before I crack it enough to call to him, Danny spots me. He jogs up and yanks the door open. "Fancy meeting you here." He may be joking, but his eyes show the real relief. He hops in and I hit the gas almost before he has the door shut.

I pause at the stop signs and run a (barely) red light, not daring to slow until we're out of sight of the airport. My gaze is on the rearview more than the road, scanning for that white van.

Finally, we hit a traffic light that's good and red, and cross traffic's too heavy to risk it. I stop, but my heart keeps racing.

To complete that effect, Danny leans across the car and draws me in for a kiss full of all the intensity and adrenaline running through both our bloodstreams.

We made it. I have Danny back. Safe.

Now I just have to keep him that way.

CHAPTER 27

THE LIGHT TURNS GREEN, and I have to pull away from Danny and drive.

"I was starting to worry," Danny begins.

"You doubted me?" My cockiness is unconvincing, so I push the conversation forward before he can comment. "Where'd you get the USB drive?"

"Hid it in my shoe before they searched me."

I glance at him—he tricked Fyodor the same way, only with a pocketknife. (Which we'd have if it weren't for the stupid TSA.) "Why?"

"It had your real name on it, all our honeymoon plans. I had to protect you."

"Sweet, but what were you thinking?"

"I was thinking I couldn't let you do that for me."

I can't believe this—I mean, I do, I just wish he wouldn't do that. "You didn't know what I was doing."

"Um, betraying your country? Didn't we just take someone down for the exact same thing?"

"What did you think would happen when the list wasn't on there?" I monitor the rearview. No white vans. Has Nadia

256

brought in backup? "What did you think they'd do to me?"

He pauses. "Send you after me." His tone carries a note of doubt.

Yeah, not the best plan. "We're lucky they didn't pick the quicker route with me and then come after you themselves. You couldn't bargain with them."

"Oh, but you can?"

The truth must be evident on my face because confusion flickers across his. "What?" Danny asks.

"The list's fake. They would've killed you too."

Heavy silence smothers us. Danny doesn't speak until we hit another stoplight. He gets the implications, but he still asks, "So your endgame was . . . ?"

"I had to get you out of there." I scan the mirrors again. One white van. Minivan. "Anything else was icing."

"I don't want you to do that for me. Ever."

"I know. You didn't ask me to." But I'd do it every day to keep him safe. And to keep him safe now, I consult the rearview again. "I need to pick up some things." And then? If we don't want to go back to the Rostov airport, the nearest one is in Donetsk, three hours and the Ukrainian border away.

Maybe a train. The station should run to Volgograd, Sochi, Moscow—hours away. If they catch the same train, or warn someone at the end of the line—it only takes a phone call—

"Wait a minute." Danny breaks into my thoughts, and I jump. "You went in there to *die* for me, and you don't even trust me to check a locker for you?"

"No, Danny—" I cut myself off to change lanes.

I brace myself for his argument, but he doesn't say anything. When I look, I find him staring straight ahead, his eyes . . . resigned.

This—this is what I've gotten wrong the last two days. "I'm stupid, okay? I just didn't put it together."

"What, that I might be capable of doing something?"

Why do we have to have this conversation while driving? I make a right and hit a red light. First time I've been glad for that today. I grab Danny's hand. "You know what?" I say. "Maybe. Maybe I did think that. But I was wrong—and you've proven that by a lot more than opening a locker."

A smile lights his eyes and Danny starts to lean in, but the light turns green. I have to hit the gas. He settles for squeezing my hand. "So glad you made it out."

"Me too."

"How'd you manage?"

"Distracted Nadia—mentioned Borya's date with an arms dealer—until she realized you had the list and took off after you." I consult the mirror again. White van. Time to turn. "Then I got away."

"Wait, what?"

I pause the conversation to take a left; the van doesn't follow. "Which part?"

"Borya's doing what?"

"Meeting an arms dealer." We run into another red light. "Think I found his plan to save Shcherbakov."

"No, *I* did."

I whip around to stare at Danny. "What?"

"I take it you didn't get my text saying I found something?"

My brain runs in three different directions, trying to figure out what Danny's talking about, trying to remember when he texted, trying to watch for white vans tailing us.

Danny jumps to the conclusion for me. "We have to stop him."

"Wait—what did you find?"

"'P' is an 'R' in Cyrillic, right? As in CCCP—USSR?"

"Yeah?" I monitor him from the corner of my eye, waiting for him to explain the non sequitur.

"I can figure out the rest of камера. They were on one of the drives you copied."

Aerospace plans with a camera—just like the ones Fyodor stole. "Are you sure? They're yours?"

"That's like asking if I'd recognize you."

A chill crawls across my skin to curl up in my stomach. If Borya has Danny's plans, and Borya's meeting with an arms dealer, even if they're talking about floral arrangements, we need to be sure. We've got to get over there and stop him. But I can't put Danny in harm's way again.

He cuts into my thoughts. "How do you know he's meeting with an arms dealer?"

"He warned me to keep you away. He likes you, too."

"When was this? During your copious amounts of private conversation?"

If I didn't know better, I'd say he was getting jealous (but considering I had zero alone time with Borya that Danny knows of, I'm pretty sure that's just sarcasm). "Last night. He basically kidnapped me to tell me not to tell you this."

Danny simply gapes at me. "When?"

"After—" *After you told me this was all in my head.* For obvious reasons, I can't say that. "—the hospital. On my way back."

Danny takes my meaning and falls silent.

I check the mirrors one more time, then pull onto the first side street that isn't a dead-end. I grab my phone and dial Semyon.

"We have backup?" Danny guesses.

"Maybe." Maybe not. Not like Semyon wants to hear from me. It's already rung four times, five. Six. "No answer." I end the call and open the encrypted texting app. *B has the plans; possible incomings to ul. Novatorov.* Seems like enough, right?

The app adds a delay, but I can't imagine it takes a lot of processing power and time to encode nine words. Silence settles over us like the cold, humid air as I wait. And wait. And wait.

In case it's merely stress playing tricks on me, I check the clock on my phone. Nope, it's been five minutes. Plenty long enough. Unless you're trapped.

One more chance. I hit the button to dial him again, and let it ring. (No voicemail—wouldn't want an agent to leave a message someone might hack.)

We really do have to go in. I end the call.

Danny doesn't need an explanation. "We have to stop him."

"Guessing I can't ask you to hide in an airport bathroom until our flight?"

"Uh, let's see. Last time your plan was to die, so . . . no."

"Worth a shot," I mutter. I stare at my white knuckles on the steering wheel, like that will somehow let me control this situation. My instincts scream I've put Danny in too much danger this week—not just this week. Over the last three months. How can I risk him again? How can I make him—?

I can't make him do anything, just like I haven't made him do any of this: today, the mission, our marriage. He's totally on board, and whenever I've needed him (and let him), he's executed perfectly.

We can do this, and we will—together. Because I'm not just on my own anymore. We're building a marriage, a team, a new thing. Scary and uncertain . . . and right.

Danny's eyes scrunch like he's really contemplating something. "What if I told you I had an idea?"

Against my will, one eyebrow creeps up. "I don't know," I say, carefully working around each word.

"Hey, give me some credit here. I *did* put the pieces together on this."

I shoot him a *touché* expression—but I'm still hesitating.

And it's still obvious. Danny gives me a look of *seriously, come on.* "Need I remind you whose idea it was to get married?"

My *touché* turns into a skyward glance. "Are you trying to

convince me that was a good idea or a bad one?"

"Fine, let's go with your plan." He avoids all sarcasm, keeping his tone neutrally magnanimous. I'd be convinced if it weren't for the underglow of gloating in his smile.

But he's got me and he knows it: I don't have a plan. "Okay, let's hear it."

For half a second, his gloating grin turns into his eye-crinkling, Talia-melting, heart-catchingly-genuine smile. And then he starts into his plan.

Just when I thought I couldn't love him any more. Don't know if I've ever been so happy to be so wrong.

CHAPTER 28

WE'VE PICKED UP OUR BAGS FROM THE HOTEL (Danny had sent his down to the front desk before they kidnapped him; I'm telling you, he's brilliant), and changed back to our "regular" disguises: Danny's coat is right-side out and he's lost the hat; I'm back in my red coat and wig. We've done all we can to prep. Time to put Danny's plan into action. Together.

We roll down ulitsa Novatorov in our borrowed SUV. The area's deceptively quiet for the residential and commercial mix.

Danny points across the street. I look: amid the evergreens, a camouflage-painted combat helicopter on a pedestal. Fitting for someone going into battle.

We've found the Rostvertrol complex. Good place to start searching.

I take the next left into their parking lot—and there's a gate. I roll up to the guard station and roll down my window as slowly as possible, giving me a whole three extra seconds to think.

I'd love to use elicitation or mind tricks or other impressive spy skills to get what we need, but we do not have the time for the observation and persuasion and finesse required. So I go for the sledgehammer of social engineering: all-purpose, appealing to baser instincts, and fast.

I hold out a banknote in the largest denomination they print, five thousand rubles.

Bribery is a line-item in our budget. The guard accepts and raises the boom barrier. We roll past.

"You know, you're pretty awesome," Danny comments.

I stop scanning my side of the street to cast him a smirk. "Just learning this?"

"No. I've known it a long time."

We head deeper into the helicopter complex, following the road until I see a sign: СтАлюминия, Компания Щербакова. *StAlyuminiya*—steel aluminum? *Kompaniya Shcherbakova*: a Shcherbakov company.

"That's it." I nod at it, but I don't slow down or stop.

"Park at the next building." Danny nods at the next warehouse beyond the trees.

"I've done this once or twice."

"Right, sorry."

I look over at him. "Actually, I appreciate it—it's nice working with you."

A grin hides in his eyes. Around the corner from the Shcherbakov place, I pull into the lot of a neighboring building and park in its shadow. I look to Danny one last time. "Ready?" I breathe.

He holds up a red USB drive. "Close enough."

"Okay." I signal for us to move out, and Danny obeys without hesitation. But that might be the last time I'm in control today. I step out of the car, too, and lock it (like that'll do us any good). Danny's already starting toward the Shcherbakov warehouse. I jog to keep up. "Hey!" I whisper-shout.

He stops and waits for me. "Sorry," he says. "Want to get it over with."

I take his hand for a quick squeeze. Together, we reach the

corner of the building, peering out at the black Jeep Cherokee parked near the front of the Shcherbakov warehouse. Borya's car. He's still here; one factor in our favor. Now, if only we could see inside. There have to be others here—a couple cars sit beyond Borya's. Can we sneak up on them?

"Security cameras." Danny indicates the roof's corners. Nadia had tapped into the cameras at her rendezvous. Has Borya done the same?

And then I notice something beyond the opposite corner of the warehouse: the back of a white van.

Right. Because I told a federal agent where her boyfriend was meeting with a wanted arms dealer. I'd be here too—but it doesn't make it easier on us. "Nadia's here," I tell him.

"Do we avoid her?"

"She'll be watching the cameras if she can. Don't like adding an unknown variable."

Danny studies the building. "Find her and add her to the plan."

"Easier said than done."

He turns to me. "If I said the words 'Wookiee prisoner,' would you know what I meant?"

I release his hand to grip his coat lapel. "I love you."

"I know."

I catch *that* allusion too and groan. I throw that mostly-fake aggravation into my cover and start out, dragging him behind me, my expression annoyed in case someone's watching. And on that note—"Resist some more. This was your idea."

He immediately obeys, stopping so abruptly that he jerks me backward and nearly wrenches free. "By the way, you know what you just said sounds totally crazy."

He has a point. I tug on his coat and raise my voice for any-one who might be listening. "Come on."

We cross the last feet to the Shcherbakov warehouse,

aiming for that white van. Clear of the cameras a minute, I press myself against the back of the building and Danny does the same. I exhale slowly and barely peek around the corner. The rolling garage door to a high loading dock is open beyond the apparently empty van. Could be a trap, but Nadia has no reason to believe anyone's following her.

"'Kay," I say. I pull Danny around the corner after me. I can't drag him onto the loading dock, but we climb up, and I grab his coat again.

I lead him in, blinking like that'll make my vision adjust to the dark faster. "Storage," Danny mutters, his eyes on the tall metal racks holding various metal parts. Nobody in sight.

Tough enough to choreograph a Russian ballet on the fly, but when your principals are unaccounted for, it's nearly impossible to get your timing right. "Nadia?" My call echoes. No answer.

Is she out front with Borya? Who else might be out there—or in here?

As soon as I think it, a hand seizes my arm. I whirl around and whip free of the stranger's grasp.

But it's not exactly a stranger. It's (a very surprised) Eager Igor. And I just dragged my husband back to face him. Sometimes I'm a genius.

This was all part of the plan—Danny's plan. We're going with it. I shake my handful of Danny's coat lapel. "He has the list."

Eager Igor suddenly isn't so eager. "We should wait for Nadezhda Vasilyevna."

"Get her in here." But if that isn't her van out back . . .

"I will search him, then I will get her."

Nope. Not only am I *not* letting go of Danny, but if Eager Igor takes our game-changer bartering tool, it might negate all our careful choreography.

"Don't you think I've searched him already?" I shake

265

Danny's coat once more for emphasis and he shifts away from me slightly, enough to complete the effect.

"I'll call Nadezhda Vasilyevna."

We've got time to kill, and we have to make this look believable—and not give Eager Igor the chance to think too much—so I grope for one of our script ideas. "What were you thinking?" I ask Danny. "Why would you jump into something that didn't involve you?"

"Didn't involve me? Pretty sure kidnapping me from my hotel is 'involving' me."

"You had a chance to get away, and you didn't take it." The instant I say that, I realize I've made an excellent argument if we're both in our covers. Taking that list makes absolutely perfect sense if he's my husband. It makes absolutely no sense if he's my interpreting client. Clearly Danny sees the logical fault. (It'd be nice if Eager Igor really didn't speak English.)

"You know," comes a woman's now-familiar voice reverberating through the shadows, "for someone who worked this hard to free Danny, I am surprised you bring him back."

Danny shoots *me* a glare so cold, the Russian winter outside seems inviting. (I've never been so glad to have married a man who was a drama geek. In high school. Briefly.) "Yeah," he agrees with Nadia.

I pitch my response toward the corner where I think she is. "Oh? So you were lying when you threatened to hunt me down if you didn't get the list?"

"Not at all." She strolls out of the dark and into the column of light from the door, her footsteps echoing over the cement floor like mine did not that long ago. Her dark coat and hat set off her platinum hair in a stark contrast that matches the stern set to her face. She can make an entrance when she wants. (Should've picked up on that with her dramatic setup earlier.)

"Yeah, well, I like being alive, and I'd like to stay that way."

Instead of acknowledging me, she focuses on him. "And

Danny. Why *did* you interfere?"

He scowls at her, then me. "I want what's mine. You people have no right to take it. I'm here to get it back." For a minute, I'm not sure if he means the plans or me.

Nadia doesn't notice any double meaning. She glances at the tablet she's holding (security cameras?), then over her shoulder. I track her gaze to a window to a front office. The shade's drawn, but the light silhouettes two men, one freakishly tall. Borya.

"Give me the list, and we'll all go," Nadia says. She speaks to Eager Igor in Russian. "We can still get out without him knowing."

Who knowing? Borya? That's my cue. I release Danny to reach into his pocket and snatch the red USB drive. "Here!" I step to the edge of the light. "I've got your stupid list. Now will you leave us alone?"

And all eyes are on me, and the prize I'm holding aloft. For a moment, we all stand there—and then the chaos begins.

Nadia's the first to move. She nearly drops the tablet and runs for me.

Danny's turn. "No, wait," he shouts. He reaches for the USB drive, but I plant my free hand on his chest and keep the drive as far away as I can. He tries to maneuver around me, but I can hold a man-to-man defense (not that it did me much good fighting off three older brothers).

Nadia plucks the USB drive from my fingers, and I push Danny back a couple feet, still holding him at bay. He comes at me again, but I grab his arms to stop him. He keeps shouting at Nadia. "Don't! That's the wrong one!"

She aims a skeptical eyebrow at him, not about to be persuaded. A cold weight sinks in my middle. I hope that's the curiosity we want and not the suspicion we need to squelch.

No. We've got this. "Shut up," I snap at Danny, and shove him back another step. "I saved your life with that list, thank you very much, and you had to go screw it up."

"That's the wrong one," he insists—and loudly. At least we're getting that part right.

"*Tsss!*" Nadia attempts to quiet us. "*Zatknis'!*"

Shut up? Yeah, right. Nadia pulls an adapter from her coat pocket and hooks up the USB drive. While her attention's away from us, I nod for Danny to continue.

"Stop her," he pleads with me at full volume (and then some). "That's not your drive."

He's supposed to be doing more than arguing with me. I give him a look of *come on already, just do it.* He shoots back an I-don't-want-to expression. To which the only possible response would be a face that says *don't be a wuss.* We have to sell the lie.

That probably wouldn't be enough to goad my husband into what he needs to do, but the situation is adding urgency. Enough to cut off the argument.

Danny shoves me aside. I was expecting it, but my stumbling heel snags on a crack in the cement. I twist to catch myself. Hot, icy pain ignites in my ankle and I slam to the ground.

Bad. Really bad. I freeze on the floor, trying to recover my breath, hoping Danny plays his part. He doesn't stop to help me, he doesn't look back—he does exactly what we planned, exactly what I need him to. He strides over to Nadia to get his USB drive back.

"That isn't what you want," Danny tells Nadia (still loudly). He reaches around her to snatch the drive away.

"Get him off me," she snaps.

Eager Igor moves in to defend her. I clamber to my feet, favoring my good leg. But when I try to move, pain slices through my ankle like a shard of freezing glass. I barely manage to stay upright, and I can't stop the yelp that escapes.

Danny whips around to look at me at exactly the wrong

time. Eager Igor has to hop to grab him by the collar, but he yanks Danny right off his balance (and I've barely kept mine).

Eager Igor wrestles Danny's arms behind him. I start for them in an awkward limp, but I'm too late. Nadia strolls up and gets in Danny's face. "*Dotron'sya do menya eshcho raz*," she says, her voice dangerously quiet, "*i umresh' prezhde, chem uspeyesh' pozhalet' ob etom*." She stays there, an inch from his face, but she's talking to me. "Translate, Lori. Tell him what I said."

"I think he can figure it out from context," I murmur.

"Tell. Him."

I take a deep breath. A week ago, a day ago, an hour ago, I would've pegged out the terror-meter. Part of my brain is scared—I'd have to be crazy to not be—but suddenly, even though they have Danny, I'm not panicking.

Because no matter what happens, we're in this together. It's not just me fighting to keep him safe, or him fighting for me. We're a team, fighting to get through this together.

Maybe Sylvie and her forty-two years of marriage were onto something.

I translate Nadia's threat, though it's a little hollow now. "She says, 'Touch me again and you won't live to regret it.'"

Danny, to his credit, doesn't flinch or react, holding her gaze, calm and level. Nadia stands there glowering at him for another second.

No time for pain—and neither of us can afford it. I have to *not* be hurt. So I won't. I gingerly place my foot on the floor, keeping my weight on my good foot. Distraction. I need—I need to keep up the cover, too. "What do you mean that's not what she wants?" I yell. "What did you do with the list?"

"I have it, I have it." Danny turns to me to make the argument.

"Shut your jaws!" Nadia shoots us a glare. She plugs the USB drive into the adapter.

"Where is my list?" I insist. "Do you have any idea what I went through to get that?"

Danny tries to pull free from Eager Igor's grasp. "I have your list! Just give me that drive and I'll give you the one you want."

Nadia pauses, cagily watching him, clearly trying to gauge whether he's telling the truth.

Yeah, I definitely don't want her scrutinizing him too long with that intent. Danny's far enough away to justify a real shout from me. "If that's not my list, what is it?"

"What is it indeed?" A new voice—a familiar voice—carries from the shadows past the table. "What is going on?" he demands.

Every single one of us goes still. The footsteps approach, measured and calculated. Finally he reaches us, and we can see him past the bright light over the table. But we already know who it is: Borya.

CHAPTER 29

"**W**HAT ARE YOU DOING HERE?" Borya looks over each of us with varying degrees of hurt. "Danny?"

Nadia pointedly waves Eager Igor off, and he releases Danny.

"I'm sorry," I break in, half-hopping to him. "This is Nadia's fault."

But Borya's not listening. He turns to Nadia, the real hurt playing across his face. "*A ty zhe?*" *And you too?*

"You don't know what's going on, Borya," she says—but the set to her jaw, uneasy and forced, says the cold voice is a brave front that she's hoping all of us, all the way up to Borya, will buy. "You need to go. Now."

"I can't."

Danny cuts his gaze toward me, but I don't dare translate. I'm too busy watching Nadia's reaction. Whatever Borya's meeting al-Ansari about, it's not good for Nadia.

Is Borya a double agent? Probably should've considered that sooner. I certainly don't want to jump in the middle of an FSB internal affair. Is this a setup for me?

No. No way. I saw Nadia's reaction to Borya and al-Ansari.

I know what I'm doing. I'm stirring the pot, and I'm doing it on purpose. And I'm about to do it some more. "So who is al-Ansari?" I ask.

Nadia rounds the table to advance on him, still clutching the tablet. "Yes, *Borya*." The emphasis suggests she normally uses a much more familiar nickname with him. "Tell me about this al-Ansari."

"None of your concern, Dinyushen'ka." Borya turns his tone somewhere between *don't worry your poor little head, Naddiekins,* and *do not interfere in my affairs.* "A business meeting."

Whether it's the tone or the situation, Nadia bristles, the lines around her mouth tightening. "I'm your secretary," she says. "*I* schedule your business meetings."

"You're my secretary," Borya repeats, his own jaw almost too tight to squeeze out the words. "Not my mother."

"And what would Yelena Petrovna say about her son secretly meeting an arms dealer?"

Borya does a double take. "How do you know that?"

This would be a great time to make our escape, but there's one little obstacle in our way—the entire reason we came here. Borya still has those drone plans, and unless al-Ansari is driving off into the sunset now, we still have a shot at stealing it back before it goes up for auction. Kinda of crucial, you know, for the safety of Americans and the security of Canadian drone technology (which I understand is important to Danny).

"Leave," Nadia insists to Borya. My pulse counts the seconds of a tension-filled minute before her intense stare becomes more earnest—more pleading. "Leave while you can."

And that's enough to (finally) tip Borya off something more's going on. He surveys me and Danny, Eager Igor, and then Nadia until, at last, his gaze drifts down to the tablet and red USB drive in her hand. "What's this?" he asks, his tone hushed. Like he suddenly realizes all this time he's been a fool.

Even the golden child of Shcherbakov doesn't have enough info to put together the pieces. Nadia won't clue him in, either. Her tone turns imploring. "It's not about you. Please."

He scoffs. "You're upset I'm meeting al-Ansari, while you're with *my* business contact?" With that expression, he doesn't have to speak to add a final *you're unbelievable.*

Borya nods at the USB drive and tablet and switches to English for Danny's benefit, since this is something Danny should hear (and verify). "It's his, isn't it? That's what all the shouting is about?"

"Of course it's mine," Danny interjects before Nadia responds. I realize he's been maneuvering closer to me.

"You need to give it back," I insist to Borya. I pivot to Nadia. "If that's not the list, it's none of your business."

Borya ignores her, contemplating the tablet. While he's distracted, Danny moves the last couple feet to take my arm, taking my weight off my hurt ankle.

I glance up at him with a head jerk/eye point to say *aren't you going after them?* Once again, he gives me the slightest are-you-really-really-*really*-sure? expression. "Go," I mouth, extracting my arm from his grasp.

Danny crosses the distance to Borya. He yanks the USB drive from the adapter. Borya's too stunned to move, but Eager Igor lunges for Danny—until Borya shoots a look at Nadia, who ricochets the kill signal to Eager Igor. Spared, Danny falls back to stand by me again.

Borya snaps around to meet Danny's gaze. "What *is* that?"

"Nothing. A stupid project."

Borya looks back at the tablet, like he can keep the plan on the screen from slipping away. Golden Child of Shcherbakov, meet Golden Child of NRC Aerospace. "This is the one," Borya breathes. Now *he's* the awed one. "The 'pet project' you were telling me about."

Something twists in the pit of my stomach. I don't know

what's on this USB drive. Danny told me he had a plan, something that would work—bait. I didn't think I needed to press my own husband for details.

But could this be worse than letting the original drone slip out of our grasp?

Hello? Is my husband stupid? Of course not. (Rocket scientist.) And I trust him. I have to.

"The one you speak about with . . ." Borya searches for the right word, but gives up after a minute. "You speak about this like a beautiful woman who somehow said yes to you."

I dig my nails into Danny's arm (not the best way to remind him *not* to turn to me, if that's where his mind was going in the first place). "I guess, yeah."

"I've seen your work," Borya finishes, "but this is . . . *isklyuchitel'no.*"

"Is that a compliment?"

I don't know if Danny's asking me, but I interpret. "Exceptional."

"So when did you see my work?" he asks Borya.

He raises his gaze to Danny's again, and the hunted, haunted look there is exactly what none of us wants to see. He's psychologically backing into a corner. "You showed it to me. That drone is nothing compared to this, but—"

"I never said whether I worked on drones."

I fight back the smile. Even that statement's carefully calculated: he doesn't actually indicate he worked on drones, eluding some clever elicitation.

"'That drone is nothing'?" Another voice carries from behind Borya. Our final principal, the wild card: al-Ansari. He emerges from the shadows. Curly black hair cut short, well-trimmed, well-tanned, well-tailored, the image of the refined, Westernized Arab businessman. He strolls over, hands in his pockets (rude in Russia), surveying our little tableau. "Am I interrupting?"

Yes, of course, everybody speaks English. (Why do I bother?)

Al-Ansari turns to Nadia, then me, but he's still speaking to Borya. "I see you've already invited the guests. We should hurry to conclude our business and continue this party."

Borya doesn't hesitate: he moves to block al-Ansari's view of Nadia. "Let's finish our business, and we'll have something to celebrate. But not with these people. They're no one."

Al-Ansari's lip twitches. "These ladies must join. Then it will be a celebration."

"They have no reason to join us," Borya repeats. "They're not important."

Under other circumstances, I might be insulted, but I'll let the man defend us.

"I know Fyodor took the plans," Danny says. Even from behind, Borya's flinch is obvious. He slowly swivels to regard Danny.

"What are you talking about?" Apparently he's burned through his bluff budget, because the lie lurks too close to the surface.

"Fyodor stole plans from my office. I came to get them back."

Nadia barks with laughter. "You bargain for them now? In your position—"

Borya interrupts her. "You don't know what you're talking about."

"You're not good at pretending. You're selling *my* plans, *my drone*, to—" Danny jerks his chin in al-Ansari's direction— "this guy."

Al-Ansari turns his attention away from me and Nadia to narrow his eyes at Danny. "And who are you?"

Borya steps up first. "No one." He looks to Danny. "Leave, Danny. Go."

"Give me my plans and I will." There's no messing with the

mettle in his tone. Danny shakes off my clutching fingers and holds out his hand, ordering Borya to surrender his drives.

"I . . . I can't."

Then—did he already give it to al-Ansari? You can almost feel the attention in the room shift to al-Ansari.

"*Nyet,*" Nadia murmurs, gaping at Borya in utter horror. "Tell me you haven't."

Al-Ansari ignores their personal drama and ambles past Borya to talk to Danny. "So, you are the designer?"

"And I came here to get what's mine."

Al-Ansari pulls out a USB drive. Not one of ours. "I think you are too late. Unless—" He hesitates, then eyes the tablet Borya's still holding. "What is this 'exceptional' prize?"

"It's nothing," Danny insists again. "*My* nothing."

Al-Ansari snorts in Borya's general direction. "'Nothing'? Funny, that's what Zverev said about this." He holds up the drive. "Compared to what you have there. A beautiful woman who is outside your grasp."

Danny doesn't respond, just slides his USB drive into his pocket. I hope al-Ansari wants to play hard to get. He heads for Danny. "I propose an even trade."

Borya, still in a daze, turns away from Nadia "What about my money?"

Al-Ansari give him a condescending smirk. "Don't you mean *his* money?"

"Letting you hold that drive was a show of good faith," Borya says. "It's still—"

"His," al-Ansari cuts him off. "Because if you want to argue that simply holding the drive made it yours, it would appear that I am holding it now. You have no ownership."

Logic steals the final gust from Borya's sails (and sales). He looks from al-Ansari's drive to Danny's. Al-Ansari dismisses Borya, deflated and defeated, and focuses on Danny. "You want what's yours?"

I realize Danny's not only taken my arm with his free hand, but his grip grows tighter every second. "I want all of it," he says.

A muscle in Al-Ansari's temple twitches. "Do not take advantage of my generosity." He casts me a pointed glance, silently adding that threat: *I could take this woman, too.* (At least he's dismissed the "nothing" plans.) "Did you think a man like me travels without security?"

At the signal, three bulky guards in suits materialize from the shadows. Even Nadia and Eager Igor are outgunned now. (And you'd think an arms dealer would be armed.)

"So," al-Ansari concludes his argument, "your drive for mine, or—"

"Fine." Danny holds out the red USB drive. I hold on to my faith in him, that this "exceptional" aerospace plan is somehow okay to give to an arms dealer.

They exchange drives, but Danny's grip on my arm doesn't loosen, and I don't think it's just because he's supporting me.

"Pleasure." Al-Ansari bows from the shoulders. His guards evaporate into the shadows again, and al-Ansari backs away. He simpers at Borya one last time and turns for the door. Borya stands there, too stunned to do anything but let him go.

"Impossible." He takes two paces after al-Ansari, but Nadia catches his elbow.

"Don't." Nadia's gaze is as desperate as her voice and her grasp. "You don't know what you're doing."

He wrenches his arm free. "This money is supposed to save the company."

"Shcherbakov isn't the only thing that matters." Nadia drops to a whisper. For a split second, I'm not watching two enemies self-destruct: I'm watching me and Danny, the fight we have over and over, the same expressions, the same exasperation, the same extremes.

Their team's cracking, and all the fractures feel too familiar.

We need to go. I tug Danny backwards, but we have to creep along unless we want to attract their attention (and injure me worse).

"Don't I matter?" Nadia asks.

"Certainly." But Borya's eyebrows knit together, like he has no idea what she's asking.

If they keep fighting, we can escape. "Don't you get it?" I call. "Can't you see who she is? Why she's here?"

Nadia turns to us, dread and hatred practically shooting from her eyes. Borya looks to us, too, slow and hesitant. "My plans for Shcherbakov?"

"Your plans?" Danny challenges, but I cut him off.

"All this time, I thought you were the one with the FSB." I shake my head.

Borya blinks in slow motion, the lies she told him dawning. (Who's the *durochka* now?) He wheels on Nadia. "What?" His voice doubles in volume.

My work here is done. "Let's go," I murmur. I edge toward the door again, ignoring the pain ripping through my ankle with every step, clamping down on each gasp. I make it five feet before I'm clutching Danny's jacket tighter than when I dragged him around.

"Don't listen to them." Nadia dismisses our claims with a wave. "They're CIA."

"How would you know?" Borya closes his eyes, pain passing over his features as each wave of implications crashes over him. "It's true then."

"Boryasha." She pleads again, a more intimate nickname, reaching to bridge the rift. "Please. What you're doing, you're breaking the law. Al-Ansari's a wanted criminal."

I have to pause before I can take another shuffling step.

"Are you—" Borya backs two steps from Nadia, as if his words can't chisel a chasm between them fast enough. "You're spying on me."

"That's not how—"

"It ends now. All of it." His tone leaves no room to argue.

Danny glances at me for a Russian translation, but I'm off the interpreter clock. I keep moving. (When did this door get so far away?!)

Nadia tries for Borya's hand. "Boryasha, for me. I won't report anything, just stop now."

Maybe it's my experience talking, but if that's what she's willing to sacrifice for Borya, she's giving up everything for him to make it right. She's still trying to span the space between them, if Borya will just choose her, choose them, reach back.

He snorts. "Yes, you excel at withholding the truth. But guess what? I don't."

"Boryashka—"

"You're fired."

The realization rocks Nadia, and her strong façade shatters, sending her reeling back a few feet. "What about us?"

"Us?" Borya laughs. "Finished." He backs up farther. Fifteen feet till we're clear.

Nadia reaches after him, and Danny doesn't need translation. Her hand hangs in midair, and Borya glares back, colder than permafrost.

Finally, her hand drifts down.

"I can't believe I'll have to tell the company this." Borya wheels away and marches into the shadows.

Ten more feet to the door. We're almost free.

"Nadezhda Vasilyevna?" Eager Igor comes to stand by her side. "Should we let him go?"

"He could do this with Russian files, controlled exports." Every word falls on her shoulders like deadweight. "He broke the law. He'll ruin my cover."

"We don't know that." Eager Igor's reassurance holds more sympathy than I thought him capable of (but I didn't think the guy had much in the way of feelings when I was evading and escaping him).

"You don't know *him*." Her rasping echoes in the warehouse. The door to the front offices latches behind him at last. Nadia flinches with each reverberation in this metallic cavern like it's a slap.

She cowers there, hunched against the reality until slowly, she raises her face. The look there makes Siberia sound like a vacation paradise.

Suddenly this is really, really, really the wrong place to be. We're almost to the door. "Run," I whisper to Danny. I tug him along, but I can't move faster with this stupid limp.

"What?"

"Run. I'll catch up."

He meets my eyes and even in the shadows, I can see he recognizes the lie I told him in the bunker an hour ago, when I had no intention of surviving that long.

"We have no choice." Nadia's tone is flat. Eager Igor stares in the direction Borya went.

"Hurry," I breathe.

Danny doesn't hesitate: he scoops me into his arms and runs the last yard to the open door. I don't have time to protest before we're in the parking lot, and Danny's still running. He pauses long enough to check the building.

"I didn't know you could run like that carrying me," I say.

"Adrenaline," he says between catching his breath.

Ah, the romance of an engineer. "You're supposed to say your love gives you the strength of thousands."

"Uh . . . sure. What just happened?"

A gunshot answers. For an eternity, we stand there, gaping at the low white warehouse.

"She killed Borya." Danny's voice rings hollow. "She killed him."

I shouldn't be surprised, but I am. Another gunshot rings

out, and Danny isn't dillydallying for the details. He takes off at a run again. I do what I can to not interfere, clinging to him like the rescuer he is.

Not a fringe benefit I expected from marrying him, but I'll definitely take it.

He reaches the SUV and sets me down (leading with my good foot) to open the passenger door. I hope he isn't planning on sticking me there. Only one of us knows where we're going. I hop-limp-hop around to the driver's side.

"No, no, no," he says. "Let me drive."

"I can't navigate from memory." I hold up the keys.

Danny frowns, but I cut off his objection. "Unless you want Nadia coming after the witnesses, we need to get moving."

He says no more. I unlock the driver's side and hop in, unlocking his door. He climbs in, his face still slack from shock. "She *killed* him."

We can't know what happened, but I try to reassure him anyway. "Nah. You can survive that. Get my phone."

Danny grabs my cell from its hiding place under the seat and gives it to me. I toss the phone back at him. "Dial 112. Russian 911."

I don't wait for him to call before I start the car and pull out. He hands the ringing phone to me, and I report the crime and end the call. But help's only on the way for one of us.

We're not down the block when Danny adjusts his mirror. "What did you say about coming after witnesses?"

I consult the rearview. Company. A black sedan, and a white van.

Precisely what we need.

CHAPTER 30

GUN THE ENGINE, gritting my teeth to get through the gears. When I have a second, I thrust the phone at Danny. "Call the last number before 112."

He obeys and gives me the phone again. It rings once, twice—"Lori," Semyon answers. "Thanks for the heads up—"

"We're leaving ulitsa Novatorov, and—"

"Tell me that gunfire wasn't you."

He must be nearby. "Not us, but we made some new friends who are eager to catch up." I have to lower the phone and use both hands to turn onto the main road without slowing. Consult the rearview. The black sedan makes the right, too. And the van.

Back to Semyon. "Sorry. We've got Nadia . . ." I rack my brain for her surname. "Obolenskaya on our tail. She's the real FSB officer. Got a henchman with her."

"Our hands are full too, here. Separated al-Ansari from his entourage in the Rostvertrol complex, and we're getting ready for a nice, long talk about where his allegiances lie."

Semyon might talk big, but last I checked, we haven't successfully beaten anyone into spying long term. "Good luck,"

I mutter. "Trying to lose them and get out. Got anyone to spare?"

"I'll try to send an intercept. What are you driving?"

"Škoda Yeti, gunmetal—dark silver."

He pauses a minute. "Might have a decoy. Let you know. Lose them if you can."

Gee, thanks, that hadn't occurred to me. But all I say is, "Yeah. Nice working with you."

We reach a traffic artery and wait for a break in the flow of cars. I'll take a left if I can—harder for him to follow—but traffic isn't clear on the far side of the road, so I take a right again.

Danny cranes his neck to monitor his side mirror. "Still in pursuit."

"Thanks." I mean it, even if it doesn't sound like it through the accents of stress. We need a plan, and a surveillance detection route won't cut it. We've already detected them. Too late to convince them we're harmless—but can we lose them?

The text message comes through. "Take the wheel," I tell Danny. He does, and I check the text. Encrypted, of course.

"Ease up on the gas," he says. I pull back, still waiting for the decryption app.

An address. It's on a big enough street that I know it, though it's in the opposite direction of the airport. And the last word: *manok. Decoy.*

"All right." I take the wheel again. Monitoring the rearview, I navigate a long, winding path across town. The white van can't keep up. The black sedan falls back or speeds up, but he makes every. Single. Turn.

When I'm two minutes out, I dial Semyon again. "Send him in," I say once he answers.

I hit the gas and slingshot around a corner. I have to support myself on the window, and I miss Semyon's answer— but there, up the street, an SUV, identical to ours, idling at the sidewalk. Hope that's him. "Hang on," I say, as if Danny hasn't already steeled himself.

We shoot past the decoy, and now I'm watching the rearview even more closely. He joins traffic, going slow.

"Stop!" Danny shouts. I jam my boots on the pedals and we skid before coming to a dead stop in front of a pedestrian. The babushka gives us a sharp glare, then slowly limps along her way. My ankle answers with a shrieking throb, and I realize I jammed both feet on the brake.

And I killed the engine. Trading with the decoy will be hard enough without this delay.

I restart the car and scan the rearview. The black sedan's between me and the decoy. Great. Does the decoy have two people in his car? Maybe one of our pop-up dummies?

The babushka clears our bumper. I put the car in first, straining against the pain. "Go, go, go," I urge the little SUV. I swing a right and get us to a bigger road—big enough for our decoy to maneuver.

And maneuver he does. As soon as we're on a straightaway, he gets in the left lane and accelerates—right past us. My stomach dips, and a spark of hope puffs out. It's not him. Is it? We were at the right address; who else could it be?

He pulls into our lane, and I switch into the other lane. To confuse our tail, we'll have to play a couple rounds of this shell game, but the best solution might be to switch *cars*. Preferably to one that isn't identical, but we can't really be picky.

New plan. I glance at the phone. The call timer's still counting. "Semyon?" I practically shout. "You there?"

"You said to hang on," he says.

Oh, did I say—to Danny. Good enough. "New plan, Semyon. Have him head to ulitsa Tsvetkova and ulitsa Molodchaya. There's an alley behind the *produkty*. Park there and wait." This time I make sure to actually end the call, and I turn left at the next light.

Danny needs to be in on it, too. "Pulling the old switch-aroo." I flash him a we're-okay smile (but I'm shifting at the same time, so it probably looks more like I'm-seriously-*not*-okay).

Within a few minutes, I'm on the familiar street—the street I lived on for six months. And right there is the *produkty*, the quaint little market with green trim along its plate windows. It belongs closer to Sesame Street than Siberia.

The black sedan's still on our tail. I cruise past the *produkty*, but at the last second, I take the corner. The sedan doesn't have time to turn.

Once he's out of sight, I pull to the curb.

"Are there details to this plan, or are we winging it?" Danny asks.

"Little of both. Hurry before they double back." I squeeze his hand and get out of the SUV, careful to plant both feet before I stand, keeping my weight to my good side. The car makes a decent enough crutch, and I slide around the back. Danny meets me at the trunk—no time to mess with our bags, and I can barely drag myself around. He helps me hobble to the sidewalk.

I hate to admit it, but this is getting serious. Not, like, hospital serious (I've been a patient in a Russian hospital; I'd rather take my chances), but like *I really hope Russian TSA doesn't require you to remove your shoes because I'm not sure I could get it back on* serious. A blowtorch is attacking my ankle, and it might be my imagination, but I can see swelling through the leather.

Danny steadies my waist again. "I got you."

I can't clutch his arm any tighter, but I'd squeeze it if I could. "In here." I start for the *produkty* doors. I can already smell the warm bread and slightly overripe fruit inside.

The door hinges screech open, and a babushka toddles out to the counter mostly by feel. Olya. "*Biznes-lanch?*" she calls, offering their "business" meal deal, though it's long past lunchtime. If I weren't hurting or hurrying so much, I'd drop the cover, stop to talk. Whenever Sestra Carter or Sestra Bulovskaya and I stopped in, Olya's two-gold-toothed smile and sparkling-but-cloudy eyes always brightened our day. But using her name would raise questions today. "I'm sorry," I start, "but do you have ice? I slipped on the sidewalk."

"Are you hurt? Sit." She dodders to the back. I move to follow her behind the counter.

Danny doesn't. I tug him forward. "Come on."

"I can tell she didn't invite us to come with her."

"It'll be okay. I've been here before—and I can't count the number of times I've gotten strangers to do things for me. Social engineering might actually be my most useful skill."

Danny groans. "You call what you do 'engineering'?"

I roll my eyes and he helps me to the door to the back room. Olya's disappeared somewhere in the cramped kitchen. (Where could she hide?) "Do you mind if I sit down back here?" I call to her. "It's pretty bad."

"Yes, sit. You don't need ice. You need a poultice."

I'm an idiot. How could I have forgotten every Russian's pathological need to push their homeopathic, old wives' remedies? Even doctors do this—my companion had one instruct her to use a vodka poultice for this same injury.

"You know what?" I say. "I should go home and rest."

"This will only take a minute."

I nod for Danny to help me into the narrow passage to the back door, ignoring Olya's answer like she ignored mine. "Do you have a back door we could use? We're parked out that way and it would save us so much time."

"Yes, one more minute."

Is her hearing going too? I crane my neck to search for Olya. She pokes her head out from behind the tall shelves. I point to the door. "We'll just be going—thank you!"

Olya continues talking, extolling the virtues of this poultice and its secret ingredients. Fortunately, the back door is unlocked from the inside and we can slip out to the dingy alley.

Where the decoy car's *not* waiting.

Great.

This may be our last chance to talk. "Danny?"

He stops searching the alley to look at me. "What?"

"We have to split up. Can you get on the plane, no matter what happens?"

"How would you find me?"

"Trust me, Danny, I will find a way. I'll catch up."

He looks at me, face to face. "You keep saying that—don't lie to me."

I hold his gaze. "I *will* make it back to you. Just, please, trust me?"

"I do."

Danny starts to turn away, but I take his shoulder and turn him back to me. "You keep saying that. Don't *you* lie to me."

"I do trust you. Will you trust me?"

Then it hits me. From the moment we accepted this mission, I've obsessed over all the things I've trusted Danny with. But I haven't trusted him with the one thing most important to me: him.

And like I told him: he's more than proven himself. It's definitely time. "Yes. If we wait for our flight, they'll find us for sure. Buy a ticket for the first international departure, and no matter what happens—get. On. That. Plane."

"What about you?"

I try to toss off a nonchalant smile, but it'd be more convincing if I weren't covering a grimace. "I'll be fine."

"I know you'll be fine. I just want to be the one who makes sure of it."

The understanding finally clicks into place for both of us. He wants to do that for me, and I want to do the same for him. "I love you," I say.

287

"I love you too. Makes this tough, huh?"

"Tough, but . . . it wouldn't be worth it without you." I grit my teeth, prepping myself for the conversation I never want to have. "If we don't—" I can't even say it, but I have to. "I want you to be happy."

He squeezes me closer. "I am. You know, other than that 'running for our lives' part."

"Kinda put a damper on the honeymoon. Sorry about that."

"I knew what I was getting into."

At first, I think he means in Paris, agreeing to this insane assignment. But I look into his warm brown eyes, and I see exactly what he means: he knew what he was getting into when he married me. And he did it anyway.

"You're probably crazy," I murmur, pulling him closer.

"Probably."

I think that's supposed to pass for romance. Engineers.

He traces a finger along my jaw, drawing me in for a kiss. The instant our lips touch, a car horn honks. I glare at the intruder, but the blue sedan's driver gestures us over. Okay, I guess I can't complain *too* much. "Hold that thought," I tell Danny. "Our ride's here."

"Better be our ride." Danny helps me to the car.

"Sorry it takes so long," the driver apologizes (native Russian?). "Had to get your bags from other car."

"Good thinking." We're going to need those. I give the driver instructions to return Garo's neighbor's SUV to her, and he starts down the street. At our trunk, I dig out what we need from my bags—a fake passport for Danny with forged entry visa—and hand them to him. "They'll be hunting for us at the airport. You're Louis Michaud."

"French." He checks the maroon cover, flips it open and pulls out matching credit cards. "Holograms and everything."

"And biometric chip." I tap the symbol on the cover where the chip's embedded. (Yep, we're good. Apologies to France; I hear your passports are tough, if it makes you feel better.)

"*Bonne job.*"

I clear my throat. "Didn't you tell me that's a Quebecism?"

"I'm kidding." He tucks the passport and cards in his coat. "What about you?"

"I have mine."

Danny holds out a hand. I stand there, uncomprehending. Does he want my passport?

"Keys," he finally says.

"No, Danny, I—"

"Louis," he corrects me with a hint of a smirk. But the smile disappears. "I'm not sitting there watching you hurt yourself. You navigate."

"Danny." I aim my tone to quash any arguments. "I can do this."

"No." The rejection is simple and calm, and now I'm the one who can't argue with him. "Let me help you."

"But you can't—are you willing to be 'paranoid'?"

He casts a quick glance heavenward. "For someone who claims she's seen a lot of unhappy marriages, you don't know very much about fighting, do you?"

Huh?

My confusion must show because Danny continues. "Did you ever see someone fight about something stupid, instead of what they really meant?"

Searching my memory doesn't take long. I highly doubt my parents cared enough about the remote control or what brand of bread we bought to fight about those things for literally years. "Then what were we really fighting about?"

Danny counts off the reasons. "You wouldn't trust me—not to take care of myself, and certainly not to take care of you. You kept hiding behind Lori, and—I thought that was the problem. I thought I was losing you."

I grab him for another hug. Because I know exactly how

that feels. When I pull back, I slap the keys in Danny's palm and we hop in—literally for me. Aside from me meticulously monitoring my side mirror and Danny updating me on what cars are behind us, the trip to the airport is uneventful.

But, hello, the FSB has resources everywhere. No time to let our guard down.

He parks and kills the engine. The sudden silence falls on us like a winter coat, thick and heavy. In the rearview, the sun sneaks below the horizon.

"Okay," I say. "Be careful. Be safe."

"Be paranoid."

For a minute, I'm sideswiped. Is this argument bouncing back to bash me on the rebound? Then I look at Danny—he's serious, not snarky.

"If there's even a *chance* you're in danger, be paranoid. Totally, completely, crazy-as-they-come paranoid."

I take back what I said about engineers. "That's the most romantic thing I've ever heard."

Danny scoff-laughs, but leans across the seat to kiss me. "I love you," he murmurs. "Be safe. See you in a minute." And he gets out.

I watch him walk away, my heart screaming to go with him. But I can't. This is more secure. Danny reaches the sidewalk. He checks behind him, but nobody's interested in his approach.

A black sedan pulls up to the curb, blocking my exit and my view of Danny—and thrusting my heart into my throat. Is it them? Are they hunting Danny?

A short guy in a suit climbs from the black sedan. Could be anybody. But my frozen lungs won't listen to that weak logic. It's Eager Igor. He doesn't go for the trunk to retrieve luggage. He heads for the doors.

I have to get in there faster. I hop out of the car (again, literally) and search the trunk. No cane or crutch—even I'm not crazy enough to tote something like that around. I grab my bag and clench my jaw so tight my molars might crack.

I test my hurt foot. The pain streaks up my calf, but I'll make it. When Danny's life might be on the line, I have no choice.

I can't hide the limp entirely, but I hurry to the doors behind Eager Igor. He reaches the entrance far ahead of me, and by the time I trail him in, sweat's beading on my forehead from the strain and searing pain of every step. I shove the pain into the background and scan the busy ticket desk.

No Danny.

No Eager Igor.

No good at all.

I hobble to the check-in line, relieved to finally rest my foot. Between the weight of my boot and the swelling, I can't hold it up long, but I wait, surveying the area every three seconds—and the flight schedule board. The first international departure: Helsinki. Someone's definitely watching out for me. I think I even have a Finnish passport or two, so I'll look like someone just heading home. At the desk, I request a ticket to Finland.

"Better hurry," the clerk tells me. "They'll board soon."

I thank the clerk, pay for the ticket and navigate through security without arousing suspicions (thank heaven they don't flag me to take off my shoes). But pain etches through my tough façade faster than acid. I don't dare sit—don't know if I'll have the mental or physical strength to get up. I keep moving, slower and slower, but steadily closer to my destination. I have to find Danny. I grit my teeth and push on, though I'm visibly limping.

Finally, I reach the waiting area. But I can't go straight in. I hide behind a brood of babushki at the opposite (naked) wall to observe the waiting passengers. He's not in the seats. My fingers tighten on my suitcase handle. He's not in the line.

And then I catch a glimpse of him, standing by the window, gazing out at the planes in the gathering dusk. That's my Danny.

I can't approach yet. If Igor's around, he'll be searching for us together. We have to board that plane separately.

I check the waiting area. An ice-fist socks me in the stomach: Nadia. Here. Blending in with her coat and hat. Eager Igor enters from the opposite direction, scanning the area, clutching a couple papers. The light shines through them, illuminating our passport photos.

The line files out the doors for the bus to their plane. Igor stands at the doors, silently touching base with one guy, vaguely familiar, on the other side of the waiting area, then another. Nadia's other guards. All closing in on our doors.

Of course. The next flight leaving the country. They could stay here all day and check every departing flight, blocking every escape.

I look back to where Danny's observing the planes, obliv— he's not there. He's gone.

Fear floods into my throat, my chest, my heart. They can't possibly have him. They all wouldn't still be hunting. Unless they've got someone else here, and he's taken him—

No. I have no choice. I have to trust Danny's doing exactly what he's supposed to, and I have to change too. I should've done it sooner, but I was so obsessed with getting Danny out safe, I let my own tradecraft slip. I can't let that hurt either of us. I have to change disguises.

Oh, crap. I have to move. On this ankle.

Gotta suck it up. I flip up my collar and pull on the knit hat I bought yesterday. I change my walk as part of my disguise, shuffling past my waiting area on the other side of the thoroughfare, averting my gaze, praying Nadia, Igor and friends keep focusing on that crowd until I'm clear, praying to survive the next step, the next bolt of pain.

The bathroom's approximately ten miles away, but finally I make it. Though the interior's no cleaner than any other public bathroom in Russia, it's cool, protected, safe.

I hobble to the mirror to undo the last week. Off comes the copper wig. Off comes the makeup thicker than a runway model's. Off comes the red coat. My cheeks are pink from scrubbing and a new set of zits greet me—a positive for my cover. (Russia makes you appreciate the little things: advertising, pimples, not having to run for your life every day.)

In under a minute, I have dark hair wavy from braids, residual liner smudgy around my hazel eyes, black coat to (finally) blend in with Russians, like my black carry-on does. A slouchy beige hat finishes the disguise, and I'm me again.

Well, I'm almost me. My ticket and my passport will tell you I'm Merja Härkönen.

I have to stay near the wall, stopping every couple minutes to rest, to make it back to my doors. Still no Danny. Eager Igor's scrutinizing every person that passes the stewardess looking over tickets. The other two guards are still in the waiting area, pretending to read their phones.

Nadia's got to be here somewhere.

I get in line, inching toward the tarmac doors. Eager Igor takes up pacing. Back and forth. Staring everyone down.

Most people ignore him and avoid his gaze, and I try to do the same. After a couple passes, I'm three people away from the front—and Eager Igor plants himself by the ticket agent. He whispers to her.

And then I see who's in that uniform: Nadia.

My heart rate hops into fifth gear.

The man before me gives his ticket to Nadia. "Your passport too," she orders him.

I reach in my coat and check one of my passports quickly—right country, wrong photo. Red hair. I put it away, careful to note the order of the booklets in my pocket.

Nadia lets the guy go. My turn. "Passport and ticket."

I pick the right passport (I hope) and hand it over with my ticket. I draw a bracing breath to calm my palpitating pulse. She shields it from the sun and shines a special flashlight on it—black light. Does she have a retinal scanner to test the biometric chip?

I sigh out that deep breath, bored and Finnishly reserved. I sneak a peek at Eager Igor—he's watching me. Crap. Will he recognize me, my eyes? Hazel isn't exactly the world's most common eye color.

I force myself to wait to look away until it's not suspicious. And I catch Nadia staring at me. My mind keeps running through the same logic I presented in Paris: without their heavy makeup, celebrities are unrecognizable. I should be, too.

This is taking too long. Forget fifth gear; my heart rate hits the redline. Could Danny have gotten past these people?

Finally the burgundy passport appears in front of me. "*Ole hyvä*," she says. Finnish for *be good*. Oh the irony—though I'm sure she doesn't know what it means, a phrase a foreign-speaking "flight attendant" might memorize. If that's the best test they have, try again. I've spoken Finnish since before I could . . . um, speak English.

"*Kiitos*," I say. *Thanks*.

No, *this* is the final test: I accept my passport and brace for those last feet to the glass doors. I can sense Nadia's scrutiny on me, and Eager Igor's. Watching to see if I can walk.

I fall into the tired-of-travel shuffle, fighting back every wince.

Nadia regards me for a second that lasts an eternity. I almost count the heartbeats I'm skipping—then she turns to the next passenger. I make it to the doors, and Eager Igor jogs off for another waiting area.

We're in the clear. I hide the limp the best I can to the bus. Danny's not on the bus, but they have to have taken passengers there once already.

Now, what if Danny's not on the plane? Do I run back to Nadia and Igor? Gee, that's not obvious. The flight leaves in twenty minutes and I—I have no backup plan. I'm all in on this bet.

Because I trust Danny.

The bus deposits us at our plane, and I haul myself up the stairs. Every row of passengers, clutching onto every seat, I'm scanning faces. Row five, no Danny. But he's here. I know it.

Row ten, no Danny. He's here. He's got to be.

Row fifteen, still no Danny. Panic pools in my chest, ready to well up and overwhelm my brain.

I know he's here. I know he is.

Row twenty. I stop in the aisle and scan the last few rows.

No Danny.

I left him. I left him when I should've taken care of him and let him take care of me. I fight back the tears, but they prick to the surface anyway, blurring my vision of people who aren't my husband.

I try to breathe, but I can't, I can't, I—

A hand lands on my waist. I try to jump away. A shock-wave rips up my leg, and I lose my balance.

I steel myself for the impact—but my fall abruptly stops. I'm caught. (The good kind of caught, I hope.)

"Careful there," says a familiar voice. He pulls me to stand. "You could use some help."

I blink past the tears and almost laugh: Danny. In that stupid gray hat and reversed jacket. The disguise fooled even me for a second. He used a disguise—he did everything I asked. No, he went above and beyond. And it worked.

"Thanks," I murmur. I let him help me to the seat next to him (though it isn't mine), clinging to his arm way more than I would any other day.

He holds up a plastic bag full of ice and leans down to put it on my boot. (Now *that's* love.) "Good to see you," he whispers.

"How did you get past her?"

"Who, the stewardess?"

I scan the aisle—nobody—and lean closer. "Nadia?"

"I went out a different door."

"You—I—" I cut off my stunned stuttering and shake my head in wonder. "I guess it does take a rocket scientist."

He leans even closer. "It takes a spy."

Obviously he means me, but I mirror his grin. "It takes two."

His smile turns up a couple kilowatts, and I'm so close to him, so close to kissing him—but I can't. The term in CIA slang is "wheels-up" for a reason. Nadia might have enough authority to board or even stop this plane, so we're not "safe" until we're in the air (and preferably international airspace).

I sit back. It's not just the ice or getting off my feet that feels good—feels right. I glance out at the glowing Rostov-na-Donu sign atop the airport. Once again, I'm leaving Russia, but this time it's different. Though I still love it, I'm not sure I ever want to come back, not even to visit.

I can carry off a Russian mission, but this definitely isn't where I belong.

Assuming we pulled this off, and didn't give al-Ansari something even more dangerous. I look to Danny. "So, what did we give our friend?"

"Oh, personal project."

"Nothing useful?"

Danny dismisses the idea. "Doubtful. The version on that drive's half done, a mix of one direction on the nose, another on the tail, and nothing in the middle. Borya saw some of the cool elements, but it'll never fly. Can't even be built."

"'Cool elements'? Sounds like an understatement."

Danny shrugs one shoulder, his smile saying, *Aw, it was nuthin.* (Only "nuthin" to him.) "It's an updated version of the

Avro Arrow."

I cover my face with my hands. "You're terrible, you know."

"I know." At the front of the plane, the doors seal. Almost home free.

I touch his knee. "You were right about Borya. Mostly."

Danny gives me a consolation-prize smile. "You were right about the situation, mostly."

The plane starts rolling and my stomach flip-flops. I hate flying, hate, hate, hate. I close my eyes and focus on my oxygen intake while we start forward at a slow, bumpy roll.

"I was thinking," Danny says. If he's trying to distract me, it's not working. "Could we raise the money for your friend's daughter? Maybe ask people at church?"

After what I put Valya through, it's the least I can do. "Great idea."

The plane lurches, then stops. He takes my hand, and I latch on, clinging to him like he'll save me from my inevitable, fiery death. (I know we're on the ground, but that doesn't help. Did I mention I hate flying?)

"You're okay," Danny says in my ear. "Remember the principles of flight?"

"Lift, pressure, speed. Not reassuring."

Danny laughs and pries my fingers loose from his—why, why, why?

I look to find Danny examining the pocket of his suit coat. Seriously?

The plane does a 180, and I *really* contemplate sticking my head between my knees or breathing into a paper bag.

I can do this. I can. I just don't like it.

Danny pulls something from his jacket's lining. Wonder where he picked up that trick.

"You can keep the passport for now," I tell him.

"For now? Or next time?"

"Next—there is no next time. I don't know if there's a next time for me."

Danny frowns. "What? Why?"

"I can't put you in danger anymore—"

"I knew what I was getting into."

The same double meaning as before hangs in his words. "But I—"

The engines whir to life, cutting off my response. I'm not ready.

If that wasn't enough, Danny shoots me a look of *can I say something seriously?* "I don't want you to do that for me."

"But *I* want to."

"But would you be happy if you quit, right now?"

I open my mouth to answer, but nothing comes. "I don't know."

Danny raises a *really?* eyebrow. I have to admit the truth: "Maybe not right now."

"How is making you unhappy supposed to make me happy?"

"Safe, Danny. Safe."

"I want you to be safe, too—even if it means being crazy-paranoid. Because I love you."

I look into those brown eyes as my favorite genuine, he-is-who-he-is-all-the-time-even-when-he's-a-spy smile dawns. Yes, he wins this round—because I can't argue with that.

"I love you too," I breathe.

"If you do want to quit, I won't stop you—I just don't want you to feel like you have to for me."

Okay, they may not be the best at romance, but engineers can definitely do *love* right.

The plane starts forward. I clutch Danny's hand again and scrunch my eyes, my face, my whole body as we pick up speed.

Danny leans close enough I can feel every breath of his whisper against my cheek. "I know you're used to making sacrifices for work, but I'm not asking that," he says. "I just want to take care of you—"

That's got my attention. "Danny, I can take care of myself." And I've spent my whole life trying to prove it to the people around me—my brothers, my classmates, my coworkers.

Danny searches my eyes a minute, and the plane's lift isn't the only reason my stomach swoops.

We're wheels-up. We're safe. We're together. (And we didn't die a fiery death!)

He frees his hand from mine. I pretend not to notice the white imprint my fingers leave. And then he slides on my rings.

I'm sure my shock's showing, because Danny explains, "Got them from Lori in Paris. You're not the only one who can use a travel sewing kit."

"But if you'd gotten caught with them—"

"I'd say my wife lost them in my suitcase."

I can't even fault his explanation. "Okay," I admit. "You're not terrible at the spy stuff."

"Thanks. I guess." His gaze turns serious. "Talia, I know you can take care of yourself—but you don't have to do it alone."

That last piece clicks into place. Because we're a team now.

"How about this?" He lets that smile I love light his eyes. "I take care of you, and you take care of me, and that should cover all the bases."

I lean the last inch to kiss him. Because finally, that sounds like a perfect plan.

Dear Reader,

Thank you so much for reading *Tomorrow We Spy*! I don't know if I've ever been quite as happy to share a novel as I am to share this one. It took a lot of effort to get it exactly how I wanted it, but not so much that I came to loathe working on it, and I'm thrilled to have shared this series with you.

I hope you've enjoyed the Spy Another Day series as much as I've enjoyed writing it! I'd love to hear from you! **You can write me at Jordan@JordanMcCollum.com or find me (and fun bonus features!) at http://JordanMcCollum.com.** If you haven't already, be sure to check out the prequels as well to see how Talia met Danny and Elliott!

Finally, can I ask a quick favor? **Could you please leave a review of *Tomorrow We Spy* or other books in the series online, or tell your friends about it?** A book's success truly depends on readers like you spreading the word—and who *isn't* looking for a great read? To make things easy for you, I have review site links on my website at http://JordanMcCollum.com/loved-tws/.

Thank you for reading!

Jordan McCollum

P.S. Want to be the first to know about my next release? Join my mailing list at http://JordanMcCollum.com/newsletter/. (I will never spam you!) The Spy Another Day series is complete (for now . . . ?), but I have many more adventures and fun stories planned to share in the future.

ACKNOWLEDGMENTS

Once again, my husband Ryan, and our children, Hayden, Rebecca, Rachel and Hazel, have supported me through long days and evenings at the computer, drafting and crafting. Without any one of them, my life would be so much less rewarding.

As always, my parents, Ben and Diana Franklin, taught me so much about the science of writing (tense shift!), and their continued support means so much to me. Along with my sisters Jaime, Brooke and Jasmine, they've always encouraged me to do my best and make it shine.

My critique partners, Julie Coulter Bellon and Emily Gray Clawson, deserve tremendous, groveling, I'm-not-worthy thanks. Their guidance and encouragement helped to make this book, this series, and these characters into more than I could ever have done on my own.

My beta readers helped to smooth out those last little blips, and I appreciate each of them: Heather Baird, Ranee´ S. Clark and Sarah Anderson. Once again, my dad, Ben Franklin, was a huge help as a technical consultant and beta reader.

Obviously, this book required more language and cultural

help than any I've published to date, so I have many people to thank here. *Spasibo* to Angela Millsap and Anastasia Kasakova, who reviewed all of my Russian and cultural notes (but any mistakes are my own), and to (Sestra) Courtney Leavitt, who acquiesced to my requests to hear more about Rostov-na-Donu, even going to the trouble of describing the church building there for me. *Merci* to Kathleen Perrin for fixing my French and to my cousin Ammon Franklin, who came through with some invaluable last-minute help. As always, *kiitos* to my dad, Ben Franklin, for Finnish help.

Jason Hanson of Escape & Evasion and formerly of the CIA was kind enough to answer my Agency questions, and my awesome experience in the field exercise of his Spy Escape & Evasion course inspired several of Talia's surveillance-evading experiences in this book.

My editor, Jenn Wilks, once again whipped my prose into shape—thank you!

Finally, I want to thank you, my readers. Your support and encouragement mean so much to me. You have made my stories come to life in more than just my imagination. Thank you so much for joining me on this journey. I hope you've enjoyed it as much as I have!

Thank you!

ABOUT THE AUTHOR

PHOTO BY JAREN WILKEY

AN AWARD-WINNING AUTHOR, JORDAN MCCOLLUM can't resist a story where good defeats evil and true love conquers all. In her day job, she coerces people to do things they don't want to, elicits information and generally manipulates the people she loves most—she's a mom.

Jordan holds a degree in American Studies and Linguistics from Brigham Young University. When she catches a spare minute, her hobbies include reading, knitting and music. She lives with her husband and four children in Utah.